All of Me

NEW YORK TIMES BESTSELLING AUTHOR
A.L. JACKSON

A.L. Jackson
www.aljacksonauthor.com
Cover Design by RBA Designs
Editing by AW Editing and Susan Staudinger
Formatting by Mesquite Business Services

The characters and events in this book are fictitious. Names, characters,
places, and plots are a product of the author's imagination. Any
similarity to real persons, living or dead, is coincidental and not
intended by the author.

Print ISBN: 978-1-946420-73-2
eBook ISBN: 978-1-946420-25-1

All of Me

More from A.L. Jackson

prologue

GRACE

A chilly breeze twisted through the intense blue sky.

A warning of the coming winter.

A cold, quiet whisper.

A premonition.

His voice twisted with seduction as he murmured the words close to my face. "I warned you who I was."

Selfish.

Greedy.

Incapable of love.

The devil.

Maybe I'd been the fool who hadn't believed him. The one

who'd seen more in him. Something better than the powerful, callous man who stood in front of me right then.

I hugged my arms across my chest as if it could shield me from the brutality of his words. As if they could protect me from the truth I should have seen all along.

"No, you're wrong. You're so much more than that. I know you are. I've seen it."

"You only saw what you wanted to see."

"You told me you loved me. I trusted you. I trusted you with everything."

"And look what that got you."

A gust of wind whipped through. The spindly branches of the ancient oaks hissed and howled, sending a tumble of dead, dried leaves across the ground.

It stirred the chaos that raged inside me.

I don't believe you.

I don't believe you.

My spirit screamed it while my mind struggled to accept the reality. The truth that he could hurt me this way.

It ripped and tore at my insides.

Loss.

A grief unlike anything I'd ever felt.

Hope scattering like the leaves.

"How could you do this?" I forced myself to look up at his beautiful face.

Too beautiful. Too mesmerizing. Too dangerous.

"How could you, when you know what is at stake? When you know how badly I need you? *I trusted you.*" The last raked from my raw, aching throat.

As raw and aching as my heart.

He reached out and brushed his fingertips down the side of my face.

Tenderly.

A stark contrast to the wickedness that blazed from his soul.

Then his voice twisted with that dark, bitter hatred—hatred I was sure was completely directed at himself.

"You shouldn't have."

one

IAN

"*Ian*, my good man." Kenneth Millstrom clapped me on the back. "How are you tonight?"

Good man.

Right.

As I shook the hand he extended, I kept myself from scoffing at the way he'd phrased his greeting.

Grin and bear it.

"Terrific, Mr. Millstrom. How are you?"

"Better than you can imagine."

I let out a low whistle as I edged back, still shaking his hand as I took in his appearance.

"Look at you. Are you trying to make the rest of us look bad?

Leave some ladies for the rest of us, why don't you? It's hardly fair."

The guy was in his late fifties and stuffed into his tux. He was also the senior partner in my firm, so that meant I had my nose shoved so far up his ass I was surprised I hadn't convinced myself that the sky had turned brown.

But a man had to do what a man had to do.

I had one singular goal. And I'd do whatever I had to do to reach it.

Kenneth chuckled. "Ahh . . . no need to worry, son. My Sally is plenty for me. I'll leave the rest of these young things to you."

One thing I had to say? Dude loved his wife. I didn't get it. But whatever.

He took a sip of his champagne before he lifted his flute and gestured around the packed ballroom. It took up the entire top floor of the posh, historic hotel in Charleston, South Carolina.

It was where our annual gala was being held, the fundraiser a mecca for Charleston's elite year after year.

"So, what do you think?" he asked.

My eyes scanned the room.

People mingled in gowns and suits and tuxes.

Voices lifted and laughter loud.

Egos bloated.

Pretension so heavy there was no air left in the glitzy room.

Sucked dry by the people parading around in their pompous best.

There they all were, acting like they actually cared about what they were raising the money for when, really, they were only there for the sake of being seen.

I hated this bullshit.

But it didn't really matter what I felt, did it?

I sent Kenneth my best counterfeit grin. "It's fantastic. I couldn't imagine a better way to spend a Saturday night. You've outdone yourself this year."

"You think so?" he asked, just begging for the affirmation, chest puffing out, meaty palm clutching his flute.

"Absolutely."

So yeah. I was laying it on thick.

But the thing was? I was *right* there. So close to getting what I wanted that I could actually taste it. A sweet, frantic desperation that danced on my tongue and spun through my insides. Fingers itching to finally possess the prize.

I learned at a young age that I was the sun. It was up to me to make the world gravitate around me.

If I wanted something, I reached out and took it. Made it mine. I didn't wait around to stumble upon something good. For something to fall into my lap or for some good fortune to come my way.

I worked for it. Gave it whatever it took. What was it they said? You can't win if you don't play?

I played hard, and I fought harder.

Took what I needed because I couldn't sit around relying on someone else to hand it to me.

Some people might call me an asshole. Callous. Ruthless.

Fuck that.

I called it tenacity.

I was a warrior.

A survivor.

I'd never go back to that place where I was hungry. A scared little kid dressed in tattered, dirty clothes, curled up in a ball on a filthy floor with an empty stomach and bruises littering his body.

Begging for someone . . . anyone to help.

The only person who ever had was my brother, Jace. He'd been my protector. The one to stand up and take the blows, the one to lie and steal, providing for me the only way that he could.

He taught me from the get-go that the only thing we had was each other. He and my best friend Mack were as far as my trust went and that was exactly where it ended.

Because I'd never allow myself to go back to that disgusting place of depravity and poverty and desolation.

A memory hit me faster than I could stop it.

Disgust crawled beneath the surface of my skin. I almost wanted to squeeze my eyes closed against the image. To refuse it. Forget it.

But I didn't.

I held on to it.

Embraced it.

Let it become a weapon and a reason.

Truth was, there was no forgetting exactly how that horror had felt. I'd been seventeen when I'd stood there in that doorway, blinking into the hollow, vacant room. Death screaming back.

It was the exact moment I'd felt a light go dim inside me, and I could physically feel the darkness rushing in to take its place.

It had obliterated a hope and a love and a loyalty that I never should have felt in the first place. I'd been nothing but a stupid kid who'd clung to an idea that was ignorant and pathetic.

It was the first moment in time when I knew I would do whatever it took to make it. When I'd made an oath to myself I'd never again allow someone to hold me back or push me down.

So, there I stood.

One step away from the goal I'd set for myself that day. I'd promised myself that whatever direction I went, whatever career or profession I chose, I would land at the top of it.

I'd reach the pinnacle even if my fingers and nails were ripped to shreds and bleeding from clawing my way there.

Even if it meant pinning a fucking fake smile on my face and pretending like I wanted to be here.

Besides, it wasn't really Kenneth's fault that he was the *bossman*. He actually was a decent guy. Didn't mean that I liked that what he said was final. That he was the one who held my ultimate success in his hands.

There was always a hierarchy.

I was almost to the top of it. I wouldn't stop until I took his place.

Kenneth sent me a searching glance, right back to business. "How's Bennet? Tell me you're keeping him happy."

Lawrence Bennet.

My guts curled with the name. Lawrence Bennet was one of the firm's biggest clients. One I'd brought on.

He'd taken me under his wing when I was seventeen. Becoming a father figure when my life had gone to shit. Getting behind me on my quest to become who I was today.

I'd thought he was there to help me.

Thing was, the asshole had had me involved up to my nose in shady shit before I even realized he was putting me in shackles. Dragging me into a seedy world I never should have stepped into.

Over time, it'd only gotten worse, his hold cinching tighter.

He was a loose end that needed to be snipped.

Problem was, I wasn't sure how to cut that thread without sending myself falling. Fucker had ensured that when he became my firm's most important client.

"I can assure you Bennet is taken care of, sir. He's my first priority."

"That's what I want to hear." He lifted his drink in approval. "You keep going the direction that you are, and you're going to do big things. Big, big things."

That was the plan.

Kenneth downed his champagne and tipped me a knowing grin. "Guess we'd better get back to it, eh? There are asses to be kissed."

A light chuckle rolled out. "I think I might have kissed plenty for the night."

He quirked a playful brow, his voice only half-horrified. "Don't tell me you're talking about me?"

Surprise tumbled out in my laughter. "Never," I told him, something wry in my grin.

He squeezed my shoulder, all too knowing. "You're a sly one, aren't you, Jacobs?"

There was a gleam to his eyes, a hint that maybe he did have an inclination of the lengths that I would go. That he knew I'd do whatever I had to do, in every and any situation, to get the result to land in my favor.

"Nothing but an open book."

Right.

I was a fucking impenetrable safe.

A goddamn tomb.

"Ah, we all have our secrets. Main thing is knowing when they're worth keeping." With a parting wink, he left me with that thought to chew on.

Got the sense he was leaving me some kind of prediction. An omen. Like he knew something he shouldn't.

Unease spun, and I blew out a frustrated breath before I turned and wound deeper into the party.

Chin lifted like I owned the place.

One day I would.

One day I would own everything.

I made a beeline for the bar that lined the back of the luxurious room. Everything was shiny and gold and gaudy, ornate tapestries hanging from the high walls supported by massive columns, the sky-high ceiling painted blue and dotted with cherubs and clouds to give the effect that you might have actually spent enough dough and bought yourself a plot in heaven.

I lifted a finger toward the bartender, who gave me a slight nod in response. If I had to be here, I was going to make the best of it.

He poured me two fingers of my favorite scotch and slid the glass across the bar. My shaking hand settled around the tumbler, relief in the sensation of the alcohol on my tongue when I lifted it to my mouth.

For the barest beat, I almost felt human. Like I was the same as every other asshole in the room. Like I hadn't fought and clawed and cheated my way to get there.

I started to push away from the bar to go do some more of that ass-kissing I was supposed to do, when my gaze tripped.

Snagged.

Usually these events bored me to death, but my dick was suddenly very interested in what the benefit had to offer.

Good God.

All I saw was legs.

A mile of them.

Toned and thick and delicious.

Shown off by this beige gown that should be illegal with the way a slit cut all the way up to the center of a lush, creamy thigh, a sparkling jewel gathering the fabric of her dress to that spot.

A motherfucking beacon guiding some poor soul who'd been lost at sea.

I might not be poor or lost, but I sure as hell could use a night of saving.

I let my gaze roam, higher and higher, inch by inch, eyes devouring this girl who was nothing but ample curves and tempting flesh.

I trailed all the way up until I was taking in the profile of her face.

Angled chin and a narrow nose. The girl was nursing a bubbling glass of champagne where she sat by herself at the opposite end of the bar.

Aloof and unapproachable . . . and somehow . . . soft.

That alone made me want her.

Blonde waves tumbled down her back, so long I was pretty sure the locks touched her ass, lips pouty and plump as she brought the rim of her glass up to take a sip.

Shit, she was stunning. Like maybe she'd been carved into the elegant room. A part of the décor.

My mouth watered. It was instant, the way I was imagining running my hands over that soft skin, wrapping those legs around my waist as I pounded into her, all the wicked things I'd do to her.

Transported.

Lost for a night.

That sweet body a sanctuary.

Discomfort radiated from her in crashing waves, her spine stiff like she didn't want to be there any more than I did.

I'd put down money she was married to one of these pompous douches who forked out a thousand dollars a plate just so he could be seen.

It wasn't like any of these assholes had any actual interest in feeding some impoverished, ratty kid.

Knew the reality of that firsthand.

Like she could feel the weight of my stare, she glanced my way. She froze when she saw me staring back, tripped up, too, both of us getting swept up in an instant of attraction.

Her eyes flashed.

A bright, bright blue.

So distinct that her penetrating gaze almost sent me reeling back.

They shined like crystallized, teal marble. A thousand shades that twisted and spun into something endless. So deep that, if I were to stare too long, I'd tumble right in.

Lust billowed in the space between us. Hot and intense.

That instant attraction had become a bluster in the air. Every single muscle in my damn body went hard just from that single glance.

It was what I craved. Something raw and intense and unbridled. Part passion, part rage.

For a few blissful moments, fully letting go.

Mindless sex.

Bodies giving.

No consequence.

I could feel it. The fever that radiated from her just as intensely as it radiated from me.

Crashing in the middle of us.

Compounding and amplifying and coming alive.

No doubt, the girl was a ticking bomb ready to blow.

Straightening my shoulders, I tried to pretend like I wasn't affected as I watched those crystalline eyes rake over me, fire and ice, and I had to wonder if she was imagining raking her nails down my back instead.

That lasted all of a second before she jerked her attention away and fumbled for a gulp of her drink.

All coy and shy as she put me off, inciting that need inside me to reach out and make her mine.

Grabbing my glass, I sauntered her way, hand stuffed into my tux pocket as I slipped into the stool next to her.

She stiffened, awareness floating from her like a hot breeze.

I fully swiveled her direction, sitting sideways with one elbow resting on the bar and the other on the back of the stool as I leaned back and blatantly took her in.

The girl was so gorgeous she somehow managed to make my insides quake.

I was having a bitch of a time stopping myself from leaning in and pressing my nose to her neck, right at that delicious sweet spot at the back of her ear. From sliding the tips of my fingers up the silky flesh exposed by that dress, taken over by the overpowering urge to get lost in those long, long legs.

"Having fun?" I asked, voice rough, grating with all the visions of what I wanted to do to her.

Her head barely shook. "I'd rather be left alone, if you don't mind."

"Hmm . . . looks to me like you could use some company."

She released an incredulous sound, and she shifted to look my direction, a flash of that icy fire in her eyes.

God, she was pretty.

The kind of pretty that struck you somewhere deep.

I knew well enough that beauty like that was only surface.

"Just don't," she hissed.

My brow lifted in amusement. "Don't what?"

"Oh, please, you think I can't mimic some variation of exactly what you were gettin' ready to say? I'm not naïve. Believe me, I've heard it all before."

Humor ridged my mouth at the same time as it was watering with the sound of her voice.

Southern and sweet and somehow bitter to the bone.

Hard and mad was exactly my thing.

"And what's that?"

A scowl knitted up her forehead. "'What's your sign?' Or was it going to be something along the line of 'what is a girl like you doing in a place like this'? Or maybe you were getting ready to play it off that you knew me from somewhere. That one's my favorite. Whatever it was gonna be, no, you can't have my number."

A rough chuckle rumbled around in my chest, and I moved so I could lean in closer, my head angled so I was about six inches away from her.

Which was apparently too damned close.

Because the energy coming from her hit me like a punch to the face.

Full force.

Fierce and furious.

Didn't help that she smelled delicious.

Like a plump, juicy plum.

The same color as those damned lips.

Fuck me, if I didn't want to take a bite.

"I wasn't actually going to waste my time on a number. I'm more of an 'in the moment kind of guy'. I figured you and I could get out of here and find something a little more . . . interesting to do. You look as bored as I am." My voice lowered, a caress at her ear. "I promise you won't regret it."

A shiver lifted across her skin, so alive I could feel it, before outrage rushed in to take its place.

She reared back, blinking through her offense.

"Wow."

That was all she said.

But I could hear a slew of other insults rambling around in her mind.

I leaned in closer, knowing I was crossing a line considering I was in a place filled with my colleagues. But this girl somehow managed to make me forget all of that.

I couldn't rationalize anything but going after what I wanted.

Right then.

In that moment.

A release.

A blissful oblivion.

A blackout.

And I wanted it with her.

I glanced down at her left hand, expecting to see a huge rock sitting on her ring finger. My dick gave a little fist pump when I found it bare.

"So, what do you say?" I asked, voice casual though I felt anything but.

This girl managed to make me feel off-kilter. Thrown from my game.

Her brow lifted and her tone dipped in disbelief. "You expect me to just . . . walk out of here with you? Just like that? Just you and me in some dark corner? No numbers required because we won't be seeing each other again? No regrets?"

The last she spat.

"That's exactly what I was thinking. Besides," I murmured, "I know exactly what a girl like you is doing in a place like this. Just like the rest of us . . . you're here because you have to be. Because it makes you or whoever you're with look good. You don't have to pretend with me that you give a shit."

Disgust rolled from her. "Who the hell are you?"

"Doesn't matter."

Huffing, she pushed to standing. "You're right. It doesn't matter who you are because you're the last person I'd ever want to know."

Glass clinked as she shakily set her flute onto the bar, and she let her gaze swing back to me, her head angled to the side as she picked up the small clutch that had been sitting on the bar in front of her. "And for the record? You don't know the first thing about me, and I'm pretty sure I would regret even a single second I spent with you."

Without giving me a chance to respond, she moved to slip out of the space between us. When she did, the top of her thigh brushed across my knee.

I jerked, and she stumbled, a sharp gust of air sucked into her lungs.

I was doing the same. Air locked in the tight well of my chest. Heavy and dense.

It felt like a torch had just whipped across my skin and climbed right into my veins.

My ears rang, and my heart started drumming an erratic, harsh beat.

I held my breath, not sure what the fuck that feeling was.

Hating it and wanting to hold it in the palm of my hands at the same time. Knowing it would scorch me if I did.

What the hell?

I shook my head to break the stupor. That was right when her spine went rigid again, and she gathered herself as she started to walk away. All leg, her slinky dress hugging those lush curves, the fabric dipping down to expose the small of her back. So sexy I could hardly fucking breathe.

She moved across the room and disappeared into the crowd

without looking back.

My stomach fisted.

"Shit," I muttered, gulping down the rest of my drink, trying to chase the unsettled feeling away.

This absurd urge to chase after her.

I didn't chase women.

They weren't interested in my proposition, they could go on their way.

No harm.

No foul.

But that sensation wouldn't abate.

Shit.

What was wrong with me?

But it didn't matter how hard I tried to convince myself that going after her would be a mistake, I was downing my scotch and slamming the empty onto the bar before my feet were carrying me across the floor.

GRACE

What in the world had just happened?

It felt as if I'd stepped right into a riot.

Unrest and tumult.

The man a disorder I could feel coming from a hundred miles away.

Gorgeous and powerful and oh so wrong.

I could feel those potent, strange-colored eyes searing into me from behind, as if he could remain sitting right there and they could still chase me down. Pin me. See everything hidden inside.

I did my best to keep my head held high and to keep my feet from slipping out from under me. I rushed through the room filled with round-tables covered in fine linens and china and crystal where dinner had been served that I hadn't been present for.

I was the damned fool who'd sneaked in after.

Uninvited.

Unwelcome.

I made it through the tables to the other side of the room where a band was set up on the makeshift stage, playing a slow R & B cover from the seventies. Below it, couples had moved onto the dancefloor.

I started to cut across it, my heels sliding across the slick floor as I rushed for the massive ballroom doors at the opposite side.

The promise of retreat was a mere forty feet away.

God, I never should have come here.

I'd been sitting at that stupid bar licking my wounds, trying to hold back the tears and the anger and the sorrow, all the while praying that Kenneth Millstrom might have a change of heart and come up to me.

Tell me he'd represent me.

That I had a fighting chance rather than him laughing at me and saying, "I'm sorry, but you have to know that's just not going to happen, sweetheart. I'd be a fool to take you on as a client. You're wasting your time."

Sweetheart.

What a douche.

I still couldn't tell whether he'd been being condescending or sympathetic. Either way, it didn't matter. Those words still had the same effect.

They'd crushed me.

Then, not thirty minutes later, I was being propositioned by that asshole.

That asshole who had my chest heaving for air as I searched for sanity.

No question, that man had the power to strip me of both.

How could I even allow a man to affect me? Even if it were only for a second?

Oh, but it wasn't only for a second. Because I felt it again. An overwhelming surge of heat that washed over me from behind.

Something dark, almost sinister, an open invitation to step into his expensive brand of sin.

I thought to propel myself faster, hike up my skirt and run, but instead I was whipping my head over my shoulder, unable to stop myself from seeking out those eyes, slowing like one of those stupid girls who stepped right into an ambush she was just too dumb to see.

Tripped up and trapped.

My heart raced, already certain of what I would find.

Oh, was I right.

That gorgeous man was making his way through the crowd. Couples who were dancing spun out of his way, as if he had the power to command a storm. To part the waters with the wicked gleam of those eyes. Or maybe it was just with the ruthlessness that oozed with every step that he took.

As if he were on the hunt.

The second he caught sight of me, his sexy mouth twisted up in an arrogant grin.

There I was, in for the fight of my life, and I was allowing myself to get all hot and bothered by some gorgeous stranger who was clearly after one thing.

A shiver rolled down my spine, and I kept backing away as he came closer.

Good lord, gorgeous was right.

Impossible, really.

So beautiful, I'd momentarily gone stupid when I'd glanced that way and saw him standing at the opposite end of the bar a few minutes ago. So obscenely sexy I'd thought I had to be hallucinating.

My mind conjuring a fantasy to make getting through the night a little less brutal.

He angled through the chaos of couples that swirled and spun and swayed.

Tux fitting that perfect body like he'd been sewn into it, shoulders wide and waist narrow, taller than any man had the right to be.

He stared at me from across the hazy glow of lights, making me fumble, the glittering light catching his eyes that were the color of cracked cinnamon and speckled with the sun.

Still wearing that sexy-as-sin grin, he roughed a hand through his brown hair that was cut short and styled impeccably.

Every line of his masculine face was chiseled and sharp, the guy carved of stone, a perfectly trimmed five o'clock shadow defining his strong jaw. I'd have said he was made of marble, all smooth and shiny and glossy, except there was something rough beneath that polished exterior.

Something raw and unbridled.

Dangerous in a way that made my stomach quake.

But after he'd opened that deliciously decadent mouth, I'd realized he was no fantasy.

He was nothing but a bad dream.

A delusion.

That pretty exterior nothing but an illusion of all the nastiness hidden underneath.

Problem was, I was held by that fantasy. Captured and entranced as he strode in my direction. I needed to up and run, and instead, I was standing in the middle of the dancefloor like a lamb that wanted to get eaten.

I'd finally just about come to my senses when he was suddenly right there, a tower of darkness that cast a shadow over me, so damned tall I had to tilt my head back to fully take him in.

But it wasn't really me who was doing the *taking*.

He was devouring me with that potent gaze, exactly like I'd imagined.

"Dance with me." It was a rough command.

A lure.

That energy moved.

A stir at my feet.

I tried not to get trapped by it, by the feeling of it crawling up my legs and spreading over my body. Chaining me to the spot.

I swallowed down the attraction. "I don't think that's a good idea."

He came closer. Stealing the air and making me shiver.

His mouth was so close to my ear that I couldn't tell if it was his breath or his lips that were sending tingles rushing as they brushed across my skin. "I think it's a brilliant idea."

"That's because you don't have anything to lose."

"Don't I?"

If I wasn't watching him so closely, I might have missed the way he grimaced, the way something struck him deep.

It only lasted for a second before that smirk slipped into something seductive.

"Besides, what could one dance hurt?"

"Oh, I'm sure it could hurt plenty."

I knew it in the way I'd started to move around him, attracted and repelled, as if this man was the gravity in the room. We were suddenly in a slow dance. Not even touching, and still, I could feel him everywhere.

As if those big hands were roaming over my body. Making me scream and shiver and quake.

And my body was already making the foolish decision for me, drawn toward him, compelled by the rhythm of the music as everything pitched into a mesmerized sway.

He leaned in, his mouth back at my ear. "You're worried about being hurt, when the only thing I'm thinking about is how good I could make you feel. I'd make you lose your mind, beautiful."

"I don't doubt that."

Not for a second.

"Everyone deserves a moment to forget," he murmured, as if he already saw all the things bleeding inside me, and then I really was shivering because he looped an arm around my waist and pulled me close.

The two of us were instantly at one with the cadence of the slow, provocative beat. "Let me be the one to do it."

I inhaled a trembling breath when I realized I was in his arms.

The man was so big. Tall and powerful in a way that should make me afraid, muscles hard and bursting with strength, but somehow, I was wanting to completely melt into the strength of his hold.

"I don't even know you," I whispered.

"Believe me, you don't really want to. That's what makes this a brilliant idea. A win-win. Tell me you don't feel it."

I was pretty sure he was no longer talking about a simple dance.

"I feel it. What I'm concerned about is the aftermath." The admission was a slip of sound, swept up in the sway of our bodies as he led me around the floor like a pro.

A pro at stealing hearts. I was sure he left them scattered all over the floor, stomped on them with the sole of his expensive shoes after he'd held them in the palms of his hands.

Tossed away so carelessly after he'd had his fill.

His mouth barely grazed along my jaw. The hint of a kiss.

Need tumbled through me in a way I'd never before experienced.

Spikes of heat.

A flood of desire.

I wondered if I'd ever truly been seduced by a man. If this was what it was like.

Spellbound and needy and hot.

So caught up in a moment that I didn't take the time to think through the consequences. In the moment, the cost didn't matter.

Careless.

That was what it was.

"I'd make sure it was worth it." Apparently, the man was the messenger of seduction with the way he was whispering promises at my skin. "I'd make you come again and again until the only thing you knew was the pleasure only I can give you. The feel of my hands and my cock and my skin and our bodies giving in. It'll leave you with a memory you'll never forget."

Wow. I didn't know whether to slap him or beg him to show me what that might be like.

A shiver of warning that ran through my veins.

"And what if that memory becomes a scar?"

"How could I hurt when we both know, in the end, I won't matter?"

He twirled us around, and I didn't know why, but my eyes peeled open at the second the opposite end of the massive room was directly in my line of sight.

It just about knocked me onto my ass.

What it did do was toss me right back into reality.

My reality.

To who I was and why I was there and exactly what I was fighting for.

A gasp ripped from my lungs, and my already thrumming pulse shot into overdrive.

Racing in fear and dread and hate.

A hate I knew all too well when my sight hooked on the man chatting with another guy dressed in a tux over near the bank of windows that made up the far wall.

My heart stopped beating. Or maybe it'd just crashed right out of my chest.

Reed was there.

Of course, he was there. Would I actually have thought he'd have missed an opportunity to toss around more of that bloated ego and his fake, shiny smiles?

Could I be any more naïve?

I stumbled back, trying to orient myself against the dizziness that swirled through my mind. To balance myself on the floor that was suddenly spinning.

Oh, God.

What was I doin'? What was I doin'?

Dancing with a man out in public when Reed was set on tearing my life to shreds?

My knees went weak, and the guy who I'd been about ten minutes from falling into bed with tried to hold me up. Confusion sliced across his gorgeous face as he struggled to catch up to what had sent me into a tailspin.

"Are you okay?" he asked in that gruff voice that spun through my senses like a rough caress.

Was I okay?

No.

Not even close.

"What's wrong? Need you to tell me what's happening, right now." His voice had shifted, his demeanor instantly protective with a sharp edge of menace slipping into his tone. The kind of menace I'd first recognized. That polished exterior dropping to expose the raw severity of the man underneath.

I had no time to explain. No reason to give him. I didn't even know his name.

I twisted myself out of his arms, this man that I somehow knew was just as dangerous as the one standing across the room. Maybe in a different way, but my guts screamed that the feeling he'd awoken in me was only gonna destroy me if I let this go on any farther.

So, I did what I should have done fifteen minutes ago.

I ran.

three

IAN

I felt her go cold in my arms, her knees going weak and panic piercing her like a stake of a red-hot iron.

"Are you okay?" I whispered, trying to keep the aggression that slammed me locked down.

Last thing I needed to do was throw down in the middle of Charleston's elite. Might be a bit of a detriment to my image for these people to get a good look at the seedy darkness that writhed inside me.

Didn't matter.

My eyes were darting all over the place, searching for a threat while I tried to gather her closer, having the intense urge to wrap her up and whisper in her ear. Promise that it would be okay.

Protect her.

Shield her from whatever had just sent her spiraling. Without a doubt, it didn't have a single thing to do with me.

Nails clung to me like I was the only thing keeping her standing, and I swore those fingers in my shoulders were dragging me over the edge right along with her, directly into a fool's game.

She didn't respond, and my voice gritted, a hard, vicious plea, "What's wrong? Need you to tell me what's happening, right now."

I couldn't afford to do this.

Slip.

Stumble.

Care or worry.

Get involved when I had absolutely nothing to offer.

The only thing I was looking for was a good time. A girl who wanted to get lost as desperately as I did. To fuck and forget.

So, I sure as shit shouldn't be showing concern. What was worse was that I wanted to show it in the first place.

Hit with this overwhelming need to fight and defend.

Thing was, I could physically feel a roll of terror crawl across her flesh like a disease. Maybe it was just the fact I was holding her in my arms while it was going down, but it was like I watched as demons slithered and scaled and scrambled over her before they jumped onto me, impaling me with steely claws and talons.

They sank deeper than should be possible. Got under my skin where I couldn't let her go.

She just shook her head, this gorgeous girl ripping herself from my hold and pushing her way through the couples who continued to dance, completely oblivious to the roil of energy pounding through the air.

She darted out the doors, that fabric of her skirt billowing behind her.

My attention flew around the room, searching, seeing nothing amiss. But that didn't mean I wasn't sure everything was wrong.

Like a fool, I chased her. I just . . . needed to make sure she was safe. See to it that the valet got her into her car and she drove away.

Then I'd step back.

Let her go.

There was something about her that warned I had to.

I pushed my way off the dancefloor and out the double-ballroom doors. Panting, my eyes scanned both directions.

She was nowhere in sight.

I moved for the elevators at the far end of the foyer. The doors were just slipping closed. That antsy feeling pulsed.

"Fuck it."

Dressed in a goddamned tux, I skipped the elevators and hit the stairwell. My shoes pounded down ten flights of stairs.

What was I doing?

This was stupid.

Goddamned stupid.

I was sucking for air by the time I made it to the ground floor, but I pushed myself harder across the slick, shiny floor, over the golden designs stamped in the gleaming, smooth stone.

I skidded as I came to the massive front doors. I dipped my head as the bellman held one side open for me.

Cool air hit my face, the deepening night growing colder as the distinct feel of fall took hold of the air.

I went straight for the valet station.

No chance would she have had time for her car to be brought around. Apprehension tightened my chest when I didn't see her standing there.

I moved for the valet who was manning the station, the kid clearly getting a hard on for the Ferrari that just rolled to a stop in front of him. Doubted he was paying me much attention.

"Did a woman just pick up her car? Tall. Beige dress? Blonde hair?"

Sexy as fuck.

Didn't need to feed any extra images into the punk's head.

He frowned at me, clearly getting ready to dismiss me before I pulled out my wallet and handed him a hundred. He didn't even hesitate to accept it.

Prick.

He gestured with his head behind me. "She went that way."

I flipped back around, heading that direction, increasing my pace with every step that I took. What the fuck was she doing, walking by herself in the middle of the night? Unease swept through, a tumble on the ground, inciting me to move faster.

I rushed down the sidewalk that lined the maintained grounds of the hotel, along the perfectly hewn hedges, the old building sitting back under the protection of imposing trees.

The entire place was lit in an ambience of wealth and affluence.

I was nearly running by the time I made it to the corner where it intersected with a side road.

Moonlight pooled like an oasis from above, painting the sky a milky glow, and it was my turn to feel like a prick when I rounded the corner and slammed right into a wall of the girl's panic.

The second she felt me, she raced across the street, her heels clicking on the choppy pavement as she ran.

Running for her life.

Sounds were jetting from her lungs, these tiny cries of desperation as she clung to her dress and tried to make it to a nondescript white sedan parked on the opposite side of the road.

By itself.

The area desolate and deserted.

The girl was nothing but a sitting duck.

I'd seen enough monsters lurking in dark corners to know this was a bad call.

She knew it, too, because she pushed herself harder, like she felt a menacing presence slip in from behind.

I was a second from grinding to a halt. Calling out to her like some kind of blathering fool that I was just checking to make sure she was okay and not some bastard who was there to hurt her.

So yeah, I wanted to fuck her. But I'd never force a girl into doing what she didn't want to do. Not once. Not ever.

But it was already too late for that.

The spike of her heel caught in a crack in the road, and I watched in helpless horror as the girl went flying. Body propelled forward, arms shooting out to try to stop herself from falling.

A cry of pain struck the air when her knees and hands hit the hard, unforgiving ground. She skidded on the rough pavement, her dress tearing at the side. Her clutch slipped from her hold and sent the contents scattering across the ground.

My body jolted back like I could feel the impact. For a beat, I froze before worry and concern hijacked my veins, and I rushed across the street toward her.

She heard me coming, and she flew around, scrambling back, those blue, blue eyes going wide in fear.

Those legs were bent at an odd angle, the thin material of her dress bunched up at her thighs, one shoe gone where it was stuck in the road.

I was the sick fuck who thought he'd never seen anything more beautiful.

A battered Cinderella.

An angel with a broken halo.

I pushed my hands out in front of me in a show of surrender, trying to carve my voice into the most placating sound I could find. Kind of hard to do when it was typically filled with bitterness and hate. "Hey . . . it's okay. I'm not here to hurt you."

But I sure as fuck wanted to hurt the fucker that'd put that look on her face.

She kept fumbling backward for a second before she heaved out in both shock and relief when she finally realized it was me, like she got that I wouldn't touch her unless she really wanted me to.

And fuck, I wanted to.

That overpowering sensation hit me again, growing stronger with every inch that I took toward her. Urging me to wrap her up. Maybe rock her and soothe her and tell her everything was going to be okay like some kind of punk.

Hell no.

I needed to turn around and walk.

Turn my back.

Because this girl was making me have urges that were not okay.

I would have, too, but that was right when she tried to choke back a sob. It erupted from her throat, her bloodied palms going to her face as she began to weep.

Might be a dick, but there was no turning my back on that.

She could be . . . hurt.

I crossed the street, edging forward like I was approaching a wild, caged animal.

There was no question in my mind the girl was close to coming unhinged.

I could feel it, the helplessness that might cause her to snap seeping from her pores. Pooling on the ground around her like the blackest puddle of mud.

Slowly kneeling in front of her, I pried her hands from her face. Blood was smeared across one cheek and down her chin. I pulled her palms toward me, searching the superficial scrapes that oozed red beneath the moonlight.

"Fuck, I'm sorry, I didn't mean to scare you."

It didn't come out sounding like much of an apology, considering my teeth were clenched and my stomach was seething.

One hundred percent on edge.

Lust still blazed, and that crazy feeling of possession that left me itchy was making me feel like I was going to lose my goddamned mind.

She turned her face away, shoulders heaving as she cried almost silently. Like she was trying to rein it in, pull it back, hide it behind the strength I could see radiating from her.

Like she was ashamed to be seen that way.

Broken down.

Vulnerable.

I took her by the chin, a gentle prod for her to look at me.

And I tried to remember every reason I'd ever given myself not to get involved.

How women couldn't be trusted.

Tried to remember the oath I'd made.

But when she looked up at me with a river of mascara running down her cheeks, I fucking forgot everything.

My mind. My sanity. My reason.

"Hey. Are you okay? Tell me where you're hurt. Let me help you."

What was I saying? Offering? But I didn't know how to stop.

Wide eyes stared back at me.

Vast.

Endless.

A churning, icy sea.

"I . . ."

"It's okay. I'm right here."

"I need . . . I need . . ."

Confusion tumbled off her tongue before she was struck with panic again, and she jerked out of my hold, flipping around to get onto her hands and knees. She began to frantically scrounge around to collect her things, whimpers coming from her mouth as she did.

Keys and a compact and lipstick that she shakily shoved back into the small bag.

I grabbed her cell phone and a tin of mints and passed them to her.

"Thank you," she whispered.

We shared a glance.

A pass of agony in her eyes and something that felt like compassion coming from me.

Good God. What was that?

But it was there.

I swallowed hard, my throat dry, everything so goddamned wrong. And the question was coming free without my permission. "What's your name?"

She stilled, her body trembling while that same awareness surged between us. Thick and deep and consuming. "Grace," she whispered.

"Grace," I repeated, testing it on my tongue. I handed her a crinkled scrap of paper. "I'm sorry I scared you. I just needed to make sure you made it to your car okay. Couldn't turn my back after the way you took off like that. Are you?"

She looked at me like I was crazy. Apparently, that was the case.

"Okay?" I prodded.

A self-deprecating sound scraped up her throat, and she gave a harsh shake of her head. "No, I'm not okay."

She climbed onto her shaking feet. I followed, rising to my full height.

Had to curl my damned hands into fists to resist the urge to reach out and rub the smear of blood from her chin.

I didn't care.

I didn't care.

Didn't have the capacity.

Hell, my caring only ever led to bad, bad things. The last thing she needed was some asshole like me getting into her business. Never turned out pretty.

Still, I couldn't keep from pressing her. "You seemed . . . upset back there."

"You could call it that," she mumbled in something that was close to a drawl, something sweet and Southern and still modern.

Guilt. It was a bitch. Hated feeling it. But somehow it was there, the idea that maybe I'd been responsible for this. This broken girl who somehow managed to glow beneath the moonlight.

"Did I scare you? Out on the dancefloor . . . what I said?" And just because it was me, it still managed to come out sounding like a threat.

The shake of her head was slow. "No," she quietly admitted.

"Then what happened?"

"I was just reminded why I can't do this."

"What, dance?" I tried to inject a little lightness into the mood when there was absolutely nothing about it that felt that way.

She laughed a short, disbelieving sound, and she looked directly at me, her voice stronger than I expected. "Pretend as if things don't matter. You might be able to pretend as if *you* don't matter. As if *I* don't matter. As if the people who come into your life don't matter, whether if it's for a fleeting moment or for years."

Her delicate throat trembled. "But that isn't me. People matter. A man touching me will always mean something, and you assuming that it doesn't is a reminder that I deserve so much more than what you're willing to offer. I've lost too much, but I have even more to lose."

Her words speared me like darts, chest going tight with more of that regret. To ask her what that meant. What she'd lost and how the fuck I could help her get it back. I struggled with what to say, to apologize, but I didn't fucking know how to apologize for what had happened upstairs before she'd gone running.

The energy that had blazed between us.

Fire and heat and need. Even if she'd been able to ignore it, I wasn't sure I was a strong enough man to do it. Because even with her standing there bloodied and scraped and bruised, I wanted to erase the space, push her against her car, get under that dress, and disappear.

Hadn't had a girl make me want her this way in a long, long time. Maybe not ever. The need urgent. A thrumming command that beat through my blood.

She looked away, into the vacant distance toward the bay. A breeze rustled through the strands of her long blonde hair. It whipped around her like a disturbance that shivered across her skin. "I need to go. Coming here was a terrible idea."

"Yeah, and why's that? Seems to me you were exactly where you should be," I said, pushing more. Not wanting her to leave.

Wondering how the fuck I might be able to keep her. Just for the night.

She laughed a disbelieving sound. "And that right there is the exact reason I shouldn't have come."

She started to hobble toward her car, one shoe on, the other foot still bare. Her dress was torn and shredded on one side and the fabric was dotted with blood from the cut on her knee.

She was a mess.

A gorgeous fucking mess.

A disaster waiting to happen.

She pressed the fob and the lights flashed.

Panic welled up like the build of a surprise storm.

Coming from out of nowhere.

Hitting land without warning.

She clicked open the door and started to climb inside.

My fingers twitched with the impulse to reach out and stop her from leaving. Or maybe it was just my dick aching to get messy. Knowing this girl was somehow as wild as I was. Desperate and willing to do whatever it took to get her where she needed to go.

I could see it written all over her.

Determination.

Strength.

Courage.

All of those things made for something I couldn't get into, and the only thing I was doing was aching to get *into* it.

Let her go. Let her go, I silently screamed at myself, knowing I was begging for trouble. There was something about her that was too different—too good and fierce—that had me trembling.

She didn't need my bullshit. The only thing I wanted was to fuck her. Use her up and toss her aside before she got the chance to do it first.

Consume before you're consumed.

A motto that had served me well.

"How about that number, Grace?" If my conscience could have drop-kicked me, it would have. God, I was just asking for it, wasn't I?

But I thought the girl looked like she might be worth a little pain.

She paused to look back at me from over her shoulder. If I didn't know any better, I'd have said it was something close to amusement that infiltrated her tone. "Doesn't seem much your style. I thought you were more of an 'in the moment' kind of guy?"

A gruff sound rumbled in my chest when she tossed my words back in my face. "No. You're right. It isn't exactly my style."

Her voice was a soft surrender. "I'm doubtin' that I'm much your style at all."

My eyes roved over that tight, sweet body. Lush curves and full hips and perfect tits. If I had a style—a style or a type or a goddamned heart—she'd be it.

I was pretty sure she saw it written on me, a black emblem that pronounced my shame.

The uptick at the corner of one of those lips was nothing but a somber goodbye. "Thank you for the dance."

Then she slipped into the driver's seat, started her car, and left me standing there in the middle of the road watching as she drove away, again fighting that foreign feeling that tugged at my chest.

There were few people in my life who ever evoked any emotion in my mangled, twisted heart. Those who had gotten in through the brittle cracks.

People who I would fight for.

Die for.

Kill for.

Jace and his family and my best friend Mack.

They were only there because they were the only reason I was still living in the first place. Because they'd proven time and again that they could be trusted.

That they would do the same for me.

The rest of the world?

They could go fuck themselves.

Lies fell from people's tongues so much more often than the truth. Betrayals cast far more often than loyalties.

I wasn't pretending to be any different.

My gaze moved back to the vacant space where she had just been.

I didn't know why it felt like she was different. Why it *mattered*. I'd only met her. Sure as hell didn't know her.

Shouldn't, either. Chase it. That feeling. It was nothing but a fool's game.

A tumble over the edge of oblivion.

A freefall into ruin.

But there was something about her that whispered and soothed and sang.

Or maybe what I was really hearing was her soul screaming for help.

I roughed a frustrated hand over my face to break up the clusterfuck of stupidity that was trying to climb into my mind and started to head back for the party. Then I tripped over my own damned feet when I caught sight of the two objects that were on the ground up close to the curb where they had been concealed by her car.

Left unnoticed when we'd collected the rest of her things.

It was a small wallet and a piece of jewelry.

Stooping down, I picked up the wallet, and then moved to grab the metal that glinted in the hazy glow. I rolled it around my fingers. It was a silver bracelet, cheap and banged to shit. Dangling from it were three stones that as far as I could tell were fake.

I frowned, straightening as I held the two offending objects.

At war with what to do, not sure how to handle this bullshit raging inside me.

I should toss them. Or maybe turn them in at the front desk.

Just a regular ol' Good Samaritan, right?

Or I could dig into the wallet like I was itching to do and discover who she was. Return them myself. Maybe in return, I'd get a *reward*.

Thing was, I got the crazed sense that if I took a step that direction, I'd regret it. Could feel myself getting sucked into the girl's business that wasn't mine. Needing to know what had dimmed the intensity of those sea-tinged eyes. The magnetized vortex I could feel swirling around her.

Dragging in everything in her path, swallowed where it would be emptied in her depths.

A fist gripped my heart as my mind was struck with the memory of the voice I wished I could erase. Purge and pummel and eradicate. A voice that shouldn't fucking *matter*, the soft lull of the song she had sang.

Forever and ever.

Hatred tumbled through my consciousness, all mixed up with a howling whirlwind of grief. Memories forever fresh and raw and grating. It didn't matter how much time had passed.

One day . . . one day I'd outrun them.

One day, I'd get so far that her ghost wouldn't be able to touch me.

And still, there she was, prodding at my conscience to do something right.

"Shit," I grumbled, unable to do anything but stuff the wallet and bracelet into my pocket. Then, like a fool, I reached down and wiggled the girl's shoe free from where it was wedged.

Holding it, my gaze was pulled down the vacant road where she'd just sped off.

Motherfucking Cinderella.

GRACE

I pulled into the short driveway in front of the tiny house and killed the engine. It cast my world into silence. Into darkness.

Shimmers of despair flashed at the outside of my eyes.

Worry.

Dread.

Fear.

How in the world was I supposed to beat Reed when it felt as if the world was against me? Or really, it was the world that stood at his side. Blinded by the façade that he wore. Reed the ruler of his own world. The empire that he and his family had built.

It wasn't as if I hadn't been blinded by it, too. But that was a long, long time ago, and it was already far too late by the time I'd realized it. Before I'd unknowingly allowed myself to become a prisoner to it.

Blowing out a sigh, I flipped down the sunshade. The glaring light burst to life around the tiny mirror, and I cringed when I saw my reflection. Blood smeared on my face, streaked by my tears with an added slick of mascara for good measure.

Eyes haunted and wild at the same damned time.

I was a mess.

Most unsettling was what that stranger had whipped up in the middle of me.

I was still feeling a little shell-shocked at the reaction he'd evoked, at the fact he'd managed to pry that feeling out of me at all.

Pushing open the door, I stumbled out into the vacant, chilly night. The modest neighborhood was sleeping, porchlights glowing and the windows blackened along the narrow street.

It was as if I were a refugee in the middle of it. A stranger who'd sought asylum. The hope and the peace where I might be reinvigorated, infused with the hope and courage that I was going to need to win this battle.

It made it difficult when everyone kept telling me it was a losing fight.

Here, the houses looked as if they'd been stamped out by the same mold and deposited in a perfect row on each side. People might actually get confused which one was theirs if it weren't for the different colors they'd been painted, the additions and renovations made through the years.

Standing on the concrete driveway in front of the single-car garage, I wiggled off my remaining shoe, gaze dropping to the beige suede pump.

The beautiful stranger infiltrated my mind.

His rough, rugged care.

That polished, sophisticated seduction.

He made me feel things I couldn't feel. Made me contemplate things I couldn't contemplate. Made me want to dip my fingers into that feeling that washed over me.

That hot, hot energy that had blasted and seared and crashed against us like waves slamming against a break wall down at the marina.

Attraction.

So fierce and instant I'd known it could lead to nowhere good. I had a path I had to take. One that couldn't be diverted. Detours down a road with a scenic view included.

Leaving him standing there was the only choice I could make. It wasn't as if I could just hand over my number.

A guy like him wouldn't understand, and even if he did, the last thing I needed to do was add another complication to this catastrophe.

The last thing I could afford was a fling concealed by the darkness of night.

My heart couldn't take it, and I wasn't close to being that reckless.

I trudged up the sidewalk, trying to remain as quiet as possible as I slipped my key into the lock. I turned it quietly, wincing at the sound of the metal giving as it was unlatched.

Old hinges creaked as I pushed open the door. Silence echoed back.

Carefully latching it shut behind me, I turned the lock before I tiptoed through the foyer and toward the hall, only to freeze when I got to the arch at the living room.

A gush of regret got free of my lungs when I saw the small lamp glowing from the coffee table.

Gramma pushed to her feet when she saw me, and I swore, I could hear all of her joints groaning as she did, my rock wringing her hands together in the worry she'd clearly been swimming in since I'd walked out the door earlier. "Well? Tell me how it went."

Disappointment throbbed everywhere, as if I could feel my heartbeat in my face and my fingers and my toes.

I inched into the room.

She gasped and pressed her fingertips to her weathered face when she saw my appearance. "Oh my, child . . . what on God's green earth happened to you?"

Instantly, her face went red with anger.

"Tell me *he* didn't get to you." She limped my way, hostile rage pulsing free. If I was looking for an army, the old woman was an entire fleet.

She'd had her own share of battles and wars, and she might be broken down, but she was stronger for it. I hadn't hesitated when I'd shown up at her door asking her to be strong for me four months ago.

"I swear on all things holy that I'm not gonna let him get away with it. I'll string him up so fast he won't know what hit him."

The last had become a rumbled threat.

Blowing out a breath, I tossed my clutch to the couch and pulled off the teardrop earrings she'd let me borrow. As if looking pretty was gonna make a lick of difference. "You know he has better ways of getting at me than making me bleed."

Well, at least not the parts that were exposed.

"Then what happened to you?" She searched my face with her blue, aged eyes.

I shook my head. "I fell."

Her brow rose, digging for more, knowing there was a whole lot more to the story than I was letting on.

My grandmother knew me better than anyone.

I huffed out a breath of concession and let my shoulders sag. "Reed was there. I took off the second I saw him. Just as I was getting to my car, I felt someone behind me. I started running, afraid it might be him."

Except, I hadn't really thought that, had I? It was that energy zapping like electricity through the air that had sent me running for my life. The feeling that if that stranger got too close, he was going to trip me up, have me falling into something that my shattered heart would never survive.

Oh, and trip I had.

Worry had her gnawing at the inside of her lip. "Did Reed see you there?"

Sinking down on the edge of the loveseat, I bent over into a huddle and started rocking, like that motion might keep all the pieces together. "No. I don't think so, but I'm sure it's gonna get back to him that I was there."

Or more importantly, what I was there sniffing around for.

I looked up at her. "It was stupid going there. I knew better. Should have known he'd show up to an event like that. What in the world was I thinking?"

She moved to cup the side of my face.

There were few people as tender and fierce as my grandmother. So staunch and understanding.

The woman had held me up in my darkest times, and she also didn't hesitate to knock some sense into me when I was being crazy.

She brushed her thumb across my cheek. "You went there because you're brave enough to show your face. Making a claim that you're willing to do whatever it takes to fight that monster. That he doesn't scare you and you aren't going to back down."

A puff of discouragement blew from my nose. "And the second I saw him, I went running."

She grinned. "Galas aren't meant to be battlegrounds. You were gathering ammunition. It wasn't time for the attack."

A grin played around my face.

Only my grandma.

She lifted my chin higher, forcing me to look at her. "And believe me, sweet one, this is a battle that will be worth fighting. It's one worth getting torn up over. One that's worth every bullet and every scar. One you'll fight to the bitter end."

I stared up at her, hope a blister of energy glowing firm in my chest. Pulsing and pushing. "I won't stop, either, Gramma. Even if it costs me everything, I won't stop."

"That's right. Because the important things in life are worth everything. Everyone's fight is different. But believe me, it's always a fight. And we fight for what's most important to us."

Fear and hope swung like a pendulum inside me.

"But what if I lose?" I could barely choke out the question, the idea of it something I couldn't entertain.

"You won't, sweet thing, I promise, you won't."

"I'm scared," I told her, my admission floating into the dense, brittle air. I didn't want to confess it. To put it out into the atmosphere.

I wanted to cling to her belief in me. Cling to the idea that I was brave and a fighter.

But the truth was that I was terrified.

Each day that passed, it just got harder and harder when he didn't back down. I'd thought he'd eventually concede. Decide it wasn't *worth* it to him. But I should have known better, the way his giving up would look, the man refusing to have his perfect reputation tarnished.

What bullshit.

Gramma squeezed the side of my face with her bony hand, and still it felt like the most comfortable thing. "It's okay to be afraid. The times I've fought hardest in my life are the times I've been most scared. Only because I was *afraid* of losing. And that's what makes us fight all the harder."

I set my hand over hers, pressing her closer, savoring the warmth. The comfort she'd always given. "I love you. So much. I don't know what I'd do without you."

She sent me a grin. "Well, you'd probably starve. We could start right there."

A shot of laughter escaped me. "Are you telling me I'm a bad cook?"

She cocked a brow. "What I'm telling you is that you're a terrible cook."

"So much love, Grams. So much love," I said, voice wry.

She chuckled. "Well, we all have our strengths. It's not your fault that you could burn the house down tryin' to boil a pot of water."

I feigned a gasp. "I take offense to that. I'll have you know I've been told I make a mean pot of mac and cheese."

She patted my arm. "I'm sorry, sweet thing, but this is where that delusion needs to end. Only thing a person can do is choke that rubber down and hope they don't up and die trying. You're lucky you have me around."

A pout formed. "How'd I spend my entire life with you in the kitchen and not learn a single thing?"

"Like I said, we all have our strengths. I filled your belly to show you my love. Tucked you in at night."

"Read me stories," I supplied, my heart pressing full at the memories.

"That's right," she said.

"That was my favorite," I told her, wistfulness winding its way into my tone.

She brushed back the hair matted to my forehead. "And you show yours by writing them."

My throat clamped up. Overcome. Love and adoration and gratitude threatening to spill out.

She cleared her throat and inclined her head. "Come on, let's get you cleaned up. You're a sight."

She led me into the kitchen. She went to the sink and turned on the water. When it warmed up, she ran a cloth under it and then pulled out a stool from the small table in the center of the old kitchen.

"Sit."

"Bossy," I told her.

"Don't you know it."

"That I do."

She'd been as strict as they'd come when she'd been raising me, but not even close to clipping my wings, the woman always there believing that I could go soaring.

When she dabbed the cloth on my face, washing off the blood and the dirt and the tears—so softly, so gently—I almost felt like that same little girl she'd taken in when I'd lost my parents.

My mind drifted back to the day that she'd tended to me in this exact same spot when I had scraped my knee after falling off my bike.

I wondered if she were remembering the same thing because the hint of a smile played around her mouth. "Let me see that knee. Looks like you did a number on it."

I gathered the fabric so she could get a better look. It wasn't all that hard to do considering the dress was shredded, a rip running up the opposite side of the one where the slit was actually supposed to be.

Damn dress.

Gramma whistled low. "Look at those gams."

I tried to spread the material back out. "Gramma," I chided.

She hiked a shoulder. "What? If you've got it, flaunt it, and girl, you've got it. You come from a long line of beautiful women. Don't you know that?"

There was a gleam in her eyes.

Light laughter filtered free. "I know, I've seen pictures of you. You were a knockout."

"Pssh." She waved her hand. "What are you talking about, was? I am a knockout. You should see all the men fighting for me down at the bingo hall."

"Do I need to come down there and whip them into shape? Tell them to back off?"

As if the spitfire needed the backup.

"God no. Best night of the week."

I shook my head at her, then winced when she dabbed the cloth on my knee, the cut there a little deeper than the rest.

"You definitely need to get some medicine and bandages on this one. You're lucky you don't need stitches."

She glanced up at me from where she was bent down to inspect my injured leg. "So, if it wasn't that two-bit, no-good jackass who likes to pretend he's a man when he's nothin' but a snake slithering up behind you, who was it that sent my girl running?"

My insides shivered, rushed with the remnants of that strange energy. I still didn't know what to make of it. I released a heavy sigh. "It was no one."

She cocked a questioning brow. As if she'd climbed right into my head and sifted through every single one of my thoughts.

No doubt, she already knew there was something I wasn't telling her. That was the problem when you spent your entire life living with a woman like her. She knew you inside out and right back out again.

Hell, she usually knew what I was going to say before I ever had the chance to say it.

I huffed and tried not to roll my eyes. She'd been doing this to me since I was thirteen. "Fine. It was a boy."

A menacing, terrifying, beautiful boy.

And there was nothing *boy* about him. He was all tall, firm, delicious man.

"Running from a boy?" She tsked with a grin, dabbing a little more at the cut. "He'd better have been a cute boy to make a cut like this worth it."

There she was, reading my thoughts again. The sneak.

"No, Gramma, he was most definitely not worth it. He's just like the rest."

Selfish.

Arrogant.

Cocky and brash and after one thing.

It didn't matter how gorgeous or sexy he was. How my body had lit up with just the brush of our skin.

He was dangerous.

I knew it somewhere deep.

"Besides, you know I can't go doing something so foolish as that," I continued. "There's too much on the line."

"We all deserve to be loved," she told me.

"I think I have more important things to worry about right now than getting wound up in the arms of another man."

One day, I'd find it. Someone to love me the way she was talking about. Someone who would put me before themselves just the same way as I'd do for them.

"Besides, it was just one of those chance encounters. I won't ever see him again. It was nothing."

She stepped back, her bottom lip tucked between her teeth as she studied me. Then she reached out and nudged me under the chin, lifting it. "All in good time, sweet thing. It'll fall into place. You'll see."

I gave her a nod.

"You'd better get some rest. Lord knows, I'm worn out."

The hint of a smile worked its way to my mouth. "Sorry about that."

"Don't you dare apologize. It's my honor. Nothing could make an old lady happier. Believe me."

She touched my cheek again before she left me there, shuffling off to her bed.

Sighing, I pushed to my feet and moved toward the opposite side of the house, walking down the short hall that led to the small room that had been mine growing up.

I grabbed a fresh pair of pajamas and underwear and went across the hall to the bathroom where I turned on the shower. Steam filled the room, and I stripped myself of the dress. I balled it up, the satiny material nothing but a shredded rag, stained with oil and dirt and blood.

I tossed it into the trash.

I stepped into the close to scalding water and prayed it'd have the power to wash away the strain. To soothe away the sting that didn't have a whole lot to do with the scrapes on my hands and knees. That tomorrow I'd wake and be restored with energy to do this all over again.

I washed my hair and then squirted a bunch of my favorite body wash onto the loofa, and washed away the disappointing night.

I wasn't giving up.

Not even close.

I dried, dressed, put a bandage on my knee before I stepped back into the hall, slowing as I got to the last door on the left. I pushed open the door a crack, letting the hall light flood into the room.

My heart swelled.

So intense I felt affection crashing over me. Washing me away. Taking me under. Surrounded by the overpowering swell of it, breath stolen, chest full.

Tiptoeing inside, I moved to the right to the portable crib where Sophie slept on her belly, her little butt in the air, her thumb in her mouth and her cheeks all rosy sweetness. She was almost too big for the small crib, her second birthday coming up faster than I could comprehend.

Reaching inside, I splayed my fingers through the short locks of her blonde, curly hair, so pale it was almost white, that hope burning inside turning into a brilliant burst of love.

Quietly, I straightened and headed for the toddler bed that rested on the same wall. Without making a sound, I dropped to my knees at the side of it, leaning down to nuzzle my nose into Mallory's soft cheek.

Breathing her in.

My sweet, smart girl. She stirred, and I cringed, hating that I'd woken her. But I just needed the reassurance, to kiss my babies good night before I could fall asleep myself.

Her blue eyes blinked open, and she grinned when she saw me kneeling at her side. She hustled to sit up, pushing the mass of bed-head out of her face with both hands, way too much excitement for after midnight. "Are you still the prettiest princess ever?"

The child pulled the softest laugh out of me, her awed sweetness my own inspiration. I brushed my fingers down the side of her face, that spot inside blazing so bright I didn't know how it wasn't lighting up the entire room.

She'd insisted her momma was an actual princess when I'd been getting ready, the child's mind so full of fanciful things that I wondered if I didn't feed too many of them into her ears.

But I loved that she looked on the world as if each second held a new wonder. A new promise and a new hope and a new adventure to hold. That was what I told her when she'd wanted to know where I was going . . . on an adventure to a ballroom dance.

She'd asked if I was going to meet Prince Charming.

Not even close.

"No, Mal Pal, I'm just regular old Momma."

The tattered dress I'd tossed into the garbage and my throbbing knee were proof of that.

"Did you dance like a ballerina? I bet you were the prettiest princess there. I know it. Grams said you were gettin' ready to knock some boys off their feet. Did you do some knockin'?"

A spurt of laughter almost made its way out. I bit it back.

"I think Grams was telling you stories."

Her eyes lit up. "Storytime is my favorite," she said in her sweet way, a little drawl and a lot overemphasized and sprinkled with a dash of sass. As if every word was of the upmost importance.

"Grams read two whole stories, and I read one, but it was really hard, and Thomas said I didn't know half the words. I think he was way wrong. I think I got more like . . . two-thirds. Two-thirds is good, right?"

I swore, the little thing slayed me. So danged adorable, the child larger than life, always so excited to take on the world and make it hers.

"Two-thirds is great," I promised.

"Next time, I'll get a hundred."

From the side, I felt movement. I should have known when I'd sneaked in that I'd end up waking the whole room. But there was my Thomas, looking rumpled and tired as he slowly sat up at the edge of his bed.

My big man.

My sweet man.

He rubbed a fist in his eye. "You're home safe?"

He was also my worrying man.

My little protector.

The oldest of my children and the only one who had an inkling about the severity of our situation. That things were bad and there was a chance they could get worse.

We were riding on a hope and a prayer and fighting with every single thing we had.

My babies could be taken from me, and there was nothing in this world that was worse than that.

"Yeah, I'm home, Sweet T."

"Did you find someone to help us?" he asked, strain in the heavy bob of his little throat.

Slowly, I pushed up to my feet and crossed the room so I could kneel in front of him. I set my hand on his face. The gentlest kind of reassurance. "Not yet, Thomas, but I will. I promise that I will."

"It's okay, Tom Tom. Momma knows all the tricks, don't you, Momma?" Mallory slid off her bed and dug around under it before she pulled out a big drawing notepad, the pages a textured beige and bound in a thick brown stock. "See!"

She pointed at the pictures we'd drawn.

It had been the only way I'd been able to explain to her a little of what we were going through without instilling her with fear, a happily ever after waiting at the end the only comfort I could give her.

The last thing I wanted was to cut down the vitality that oozed from her like a spring gushing up from the earth.

"Tell us another one?" my five-year-old asked with way too much enthusiasm for the middle of the night. "Oh, please, Momma. You didn't tell one before you left. You owe us."

She grinned.

Way too big.

All little teeth with a single one missing in the middle.

I swore the child could melt a glacier.

I glanced at Thomas who was still wearing worry all over his expression. I wished I could take it from him, the terror he'd felt when I'd woken him in the middle of the night four months ago and whisked him and the girls away in the darkness.

Wished I could cover it and conceal it.

Or more importantly, make it completely go away.

Instead, I stood and stretched my hand out for him. "What do you say?"

He nodded, accepted my hand, and took a seat next to me on the floor by Mallory's bed.

Criss-crossing my legs, I pulled her onto my lap and wrapped an arm around Thomas. He snuggled into my side, my nine-year-old putting aside his shield of armor that he typically wore in favor of consolation during the late hour.

Sophie Marie continued to sleep through the ruckus, her tiny breaths filling the air as I opened the book. The pages were full of freehand drawings, and I opened my mouth and whispered the words to my older two children who snuggled closer.

"Once upon a time, there was a prince and two princesses. They were the most fearless in the land, held hostage by a ruthless king. The prince . . . the prince wore a crown of rubies . . ."

I squeezed Thomas just a little tighter. I could feel him fighting an affected smile.

"The baby princess wore a ring of sapphire, and the sweet reigning princess wore a pendant of diamond."

Mallory flapped her arms in excitement, lost in the inflection of my voice when her character was woven into the story.

"But they weren't only brave, they were also smart. So, one day, they came to their handmaiden who cared for them with every ounce of her being. They were sure she had their best interest at heart and would help them no matter what. They knew she would help them make a plan to break free from the castle. They knew of the endless maze of bushes that grew ten feet tall around the castle, confusing any reckless warriors who dared come against the king. Many had been lost to the maze, their minds sent into a permanent bewilderment that left them wandering throughout their years. But not the prince and the princesses . . . they knew a secret way, their loving handmaiden helping to guide them as they set out into the night . . ."

Only our story wasn't so much a fairytale.

It was our reality.

My children nothing but pawns in an elaborate game. In the end, I knew I'd be the expendable one.

All signs pointing to a tragedy.

For them, for us, I refused to let that happen.

I wouldn't stop until we found our way out.

five

IAN

I'd been sitting in my office for the last four hours with the contents of a file spread out in front of me. Pretending I could focus on reviewing the details for a case that was going to court next week rather than the fact I was actually sitting there, all spun up and feeling like I was going to go right out of my mind.

A fucking pussy who couldn't shake the feeling that had been chasing me down for the last two days. This cagey urge to get wrapped up in the middle of something that I had no tie to. No binding or connection to the situation other than a random encounter at a bar.

But when I closed my eyes and the only thing I saw was that stunning face, it made me feel like I was. Like I'd already stumbled into something that I couldn't climb out of.

Her wallet was burning a goddamned hole in my pocket, and not because I was itching to spend the whole fifteen dollars she had stuffed in there.

I was going to take it and that bracelet to her, make sure she was okay, and then get the hell out of there.

Put the girl out of my mind.

My phone rumbled on my desk, and I exhaled, thankful for the distraction, even though the chances were stacked high that it would be some stupid question that I'd have to grin and bear. Teeth clenched tight while I pretended like I *cared* as a client droned on about something insignificant or irrelevant.

But at least I could allay the annoyance, knowing a five-minute call was an easy five-hundred made. You'd think they'd stop with the inane bullshit when they realized how much their stupidity was costing them.

Guessed I shouldn't complain.

But this grin? The one that spread across my mouth when I saw who was calling?

It was real and unstoppable and knocked down a piece of that wall.

Immediately, I reached out and accepted it.

A face that was so much like mine popped up on the screen. The two of us resembled each other so closely that I felt like I was looking into a mirror when I looked at him.

That was where our similarities ended, though. My brother was made up of courage and strength and loyalty. I was built of greed and immorality.

I could only wish I could be as good as the guy smiling back. But I gave up on that idea a long, long time ago. It wasn't gonna happen. Some things were just embedded bone deep.

Still, I admired the asshole, the guy carving himself out a spot in my bleak, black heart. For being the one who'd kept it beating for all those years.

"Well, well, well, if it isn't my big brother, Jace. Tell me how life is in the middle of insanity."

My voice was totally wry.

Because that was what that shit had to be.

Insanity.

The guy had his phone in one hand, holding it out so I could see him, all the while trying to wrangle a squirming, squalling baby in the other. The only part of the kid showing up on the screen was a tiny fist that waved its fury in front of his face. He tried to angle his head around it.

Still couldn't believe that my brother had made his way back to the girl who he'd loved since he was seventeen. The path sure hadn't been easy for him to get there, littered with treacherous shit, twists and turns and dead ends, but it was a road he'd deemed worth traveling.

The guy was married to a girl named Faith and lived in this huge plantation that they'd restored and now ran as a bed and breakfast over in Broadshire Rim.

Lucky bastard had gotten one of the good ones. His wife, Faith, had this blooming heart, just fucking glowing.

Women like that should be impossible. She was the kind of mother every kid deserved. One in a billion. But if anyone deserved a love like that, Jace did. I was just about as happy for him as I was petrified that he might lose it.

Love precarious. Lost so easily.

The guy had taken up the family life like that was where he'd been heading all along.

Faith had given birth to their son just a few weeks ago. Not to mention, Jace had inherited Faith's little girl, Bailey, in the process.

I didn't get it.

Not at all.

Risking being responsible for *life*. Bringing more of it into this vile, vile world.

My heart skipped a nervous beat when he angled his phone a little so I could get a full view of my nephew.

Benton.

Tiny, scrawny legs flailing.

Jace chuckled a self-deprecating sound. "Things are perfect in the land of madness."

"Looks like it."

Jace bounced his baby boy. "He's just screaming, demanding his mother, who handed him over so she could get a shower. Five minutes, and the kid is having withdrawals. What can I say? My boy has good taste. I fully understand his pain."

I shook my head, a tease winding to my lips. "Never thought I'd see the day when my badass big brother handed over his balls. That's gotta hurt."

"Pssh . . . you just wish you were man enough to handle all of this. You're just jealous you're missing out on the good things in life."

"Uh, yeah, no, but thank you. I'll leave all the manning up to you. Monogamy is for the brave. Or the weak. However you want to look at it. All I know is I want no part in it."

He laughed. "You just haven't found a reason to *take part*."

My lips twitched up at the side. "I'll just keep enjoying the hunt."

"You goin' huntin', Uncle Ian? My daddy told my mama you *nofin'* but a dog." All of a sudden, Bailey was right there, jumping up and trying to get in front of the camera. My heart gave another one of those pangs when I saw her adorable face, all the while hoping her innocent ears hadn't been privy to me busting my brother's balls.

Kids were on my no-go list.

Out of fucking bounds.

But goddamn it if that little girl hadn't wound her way right into that dark, dark place inside me, a flash of light and warmth skating through my senses every time she was in my space.

Which kind of scared the fuck out of me.

I wasn't joking when I said my brother was brave. Being a parent had to be about the scariest shit a person could endure.

I turned my attention to my brother, who was wearing the damned smuggest grin I'd ever seen, brows lifting for the sky. "Dog, huh?"

"What?" he defended with a chuckle.

"I *wike* dogs," Bailey sang in her cute little drawl, like she was confused by the irritation in my voice and I should have taken the dig as a compliment.

"Well, that's good because I like you, too," I told her, sucked in a little deeper.

"See, Daddy. Uncle Ian is a good dog." She was looking up at her dad, smiling a wide smile, like she was hoping to convince him of it.

My eyes met Jace's. "You're in so much trouble when I see you, brother." I let *brother* linger like a dirty word.

The guy had the audacity to laugh. "What, are you going to deny it now?"

"No. I just didn't know my lifestyle was a topic of conversation in your house."

"What? We worry about you." His voice lost some of the amusement. "Want the best in life for you. Everyone deserves that."

The number of times he'd taken me aside to talk with me about what I was doing, how I was living, had grown exponentially since he'd permanently moved back to South Carolina. Like I was still that pathetic kid he had to protect and feed and go to bat for.

I pushed out a sigh. "There's nothing to worry about. Life is as good as it's going to get. Better than ever. I have an awesome pad I know even you are jealous of. I'm about to make partner. Have a corner office to die for and a bank account overflowing with zeros. What more could I ask for?"

"Money doesn't buy happiness," Jace said.

"You sure about that?"

He glanced down at his kids. "Positive."

"Money buys all the dolls, Uncle, but yous got to do chores first." This from Bailey, grinning again with a mouthful of teeth.

The kid pulled a soft roll of affectionate laughter right out of my chest. Kind of wanted to scoop her up and squeeze her for interrupting the direction my brother was heading. "You need more dolls? Don't you already have a room full of them?"

"A girl can never has too many dolls. Just like mommies can never has too many shoes." She was looking at me like she was worried I didn't know anything and she was affording me some worldly wisdom that I was lacking.

Apparently so.

"Well, then, I'll have to keep that in mind. Someone's birthday is coming up fast."

"Mine!" she screeched, pure unadulterated excitement. God, the kid was cute.

Her little brother kicked and let go of a shrill cry so loud I didn't know how it didn't bring down the walls of their old house.

His little legs thrashing.

His foot caught Bailey on the shoulder.

Another kid would cry.

But Bailey?

She laughed this laugh that was nothing but love, reaching out and grabbing him by the foot, swinging it around a bit. "Dids you see that, Uncle Ian? My *brover* just kicked me with his *wittle* toes. He's so cute. Do you think he's cute? I got the best *brover* in the world."

"Yeah, I definitely think he's cute."

The two of them were about as cute as I could stand. Too cute. Too sweet. Too innocent.

I scrubbed an uneasy palm over my face, pulling myself back before she had me hooked any deeper. Wrapped tighter around her little finger. I turned my attention back to Jace, who was watching me like he knew exactly what I was thinking.

He just didn't know how deep and ugly and depraved it got.

It was the one thing I'd never let him in on. What I'd done.

He'd hate me if he did.

Apparently, he had witnessed me spiral because he cleared his throat, snapping me back to the here and now. Shifting Benton, he bounced him more, trying to keep him happy. "Listen, I actually called for a reason. I need you to do me a favor."

"Anything."

That was something he could count on.

"There's a building that's going up for auction downtown. Faith has her hands full today, so I want to stick around. Do you think you could go down and check it out for me this afternoon? Take a couple of pictures and send them over?"

"No problem. Text me the address. I'll go by. I was actually getting ready to head out."

I had one stop to make beforehand.

"That'd be great. I'd really appreciate it." His tone shifted, a quiet, prodding push. "And if you want in, this one would be a good opportunity."

I sighed. I knew Jace somehow thought he was helping me out. Inviting me in.

But he'd taken care of me my whole life.

Neither him nor anyone else would be responsible for my success. That was on me.

"Nah, man. I have enough going on here to keep me busy for the next fifty-two years."

"You know the offer stands . . . if and when that ever changes."

"Thanks." I straightened, flipped the file on my desk shut because there was no chance I was getting back to that shit, and started to gather my things. "I'll text you as soon as I go by."

"Bye, Uncle Ian!" Bailey sang.

"Bye, Button."

I ended the call, sighed, patted my pocket for that damned wallet and bracelet.

Felt a sizzle burn through my blood, tried to tamp it, keep it contained.

It doesn't matter.

I strode out my office door, intent on scraping her from where she'd managed to get under my skin. Slithering in and curling up without my permission.

Making me *worry*.

Worrying about a stranger was one thing I couldn't do.

No matter how fucking sexy she was.

No matter how badly I'd wanted to carve out a place for myself between her thighs.

That's all that it was. That was all that it was ever gonna be.

For once in my life, I was going to do something nice, something that didn't require payment or retribution or a favor, and then I was going to let her be.

I rode the elevator down to the busy street. Crowds battled to get from one place to the next, the sidewalk always a clusterfuck of chaos in the late afternoon.

I headed in the direction of the address listed on the business card I'd found in the wallet, ignoring her driver's license, figuring checking out the info on that would be stepping out of bounds.

Creeper mode.

Not exactly my style.

The address on the card was three blocks over.

Dodging the masses, I ambled that way, ignoring the rumble in my chest. The way my heart beat a little too hard, and the way my dick felt a little too excited.

Not good.

That lust still simmered. Unsated. Waiting to make its claim.

But then I remembered the look on her face when she'd been weeping on the hard ground. That was something impossible to forget. The storm in those blue, blue eyes. That was the kind of raging sea that shouldn't be traversed.

Five minutes later, I stood in front of the three-story building. It was painted a yellow that was supposed to make it look cheery or some shit, the door and awnings a sky blue.

Quaint and homey like the rest of the buildings on this street.

Greed and curiosity flared.

When I pushed open the door, a bell jingled overhead, and I stepped into the small hair salon. Senses overloaded, I was hit with the pungent scent of hair dye and bleach, ears hammered with the sound of hair dryers and the lift of voices to be heard over the din.

All the commotion was coming from behind the partition wall that sectioned off the waiting room and the stations in the back.

The waiting room was completely empty, so I moved to the counter that took up the majority of the front, the wall behind it lined with shelves filled with products.

I leaned around to the left so I could see through the opening on that side.

In the back, four stations were set up on each side of the salon. A few women were sitting at them.

I angled farther, trying to catch a glimpse of *her*.

I pasted on a smile when a woman came barreling around the corner. Magenta hair and tattoos covering every exposed inch of her body and wearing clothes more fitting for a night club in LA than a business in Charleston. But whatever.

At least she didn't have to wear a mask the way I did. Conceal what was really hiding underneath.

"Hey there, handsome, sorry about that, I was tied up in the back. How can I help you?"

I shifted, antsy, not sure what to say. "I'm looking for . . . someone."

Blonde. Gorgeous. Sexy as fuck.

Have you seen her?

Like she picked up on something ulterior in my tone, she arched a questioning brow, the stud in her lip pulling up at one side.

"Is that so?" She looked me up and down, gauging me.

Protector.

I saw it written all over her.

"And just who is it that you're lookin' for?" She was tiny, but the girl so clearly packed a punch.

"Grace?" It came out like a question. Because, shit, I had no idea if she worked there or owned the place or merely had the card tucked in her wallet because that was where she got that river of hair done.

If so, they were doing a damned good job.

Like that was answer enough for her, she moved to the computer, muttering, "She is earning herself quite the reputation around here. People have been flocking in, asking for her. She's pretty booked for the rest of the day, but I can . . ."

She narrowed her eyes as she squinted at the computer screen. "I think she could squeeze you in really quick before her next appointment. Just a trim? If that's what you were lookin' for?"

She glanced up at me wearing more of that speculation, voice twisting on the last, wondering how I was going to answer. Keen to the fact I wasn't looking for a haircut at all.

I should hand over the wallet and run. Get the hell out of there like I'd planned on doing. But I needed to see her. Verify that she was okay. "Yes, just a trim."

"Perfect. She'll do you up good." The girl winked at me.

I wished.

"Right this way."

Slipping out from behind the counter, she rounded through the opening on the left, and I followed her, feeling another rush of sensation slam me when I sat down on the chair that she gestured to.

Antsy and needy and dark.

Fuck.

What was I doing? Whatever it was, I didn't want to stop.

"She'll be right with you."

The girl headed to a short hall at the back of the salon, and she leaned into a room that I couldn't see inside of, though I could hear their voices. "Hey, Grace, you have a walk in. Just a trim. You should be good on time."

"Oh, good, thank you, Melissa."

"No problem."

Grace's voice was deep. Sultry like a Southern summer. It instantly stirred that same feeling I'd felt on Saturday night. Energy and light.

And my body that hadn't stopped wanting something it shouldn't have only fired harder. My muscles tightened, and my dick—the bastard that I was pretty sure had talked me into this shit in the first place—was punching against my dress pants.

Painfully.

Need racing my blood, guts twisting up in knots, lust stalking my spine like a caged lion seeking a way out.

What messed with my head was the way I was hit with another swell of that protectiveness when I saw her round the corner and step into the salon.

A river of blonde and a sea of sadness in those teal eyes.

My heart shook at my ribs when she saw me sitting there.

Energy lapped, so fucking intense I swore I could see a shiver of it racing the floor.

I should have known better than to come here.

I'd felt the tremble of it. The warning of something unknown. Of something I couldn't afford to get involved in.

It didn't *matter*.

Because sitting there?

I knew it was exactly where I was supposed to be.

GRACE

I froze in the middle of the salon. Just staring. Heart taking off at a sprint and my mind whirring with all the possibilities of how it was possible that man was sitting there.

Cinnamon-colored eyes pinned me to the spot.

Hot, hard need coming off him in blistering waves.

I swore I had to be chained up to something solid.

Shackled.

Unable to move.

He watched me through the mirror, the ridiculously gorgeous man from Saturday night.

The guy who'd been trying to entice me with the most wicked night of pleasure who'd instead had knelt on the hard ground at my side and helped me gather my things. The man who was so rough and raw and dangerous and somehow unbearably soft.

The way he'd watched me as if I were fragile—as if he wanted to save me and then turn around and break me a little, too.

His striking reflection was captured in the reflective glass.

So menacing and ominous and intense that it about dropped me to my knees.

A shiver of fear crawled into my belly.

A different kind of fear from the one I'd felt at the thought of facing down Reed.

This kind of fear had me taking a step in his direction. Drawn toward the darkness, a prisoner to the tethers I could feel wrapping around my wrists and yanking me forward.

Tug, tug, tug.

Right there in my belly and in my heart.

How had he found me?

Better question, *why* had he found me?

Knowing it was dangerous that he had. I just didn't know who it was most dangerous for.

Lifting my chin, I edged up behind him, trying to exude as much confidence as I could, trying to pretend as if him just sitting there didn't threaten the rise of tears back to my eyes. The way I both wanted to thank him for what he'd done and scream at him to run.

Tell him I couldn't afford for him to get tangled up in my business, sure that a man like him would never be willing to pay the price, anyway.

What I really was aching to do was walk up behind him and press my nose to the skin exposed at his neck.

Inhale and breathe him in.

Feel him under my hands.

Decide if he was real or a hallucination my mind had conjured.

I couldn't help it that every time I closed my eyes over the last two days, he'd popped into my mind, haunting me with the tease of a memory, adding to all the mayhem that was already wreaking havoc on my insides.

Today he was wearing suit pants and a pin-striped white button down, the jacket gone, sleeves rolled up to reveal curls of ink covering both of his forearms.

My mouth watered, and my stomach clenched. Maybe I really had let my imagination run a little too wild. Because I felt like all those fantasies were catching up.

Taking hold.

A reality I most definitely could not keep.

He appeared every bit as powerful as Saturday night. Maybe more so. As if second by second, the man continued to gain the upper hand.

For a moment, my eyes got trapped there, on the dark designs etched into his skin, hewn like shadows and mist, as if they might be a hazy screen previewing what was written on the inside of the man.

Scored and scarred and marked.

I had the sudden urge to run my fingers over them, trace the swirls of suggestion standing out in stark contrast to his strait-laced exterior.

Discover what they meant.

The man a riddle.

Then I shook myself out of the stupor.

Come on. This guy had just waltzed in off the street. From out of nowhere. And was sitting in my chair. That had to be wrong on a hundred different levels.

Yet, he didn't give off the creeper vibe, even though I was sufficiently spun up by his presence.

This was different.

I knew it.

Was pretty sure he knew it, too.

Energy lapped in the space between us.

The same from Saturday night.

Though it was slowed. Weighed down by the questions that were clearly playing out in our minds. His coming to life in the sparks that glowed like a toss of red glitter in his cinnamon-colored eyes, mine in the way my lips parted with the concern that he'd sought me out.

"What are you doing here?" I finally managed, the words

trembling even after I told them not to.

Traitor lips.

The man hiked an indifferent shoulder, and one of those hazardous smirks lit his face, the kind of smirk that flamed my insides and fanned the attraction that rippled through the air, so hot and heavy I could feel it crawling across my skin.

What was wrong with me?

But that was the thing about attraction. You couldn't control who you were attracted to, how sudden and intense it might be. Whether it smoldered and grew or hit you like a ball flying out of left field.

You could only be wise enough not to act on it when you knew it was gonna be bad for you in the end.

I guessed I'd never been so good at heeding that.

"What does it look like I'm doing? Getting a haircut," he said as if he'd sat in my chair a hundred times before. So damned casual, as if it were just another day. As if he hadn't stirred something up in me that shouldn't have been possible two nights ago.

My brow pinched, pulse pounding fast, and I struggled for some kind of self-control. To bring up some walls of security and protection.

No doubt, it was a horrible, horrible time to leave my heart so unprotected. "So, you just happened to stumble into my salon after Saturday night? Seems awful convenient to me."

"Call it fate." Another one of those smirks.

"I'd call it stalking." I didn't know whether I was flirting, falling into that trap, or if the tumble in my belly was a true-sort of terror.

Intuition.

A warning glowing from deep within that warned me to step away.

He laughed a low sound. As if I were completely ridiculous. The gorgeous stranger set an elbow on the arm of the chair, resting one side of his strong jaw in the crook between his thumb and forefinger, smiling at me through his reflection.

"Do I look like the kind of guy who needs to stalk a woman to get her into his bed?"

Not even close.

Hell, they probably fought to get their chance at claiming that spot.

"No, you don't. But you don't really strike me as the type of man who likes being told no, either."

"I have to admit, I was . . . disappointed," he seemed to settle on with a twitch of his lips.

"Is that why you're here? To convince me to fall into your bed?" The question was a tangle I could barely force off my tongue.

"Won't deny that I wanted you the second I saw you."

His voice dropped, low enough that no one else in the salon could hear. "Won't deny that I'm looking at you right now and imagining all the things I want to do to you, and no, I won't deny that I'm usually a man who gets what he wants. But sadly, that's not why I'm here."

God. Even his voice had my insides doing stupid things. His tone both seduction and a threat.

"I told you . . . you don't know me or what I'm going through. Believe me, it was better we left it as we did."

Okay, so maybe my mind was still tripped up on exactly what he might be imagining. Insides shaking with what that might be like. Somehow feeling like I needed to throw out a defense considering the man was sitting right there, in my chair.

Looking way too pretty. Far too sexy.

Edible.

But that was the kind of craving I couldn't give in to.

"Or maybe we should pick up where we left off," he countered.

He arched a brow, voice so rough and low. "Don't tell me you don't feel this. That you don't want to explore it."

"Just because I might want something, it doesn't mean it's good for me."

"Oh, I can promise you it will be *good*."

Shivers streaked across my skin, and I tried to ignore the way he had me in knots. I huffed out in disbelief, as feigned as it was, trying to steel myself against the all-out assault that was this man.

"So that's just it? You found me because I turned you down

on Saturday night?"

In some kind of discomfort, he fiddled with the expensive watch he wore. Instantly, my eyes went back to the swirls of mystery on his arms. The only thing I could distinctly make out was a demon on the top part of his left forearm.

Screaming.

Screaming as if it were in pain.

"Didn't I already say that's not why I came here?" He was doing that arrogant thing. You know, just breathing. As if he held the power to command all the air.

Flustered, I scowled at him, not sure if I wanted to shake him or climb onto his damned lap. He was making me crazy.

"Then you'd better start talking, or you can stand up and walk right out of here because I don't have the time to play games."

"You want the truth?"

"Yes."

He fumbled out a sigh, like actually being truthful might cause him discomfort. "The main reason is I needed to make sure that you were okay. You took off before I could find out if you were really injured or not."

He lifted his chin in some kind of challenge. One I got the distinct feeling he was directing at himself.

As if he couldn't actually believe he was admitting it. "I was worried about you, and that's not okay with me. You didn't give me the chance to ensure you were safe."

So, he needed to wipe me off his conscience?

I narrowed my gaze at him. "Men like you don't deserve that chance."

He scrubbed his palm on his pants. In all his over-the-top arrogance, he somehow looked nervous. Agitated. All of it was underlined with the type of overbearing confidence that made it come off as if it made him mad. "I deserve that," he said with a tight nod.

"And . . . what else? You said mostly."

The man situated himself in the chair so he could pull something out of his front pocket.

My wallet.

My eyes went wide. "Oh, thank goodness, you found my wallet. I went back there yesterday to see if I'd dropped it on the ground. I thought I was going to have to spend my day down at the DMV trying to get things sorted."

Then he dug a little deeper . . . and . . .

My hands flew to my mouth when I saw what he was holding. "My bracelet. Oh my God, you found my bracelet. I thought . . . I thought I'd lost it forever."

My favorite bracelet.

By no stretch of the imagination was it valuable, but to me, it was a priceless heirloom.

Three dangling gemstone charms, as fake as could be.

A ruby, a sapphire, a diamond.

My babies I kept so close to me.

"I found them by the curb after you drove away."

He waved the tiny, slim card-sleeve in the air as if it were the prize. As if it would mean more to me than anything else. Which under normal circumstances, I could totally understand, but it couldn't be farther from the truth.

The only thing that mattered was that bracelet.

That was when I noticed he had one of the salon's business cards resting on his knee. I'd stuffed a small stack of them into that sleeve, trying to shove one at Kenneth Millstrom.

Praying he'd take it.

That he'd call me.

Turned out, it'd been one of the smartest things I'd ever done. That was how he'd found me. Why he'd found me.

Maybe it was *fate*, after all.

A genuine smile pulled to my face, gratefulness swelling wide. For a fleeting moment, warmth filled the expansive, empty gulf throbbing at the center of me.

"I can't believe you took the time to return my things. I . . . I thought I'd never see it again."

I slowly reached out for the bracelet that he was rolling between his fingers, and he seemed to catch on to the fact I cared more about the bracelet than anything else. I met his curious gaze through the mirror as he held it up for me to take.

That energy shifted.

Doing something wild.

A thrash of attraction.

A lash of need.

Gulping around it, I took the small bangle and slipped it onto my wrist, emotion growing thick as I traced it with the fingers of my other hand. If I listened closely enough, I could almost hear their little voices shouting in my ear as they jumped around.

"Happy birthday! Do you like it? We saved all our money!"

Moisture gathering fast, I looked back at him, meeting those strange-colored eyes. If I didn't know better, I'd say they glowed red. Like they matched that demon on his arm.

This unsettled feeling came over me, as if I were being sucked into the aura that radiated from his skin.

Cruel and evil and kind.

All of it swirled around him like a whirlwind. As if he were made of them all.

A toxic, mind-altering cocktail. A sip of bliss. A drop of wickedness.

"Thank you, so much, for taking the time to find me. To bring this back. I only took it off because it didn't match that stupid dress," I admitted.

Discomfort rolled from him, so different from the dominating stance of a few seconds ago. "It was nothing."

"Well, it means something to me. Most people wouldn't make the effort of hunting someone down like this."

"Apparently, I'm good at hunting." He said it as if he were saying it at his own expense, edged in more of that seduction and a measure of amusement.

I angled my head, trying to get a read on this man who I just couldn't put my finger on.

He shook his head. "Never mind. Honestly, I couldn't not return them to you. I didn't know if it was something you'd miss or not."

I could see what he was thinking. That it was cheap. Worthless. And still, he'd brought it back as if he'd somehow known it *mattered*.

I wrapped my free hand around it and hugged it against my chest. I gave him the most honest answer I could find. "It broke my heart that I might have lost it."

It was like a palpable, living piece of me.

Something I never should have risked taking off in the first place.

"I'm glad, then." For the first time, there was something gentle in his eyes.

"I don't know how to repay you."

Then that gaze flashed, that cocky, confident arrogance surging to the surface. I was all of a sudden realizing what I'd said, what it almost sounded like I'd implied. I started to stammer, "I-I . . ."

He laughed, letting me off the hook. "That haircut would be nice."

"Wow, you really can be a jerk, can't you?" Somehow a tease managed to weave its way into my tone.

My guard wavering.

Not sure if it should stand.

He cocked a brow. "You have no idea."

"I bet you're not so bad." Softness lined the words.

"I'm not a good guy. Don't make the mistake of believing that."

There he went again.

Attracting and repelling.

Pushing and pulling.

Warning me at the same second as he was reeling me in.

Hooking me. No hope of release.

I shook it off and gestured toward the sinks on the other side of the pony wall. "Come on over, we'll get your hair washed."

He pushed from the chair, so damned tall, so imposing as he followed.

My breaths came shorter and shorter with each step that we took.

The man all around me.

He sat down and leaned his head back against the headrest on the basin.

His striking face too close.

So close.

Carved, chiseled stone.

Jaw sharp.

Eyes deep.

I turned on the faucet and ran my wrist under the water to make sure it wasn't too hot. I took the nozzle and wet his hair, words leaving me on a whisper, "Is the temperature okay?"

"Yes," he murmured back, watching me. My movements were somehow prolonged as I pumped shampoo onto my hand and began to lather it into his hair.

As if time had been set to slow. As if the world raced around us, whirs and streaks of color and light, while we were there.

Stilled.

My fingers weaving into his soft locks of light-brown hair as if I'd gladly do it all day.

He moaned this low, sexy sound.

While my heart sped and awareness spun.

His nearness overpowering.

A vibration in the air.

A low hum running a circuit through my body.

He watched me with that fierce, unrelenting gaze.

His lips full.

So full.

I gulped and tried to look away, but I felt trapped. Completely consumed by a man whose name I didn't even know.

I gently rinsed his hair, lathered in conditioner.

His chest rose and fell in measured heaves as he sat completely still and let me touch him.

I'd never, ever had this reaction to a client before.

Never had my job felt erotic.

Never had my mind raced with the idea of letting my hands wander. What it might feel like. Wanting to experience it.

Experience him.

Oh boy, was I letting my thoughts run out ahead of me.

I needed to rein them in. Get it together.

Anything I was feeling was just plain reckless.

I rinsed out the conditioner and wrapped a towel around his

head. Trying to get some space between us, I led him back to my station and watched him fold that big body into the chair.

I rubbed the towel against his head, watching him over his shoulder. Those eyes were on me. Tracking every movement.

God, what was happening to me?

But I couldn't help it, the way my hands shook as I took the scissors and began to snip away at his hair, as my fingers danced through the locks, as I breathed in his breaths as I leaned in close and used the razor to trim around his ears and neck, then used the dryer to blow out his hair.

"There, how's that?" I asked quietly. They were the first words I'd spoken in all that time.

He ran a big hand over the top of his head, fluffing the pieces and then fingering them back into place. "It's perfect."

Redness threatened to bloom. I didn't know why. I wasn't exactly shy. But there was something about him that made me feel both timid and bold.

Modest and sexy.

Different.

I dusted off the fine pieces of hair that I'd cut and removed the robe. "There we go. All done."

He didn't get up. Instead he was still watching me through that mirror. "I have one more favor to ask."

I felt the weight of the bracelet on my wrist. "What's that?"

"Have a drink with me."

"I don't think that's a good idea."

"Why not?"

"I think you already know the answer to that."

And he could barely see what was visible on the surface.

Unaware of the iceberg hidden in the depths of the murky waters. Lying in wait to drag everything I loved into the deepest abyss, forever lost in the cold, cold vacancy.

His jaw hardened. "Actually, I don't. Maybe you could let me in on a little of that."

I huffed out a soft sound. "I promise you, you don't want to go there."

"What could one drink hurt?"

There he went again.

A soft puff of laughter rippled out, and I forced myself to straighten. To put an inch between us. "Oh, I'm sure it could hurt plenty."

"What fun is life if it doesn't hurt a little?"

"I've had enough hurt to last me a long, long time."

"Maybe it's the fun part you're in need of."

I gave him a soft shake of my head. "It's a bad idea."

"I'd make a really good memory."

Honesty came bleeding free. "Or a really bad one."

And I didn't have the time or space for that.

And the last thing I needed was another reason for Reed to go ballistic.

Then another gush of air was being tugged from my lungs when he pushed to standing.

He swiveled around and leaned over me. He fluttered his fingertips down my cheek, the man nothing but fire. "Oh, it'd be a good one. Trust me."

Cocky, cocky boy.

Why'd I like that about him?

But that didn't change anything.

"Maybe in another lifetime."

He blinked a few times as if he were catching up to another rejection, something I was pretty sure the man had probably never experienced before, and then he moved back to my station. He grabbed the same business card he'd returned to me and a pen from the container.

He scribbled something on the back of it, glancing at me as he did. "That's too bad, considering we only have one life to live."

He dug into his wallet and pulled out a stack of money.

Frowning, I rushed, "Oh, no, the cut is on me. I'm just grateful you brought my things back."

His head shook, and he set the stack on top of the card. "I think it's me who owes all the thanks. I mean, look at me."

He was all easy smiles when he pointed to his hair that was framing his striking, defined face.

Right.

As if I were even a little bit responsible for all that perfection. Some things you just had to be born with.

He started to walk away before he paused, cocking a grin at me from over his shoulder that somehow looked like a grimace. As if he'd managed to read something inside me when I'd never wanted him to have the power to peel back the cover. "Watch out for yourself, Grace. If you need to use that number? Use it."

Then he strode off, disappearing out the arch, taking that energy with him.

I slumped over from the loss of it, hanging onto the back of my chair like I'd forgotten to breathe the entire time he'd been sitting there.

Or maybe the real problem was that I'd been breathing him in the entire time. The man overwhelming. Filling me too full. Full of foolish feelings and foolish ideas.

Because I'd wanted to say yes. I'd wanted to spend a few moments prisoner to those strange eyes, lost to that sensation that swept through me every time he was near.

But it'd be a mistake. I knew it.

It wasn't as if I were still married. By the grace of God, I'd been granted that small gift. Cutting my legal tie to Reed. For the time being, I was keeping my last name until I was in the position to change the kids' last name as well because I didn't want them to feel separated from me.

Once I'd been granted the divorce, things had only escalated with Reed, and I couldn't risk my judgment being called into question. It wasn't fair, but that was just the way things were.

With the way he was watching me, I was pretty sure that he knew it, too.

I moved for the stack of money he'd left. I fluttered my thumb through the bills, scowling when I realized he'd left a pile of five twenties.

What on earth was he thinking, leaving me a hundred-dollar tip?

I really hoped he didn't think I was *that kind* of easy. Then I picked up the card.

He'd written his name and number on it.

Ian Jacobs.

Ian Jacobs.

I let his name roll around on the tip of my tongue, fidgeting with the card, trying to convince myself to toss it into the trash.

Somehow doing it felt like blasphemy.

I whirled around when the voice hit me from behind. "Um, hello, care to fill me in on whatever was just going down on this side of the salon?"

Quick to toss the card back onto my station, I lifted a careless brow at Melissa and began to sweep up the little waves of brown hair littered around my chair, fighting the urge to pick a lock up and tuck it into my pocket like some kind of weirdo.

"I was giving a haircut. What does it look like I was doing?" I tried to make it come out as if she was the one who'd lost her mind.

"Um . . . that was no haircut. That was foreplay. It's so hot in here that   I'm about to have to go relieve myself in the bathroom."

My brow knitted. "Are you always so gross?"

"Are you always in denial?" she shot back.

Three months ago, I'd come into Melissa's salon, ready to beg for a job or to rent a station, even though I hadn't actually cut hair in eight years, and even then, I hadn't done it for very long.

But for some reason, I'd always maintained my license. Maybe I'd known all along that I needed that security.

Really, the only thing I needed was an address. A place of employment to put on those forms. Something that would say that I was both working hard and doing my best to make ends meet.

Something that made me look like an upstanding citizen.

Not a thief.

She'd had a station available.

We were about as opposite as opposites could be, but we'd formed some semblance of a friendship after Reed had come in here one day, acting the asshole, trying to back me into a corner. He'd tossed his power and influence all around, as if it was going to sway me, make me forget what I'd seen and the things that he'd done.

The second he'd left, she'd come running over, holding me while I'd tried to stay standing in the wake of his threats.

I gave a small shrug. "It was nothin'. On Saturday night, I lost my wallet and bracelet. He found them and brought them back to me."

I waved my wrist in front of her face as proof.

She grinned like I was offering her a date with David Beckham, the girl basically salivating at the mouth.

"So, what you're tellin' me is the guy who found your things is a bad-boy Chris Pine. Maybe even more delicious, and that shit should not be possible. I mean, did you *see* him? All posh and suave with those tats peeking out? He's like a present just begging to be unwrapped. Yes-fucking-please."

A little jolt of possessiveness nudged at me before I rolled my eyes at Melissa. "Go for it."

"Hello . . . I wasn't talking about for myself." She patted my shoulder. "My girl here obviously needs a little lovin'. When's the last time you had yourself a nice big O that you didn't give yourself? It's just plain sad, especially when that man clearly wants to be the one doing the honors."

I kept sweeping up that hair, doing my best not to mourn for it as I guided the pile to the stationary vacuum against the wall. "And you're the one giving advice on the topic when you were the one who was just talking about taking matters into her own hands?"

She wagged a tattooed finger at me. "You know what, you're right. There are much better alternatives. Leo's is just around the corner. I'm sure there would be something yummy there to help me out. You could join me or go after Bad Boy Kirk."

"Neither of those things are an option for me."

She crossed her arms over her chest. "And why is it you have to go by jackass's rules?"

That was what happened when jackasses always had the upper hand.

"You know why."

Except she didn't know everything. I'd never put her in that kind of position.

She pushed out a frustrated sigh. "It's so . . . unfair. It makes me want to scream."

"Oh, believe me, I've done plenty of screaming for the both of us. But screaming doesn't help anything. So, I do the only thing that I can."

"But he'd never even know," she all but whined. "This opportunity is too good to waste."

"Your point is moot, anyway. I don't even know his name or have any way to contact him."

She reached around me and snagged the card from my station.

The little snake.

She narrowed her dark eyes in some kind of devious glee. "Liar."

I groaned. "Give that back."

She waved it in my face, jumping around, the girl shorter than me by about five inches, wearing her skin-tight black leathers and a corset. I had half a mind just to tackle her.

"I thought you said you didn't *want it*." She sang it while she continued to jump around and tease.

I snatched it right out of her hand.

She smirked. "That's what I thought."

I frowned at her and then looked at the number. Looked at the name. I wished I had the space, the capacity, to be wild for a little bit.

Be reckless and make bad choices.

But all my bad choices had already been made.

IAN

I slipped into the dark, secluded booth, the lights hazy and low in the cavernous space.

I shot off a few texts to Jace with the pictures and information he was looking for.

The building was shit.

Rundown.

Dilapidated.

The poor employees filing out at the end of the day looked every bit as bad.

Exactly what Jace was looking for. The guy took floundering businesses and buildings and spun them into gold.

Dude was legit. Had to say, I was fucking proud. So fucking

proud that it made me squirrely whenever he asked me to do anything for his company. Last thing I wanted was to dirty his name. Dip my filthy fingers into something good and taint it.

Just like that girl.

That girl who was still shivering across my flesh like a warm caress.

Fuck, she was sweet. So damned different from the immediate assumptions I'd made about her when I'd seen her sitting across from me at that bar Saturday night.

It only made me all the more curious. Made me want to dig a little deeper. Get lost in the sea of those sad eyes that somehow brimmed with determination.

What was really messing with my head was the way she'd looked at me like I was some kind of savior when I'd returned that bracelet to her. Like I'd given her back something precious. Like I'd done something *good*.

Funny how I'd expected she'd be excited over the wallet.

The only thing she'd cared about was that bracelet that wasn't in any better shape than that building Jace had sent me to check out. There'd been so much gratitude flooding from her that it'd made some hard part of me go soft. One warm pulse that throbbed through every inch of my body.

A shockwave.

Only got worse when she'd washed my hair. Snipped the pieces away. Touched me with those tender fingers. Her scent all around me. Like I was rolling around in a bed of sugar-coated flowers.

Lust and need and something else that I couldn't quite decipher had hung so thick in the space between us that, for the first time in my life, a girl had made me feel like I couldn't breathe.

Like she'd stolen it. Bottled it up and held it in the palm of those delicate hands.

That alone should have made me want to run.

And there I sat, itching to get back up, hunt her down, and sink my fingers into all that flesh.

Feel what that might be like.

That soft *grace* that radiated from her like the sun breaking through the clouds after a hurricane.

But even considering it was stupid.

Reckless.

That was the kind of carelessness I didn't play partner to. I knew better than to let myself get distracted, and she'd made it clear she didn't need any of that, either. She couldn't afford what I wanted to take from her.

When I felt a presence approach, I set my cell on the table and glanced up to find Mirena standing over me. She was one of the cocktail waitresses who I was . . . familiar with.

"Ian Jacobs." My name slipped out of her mouth like she was confessing a sin. "So nice to see you."

Shit.

Obviously, the girl was serving up sarcasm today.

I dipped my head, half inclined to ask for another waitress because I definitely didn't feel up to her brand of drama. "Mirena."

Monty's was my home away from home. Hell, I felt more comfortable here than behind the doors of my condo. At least here it was noisy, especially on nights like tonight when a band was set to play, Carolina George setting up to take to the stage. Dark and dim and rowdy, the energy gave the vibe that at any moment everything could slip into chaos.

A constant din of music and voices and bodies there to chase away the emptiness.

Loud enough that the ghosts had no chance of being heard.

Of course, because it was me, I'd fucked up and fucked her. Never should have given into the girl standing in front of me. I knew it the second she'd propositioned me that it was a mistake. I'd been told you should never shit where you eat. Should have taken up that advice for where I drank, too.

"What can I get for you tonight?" She was close to purring when she said it before she shook her head and released an angry chuckle. She leaned forward and tossed a cocktail napkin down in front of me and started talking before I had the chance to respond.

"Wait, let me guess. Scotch. Double. On the rocks. Because you like your liquor just as cold as your heart. Whatever leggy brunette walks through the door wearing a slinky dress. Or maybe you're in the mood for a blonde? What is it that's on the menu for tonight?"

She hadn't let it go. I wasn't really sure what she'd been expecting, a marriage proposal or a date or maybe she'd just wanted it twice.

If she knew me so well, she should have known none of those things were going to happen.

But she'd gotten one thing right. I was in the mood for a blonde. But the one I was thirsting for was the last thing I needed.

I tossed a smirk Mirena's direction, needing her to know there wasn't going to be a repeat. "How about one of each? I am in the mood for a little . . . variety."

She scoffed. "Of course, you'd want it all. Stupid me."

Her smile was brittle. Filled with regret and a shot of hurt. I refused the impulse to feel bad. I wasn't going to fucking coddle her when she knew just as well as I did that when I'd followed her home that night we were really going nowhere.

"Why don't we just start off the night with that scotch?" I told her, willing to say anything to get her out of there.

"Bluebird for me," the gruff voice came from behind her. Caught off guard, she shrieked, and then she whirled around as a true smile spread across her face.

"Mack. Where have you been all my life, handsome?" Her voice had gone easy. Because that's just the way he made people feel.

Comfortable.

Like any situation was going to turn out better when he was involved.

He was the ultimate protector.

Big and mean and probably the softest dude I'd ever met. Had no fucking clue how we were friends. The guy was always there for me when I sure as hell didn't deserve it. Watching me, ready to rush in and save my ass if I got too deep.

But there were some things we just couldn't be saved from.

My bear of a best friend slipped into the side of the booth opposite me. He ran a tattooed hand down the scruff on his face and pushed out a sigh like he was leaving behind a grueling day, all of his ink out and on display.

He chalked it up to being undercover in his early days.

I knew better.

He gave her a massive grin. "Lookin' for you, gorgeous. What else would I be doing here?"

"Drinking your weight in beer?" she deadpanned.

Yeah. I guess she did know us well.

He laughed and sent her a smirk. "You think so little of me. I take offense to that." Mischief gleamed in his blue eyes. "And here I thought you'd be happy to see me."

"Oh, I'm always happy to see you." She rubbed his massive arm. "And don't you dare think I'm judging you. You deserve it. Tell me how many bad guys you put in cuffs today? That's how many beers I'll bring you. How's that sound?"

"Ah, well there's never any shortage of them, that's for sure."

Didn't I know it.

He lifted one side of his mouth. Looking at the guy, it was hard to tell if he was a monster or a huge-ass teddy bear. Dude could win over a surly DMV agent with a grin and a wink of his eye and then turn right around and make a calloused criminal piss his pants.

You'd think women would go running from that thick shell of intimidation, but they flocked to him like he was some kind of inked-up Mecca.

That was the thing about Mack, though. He'd gone through as much bad shit as the rest of us. Still, he'd managed to come out of it wearing a smile on his face. But there was a layer underneath that he didn't let anyone else see.

"Well, that's a good thing, considering here at Monty's there is no shortage of beer." She overstated it like she was auditioning for a commercial.

Mack laughed, and she patted his shoulder again. "I'll be right back."

Her expression was totally playful when she said it before it darkened when she glanced at me.

Clearly, she was trying to put me in my place. Get under my skin. Make it hurt. But that was the brilliance about not giving a fuck.

Nothing hurt. Nothing *mattered*. That was the way I had to keep it.

Mack watched her saunter away before he pushed out an exaggerated sigh and shot me a glare. "That poor girl is in love with you."

"Pssh . . . the only thing that girl is in love with is my dick. Big difference."

He barked out a laugh. "Cocky bastard."

"That is what I just said." I tried not to grin.

"You really are full of yourself there."

"What can I say? We all have our talents."

"You mean delusions. We all have our delusions," he tossed out, grinning wide.

"Like the delusion you've been having for years that you're as good as me? That's just plain sad," I razzed.

His tongue rolled around under his left cheek, fighting laughter. "You wish, asshole. I taught you everything you know."

"See . . . that's where you've gone wrong, Mack. It's not about teaching. It's all about the natural, raw talent."

"Only talent you have is making all that bullshit rolling off your tongue sound convincing."

A chuckle danced in my chest. "Again . . . raw talent. What can I say. I was born to hold court. Just like I was born to love the ladies right."

We both sat back when Mirena returned and set Mack's beer down in front of him. "There you go, tough guy. There's more where that came from."

She'd shifted her eyes to me when she said the last, sliding my scotch in my direction.

She walked off.

Mack took a gulp of the dark amber in his glass. "She doesn't look like you did her all that right."

"Seems to me you're just pissed you didn't get a go at her first."

He shrugged his massive shoulders. "Maybe. She's fucking hot."

I took a swill of my scotch, relishing in the burn. "Go for it."

With a harsh shake of his head, he sat back casually in the

booth, one of those smirks riding all over his face. "Last thing I need is to go dipping my dick anywhere yours has been. No, thank you."

"You act like you don't love me." Humor played around my mouth.

"Uh, yeah, no. Not even close to *lovin'* you that much," he teased, lips twitching all over the place before his demeanor shifted. "You really wouldn't give two fucks if I went after her, would you?"

"Not even half of one. I don't catch feelings. Don't have the space for that."

A huff of disbelief slipped from his mouth. "I think you have plenty of space in that hollowed-out cavern you've got going on right there." He leaned across the table and poked me in the chest.

The asshole.

He sat back again. "Maybe if you started acting a little sweeter, you might sucker in one you actually might want to keep."

I swirled the liquid around in my glass. "I think both of us know there's nothing *sweet* about me, and the last thing I'm interested in is *keeping* anyone. You know better than that."

"Do I?"

Discomfort pushed at my conscience as I looked at my best friend, who was heading in a direction he knew better than to go. We both got it. Understood it about the other. Didn't need him to go changing his tune, digging up shit that definitely was better left buried.

"Maybe it's time you stop thinking with your dick and do a little thinking with your heart." There he went, pushing it farther.

Eyes narrowing, I cocked my head with the challenge. "That wouldn't be so pretty, now, would it?"

"Not sure you'd know since you've never tested it out."

"Got a whole lot of room to talk there, my friend," I sent back, trying to keep the hostility from taking control of the words and failing miserably. He didn't get to do this.

He choked out a laugh that held zero humor, harshness ridging his brow. "Circumstances are a little different, don't you think?"

"Are they?"

Redness climbed up his thick neck. The guy tried to swallow around it, while I felt like a total dick again for throwing it in his face. Because the circumstances were different. But that didn't mean they hurt either of us any less.

We'd both learned the hard way that loving someone, having faith that they were going to be around forever, that they wouldn't completely *break you*, led to nothing but a demolished, desolated heart.

I hadn't created that empty cavern inside me.

She'd left it there.

He edged closer to the table, gruff words a challenge as they rumbled from his mouth. "Yeah, they are different. Because at least I let myself feel it."

My teeth gritted. Pain lanced through the middle of me. A million cuts that would never heal ripped wide open. "You think I don't *feel* it?"

Did he think I didn't remember, every fucking day?

He was clutching his beer so tightly I was surprised he didn't crush the glass. "I think you'd prefer not to feel anything. I think you shut yourself off that day, and you haven't let a soul in since. That's gonna kill you, man. Emotionally. Maybe even physically. Because you roll without having a whole lot of fucks to give except for your climb to make partner and build your own fucking empire. One way or another, in the end, that's gonna destroy you."

"It's what will save me." It was out before I could stop it.

I suddenly felt seventeen.

Terrified and alone and promising myself it would never feel that way again. That no one would ever have the power to hurt me the way she had.

I'd break the entire fucking world before it got the chance to break me.

"Yeah, and how's Bennet?" Mack's words twisted with distaste.

I cringed, shifted in discomfort, took a sip of the scotch. "Bennet is just the same as he's ever been. My ticket to the top."

"Not if he takes you down before you get there."

I fiddled with the collar of my shirt, suddenly feeling hot. "He was there for me when I needed someone most."

Brow pinching up tight, Mack angled his head. "Dude is shady as fuck. You and I both know it. And you know I fucking love you, man. That I'd die for you. That I'll always have your back. Help you in whatever way I can."

He angled in farther, his voice dripping with a growled promise, "But what I'll never be is a dirty cop. And you know as fucking well as I do that Bennet is as dirty as they come."

"My shit's clean."

It was a lie I'd been feeding myself for so long, I should have believed it. But the truth of just how shady that shit went was impossible to ignore.

He sat back in the booth. "You better make sure it stays that way."

I tried to tamp it down, stop it from boiling up, the old hatred for owing anyone anything. But Bennet had been there for me when I'd been that pathetic, scared kid.

He fed me and had given me a job. Picked me up and dusted me off. Told me he'd always be there for me, and he'd stuck by his word.

I'd owed him. Felt loyal to him.

But as the years had passed, the side jobs he'd had me doing for him became more and more warped. Darkness concealed by the light, feigned good deeds that were nothing but a cover.

Had to wonder if that hadn't been the reason I'd been drawn to him all along. The reason I'd ended up at his feet. The lure of wickedness hidden inside him, the same kind of wickedness that thrived inside me.

Mack shook his head and swore, looking away for a second like he'd just heard every single one of my thoughts. "You're one of the good guys, Ian. Fucking good, no matter if you want to be or not. It's time to start living that way. Because I know you. I fucking know you better than anyone, and it will *kill* me if you let the grief you refuse to feel continue to own you."

"I'm fine."

A hard breath of disbelief and frustration jetted from his nose. "Do you really believe all the bullshit you feed yourself?"

"What can I say? It's a talent." My response was hard, but Mack laughed and scrubbed a hand over his face. Asshole was grinning again.

I started to tell him to go to hell when my phone dinged. I reached for it, figuring it was Jace following up about the building.

I fucking froze when I saw who the text was from.

My ice-cold heart flashed with a bolt of heat. A frenzy pumped directly into my veins.

Unknown: Thank you for what you did today. I wish I could have truly expressed to you what it meant to me. I want you to know it meant everything.

Grace.

I sat there staring at her message, fighting that same feeling again.

"Who's that?" Mack nudged me with his boot from under the table.

I shoved my phone into my pocket. "No one."

"No one?" he challenged.

"That's what I said."

Fucker grinned. "And you're lying. I see it written all over you."

I sent him a glare and tried to ignore the excitement that blazed just beneath the surface of my skin, my phone burning a damned hole in my pocket.

I had a number.

An in.

And I was fucking going to take it.

Mack laughed. "Looks to me like you're not feeling so cold, after all. Maybe I shouldn't lose hope in my best friend just yet."

"It's just a fuck, Mack."

At least, that's what I wanted it to be. Still, I cringed when I said it, as if it were insulting her, the girl who dripped sex and indecency and then had me fumbling when she looked at me with those sad, fathomless eyes.

Truth was, if I was right about the girl, that was probably all that the text was.

A thank you.

Mack was right. I wasn't anything but an asshole. A predator. After one thing. Because sitting there right then? I knew I was going to take it as an invitation.

Problem was, everything about it felt different. Body lighting up at the thought. Pulse doing something funny when it thrummed an extra beat.

"One day, some girl is going to make a crack in that impenetrable stone, and you're gonna put one on her finger. Have a small herd of kids. And you're going to be happy, Ian. Fucking happy because it's about time you had a little of the real kind."

"You want to be called Uncle? You've got Jace for that. So why don't we drop this bullshit you're trying to get at? You know what's important to me. What I live for, and you know damned well that I'll live the way I want. I won't let anyone get in the way of that."

And it sure as fuck wasn't going to involve marriage and a family.

I edged up so I could get my wallet out of my pocket, dug into it, and pulled out a twenty. I tossed it onto the table. "I have to go."

Asshole cracked a grin. "Where you headin', Ian?"

I pushed out of the booth and shot him a finger, not turning to look back. Only thing I heard was his laughter following me to the door.

GRACE

"Thomas, set the table, please."

"Oh, man, do I have to?" he whined, stomping through the kitchen and heading directly to the cabinet. Clearly, he already knew the answer to that, especially with the look I sent him.

But because it was Thomas, he was going to argue anyway.

Gramma chuckled and shook her head. "Boys. They like to do everything the hard way."

Wasn't that the truth?

"Not the hard way, Grams, the right way," he corrected, hiking up onto his tiptoes to pull down the plates.

"Right way, huh? And how do you figure?" she asked, moving around the kitchen and finishing our dinner, poking at the potatoes with a fork to make sure they were soft. All the while, I was busy washing Sophie Marie's face and hands since she'd decided to have a mud pie as an appetizer.

She'd shoveled about three fistfuls into her mouth before I'd made it across the backyard to stop her.

Mallory was spinning around in the middle of the kitchen, singing Taylor Swift at the top of her lungs as she danced and held a spatula to her mouth, the child already thinking she was a superstar.

We were all basically knocking into each other, getting in each other's way.

A muddle of confusion.

I called it harmony.

Funny, how I'd gladly trade that rambling kitchen with a cook and a maid for the warmth of my grandmother's.

The smell of a roast rising up from the faded white stove, flecks of paint missing, the counterspace close to nonexistent, and the floors a worn linoleum that had long since turned brown.

There was no place better.

No place safer.

No place that made me remember who I was and exactly who I wanted to be than when I was standing there in the perfectly orchestrated chaos.

Thomas rolled his eyes. "If we were doing it the right way, we'd be using paper plates. I mean, who even sits at a table and eats dinner together anymore, anyway? And I'm not even allowed to have my tablet."

"The horror," I told him, sending him a warning glance.

You'd better watch it, young man.

I knew he was just trying to figure out his place. Adjusting to the change. Dealing with the fear he tried to keep hidden, which worried me most of all.

"It's family time, Tom Tom!" Mallory shouted, breaking song, before she was right back at it again, the little thing singing about shaking it off as she shook her little bottom, wearing a pink satin nightgown and my grandmother's slippers with old style curlers in her hair.

Apparently, she'd had a little *Gramma* time this afternoon.

The kid was taking and giving good advice, that was for sure.

I was trying hard to keep it myself.

Hold it.

To pretend as if everything was normal. As if my beautiful stranger hadn't come into the salon today and ripped the rug right out from under me.

Sophie squirmed, jogging me out of the daze. "I down. I eat now. I eat now."

I was holding my toddler facing out, the squirming wild monkey wiggling in my arms. I finished washing the sand from her mouth and grabbed a hand towel to dry her face and hands. "We are going to eat right now. Don't you smell that delicious dinner your gramma is making you?"

"Yeah, delicious because you're not making it." Thomas sent me a grin as he swaggered passed.

"Hey, that isn't very nice."

"What? It's the truth. Right, Grams?" He turned to her, looking for confirmation.

She chuckled one of her light laughs, body swaying at the stove. "We all have our strengths, child. Unfortunately for your mother, cooking is not one of hers."

From over her shoulder, she sent me an affectionate wink.

"Hey, why is everyone ganging up on me?"

"Shake it off, Momma!" Mallory sang, jumping around. "Besides, you make the best mac and cheese in the whole world."

"See," I shouted in something akin to victory, eyes going wide as I gave my grandmother an I-told-you-so look.

"She is your child who's living in a fantasy world," Grandma said with a shrug, grinning wide and making Thomas howl with laughter.

"Fine, only people getting any of my mac and cheese around here is my Mal Pal, isn't that right?"

She jumped in front of me, those ridiculous pink curlers flopping around, one sliding right out. "That's right. None for you two boohoos."

"I down!" Sophie Marie shouted again, and I set her on her

feet. She went running through the kitchen, scooping up her plush princess doll that she carried everywhere.

It was definitely going to need to take a tumble in the washer after she went to sleep, but I so didn't need the meltdown that would come with taking it from her then.

My grandmother had taught me some battles were worth fighting. That was not one of them.

Plates clacked as Thomas set them on the round table in the kitchen nook. He went to the drawer and pulled out silverware. He waved it in my face. "Happy?"

"Very," I shot right back.

"Can I have my tablet, then?"

"Nice try, buddy."

"The TV? We could all watch a show together." That perked him up, brows riding high as if his manipulation was irresistible.

"Nope. You know the rules. No electronics at the dinner table. We can have one meal a day where we all have an actual conversation, can't we?"

Thomas's shoulders sagged. He might as well have gotten the news that he was grounded for a month. "Why do I have to have the most uncool mom on the planet? No one else has to do it."

I tapped his nose. "Maybe I just love you more."

Okay, who said I couldn't wield my own manipulation?

He rolled his eyes, but there was affection behind it, the kid trying to fight the smile that pulled to his mouth.

Such a tough guy.

Good thing I knew better.

Gramma laughed, transferring the roast to a platter, talking over her shoulder as she did. "Don't let her fool you, Thomas. Your mother used to try to pull the same stunt on me when she was growin' up. She always had an excuse why that television should be blaring during dinner. Nearly drove your Grandpa Smitty straight to the loony bin."

Thomas's mouth dropped open. "Mom got to watch TV during dinner? That's so not fair."

"Not even close. But you have to give her credit. She tried just as hard as you." She knocked him with her hip. "Might as well give it up, kid. Because I loved your mother more, too . . . just like she loves you."

It was all affection.

Devotion spinning all around us.

Thomas so comfortable that he did, in fact, give it up. He helped Mallory climb into her chair while I wrangled Sophie into her high chair. Gramma heaped a ton of food onto each of their plates, roast and potatoes and carrots.

"Grams has mad cooking skills, that's for sure," Thomas said, shoving his fork into his mouth and talking around his food. I didn't even have the heart to tell him not to talk with food in his mouth.

He'd had enough of that polishing to last him a lifetime.

Our meals had never been shared like this before.

The comfort of it only found here.

Where a true sort of family resided.

Where just being together meant more than anything else.

My gaze roamed around the table.

My grandmother who'd raised me with my grandpa before he'd passed eleven years before.

My children.

Thomas and Mallory and Sophie.

Love shining so bright.

Thomas chatted with my gramma as if he were the man of the house, which she continually told him he was, and Mallory laughed uproariously at just about everything, while Sophie babbled a little song while she flung half her food into her hair and onto the floor.

Hope filled me full.

Joy so bright.

Heart beating wild with the possibility of it all.

I'd been sitting in my room for the last two hours, trying to settle the riot inside me that writhed and heaved.

The kids had long since been bathed and tucked into bed. A continuation of our story had been made, a new twist in the *Ruby Prince and Priceless Princesses*, two new pages drawn into our sketchbook.

A dragon and his lair.

I guessed maybe it had been fed by the text message that had been waiting from Reed after we'd gotten finished with dinner.

Reed: You're running out of time to make the right choice. Do you think I don't know you were at that gala? Sniffing around? You're treading into dangerous waters, Grace. It'd be a shame if you drowned.

Terror had raced my veins when I'd read the words. It hadn't even been a veiled threat, his blatant hostility growing greater and greater with every day that passed, my worry amplifying in direct correlation to his warnings.

I knew the only thing holding him back from coming completely unglued was the flimsy evidence I had against him, which probably amounted to nothing, but somehow had worked at keeping him at bay.

The problem was, I was beginning to feel that assurance slipping. Reed's demands had gone from pleas for me to return to threats of what would happen if I didn't.

As if I'd ever trust his feigned affections. Not ever again. I'd already seen the monster hidden underneath.

I'd met Reed in college. Our love had been sweet, if not a little boring. Maybe I should have given more credit to that, but I'd been so young that I hadn't even had time to read the warning signs before he had a ring on my finger and had moved me from my dorm and into his house.

Looking back, I could see that it'd been nothing but a strategic move. A game piece.

It hadn't been long before I was just another pawn he kept under his thumb.

I refused to succumb to it.

Antsy, I glanced around my childhood room.

It hadn't been touched since I'd left when I'd headed to college.

High school pictures were still tacked to the walls and played partner to posters of my teen idols. My twin bed was still made up in the same quilt my grandmother had made for me after I'd picked out the colors for the patchwork pieces when I was thirteen.

The room was filled with small white furniture—a dresser and a desk and a nightstand that had a pink lamp sitting on top of it that matched the quilt.

From where I was propped against the headboard, I looked around, running my hands up my arms, fighting both the fear and anger at Reed and the buzz that still lingered from what had happened earlier this afternoon at the salon.

A quiet hum that drove the possibility of sleep from my mind.

More intense where it glowed beneath the bracelet around my wrist.

What I needed to do was sink down into my bed and put a pillow over my head.

Block it all out.

Maybe I was just delirious, still angry, my spirit rejecting everything Reed had implied, everything he stood for, the chains I was anxious to be free of.

Maybe it was that flicker.

The idea of *more*.

I glanced at my phone.

Just as fast, I jerked my attention away and questioned whether I'd lost my sanity.

Apparently so because just as fast I picked up my phone from the nightstand.

Quickly, I typed out a message to the number I'd gone and memorized like it was a theorem on my next high school calculus test.

Seemed fitting considering I felt as if I was officially back to that age.

A young girl who wanted something more. To experience what it felt like to be alive. Exhilarated and excited. To be touched and loved and adored.

Me: Thank you for what you did today. I wish I could have truly expressed to you what it meant to me. I want you to know it meant everything.

Somehow, none of those worries seemed to matter when I pushed send with a rush of butterflies taking flight from my skin.

Fluttering and flapping and the threat of an eager grin crawling across my lips.

His name and number had been nothing but a slip of temptation in my hand.

Part of me knew I shouldn't. That I should just let it be.

But sometimes that loneliness came on too fierce. When I could feel my spirit moaning from within, the worries growing more severe at night, in the moments when I felt utterly alone.

Or maybe I was already addicted to the way he made me feel. To the way I could feel those crazy-colored eyes raking over me, filled with the promise of the most decadent kind of sin.

It'd be a pleasure unlike anything I'd ever known. I knew it. I'd felt the promise of it radiating from his skin and vibrating from his body.

I could still feel that gaze touching me from across the space. Maybe the only reason I sent that text was because I wanted to experience it for a moment more.

Silly girl.

But sometimes, fantasy was the only thing that kept us moving.

I sat on the edge of my bed like a girl waiting to be asked out to prom, holding the phone as if I could will it to buzz.

Five minutes passed, and he hadn't texted back.

Disappointment pooled in my spirit.

I tried to push it off. It was for the best, anyway.

Even harboring the idea of something happening with us was sheer recklessness.

I wasn't the type of girl who threw caution to the wind.

Tossing my phone onto the nightstand, I flipped off the lamp and tugged the covers over my body.

My old room fell into darkness. Those sweet, innocent faces

raced into my mind the second I pushed everything else out. I needed to regroup. Make a new plan of attack.

Figure out how I was going to get us out of this mess.

Maybe I'd messed up to begin with. Done everything wrong. But sometimes the only thing a mother could do was go with her gut, and I didn't know how to regret that.

I guessed that, if I was looking at the situation, I was lucky to be here at all. Lying in this bed with my babies sleeping in the other room. The worst part was that he got to see them at all, that I'd been granted temporary custody, but he still got them two days a week.

As if he was even the one taking care of them. Wanting to see them.

But for the time being, they were mine. I just had to make sure they stayed that way. Could only pray that I was strong enough to see this through.

I jolted when my phone vibrated on the nightstand. A flash of light filtered into the room.

I reached over and flipped on the light switch, pushing up to sitting in my tiny bed as that ridiculous excitement I'd been feeling earlier sprang back to life. In a big, big way. Because there it was. A text from him.

Ian: It was my pleasure.

I could almost hear the scruff of his voice. As if he were whispering it in my ear. A rough caress. I felt it all the way down into my belly.

My phone buzzed again.

Ian: Actually, let me rephrase that. It should be me thanking you. That haircut was quite . . . memorable. You are good with your hands.

Oh, my goodness. That man went from zero to one hundred in a second flat.

Those hands he was speaking of started shaking, and I felt the flush race up my chest and hit my cheeks. Chewing at my bottom lip, my eyes darted around my room as if I'd just engaged in something illicit or illegal when the only thing we were doing was sharing a casual thank you.

But there wasn't a single thing about that mesmerizing man that felt *casual*.

My fingers flew across the keyboard.

Me: Why am I certain that you're good with yours, too?

Oh, what was I doing? What was I doing?

Begging for trouble, that was what.

I bit down hard on my bottom lip, trying to convince myself not to send it, that I was wading into dangerous, dangerous waters, playing this kind of game with a boy like him.

He'd chew me up and spit me out.

But I loved the way it felt, the erratic racing in my heart when I pushed send.

My racing heart skipped a beat when my phone buzzed again. Oh hell, who was I kidding? It skipped two.

Ian: You can rest assured that I am. Why don't you let me prove it to you?

I felt those waters lapping up to my thighs.

Steam rising up.

Scalding hot.

It'd been a long, long time since someone talked to me that way.

Brazen and bold.

No restraint.

The man was so arrogant that somehow his words fit him perfectly. Confidence oozing from him like the slow drip of honey.

The more shocking part was what he was conjuring in me.

Desire.

It was almost an unfamiliar sensation that went slip-sliding through my body. That feeling that had been there since the first time I looked over and saw him sitting at the end of the bar.

Bigger and brighter than anything else. Yet, still so obscenely dark.

I guessed I'd taken too long to respond because another message came through while I was sitting there staring at my screen, held captive in some sort of lust-induced haze.

Ian: I can't stop thinking about you. I have that number now. How about that drink?

Damn him, tempting me.

Me: I already told you that's a bad idea.

Ian: I think you're wrong. I think you're just scared to take the chance. You're afraid you won't be the same after I'm finished with you.

My spirit trembled with trepidation, whipped up with need. It was a bitch wanting something when you knew it was going to be bad for you.

On top of that, I wasn't even sure what it was I wanted. How far I was willing to let this go.

All I knew was I couldn't stop thinking about him, either. He'd invaded a secret place. A place I'd almost forgotten existed. I was terrified once he removed himself from my life, it was finally going to collapse.

Me: That's exactly what I'm afraid of . . . that I won't be the same after you're finished with me. I'm not exactly one for casual flings. I don't have any space to be hurt again.

I wasn't sure why this guy compelled me to cut myself wide open. Why I'd give him anything at all. But I felt hinged, caught up on the intensity of his response when my phone blipped again.

Ian: Why does that make me want to hunt someone down? Makes me crazy . . . knowing that someone hurt you. That you might be hurting. How is that possible?

My chest tightened, desperate for that feeling. To care about someone and for them to care about me.

To give and take.

Rely and provide.

But that was just stupidity. I didn't even know this guy.

I tapped out a quick reply, needing to get him off the phone. To end this before I said something that I'd regret.

Me: It's not your problem. Don't worry about me. I'll be fine.

I sat gaping at the string of responses that came blipping through, as if he were firing them off, not giving himself time to think his answers through.

Ian: It is a problem, Grace. It's a fucking problem because I can't get you off my mind.

Ian: It's a problem that I met you once and you affected me the way that you did.

Ian: It's a problem because the only thing I do is casual, and somehow, you have me wanting to say fuck it and see where this goes.

Ian: It's a fucking problem.

Ian: Tell me what happened that night . . . when you took off.

I didn't have time to answer before another message came through.

Ian: Actually, don't answer that. I want you to tell me to my face.

Disappointment seeped into my bloodstream, a gushing river of despondency and discontent. Because I wanted to confess it all. Tell him what I was going through. Pray that he wouldn't run.

But he would.

He should.

I couldn't expect anything different.

He didn't deserve to get mixed up in my mess. And there was no chance I could trust him around my kids.

Me: That's not possible. You aren't going to see me again.

Ian: I think you're wrong. I think you want to see me every bit as badly as I want to see you.

Ian: I want to touch you.

Ian: I've never wanted to touch a woman as desperately as I want to touch you.

Ian: Would you let me? Would you let me touch you, Grace? Touch you until you forget whatever it is you're going through?

My chest stretched tight, body rigid with shock and that blistering attraction that burned like a firestorm.

I pressed my thighs together, that river of disappointment turning into rapids of desire, sending me plunging right over a cliff.

A waterfall.

Pounding and throbbing and crashing.

Deeper and deeper.

God, this man was too much. And I was shaking . . . shaking and shaking as I fumbled to form a response.

Me: I don't want to forget. But if I didn't have all of this

going on in my life, you'd be the one I'd want. But it's for
the best if you let this go. I don't want to hurt you.

Ian: Funny, I was just going to say the same thing to you.

I could almost hear the self-loathing in his words. A shock of
angry laughter ricocheting through the air. Those eyes going dark
and dim, flashing with something wicked.

Regret had me typing out my response.

Me: Then I guess we're even.

Ian: Yeah. I guess we are. We're the perfect match.

Air puffed through my nose. The man was nothing but
ridiculous.

**Me: I think I was right about you. You don't like to be
told no.**

And I had this glowing problem between my thighs begging
me to say yes.

To give in.

To let him tempt me and touch me and make me forget.

It would feel so nice to be held in those big, powerful hands.
Hands that would chase away the emptiness. Fill my broken spirit
that was littered with debris.

But there was no question that this man would break what was
left of my fragile heart. Hell, he was already breaking it now.
Making me crumble with every word.

**Ian: I think the bigger issue is that you want to say yes.
Tell me I'm wrong.**

I couldn't respond.

Ian: Don't you? Are you touching yourself, Grace, just

thinking about it?

On all things unholy.

I could feel sex dripping from his fingertips, and he wasn't even there.

Want clamored through my senses, every nerve alive. I shifted on the bed, my body on fire, so needy I was close to panting.

So close to touching myself and telling him that's what I was doing. That I was wishing it was him doing it to me.

I knew exactly how that would end.

I really had to put an end to this conversation. It was heading down a path of no return. One where the two of us were gonna collide, and the result of that was not going to be pretty.

He could so easily crush me.

Wind me up and leave me spinning.

Chasing after something that I could never have. But my heart had taken control, and my fingers were tapping out a reply.

Me: No. I'm not. But I wish you were.

It took a couple seconds before another text came through.

Ian: Is that an invitation? Because you know I am. My cock is so hard, I can barely see. You should feel it, Grace. What you do to me.

Me: I wish it was my hands.

Ian: Let's forget these wishes and make it a reality. I want inside of you. I bet your pussy is just as perfect as the rest of you.

Oh goodness.

There was nothing I could do. I was touching myself. Imagining exactly that. That gorgeous man crawling over me. Pushing deep. Taking me.

Three texts blipped through, I had no idea how much time in

between, my mind lost to the vision of what that would be like.

Letting myself go in a way that was so out of character for me.

I shattered. Body jerking as I bit my lip to keep myself from calling out his name. I was panting by the time I made it back to the waiting messages.

Ian: You are, aren't you?

Ian: Touching yourself?

Ian: Fuck. That's so hot. I want to see it. Your fingers dipping inside your body while I watch. What could one night hurt, Grace?

Reality slowly seeped back into my consciousness, and I struggled with what to say. How to end this when really, I wanted everything the man was offering, even when I knew it was going to hurt me in the end.

Me: I'm not much of a one-night kind of girl. I'm afraid it might hurt a lot.

Ian: I'd tell you that you shouldn't be afraid, but that would be a lie.

I hesitated, contemplating how to answer, wishing there was a way when it was clear we'd hit a dead end.

Me: Then I think this should be goodbye.

Ian: I guess it is midnight. You'd better run, Cinderella. It seems to be what you do best.

IAN

Groaning, I peeled my eyes open to the blaring alarm. Darkness still permeated my bedroom, just the barest hint of the approaching morning hinting at the edges of the window. I slapped at my phone to silence it, feeling totally wrung out and off.

Not sure what the fuck I'd been thinking last night.

Pressing that girl the way that I had. Needing something I had no right to go after and wanting to pursue it, anyway.

Seriously. What the hell was wrong with me?

Grace had thrown up so many red flags that I should have been out of the game.

Whistle blown.

But it had started feeling like something that wasn't close to being only a distraction or a diversion. Didn't feel like amusement or entertainment.

It'd grown into something bigger. Something that, for the first time in my life, had me wanting to step out and take a chance. Ask for more. Even when I knew I had so little to give. So little to offer.

God, I was fucked up in the head because I didn't know this girl, and she sure as shit wouldn't want to know me.

She didn't know my true nature.

The demon inside. The monster that raged.

Didn't matter anyway, though, did it?

I'd pushed her, and she'd pushed right back.

Shutting it down.

What I should have done the second she had that foreign feeling rising up and taking hold. The compulsion to possess and protect.

Flopping over onto my back in the middle of my enormous bed, I scrubbed my palms over my face and prayed it might break me out of this fuckery, bring me to my senses, knock me back into reality.

I blew out a strained breath toward the ceiling, dick still goddamned hard from just the few minutes I'd spent talking to her last night. Me picturing her in her bed. Probably surrounded by some Pinterest shit. Chic and modern and pretty.

Just like the girl.

I'd officially become a pussy. A pussy who was picturing a girl's fucking bedroom.

I needed to get laid, and I needed to do it fast so I could scrape this girl from my mind.

Forcing myself to sit up on the side of my bed, I sighed and grabbed my phone so I could check my emails.

It was routine.

What I always did to prep for the day.

Peoples' emergencies always seemed to spike in the middle of the night.

Annoying but true.

My life centered around other peoples' drama. Their heartache.

The goal pretty much to turn around and cause more.

Payback and revenge in the form of dollars and wealth. It was always what it amounted to.

Money.

Greed.

I guessed I'd landed myself in the right industry, after all.

A breath left me on a gush when I saw I had a shit-ton of unread texts. Heart rate kicking, hammering like a beast.

The messages had come in about two hours earlier. Probably right after I'd finally drifted into a restless sleep after spending hours aching in my bed. Dying to get lost in that body and those legs and that mind I could feel sucking me inside.

I quickly read through them.

Grace: You're right. The real problem is that I want to say yes.

Grace: But I also wasn't lying when I said I have too much going on in my life.

Grace: The truth is, I'm scared. I'm scared of losing anything else. I'm scared of being hurt. I'm scared of putting myself in danger. I'm scared that, once you know me, you'll walk away.

Grace: But I need you to know something. I might be beaten down. Crippled and fractured, but that doesn't mean I'm broken or crushed. That has never been me. Someone who is too timid to live her life. Someone who is too terrified to step out and take a chance.

Grace: But sometimes taking those chances might be risking too much.

Grace: I just want you to know . . . someday . . . someday . . . I will get the chance to live again.

My chest tightened.

Painfully.

And I wondered what that might be like.

To live again.

To fully breathe.

To give rather than to take.

To love rather than to hurt.

I just didn't know how the fuck that was possible when it was the only thing I'd ever known. But there was something about this girl, something overpowering, overwhelming, too perfect and sweet and enthralling, that made me want to try.

I wove my way through the crowd on the packed sidewalk. Hands shoved into my pockets, the evening air gathering around me, heart manic where it knocked against my ribs.

Hard and fast and desperate.

I was a fool.

I was a fool.

But I didn't care.

Didn't care about anything but the girl whose back was to me as she fumbled to lock the door to the salon, shutting down for the night.

Blonde waves tumbled down her back. The girl wore white jeans, a black sweater that draped over one delicious shoulder, and the sexiest pair of boots I'd ever seen.

Everything soared.

This surge of energy and light and need.

Standing there, ten feet away, I had the sinking feeling that I didn't recognize myself.

Most disturbing was the thought that maybe it was my soul recognizing hers.

Without looking my way, she froze, like she felt it, too, a tremor rolling the length of her spine.

Slowly, slowly, she turned to look at me.

A battered Cinderella.

A broken angel.

And there I stood, the devil in sheep's clothes.

Got the sense that she'd felt the demon all along. From the moment she'd first seen me. Because she breathed out in surprise, eyes a charge of lust and fear.

I welcomed it when it slammed into me.

Held it.

Just like I wanted to hold on to her.

GRACE

"*Ian.*" His name was a whisper that fell from my tongue, my mouth parting on fear and need and a breathy sigh.

Everything trembled.

My heart and the air and the ground beneath my feet.

"What are you doing here?"

But I already knew, didn't I? I already knew what I'd set into motion when I'd texted him in the middle of the night. Unable to sleep. Only able to think of him. Wanting something I shouldn't take.

But some things were unstoppable. Impossible to resist when the temptation was too great. Right there, begging for me to dip my fingers in so I could take a taste.

He edged forward, that severity a bluster from his perfect body.

Today, he wore a full three-piece suit, dark gray and sleek and fitted. It showed off every inch of the strength that rippled below the expensive fabric.

Shoulders wide.

Waist narrow.

Tie around his neck and desire on his lips.

I could feel it.

Passion.

Lust.

Need.

It radiated from him with the force of a thousand suns.

The man edged closer. Each step that he took robbed me of a little more of my sanity.

Because this was truly crazy.

He stopped when there was only the fraction of a breath between us, his heat wrapping me whole, his words warmth where he dipped down to utter them close to my cheek.

"You told me in that text that you've never been a girl who was afraid to live her life. To step out and take a chance. And fuck, Grace, I'm standing here, right now, asking you to take a chance on me."

Oh God.

Crack. Crack. Crack.

I could feel every reservation crumbling out from under me.

There was no missing the way his mouth tweaked into one of those arrogant smiles where it barely brushed my skin, the words so soft but laden with a demand. "Have dinner with me."

Need spiraled. I inhaled, drawing him into the well of my lungs. Power and influence and dominance. Cinnamon and orange and sex boiling on a stove.

Fingertips fluttered along the side of my neck, trailing my pulse that throbbed out of control. "What could one dinner hurt?"

There was a tease to his tone, a tease to his question.

The man was so damned good at winding me up. Hooking me in all those places where I'd never be released.

I almost laughed.

"Oh, I think you could hurt, all right." I edged back so I could look up at him. "Men like you should come with a warning."

Cinnamon eyes flashed. Red and gold and black. He was cupping the side of my face in one of those big hands, his thumb running across the hollow beneath my eye. "I think it's a woman like you who bears all the threat."

"How's that?"

"You're so sweet that you don't have the first clue just how dangerous you really are."

The man managed to pull a giggle free. "I'm not all sweet."

He quirked a sexy grin. "I don't believe you."

"I just might surprise you."

He was back to whispering in my ear, his aura all around me. "Oh, you surprised me. You knocked me off my feet."

I peeked up at him. "I think it was the other way around."

Literally.

The man had knocked me on my ass. I hadn't fully been able to stand on my feet ever since.

He took me by the chin, eyes searching, so close I was terrified he was going to dip down and kiss me right there. I was most definitely not ready for that. Especially out in the open.

Exposed.

Hell, this was as reckless as could be. Just standing there with him that way.

My gaze flicked around, searching the packed street for eyes that might be watching. But Reed had the kids today. Their days at his place tended to keep him preoccupied with keeping up that charade. The parody of a caring parent.

Ian must have sensed the shiver of unease that rustled through me because he put an inch between us. "Just dinner . . . then you can decide where we go from there."

His voice shifted, dripping pure sex. "I hope you let me take you where I'm dying to go. Follow me, Angel Girl."

I guessed he thought I was getting ready to say no because he pushed me back against the door to the salon, his big body pinning mine.

Heat ran wild.

"Please, Grace. Just dinner."

I hesitated for only a second before I gave a nod. I was going to regret this, I knew I would. But the last thing I wanted right then was to go to my grandmother's house and face the reminder of an unthinkable possibility.

The vacancy and emptiness echoing back.

"Just dinner."

I think we both knew it was more than that when he wrapped an arm around my waist and tugged me close to his side.

Once again, my attention jumped around. I hated that Reed still held a thumb over me, but I had to be careful. Remember what was riding on the line. A line I needed to toe.

Ian Jacobs had me sliding off.

I turned my face into his neck to hide it.

The only thing I managed to do was breathe his aura in.

He began to lead me through the mob of people that hurried this way and that as they rushed home at the end of their day.

I think we both knew it then.

That this was different.

That this moment *mattered*.

We knew it because it felt like a start. As if we were standing at the beginning of something great. Which was impossible because this man didn't know what I was up against.

Who I was or what meant the most to me.

Their little faces flashed through my mind. It stabbed me with guilt. Because I shouldn't be seeking any pleasure until I knew their happiness was secure. Until I'd finished this fight.

Until I'd won.

With the thought, I peeked out again, darts of anxiety impaling my senses. A warning to be careful. To take heed.

Push.

Pull.

Push.

Pull.

I felt as if I was being yanked in every direction.

My heart propelling me forward, and my rational side attempting to reel me back in.

Being reckless wasn't going to win me any points. But it wasn't like going to dinner with a man was wrong. I was committing no crime, and I certainly wasn't partaking in some kind of disloyalty.

All the betrayals had been perpetrated on me.

I guessed the real test would be if Ian wanted to fight alongside me when he knew.

If he'd be the one willing to take the chance on me.

The problem was, I had no idea when I should tell him or how he would react.

"Just dinner," he whispered at the side of my head. As if he'd felt every single one of my insecurities crawl across my flesh.

"Just dinner," I agreed.

I wondered if that was the moment Ian and I told our first lies.

IAN

She leaned into me, and I pulled her closer.

I couldn't help but wonder why it felt so right.
Why I wasn't repulsed.
Why I didn't want to push her away.
Why I wanted more.
Why I loved it when she snuggled deeper into my hold.
I didn't do this.
Not ever.
Didn't want it.
But right then, the only thing I could think was that I did. That this was a chance worth taking.
Just dinner.

What bullshit.

She and I both knew it. Because she was trembling in my arms, nerves wracking through her, like she was holding back a secret she wanted me to keep.

To hold.

It fucking terrified me that I might want to.

I knew something was up. No doubt there was shit going on with her that I couldn't see.

I held her close as I led her through the droves of people who were flocking from their workplaces as evening began to settle on the city, the sky hewn in a dusky gray, streaked with pink.

Finally seeming to settle, she exhaled in some kind of relief and peered up at me. She was tall, but she still felt small where she was tucked against my side.

"So, where are you taking me for *just dinner*?"

A light chuckle rumbled out. "I figured since I need to make a good impression, I'll have to take you to my favorite restaurant."

At the intersection, cars stopped at the red light, and I quickly guided her across the street toward the glitzy building that housed Eve's on the top floor.

She almost rolled her eyes, but there was still something playful about it. "Of course, this is where you would take me. Only a boy born with a silver spoon in his mouth would have a taste for a place like this."

It was instant. The way turbulence rippled through my senses. The air I was breathing suddenly choppy and rough. "Hardly."

If she only knew. If she only knew the way I'd lived. The things I'd overcome. The things I'd done to survive.

The only delicacy I'd known as a child were the ones I'd scraped out of a trash can. I wondered what she'd think then?

"That's good then . . . because you should know, I'm not going to be impressed by the location. The only thing that can impress me is the man."

God, this girl. So damned different.

"I guess I already have everything going against me then, don't I?" I tried to inject some humor into it, but I realized I was sending her a warning. If she looked too deep, she wasn't going to like what she'd find.

She turned that teal gaze on me as we entered through the revolving door, my hand at the small of her back as I ushered her inside.

With a glance over her delicate shoulder, her stare scattered over my body. Or maybe it was just breaking me into pieces. "Is that what you think? That you aren't worth it? That you aren't worth the chance you're asking me for?"

Apparently, when it came to this girl, I had no impulse control. Because I had her pushed against the interior wall in a flash.

A gasp of air shot from her lungs, and I was immediately sucking it down. Wanting to breathe in every element.

Earth and water and sky.

I gripped her by both sides of her gorgeous face. "Make no mistake. I'm not worth it. I'm not ever going to be. I'm an asshole, Grace. The greediest bastard you'll ever meet. But with you . . ."

My words trailed off, my eyes moving over her face, wondering what the fuck it was she was making me feel. "With you . . . for once in my life . . . I wish that I could be someone else. Someone better. That I could be worth it."

She blinked up at me, guilt and hope and belief blazing through the depths of those eyes. A dark, mesmerizing sea.

There I was giving her an out, and she was looking at me like I'd just given her a gift.

"I guess we both want to be. To be worth it," she murmured, her words wrapping me like a caress.

An extension of *grace*.

And I didn't deserve it. Not after all the things I'd done.

"Isn't that what everyone wants? To be worth taking that chance on? To *matter*?" she continued, voice so soft.

So sweet.

So real.

I thought she might be the most honest thing I'd ever held.

Taking her by the hand, I threaded our fingers together, relishing in the flash of heat that skidded up my arm.

A jolt that threatened to shock my heart back to life. I pressed my mouth to her temple and whispered as I guided her toward the elevators, "What are you doing to me, Angel?"

She didn't have time to answer before the elevator doors swept open and a drove of bodies came flooding out. I stepped back in not-so-pleased surprise when I saw the huge body in the middle of it.

Shit.

Just what I needed. Hell, this was probably exactly what I deserved.

Instant karma, baby.

The second Mack saw me, he angled his head as if he were trying to make sense of the scene in front of him.

I kind of wanted to grab Grace. Wrap her up. Take cover and hide.

Instead, I shuffled my feet like a pansy bitch.

I roughed an uneasy hand through my hair.

"Ian," Mack said, amusement in his voice as he looked between Grace and me, clearly making the calculation between the text I'd up and ditched him for last night and what had led me to be standing in that spot right then.

His voice twisted with knowing emphasis, a razz fraying from the seam. "What are you up to, man? Long time no talk."

Right.

I tried not to grind my teeth, but they were instantly getting mashed to shit.

His gaze darted between me and the girl tacked to my side, his blue eyes riding high as silent questions fired from him like arrows.

Are you on an actual date?

Seriously?

Where is my best friend and the bullshit he was feeding me last night?

This was something he'd never once witnessed before. He knew full well an exchange of names and numbers and dinner as a prelude had never been my style.

Discomfort and a shot of something unexpected rushed me.

This protectiveness that whipped and gusted and blew.

Gale force.

Like I wanted to make a statement.

Tell him she was *different*.

116

That this was *different*.

That it *mattered*.

But I didn't have time to evaluate any of those things before her sweet voice was filling the space—a soft giggle and a glance of those eyes as she raked her teeth over her bottom lip. "We're *just* having dinner."

I couldn't stop the bolt of surprised laughter that came rumbling from my chest, this girl a confusing mix of hard and bitter and soft and sweet. Then she went and was throwing out a tease to my big-ass, burly best friend as if he didn't intimidate her at all.

I liked her.

That was exactly what was wrong with me.

Exactly what had gotten into me.

I like her.

Liked being in her space and standing at her side.

Shaking my head, I cleared the roughness from my throat. "Grace, this is my best friend, Mack."

He shoved a big hand her direction. She released mine and reached out to shake the one he had extended.

"Mack, this is Grace."

"It's nice to meet you, Mack," she said, offering him one of those genuine, mind-bending smiles.

I was suddenly fisting my hand where hers had been, wondering why she made me feel that way. Possessive and needy as I watched him looking her over.

He continued to shake her hand, not releasing it as his attention bounced between the two of us.

"Grace . . . who you're having dinner with tonight?"

It was a prod and tease and a challenge, the last fully aimed at me.

"Yes. We're having dinner." I tried to keep my response even. To keep my cool.

And you know, not go and do something stupid like rip her hand from his.

He definitely didn't need any more ammo than he had.

He had plenty.

He was clearly in the mood to use it.

"Is that so?"

I angled my head at him, the flare of a threat in my eyes.

Don't say a word, asshole.

He chuckled, looking back at Grace. All that amusement drained from his face and something tender took to his expression. "It's really, really great to meet you, Grace."

"It's really nice to meet you, too."

She glanced over at me as if she were asking for help. Unsure of what was passing between Mack and me, their hands dropping just as I wrapped my arm back around her waist and tucked her close to me.

Right where I wanted her.

Didn't give a fuck if Mack watched it with speculation or not.

"I'll talk to you later," I told him, a little harder than necessary.

A cue to drop it.

He could give me all the shit he wanted to later.

A deep chuckle rolled from him, and he started toward the main entrance, walking backward. "Yeah, we will."

He gave me a salute before letting it fall into a grin that he cast at Grace.

She gave him a timid smile.

Without saying anything else, I reached out and pushed the button for the elevator that had given up waiting for us to enter. Immediately, the doors slid open, and I led Grace inside.

"So, that was your best friend, huh?"

"Yup," I told her.

"Not your enemy?" There was a bit of a laugh that came out with her question.

I shook my head, letting a smile pull to my face. "Let's just say he can be a little . . . overbearing."

What I really meant was he loved having his nose up in everyone's business. I'd been made to be an attorney, and the dude had been made to be a detective.

"Frenemy?" she tossed out with an arch of her brow.

Light laughter rumbled. "Something like that."

Though that wasn't really true. He was my closest ally. The one

I could trust, or turn to for absolutely anything. It also meant I could count on him to give me the most shit.

"I like him," she said, casting me a soft glance. As if she was adding a checkmark of reasons to be impressed.

"He's the best guy I know. Him and my brother. Both of them would do absolutely anything for me, and I'd return that favor in a heartbeat."

There was no stopping the bit of honesty that came riding out. This girl getting deeper. Every second, coming closer.

The elevator sped, sweeping us to the top floor, me watching the girl as we went.

Her spirit and scent all around me.

Closed in.

If I thought she'd been driving me mad before, I didn't know what hit me when I was caged in with her in that tiny space.

The girl so fucking pretty.

So soft.

So right.

The demon was itching to come out and play.

It was almost relief I felt when we landed at the top floor. We stepped off into the posh foyer, the clatter of dishes and glasses and laughter echoing from the restaurant beyond.

I set my hand on the small of her back.

Shivers.

Fire.

Hers or mine, mine or hers.

I wasn't sure.

Maybe both.

Only thing I knew was that intense connection lit with the mere brush of a hand.

I pressed my nose to her neck and ran it up behind her ear, inhaling that lust-inducing scent.

Lace and desire.

The juiciest, sweetest plum.

Content thrummed through my chest.

I had the crazy urge to eat her all day long and then maybe snuggle up with her afterward.

That was right when I got to worrying that was exactly how addictions were started.

GRACE

The hostess led us out the side door and onto the rooftop patio.

The fire in a gas firepit whipped and lapped into the dusky shadows, the heavens growing the deepest gray as swashes of fading color crawled across the sky.

A few other couples were dotted around, tucked into the private alcoves of couches and low tables.

There was a view of the city on one side up against the stunning expanse of the darkened bay on the other.

I hugged Ian's arm. "No wonder this is your favorite restaurant."

"Wait until you taste the food."

His nose kept dipping to my neck, inhaling deeply, and I

shivered with the thought that what the man really wanted to get a taste of was me.

I understood the impulse. The compulsion that shimmered and shook through the twilight. This feeling that came to life every time the man stood at my side.

We were seated in one of the private nooks with a horseshoe-shaped couch. Ian and I sat opposite of one another. Flames licked out from the small fire at the center of our table, jumping and tossing and playing in the air.

Adding to the heat.

I pressed my thighs together.

Not having the first clue what I was going to do with this man.

The hostess handed us each a menu. "Enjoy your dinner."

She walked away, and Ian slung himself back against the cushions, one arm draped over the back. The man was so casual and powerful sitting there staring at me with the flames casting shadows across his face.

I didn't think I'd ever seen a more deliciously seductive man.

He watched me with those intriguing eyes, those cinnamon hues a dance of disorder in the jumping light.

"You are stunning. Do you have any idea?" His voice was so low it was close to a growl.

I felt my heart nearly leap across the space where I was sure it would land right at his feet.

My tongue darted out to wet my lips, my voice low and filled with all the things he'd brought to the surface. "The first time I looked over at you standing at the bar, I thought I had to be hallucinating. I thought you had to be nothing but a figment of my imagination, and my mind was sending me a gift to get me through a horrible night."

He cocked one of those grins. The one that touched me from across the distance and made that fluttery feeling flap and rise.

His long fingers picked at the back cushion on the plush couch, as if they were itching to jump in and play a part. "You shouldn't say things like that to me, Grace."

"No?" I was kind of surprised I was actually flirting. It was as if Ian reached in and plucked something from the depths of me.

Something that had been lying in wait, desperate for release.

I ran my hands over my arms, covered in chills of need, realizing right then how much I wanted to find that with him.

In him.

But he was right . . . I was terrified I was never going to be the same if I let him have his way with me.

I knew it'd be a little wicked.

A little wild.

I knew it'd require completely letting go.

"Not unless you want me to haul you onto my lap."

He leaned forward, voice a billow across the space. "I've had to temper myself since the second I saw you. I've always been a man who goes after what I want, and I don't think you have the first clue how much I want you. Right now. This second. I warned you I was an in-the-moment kind of guy."

I should be scared.

I knew it.

I saw it in the way he was watching me. As if he were half deranged. Hovering on a heartbeat before he went in for the kill.

Sitting back, I tried to see through all the attraction that blazed between us, to the man who I knew was right there, waiting underneath.

"Are you, though? It seems to me that there is a lot more to you than you're letting on."

He chuckled out a raw sound full of uncertainty and self-deprecation.

"Believe me . . . all the things I'm not letting on, you don't want to see."

"And what's so bad about them?" I asked, inclining forward. Needing to get closer. This man who was so rough and raw and somehow intrinsically sweet. There was something good stitched into all that hardness.

I could see it.

Feel it.

He mimicked my movement, edging closer, filling the space as the darkness continued to fall around us.

I got the sense that neither of us could help it.

Stop it.

Resist whatever it was that drew us across the flames.

He edged my way, his hand on the couch as he scooted a bit to the inside of the horseshoe, angling in my direction.

A tremor of need slipped through me.

That seemed to be the only invitation he needed to slide the rest of the way over. Then he was right there, leaning in, his mouth a brush at the edge of mine as he issued the word, "Everything."

He brushed back a lock of hair at the side of my face, his mouth taking its spot, the heat of his lips caressing across my skin. "I'm the devil."

There was no lightness in it.

No playful caress.

It was bitter and hard and ugly.

This was the guy who'd first propositioned me at the bar that night. The one who'd outright warned that the only thing he wanted was to use me, fine with the idea of someone using him.

But I was coming to the quick realization that guy was really the illusion. A mask that wasn't real. Bred for cover and protection.

"I don't believe you," I whispered.

Because I'd already seen it—something good. A flash of vulnerability.

He leaned in closer, sliding his hand across the fabric until our fingertips were touching. "You should."

I gulped and pushed out the words, barely heard as they fell from my tongue, "And what about the guy who asked me for a chance? For someone to believe in him? The guy who wants to be worth it?"

Ian angled his head, his voice the rasp of a murmur across my cheek. "He's praying you won't hate him when you really get to know him."

His breaths came out in pants, mingling with mine.

It was crazy, the way sensation went streaking through my body.

My nerves alive.

I felt as if I hadn't been able to breathe for a long, long time.

And suddenly, I felt as if my lungs were expanding. Filling full. Saturated with his presence.

Taking a chance, I let my fingertips trail across his plush lips. "We all have secrets, Ian. Mistakes that we've made. We all have reasons not to step out and take the chance. But just the fact that you're sitting here reveals the part of you who wants to be better. The guy who wants something more. Because I don't believe for a second that you don't have anything to offer. That there is anything cruel about you. I think you're just scared."

I realized it right then . . . that's what I'd seen beneath that harsh, brazen exterior.

"You think you know all that from the few times that we've talked?" It was a hard, savage defense.

I inhaled, my heart a clatter in my chest, affection coming on fast. Just the way I knew that it would. So quick to get attached.

Craving the feeling he incited.

The feeling as if I could maybe be important. Something more than waste. And I was certain he needed to know he was important, too.

I could feel my fractured heart splintering a little more, opening up to make him room.

"I see you . . . looking so flashy in your expensive suit. So proud. Covering something broken inside."

I touched the tattoo that peeked out from the cuff on his wrist, as if the design were dripping sorrow, mourning for something unseen.

The demon.

And I wondered what could have possibly gone so wrong in his life that he'd ever think himself evil.

I was overcome by the urge to peel back his shirt, push it from his shoulders, explore and discover.

"Am I wrong?" I pushed.

His thick throat rolled. "No." He fiddled with a piece of my hair. "No, Angel Girl, you're not. Maybe that's what scares me the most."

His teeth gritted. "But it's those broken parts you recognize inside me that make me who I am. They are what make me cruel.

I learned as a little boy that the only person I could look out for was myself. Learned it was the only way to survive. I've done horrible things, Grace."

Shame passed across his face, and his voice dipped, churning with grief. "Things that haunt me. And still, I know at the root of me, that I will continue to do whatever it takes to survive. I look out for myself. The only people who get any part of me, who hold any part of my heart, are my brother and his family and Mack. That's it. They are the only people I know I can rely on. They're the only people I have space for. The only people I can trust."

If it was possible, he got closer.

Winding and winding. Drawing me in.

"And then there's you. This girl who I don't even know who I feel like I might fight to the death to keep."

Tears gathered in my eyes.

Why was I close to crying?

But sometimes we all needed to be held. Supported. Fought for. I let my fingertips run down the side of his gorgeous face. "And what if you don't like the parts of me that you don't know?"

He gripped my hand, his lips to my knuckles, kissing them softly.

I sucked in a breath, so close to coming undone right there.

"I don't think there's anything you could tell me that would make me unwant you."

There was the threat of a smile.

A hint of seduction.

Hell, there was an avalanche of it. Knocking me right off my feet. Apparently, the boy was a pro at that.

"I'm sorry for the wait. Are you ready to order, or would you like me to start you off with something to drink?" We both jumped when the server's voice hit us from the side.

Ian cleared his throat and glanced at me. "Share a bottle of wine with me?"

"Yeah, that would be nice."

This time, she returned quickly, and Ian poured us each a glass. Lifting his, he clinked it to mine. "To misplaced slippers."

He let one of those wicked grins ride to his lush mouth, and I felt a blush rushing to my face. "That was probably the most embarrassing thing that's ever happened to me."

Shifting to sit a little to the side, he watched me, his expression soft. "Is it wrong that I'm not feeling so sorry that you fell?"

I took a sip of my wine. "I'm having a hard time feeling sorry that I did, either."

He reached out, a finger running the angle of my jaw.

Tingles spread. So fast. So hot.

It was a little terrifying the draw this man held over me.

"I still have that shoe."

My head jerked back an inch. "You do?"

Amusement played across his features. "I figured I'd keep it as a memento from an unforgettable night."

I chewed at the inside of my cheek, warmth slipping through every inch of my body.

There was something about him that made me feel that way.

Comfortable and safe.

Like maybe he really would fight to the death for me.

"Tell me you don't have some kind of weird shoe fetish?" I teased.

Laughter rumbled in his massive chest, and one of those wicked smirks climbed to his mouth. "I wouldn't go so far to call it a fetish, but I'd be a liar if I said I didn't want to see you wearing those shoes again."

He leaned in, words spiraling through the middle of me. "Wearing nothing else but me."

My skin felt sticky and hot, and my belly did a tumble and flip.

Needy breaths pulled from my lungs, and he was back to searching me, fingers playing casually in a lock of my hair.

But there was nothing casual about the way his tone shifted. "What were you doing there that night?"

I looked at him, hoping he'd understand. "I was taking a chance, Ian. I was stepping out and taking a chance. Praying someone might see me. Might listen. And when I looked up, what I found was you."

Cinnamon eyes flashed.

A shockwave of need.

Heat blistering across my flesh.

He might as well have tossed me into that fire.

Because flames lapped, burning up my insides.

One of those big hands landed on my neck, trailing south, gripping at my waist. He breathed out, a plea of words that he whispered at my mouth. "*Just dinner* isn't going to work for me, Grace. Not when there's so much more to you. So much of you waiting to be discovered."

"You make me feel like I'm standing at the edge of something brilliant. Something significant," I confessed in a twined rasp of words. "You make me feel something . . . want something that I don't think I've ever wanted in all my life. Something I'm not sure I even understand."

Ian set his wine aside, took my glass, and did the same. He stood, a tower of shadows that lapped over me. He took out his wallet, pulled out a hundred-dollar bill, and trapped it under one of the stems.

Then he reached out his hand. "Let me show you."

thirteen

GRACE

I stood anxiously facing the double-doors in the foyer on the top floor of the new building just two blocks over from where we hadn't gotten around to *just dinner*. There were only two condos on this floor, and Ian had punched a code into the elevator to gain us access.

Standing behind me, he snaked an arm around my side and slipped a key into the lock. His big body was at my back. Covering me like a shroud.

Nerves rustled through my body, making me shake.

Was I really doing this? It was so unlike me. So far removed from who I was. But I didn't know how to stop from following this man.

Enthralled.

Spellbound.

The lock clicked, and one side of the door swung open. A murky darkness billowed out from within, his condo darkened, the rambling space only illuminated by a long row of windows at the far end of the open living room.

It overlooked the bay, the view beyond a hazy glow of moonlight and glitters of sparkling city lights.

I took a tentative step forward, my gaze jumping around his home as if it might give me a clue into the man.

From behind, he edged forward and shut the door. The lock clicked back into place.

It resounded around the expansive room that was so sparsely furnished you'd think you'd just stepped into a sales model that had never been lived in.

Everything was perfectly in place.

A designer sofa that faced a television on a designer stand. A white marble table set for ten that gave the impression that it'd never been used. An immaculate kitchen that I doubted had ever seen a dirty dish.

As if he thrived on control.

Ian stepped forward and plastered his chest to my back, his head dipping down and his nose digging through the strands of my hair to find the sensitive flesh of my neck. A big arm looped around my waist and tugged me firmly against all that hard, hard man.

Rigid muscles and massive, rock-hard cock that prodded at the small of my back.

A threat.

A promise.

A shiver rolled through every inch of my body, and a trembling breath left my lungs. I gulped around the knot of desire that climbed my throat, nerves of uncertainty only amplifying the sensation, fear and need and a desperation unlike anything I'd ever experienced before.

I tried not to fidget as I forced the words from my tongue. "I've only been with two men in my life. I'm not sure I know what

I'm doing."

I felt so far out of my element.

Gone to who I was.

A prisoner to this man who was commanding all of me.

A harsh gush of surprised air left him, and I felt the tension fill that beautiful, powerful body, the pants he released at my neck rippling with restraint and hesitation and questions.

Ian ran a hand down my left arm, his touch searching as he hit my left finger, as if he were looking for the proof of a rusted ring.

"There's so much you don't know about me," I whispered.

Slowly, he spun me away so I was facing him, which didn't help matters at all. Because all that energy spiked, a thrum in the space between us.

He backed me deeper into his condo, his presence so profound as he edged closer and closer. "There's plenty that you don't know about me, either."

He'd taken on a predator's stance. Lust a gleam in those crazy-colored eyes. Maybe there was a bit of demon to him, after all.

"Two?" he continued. The grit grinding from his tongue made it sound like a challenge.

My belly tightened, and I could barely nod as I was taking a fumbling step back, then another, until I'd backed myself into a wall.

He watched me from the middle of the room. So gorgeous I couldn't see straight.

"You want to leave?" he asked, so low I felt his voice scrape across my skin. "Because I'm about to make it three."

"No," I managed.

Not even close.

I wanted to run to him. Let him hold me and keep me and pray that he wouldn't break me.

But I knew that he would.

Knew it so deep with the way he was watching me, with the way a storm of mayhem and chaos and menace whipped around him as if he were commanding the night.

I think we both knew that's exactly what it was.

He'd taken control. He had me, and he was going to annihilate me.

"Good," he almost growled as he kicked off his shoes and socks. "Think I might die if I don't get to show you. If I don't get to feel you. If I don't get to touch you. I don't think I've ever needed to be inside a woman the way I need to be inside of you. Is that what you want? To feel me inside you, Grace?"

His words hung in the dense, thick air, his chin lifted as if he were daring me to deny it.

To deny him.

Impossible.

He stayed in that same spot as he worked his tie the rest of the way from his neck.

Purposed, he ticked through the buttons of his vest, peeled it off his massive shoulders, and dropped it to the floor.

Then he started to do the same to his shirt.

I leaned against the wall, my knees weak with want, pressing my thighs together as if it might relieve the flames that lapped higher.

He shrugged his shirt off his shoulders.

I nearly came undone right there.

"Is this what you want?" he challenged, those words he fired from his mouth nothing but seduction.

The man was an overwhelming surge of severity that washed over me.

Oh God. Was this really happening? Or was I just having another one of those hallucinations, my mind conjuring the most dangerous sort of perfection?

My lips parted on a needy gasp, and my mouth went dry at the sight in front of me, my back hitched to the wall as if I were hanging from it.

"Yes," I managed.

From where I was pressed to the wall, my eyes raced over him, trying to take in every inch where the man stood there like a fortress.

A predator sent to protect or destroy, I still wasn't sure.

The only thing I knew was he was nothing but packed, solid muscle.

Carved, chiseled stone.

Chest and shoulders so wide. Abdomen flat and defined, muscles shaking with his own need.

It left me feeling half deranged, half a second from dropping to my knees and licking across the deeply cut grooves.

Bowing at his feet.

"You should see what you look like right now, Grace. Like art hanging on my wall. I don't think I've ever come across a girl as beautiful as you."

"Ian."

He took a step forward, and I was slammed with another blast of his potency.

My eyes moved everywhere, from that gorgeous face and down that striking body. The waistband of his pants hung on his narrow hips and barely concealed the v that dipped down beneath the fabric.

But it was the marks written all over him that had my own chest pressing full.

Heart beating manic as my gaze traced over the designs etched and marred across his skin.

Scarred like brands of anguish.

A trademark of torment.

More of those demons screamed across his flesh. It appeared as if they were howling as they flew into his world that had been dimmed in the blackest night.

Roman numerals were stamped across his collarbones, and his abdomen and sides were covered in barren trees and devastated landscape and a watch that seemed to have run out of time.

Everything was a little warped, a dark fantasy, as if it all was being viewed through a veiled, distorted mirror.

But it was the words printed on his side as if they had been scribbled onto his skin by a small child with a crayon that had my spirit screaming.

Forever and Ever.

There was something so heartbreaking about it that I felt mine reaching for him, every inch of him something I wanted to touch and soothe and ease.

Because all of that ink was covering scars.

As if he'd been whipped and burned. Battered and bruised.

It seemed impossible that he had grown to stand the most powerful, influential kind of man.

I was overcome with the need to know him. To climb inside. To search and hold and stay.

Did any of my worries matter, anyway? Because something about this felt so fleeting while there was a huge part of me that wanted to reach out and hang on for forever.

See him, know him, understand him the way I wanted him to understand me.

He started to edge toward me, barefoot, wearing only his suit pants.

Menacing and persuasive.

Sexy and sure and brimming with that arrogance.

Tension held fast to the atmosphere, the man more intense than I'd ever felt him before.

"Don't ever fucking feel pity for me. I know what you're thinking. Don't fucking go there. Just know that every one of those scars made me who I am today."

I wanted to shout it back. Beg him to let me in. To show me what that meant. Tell him that my scars made me who I was, too. Though mine were invisible. Written deep. My children a gift given in between.

But my tongue was locked up, held in a blast of that energy that surged, higher and higher with each step that he took in my direction. My empty lungs filled up with the scent of cinnamon and orange, an insinuation of sex that dripped from his skin.

The man a bottle named *Bliss*.

He planted his hands on the wall over my head.

Towering.

Obliterating.

Casting me in shadows.

I didn't know whether to hide or run toward the mayhem.

To dive into his disturbance or crawl for safety.

But I was stuck, helpless but to fall for him.

He trailed his fingertips from the cap of my exposed shoulder, dipping it down across my collarbone.

A shiver rolled, trembles shaking me all the way to the core.

"Cold?" he murmured, his voice a blast of heat across my skin.

"No," I barely managed to choke out.

Ian ran his nose up my jaw, and he inhaled as he went.

All the while I struggled to breathe, emotions flying at me from everywhere. Questions and concerns and worry, my judgment cast into the surety of his hands.

His chest expanded, his heart racing just as fast as mine.

As if the two were catching time.

Was it possible that he felt this, too? As if he were standing at the precipice of something great? That one second more, and we would never be the same?

Because I knew in another breath, I would forever become a part of him.

He pressed his pelvis to my belly. "Grace."

The man was so hard. Enormous.

"Ian . . . I . . . I don't understand how you make me feel this way. How you make me want things I don't want. Give myself in a way that I don't."

I watched his expression sift through a million emotions— anger and need and lust and fear.

I wanted to reach out and hold every one.

Oh, I was in so much trouble. Stumbling over the edge as the ground crumbled out from under my feet.

He pressed his hard length deeper against my trembling belly. "And you've been driving me out of my mind because I can't get you off of it. Who do you think you are, Angel Girl? Stealing my time and my thoughts and my sleep?" He ticked each one off like a threat.

A quiver staked at my center, and I was speared with my own arrows of need. Greed and lust and things I didn't realize I'd been missing. But the truth of it shined bright, red embers that singed my insides and glowed white hot at my throbbing center.

I wanted this.

I wanted it so desperately that I no longer recognized who I was.

"Do you know what you are, Grace?" he murmured at my jaw, running those soft, soft lips all the way up to my ear. "A goddamned temptation, that's what."

His intoxicating scent came off of him in waves.

The man an ocean. Liquid. I could feel him seeping into my veins.

He nipped the lobe of my ear, and I moaned just as he scraped his teeth across the sensitive flesh.

"Ian, what are you doing to me?"

Tingles flashed, and my entire being rocked toward him.

"I think the better question would be what am I not going to do to you, Angel Girl."

That mouth was moving over my jaw. My chin. A whimper bled free like a pathetic plea.

A dark chuckle rumbled from Ian's tongue that licked out to taste my flesh. "I love that sound, Grace. That I'm the one responsible for it. Do you have any idea how much it turns me on? How fucking hard it makes me?"

His words coaxed another whimper right out of me.

I could feel the wicked grin against my throat. "That's it. Just like that. I want to hear you making those sounds all night."

His lips traveled up and down the racing pulse at my neck. "Want to hear them growing louder until they're screams. Are you a screamer, baby?"

Oh my God.

I couldn't stop shaking. This man too much. Overwhelming. *Everything, everything.*

His mouth moved to my ear, his words a deep, growling rasp. "Because you're going to be tonight."

This time the whimper was nothing but a needy moan, my body vibrating with want.

Everything stretched taut and tight, my breaths shallow. My heart was stampeding so far out ahead of me that I couldn't catch up.

I couldn't catch up to his touch and his hands and the words from his mouth.

The air flames and friction, his body a match.

The man was going to devour me. Ruin me. I knew it. I knew it.

I should stop. Put an end to this madness. Heed all the warnings I'd given myself when he'd first come into my space.

He nipped at my chin. "Tonight, you're mine."

And I knew he was right, because I wasn't going anywhere. I was a prisoner.

Willing to lose.

If only I got to experience this one moment with him.

I felt desperate to taste him on my lips. To taste him on my tongue. I angled my head, lips parted, begging for relief. "Ian, please."

Those eyes flashed to mine, intense and hard. But he angled back and let his fingertips flutter down my cheek.

A tease. A tease. Two seconds in, and the man was already wrecking me.

My hands landed on his shoulders, nails scraping, sinking in. I ran them up the sides of his neck, trying to get closer to him, for him to put me out of this achy misery.

My lips sought his, and he dipped down and away, his lips carving a path down one side of my quivering throat and up the other.

My head rocked back on the wall. "Ian."

"Grace," he murmured at my skin, the vibration traveling to my bones. Those big hands traced my sides, gripping and kneading and exploring as his mouth delved to the cleft between my breasts and licked back up again.

I chased his mouth again, and he kissed up to my ear. An unfair game of cat and mouse.

"Please," I begged, holding onto his shoulders as I angled my head to press my lips to his.

He moved the other direction, and I tried again.

His head rocked back, and his teeth ground so tightly I could hear them grating.

"Don't," he forced out.

Rejection sank to the pit of my stomach. "Ian—"

Two of his fingers flew to my mouth, the pads pressing the

words back inside, his tone coarse with his own desperation. "Don't. Please, don't."

Confusion spun, and I searched him where he hovered two inches away. His breaths mingled with mine, his stare fierce, his eyes blazing when they captured mine in his warning.

Mouth parted, I was gripped by the overpowering emotion that spun, lost in the flare of vulnerability that erupted from the churning depths.

A silent conversation transpired between the two of us.

A wall he barely allowed me to peek over.

Hurt and misery and pain.

Sorrow, sorrow, sorrow.

So deep and dark that my heart fisted in my chest. Emotion squeezing so tight, the tension binding us in that bare, naked moment crushing us under its weight.

"Don't," he commanded again, and I knew he was back to making demands.

Pride and arrogance filled his demeanor. The man control and dominance.

And I wanted to beg that he let me in. Let me hold a little of that pain.

"Tonight, you're mine," he repeated, those eyes spinning that ferocity through the air as he slowly climbed down onto both of his knees.

A god making an offering.

I didn't know what to do with my hands when he reached down and unzipped one of my boots and pulled it from my foot, then turned and did the same to the other.

Ian never released me from that unnerving gaze as he did.

His tongue darted out to wet his lips when he edged up a fraction and tugged at the button of my jeans, and I was shaking more, this moment becoming so unbelievably real.

The fact I was going to give myself to this man.

Wholly.

Completely.

The sound of him dragging the zipper down hit the air like a sonic boom.

"Oh," I whimpered at the sound, at his stare, at the emotion that twisted so tightly, as tightly as the need that rose higher and higher inside me when he hooked his fingers into the heavy material of my jeans, digging all the way down to get my underwear in his grasp.

He dragged both down my legs.

Slowly.

Purposefully.

"Shit," he hissed, head dropping for a beat as if maybe he could possibly be half as affected as me, those hands at my calves and working the jeans off my ankles and tossing them to the side.

"You are a fucking vision."

Hot hands smoothed up the outsides of my legs, from my ankles, over my calves, to my knocking knees, all the way up to caress my thighs.

"Did you know the second I saw you, I wanted to get lost in these legs?" He glanced up, so damned beautiful the breath I was trying to inhale hitched. "I chased you down that night, Grace, because I couldn't imagine not getting the chance to feel them wrapped around my waist."

His fingers dug deeper into my thighs, but I swore that it was vulnerability that flashed through his gaze. "Because I hadn't ever been so instantly attracted to someone in all my life."

He pressed his nose to the inside of my thigh, inhaling deep. "It was so intense, I knew I had to take the chance and go after you. The thought of never being inside of you was almost unbearable. I wanted you that fucking bad."

His hands rode higher, under my sweater to my bottom that was bare underneath. "And now I'm going to have you."

Those big hands squeezed my ass.

Possessively.

As possessive as his stare as he looked up at me.

And the words were falling free before I could think to stop them. "You have me. You have all of me, Ian. You have me in a way I'd never imagined a man could."

Ian nudged my legs apart, teeth raking his plush bottom lip as he hissed, "So sweet."

The movement inched up my sweater and bunched it at my waist.

My bare pussy was right in his face.

And I was trembling. Trembling and trembling as he looked at my nakedness as if he were being offered a gift.

He slicked a single finger through my lips, my body so wet and achy and needy that I whimpered again. "Ian. Oh God. Please."

A dark chuckle rumbled from his massive chest. "Barely touching you, and you're already shivering. How bad do you want me, Grace?"

He pressed two fingers into me, my walls clenching in a plea. "Why are you teasin' me?" I whispered.

"Teasing you? I'm not teasing you, Grace. I'm just making sure you're prepared for what I'm getting ready to do to you."

"Ian." It was a choked sound of surrender. My body on fire. Flames and lashes of need. A dark intensity held fast to the atmosphere, bouncing from the walls, the man the air that I was breathing.

I only sucked it down deeper when he burrowed his shoulders between my thighs and dragged one of my legs over his shoulder.

It spread me wide open.

Exposing me in a way I was sure I'd never been before.

Heart and body and soul.

All of it for him.

My fingers scraped at the wall, searching for something to grasp onto when I was certain it wouldn't matter anyway.

I was falling.

Falling fast and hard and completely.

Crashing to the ground was going to hurt. But somehow, my spirit understood that one night with this man would be worth the pain.

Angling down, he swept his tongue through my throbbing center.

On a growl, he jerked back, those eyes flashing like a red, violent storm. "Just what I thought. A sweet, juicy plum. I want to fucking tattoo the way you taste on my tongue. Or maybe I could just taste it every damned day."

Quivers rocked my legs, and I was having trouble standing under the impact of his words. Under the impact of his touch as he continued to drive his fingers into me.

He watched as he did it, movements sure and strong and making my mind go numb.

"Your pussy is perfect. So wet. So wet for me. Aren't you, Angel Girl? Have you been thinking about this? Dreaming about this? Me touching you?"

I wasn't sure I was coherent enough to give him a response.

But I was nodding, whispering, "Yes. I close my eyes, and you're the only thing I can see. I've never wanted a man the way I want you."

"I'm going to make sure I keep it that way."

A surprised cry jetted from my mouth when he dove in, his tongue lapping and licking and sucking as his fingers drove deep.

That fire I'd been dying in was doused in gasoline.

Consuming.

Incinerating.

I knew this man would leave me nothing but ash.

He pulled his fingers free, and I was crying out in some kind of despair. He only pulled me further from the wall, angling my leg so he could lick all the way back.

Tongue circling my most private places, a gasp of shock leaving me in an unfound sort of pleasure, the man never slowing to give me time to catch up before he fucked his tongue into my pussy and then moved back to assault my clit with little bites and long, toe-curling licks.

And I was going mad. Crazed with greed and lust, begging his name.

Pleasure binding and wrapping. Gathering fast.

"Ian . . . please . . . oh God . . . I can't take it."

He drove those two big fingers into my body, finding me, filling me, his aura and his presence and his gravity.

My back rocked against the wall, one foot barely touching the floor.

Ian holding me up.

Consuming me in a way I'd never been consumed.

Low, growling sounds were coming from his mouth and pulsing against the sweet, sweet spot that he greedily devoured.

The man pouring out that bliss all over my body.

It sizzled through my being, nerve endings alive, until I knew I was close to bursting.

Higher and higher where I rode the sharp, blinding edge of ecstasy.

He curled his fingers and sucked.

Light burst and the most intense pleasure streaked through my body, laying siege to every cell.

Shattering.

Splintering.

Fractures of myself spilling all over that no longer belonged to me.

I floated there, where he held me in his rapture, the man keeping me there.

Floating. Falling. Flying.

Everywhere in between.

"Ian." It was a cry. A plea. A promise that I'd never felt anything more perfect than his mouth and hands on me.

That I'd never felt so connected to a man.

That I'd never wanted anything more.

That was until the man was pushing to his feet, straightening to his full height. He watched me with those darkened eyes as he stepped away to dig a condom out of a drawer in a cabinet five feet away.

That gaze never wavered as he returned, towering over me as he shrugged out of his pants and underwear.

They dropped to his ankles, and he kicked them free of his feet.

A shiver flashed across my skin, a blister of that ferocity.

The air heaved from my lungs.

The man stood there, completely bare.

So beautiful I could barely see.

That polished exterior stripped away and revealing every rough, raw inch that had been hidden underneath.

A mystery he was quickly writing on me.

He stroked his massive length. "This . . . are you prepared for this?"

"I'm not sure I could ever fully be prepared for you." It was a mumbled confession that climbed into the dense air.

"Do you want it?" His question was nothing but a lure because my mouth went dry, and I tried to swallow.

"I want it . . . I want you. All of you."

Something flashed through his expression, something deep and dark, as if he couldn't make sense of what was happening between us any more than me.

A needy gasp parted my lips when he slowly rolled on the condom.

Stepping into the space that separated us, he reached out and pulled my sweater over my head.

"Sweet," he mumbled almost incoherently, eyes sweeping my chest, before he dipped down to make quick work of my bra and slid the straps free.

Instantly, those palms were cupping my breasts, and chills were skating in a flashfire of need. He ran his thumbs over my nipples that instantly puckered into hard, pebbled peaks.

"Fuck . . . fantasies just didn't do you justice, Grace. What it might be like to see you like this. Bare and trembling for me. It's the best thing I've ever seen."

Raspy pants lifted from my lungs. "I couldn't have even hoped to imagine what being with you would be like. You are the best thing I've ever felt."

His mouth fell to my ear as he continued to stroke and flick my nipples. "Don't worry, baby, I'm just getting started."

And God, he was about to make good on that promise.

He carved out a space for himself between my thighs, his big penis pushing between us, the head of him hitting my belly button, the juts of his harsh breaths only spurring me on more.

Desperate to feel him. All of him.

I whimpered. "Please."

The words he released were nothing but a growl. "I'm going to fuck you, Angel. Don't ask for it soft."

There was no hesitation left when he hoisted me from my feet and surged into me in one mind-bending thrust.

I might have blacked out right there.

This had to be a dream.

A fantasy.

Because the feel of him shouldn't be possible. The way he stretched and filled, so huge I was gasping and clawing and trying to adjust.

Ian stilled, his hands shaking where he held me by the outsides of my thighs, his big body pinning mine to the wall. His chest heaved, his eyes wild like he'd slammed straight into shock.

"Perfect." His throat bobbed when he swallowed, and he seemed to struggle to gather himself. "Fuck . . . you're perfect. Angel Girl. Angel Girl. Tell me that tonight you are mine. You're mine."

There was something frantic about this command.

"I'm yours. Tonight, I'm yours."

But I knew it was so much greater than that. That I hadn't only given him tonight. I'd given him a piece of myself.

I'd never been so sure of it until he began to drive into me, slow drags out of my body that sent me reeling with shivers of pleasure, hard thrusts that took me so deep that a cry left me on each one.

Those fierce eyes pinned me just as fiercely as the thrust of his hips.

Measured. Hard. Possessive.

The air and his fucks and the intensity that swam and billowed and blew.

The man owning me where he held me in the power of his hands.

Those eyes flicked all over my face, searching, knowing, this feeling coming over me that I'd never been so close to someone before.

That we were both broken open wide.

Giving and taking. Giving and taking.

Oh, did Ian take as his hips began to snap. Deeper and faster, working both of us into a frenzy.

Heat blazed and flames lapped.

Rising up at our feet.

Emotion thick, my heart threatening to batter right out of my chest.

"Grace," he gritted, his fingers sinking deeper into my thighs as if he couldn't get deep enough, his cock surging into my pussy at a punishing pace, those mesmerizing eyes on my mouth as if he wanted to lose himself there, too.

"What are you doing to me?" he whispered in some kind of awe. In fear and confusion and need.

It only drove him to take me harder. Demanding more. As if he didn't understand that I would willingly offer everything.

I wanted to touch his face.

Kiss his mouth.

Taste his tongue.

But I let him have me the only way he would let me.

The man fucked me as if we had no time left. An uncaged animal who was taking his one chance.

Making his claim.

Marking me.

Every inch.

Body and heart and soul.

I was right.

I was right.

I was never going to be the same.

Our grunts filled the air, our bodies slapping as he drove deeper and harder and seared himself to my flesh.

"Fuck . . . so sweet . . . this body. It's mine, Grace."

Big hands grabbed me by the knees and pushed me open wide where I was splayed across his wall as he banged me into oblivion.

That's what it was.

Oblivion.

And I was screaming out again, an orgasm splitting me in two.

Riding a river. Burning in his flames.

"Ian." His name had become a prayer. A shout of my heart.

He only fucked me harder, faster and deeper and madder before the man was growling, hands everywhere, searching, as if he were trying to find a place to latch onto me forever.

He cinched down tight, body going rigid as he fully seated

himself inside my body.

Ian's grunts became a roar, and the man shuddered and shook, shouting my name with his release.

His cock was so full and thick as he throbbed inside me that I was slammed with a rebound of pleasure.

Streaking ribbons and binding bows.

Shot somewhere into heaven or hell or purgatory, I didn't know.

The only thing I knew was I wanted to ride on it for all of eternity.

So, it was me grasping for him, hands sinking into his skin as I clamored for a breath. For a way to slow my body down, my heart down, when it was already racing for him.

He buried his face in my neck, gasping, his chest heaving as he struggled for a breath. "You are a goddamned miracle."

My mouth went to his shoulder, kissing at the flesh, tasting his sweat-drenched skin. "Ian," I whispered through shallow rasps, "Ian."

My mind whirred as I tried to catch up to what I'd just done. Waiting for guilt to come flooding, this selfish act that I'd taken for myself.

But there was none to be found.

Only this feeling that I needed more.

His rock-hard abdomen rippled with aftershocks, and he stayed inside me while he caught his breath, before he slowly eased out and helped me onto my unsteady feet.

I wanted to weep at the sudden emptiness.

Eyes moving softly over my face, he brushed back my matted hair, his breaths short and heaving as he stared at me, brow pinching as if he were struggling with what to say.

"That was . . . incredible. You're incredible. I knew I wanted you. Finally understand why."

I was silently begging him to give in to me.

Kiss me. Why won't you kiss me? What are you afraid of?

I wondered if he knew it, where my mind had gone, because his eyes dropped to my parched, dried lips.

A sorrow so old flashed through his expression that I got the creeping feeling that I might be chasing down a ghost.

He sucked in another breath, and he wound a hand gently into my hair. "I knew you would blow my mind. I just had no idea you were going to rock my world."

I had to swallow down the emotions that were making a play at climbing up my throat. Words I wanted to release but knew neither of us were ready to hear. "I'm pretty sure it was you who just blew mine. Three times."

"I promised you I'd make a good memory."

I tried not to let those words cut through me like a blade, the horrible, empty feeling with the thought of him walking away after what we'd just shared.

The connection between us so tangible I felt like I could hold it in my hands.

I forced my mouth into the semblance of a smile. "I like your brand of promises."

He nipped my chin. "There are plenty more of those kinds of promises where that came from."

Surprise had me squealing when he suddenly dipped down and swept me off my feet. He cradled me like a bride against the strength of his naked body, those tattooed arms wrapping me tight.

He might have been holding me, but I was only falling farther. Faster and deeper.

Still, I latched onto the playfulness that had taken over his mood as he began to rush with me through the massive room. "Oh my God . . . don't you dare drop me, Ian Jacobs. The last thing I need is to be explaining away how I ended up with a broken leg."

Ask me who I'd be explaining it to, I wanted to beg.

I didn't know until right then how desperately I needed to tell him. To let him hold it. Wondering if he'd run or stand at my side.

That raspy voice came low at my ear. "Drop you? Never."

If only that were the truth.

I looped both arms around his neck. I realized in that moment I didn't care where he was taking me.

He carried me down a short hall, passing by two doors on

either side. He continued to the end of the hall toward another set of double doors.

He edged around so he could turn the knob, trying to balance me at the same time.

Another ripple of giggles rolled up my throat. "So strong." I let the words play from my tongue when I meant them one hundred percent.

He cocked me one of those arrogant smirks, the man so damned pretty it made my heart hurt. "You're really just a skinny little thing."

I rolled my eyes because that wasn't even close to being the truth. "Hardly. I rock my curves. Don't pretend like you haven't noticed."

"Who me, ogling you."

I swatted playfully at his chest, the man bringing out a side of me that I'd almost forgotten. "Pssh. All you do is ogle me. Don't act like you haven't."

"Fine. You want the truth? I've been eye-fucking this fine-ass body since the second I saw you." He nuzzled his face into my hair. "Guilty as charged. I want to get lost in every lush curve. Get lost in all of you."

Do it.

Let go.

Love me.

Oh, but that was just stupidity, just asking for the worst kind of trouble. I couldn't even believe I'd let the thought enter my mind.

One side of the double doors swung open, and he carried me through the shadows that played along the walls of the darkened bedroom.

It was the only room that appeared to be halfway lived in, a pair of shoes at the foot of an enormous bed and a tee shirt tossed on a fabric chair over near the floor to ceiling windows that were covered in wispy, sheer drapes.

I was expecting him to carry me to his bed, but he bypassed it, going straight for the en suite bathroom through an open archway to the right.

He flipped on the overhead lights, and I blinked against the harshness.

I was taken aback again by just how strikingly beautiful he was up close beneath the glow.

A bronzed, tattooed statue.

It only made me hold on to that strength more tightly, clinging to the erratic beat of his thrumming heart, wishing that he might let me hold it.

He set me down in front of a glass-walled shower.

My legs wobbled.

He grinned. "Knocking you off your feet again."

A blush rode up to my cheeks. "I'm not sure I'll ever stop shaking when I'm standing in front of you."

"You'd better not." The sweetest kind of smirk rode around his full, full lips, as if another side of him was trying to break out.

Keeping a hand on my waist to keep me steady, he reached through the door and turned on the showerhead. I watched him, the profile of his masculine face, the bristling strength of his beautiful body as he removed the condom and tossed it into the trash.

The man was like raw, unedited art. The purest form of beauty.

Steam filled the room, and he stuck his hand under the fall of water as if he were checking the temperature the same way as I'd done for him.

There was something about it that felt the same. As intimate as that day he'd come into my salon.

The connection that stretched tight between us something neither of us could escape.

As if he felt the draw of it, he backed me into the spray.

Goosebumps crawled across my flesh.

From the change of the temperature or the sheer heat of his gaze, I didn't know. All I knew was sensation was still racing everywhere.

Somehow growing even stronger.

The man had just obliterated me, heart, body, and soul, and I got the distinct sense that he was aiming to do it again.

His dick swung at half mast, and there was nothing I could do but reach out.

Touch him.

I fisted the velvet flesh, and my heart gave a quiver.

Overcome.

But I didn't know how to stop. Not when I'd already been swept away.

He groaned out a needy sound, the man growing hard and long and thick where I held him in my hand.

I stroked him, relishing in the power of doing it. In being in control of his pleasure. Of his need.

He stepped closer, and my other hand felt along his hip, gliding down until I was cupping his balls.

His jaw came unhinged, and he dropped his forehead to my shoulder as I continued to stroke him.

"I thought you said you didn't know what you were doing?" he rasped.

"The only thing I know is I don't want to stop touching you."

Pants rose into the air, at one with the steam that billowed between us.

I could feel it, the energy that lit into a frenzy.

Wild.

And I was stroking him harder and faster as need blossomed in my body, my belly shaking and center throbbing for him again.

Faster than I could make sense of it, he had my back pinned to the cold stone of the shower wall. The impact made me release him, and instantly he was the one in control.

A big hand gripped me by the chin, his fingertips sinking into either side of my cheeks.

There was some kind of war on his face, eyes flashing dark as they darted between my eyes and my lips.

"Fuck . . . Grace . . . what are you doing to me? You're making me crazy. Making me want things I don't fucking want."

Pain.

It reverberated through the space.

The man giving me another glimpse.

My hand was trembling when I reached out and let my fingertips trace against his bottom lip in a silent question.

Why won't you kiss me?

His mouth parted on a sigh, and his eyes closed, throat vibrating with a low, urgent sound.

In another flash, he had me spun away from him.

Whiplash.

My hands flew out to the wall, and I gasped out in shock when he tumbled his mouth down the length of my spine.

Desperate, needy kisses.

Flicks of tongue and soft, adoring lips.

Oh, God, he was undoing me.

Wholly and completely and permanently.

I had no idea how I was going to recover from this. How I would ever be the same when he gripped me by both hips, his rigid, hard cock sliding through the crease of my bottom.

"Ian." It was a plea of confusion and need. His hands kneaded into my thighs, and my head turned to the side so I could watch him through the mirror.

He rocked his cock through the cheeks of my bottom like some kind of illicit threat.

Want gripped me everywhere.

Everywhere.

Everywhere.

A tight fist that squeezed my heart, so tight I thought it might shatter under the pressure.

"I want you everywhere, Grace. I want to fuck you until the only thing you know is my name. That sweet cunt and your mouth and this perfect ass."

I was pretty sure what the man was fucking with was my heart.

He was taking over. Invading the places where I never should have let him go.

I should have known better.

I should have known better.

But none of that seemed to matter when he kept sliding along my bottom, grunts coming from his mouth. He dragged me by the hips farther from the wall and bent me over.

He shoved himself into my pussy.

So deep I swore the man destroyed me right then and there.

"I want to keep you," he muttered in some kind of frenzy, so low and garbled I wasn't sure I'd heard it right.

But that didn't matter. It didn't matter because I felt it. Felt that ferocity. The energy that wound and climbed and claimed.

He started to pound into me.

I couldn't stop from watching him through the mirror, his cock drawing almost all the way out before he pounded into me again.

Over and over.

His body so strong and massive and in control. Big hands clenched down possessively on my hips, fingers sinking in.

He dragged me back to meet him with each trust.

All those scars lining his back flexed and curled, hidden in the ink, haunted memories that couldn't be found. Demons howled as they dragged me into his darkness, the words written on his side gnarled and disfigured.

Never had I seen such a beautifully broken man.

And I wondered if he saw mine, the silvered stretch marks that were close to invisible on my bottom and hips. My marks treasures. My pain. My perfection.

Those arms came around to my front, and with one hand he gripped me by the chin as he tugged me up against his chest.

Fingers went to work on my clit.

Playing me.

Coaxing me.

He continued to drive into me from behind, this position leaving me a hostage to the power of his hands. No longer was I on solid ground.

"What are you doing to me, Grace?"

This time, he sounded almost angry. As if I was weaving my way into him, the way he was weaving into me, and he hated me a little bit for doing it.

I reached back and clung to the back of his neck while he held me up with the force of his body.

Pleasure gathered so fast.

A flashflood from out of nowhere.

I screamed his name when another orgasm ripped through my body.

Potent and wild and unending. Surging and possessing the same way as the man possessed me.

Before I could make sense of it, he had my hands planted back on the wall, and his hand was on his dick.

He stroked himself as he came all over my bottom, grunts tumbling from his mouth.

I guessed it was the first time that night that reality caught up to me. Still, I watched it play out like a horror story. Through a screen of steam that fogged up the mirror. Me losing absolute control. Forgetting myself. Letting this man who was little more than a stranger take me with no barrier between us.

He grunted and shook, then burrowed his fingers even deeper, freezing, those crazy-colored eyes blinking frantically as if he too had to break himself from the fog of passion that made us do stupid things.

He seemed almost horrified himself as he reached out a trembling hand and let his fingers swim through the mess he'd left on my body.

"Shit," he cursed, a low, guttural wheeze, his throat bobbing. "What the fuck?"

Then he was cleaning me off, hurrying like he could erase the evidence, before he cut the showerhead and stepped out. He took my hand, helped me out, and wrapped me in a fluffy white towel. Without saying anything, he picked me back up and carried me to his bed.

Gently, he laid me in the middle of it, his brow knitted up when he did.

As if maybe he weren't in control of his actions any more than I seemed to be.

Both of us lost.

Wanderers who'd forgotten their way.

"I'm so sorry," he muttered, voice urgent. "I'm clean. I swear to you, I'm clean."

I gulped, having no idea what kind of promises to make him.

Slowly, he set a knee on the bed, hesitation taking over his movements as he climbed to hover over me.

Caging me in.

As if I were the wild one that needed to be tamed.

Those eyes searched my face.

Almost painfully.

"What's wrong?" The question felt raw in my throat. And I realized I was already in too deep when a ripple of terror washed over me at the thought of what the answer might be.

His throat bobbed, and he was watching me as if he was in shock, the words choked as he forced them out. "I've never had a woman in my bed before. In my personal space."

My fingertips fluttered across his strong chest. "Do you want me to leave?"

There was no shame in my question. No rejection. Because I saw no hardness in his eyes. I only saw stark vulnerability vibrating with the power of the man.

He grabbed me by the hand and pressed my knuckles to his plush, soft lips. Mouth open as he kissed each one. "No . . . what scares me most is that I want you to stay. That I want things with you that I've never wanted before."

"Is it wrong that I want to stay?" My gaze roamed his striking face, his expression so different than I'd ever seen it before.

Open and raw. A room with the most magnificent view.

"Is it wrong that every time I'm with you," I continued, "I feel different? Beautiful and strong?"

"That's because you are." He threaded his fingers through my soaking wet hair. "Angel Girl."

My teeth tugged at my bottom lip. "Why do you keep calling me that?"

"Because the night I chased you out and saw you fall, that's what I saw on the ground . . . an angel. I don't want to be the one to taint that goodness."

A frown marred his brow. "It's crazy that I even want to be in your light. I usually run from it. As far as I can. You're exactly the type of girl I stay away from. And when it comes to you, the only thing I want is more. Again and again. What scares me most is I'm not sure I could ever get enough."

A burst of heat blazed across my flesh. Unable to stop myself, I arched toward him. "Take all you want."

Possession rumbled in his chest. "You shouldn't offer things like that. You have no idea what I'm capable of."

God, he was rough. So raw and brittle and, still, he was melting something inside me. Goodness shining out from beneath all that brash.

"I think I'm willing to take the chance."

Something hard flashed in his eyes. "Awful brave of you, considering you don't know me. Believe me, when you do, you'll go running."

"Isn't that what taking a chance is all about?" I gave him a small nudge, and he rolled onto his back. I started to move over him, stalling out when I caught sight of him laid on his back in his bed looking like a drawing.

A masterpiece.

Impossible.

My mouth was back to watering, and I slowly straddled him, loving the feel of those hands when they slipped around my sides.

I dipped down, wanting to kiss him, wanting to respect him. I let my lips tumble along the scruff on his jaw. I ran them all the way up to his ear. "Doing this again and again. Day after day. Getting to know each other. Figuring out if we fit. That's what taking a chance means."

I forced an edge of playfulness into my tone. "Just be careful not to go falling in love with me, Ian Jacobs."

He tightened his hold on my hips, so much sincerity in his voice that I broke a little more. "Don't much have the capacity for that. But if I did? If I were capable of it? I think I'd already be in love with you."

"I think it's you who needs not to be saying those things to me," I whispered.

Fingertips traced the curve of my cheek, his expression something close to awe. "Think I'm a goner, baby."

My chest stretched tight. Break. Break. Break. I was the goner.

Humorless laughter rolled from him as he studied me through the shadows. "I don't even know you. Did you always want to cut hair?"

There it was. My opening. An open door. I shifted so I could lay down at his side, preparing myself to find the right place in this conversation to tell him.

It wouldn't be a confession. No shame.

It was the claim of my life.

I let my fingertips play across the deep grooves and flat planes of his abdomen. "No, I didn't."

Shyness weaved into my tone. "I've always wanted to write children's books."

He brushed his fingers down my arm, and I could feel his tender smile, and my spirit shivered with the realization that I was right about him.

I cuddled closer, letting my mind and my voice wander. "These outrageous stories have always come out of me. As a little girl, I'd imagined them novels, that I was writing the next epic fantasy, but really, they were fantastical stories that at the heart were nothing but simple. Simple stories about growing up. The fears and hopes and dreams that come along with it."

I dared to look up at him again. Ian was watching me so tenderly, something melted in the middle of me. "And of course, they have a dash of adventure to get you there."

"You're a dreamer," he mused, as if he'd just caught on. As if I all of a sudden completely made sense.

"Aren't we all?" I asked quietly.

He huffed out a strained sigh that billowed toward the ceiling, his attention cast there, as if he were getting drawn back to a simpler time, too. "I used to be. Until the day all my dreams dried up."

He glanced down at me, a bold flash in that intense stare. "But that doesn't mean I'm not driven. That I'm not chasing after a goal. That I won't do everything it takes to achieve it."

My brow pinched, and I shifted a little so I could look at him better. "Isn't that the same thing?"

"No." There was no hesitation, just the grim set of his mouth. "Dreaming only ever gets you hurt. A goal is acting on a calculated risk."

Confusion wound through me, and I shifted more so I was almost completely facing him. I had the overwhelming urge to dig deeper, push through, feeling myself butting up against a wall.

Taking a chance, I reached out and played with a lock of that soft, soft hair.

"I don't even know what you do," I told him, inviting him to let me in. To ask me to meet him there. I let my attention traipse around the luxury of his bedroom. "Although whatever it is, it looks like you're doing just fine for yourself."

He'd been there at that fundraiser, no doubt an investor or bigwig at some corporation, doing exactly what he'd assumed about me that night.

Putting on a show.

Making himself and whatever company he owned look good.

What had struck me most was how bitter he'd seemed about it. As if he were angry anyone would show up there at all.

His fingers roamed down my side, his voice casual. "I'm an attorney."

That was the thing about shock.

It was instant.

And that was the very second my heart froze in the middle of my chest before it took off at a sprint. Running wild. It dragged the thoughts in my mind right along with it.

He is an attorney.

Oh, God, he is an attorney.

Ian must have caught onto the way my world had started to spin because his tone twisted into what was close to a question. "I'm one step away from being partner at Millstrom, Garcia & Grant. But I won't be stopping there. Soon, I'll be in control of everything. The firm, the biggest clients, making sure I'm getting a cut of the biggest cases. Everyone in this city will come to me."

It was strange that I'd never even considered it. He just seemed so . . . different than what I'd anticipated of one of the stuffy attorneys I'd been hunting down.

And I definitely hadn't come across his name, considering I'd only looked up the names of partners at firms when I'd gone on my search. Seeking out powerful names that might be willing to take down an even more powerful empire.

When I'd been crawling around on my knees begging for

anyone to listen.

To hear.

To understand.

It felt like my throat was a landslide of jagged rocks. "And that's your goal you were talking about? Becoming partner. Becoming the head of your firm?"

He gave a tight nod. "Since I was seventeen, I wanted to be an attorney."

"And you chased it?" I asked.

Something fiercely sad wove through the sharp lines of his stunning face. "I guess I did, didn't I?"

He smiled softly, and I was pretty sure that was gonna be the end of me.

Because when he tucked me into his side, his big body wrapped around me from behind, I knew I'd come to a crossroads.

Too late for a detour, Grace.

I was already there.

Falling.

And I knew this was going to hurt. But there were some things in our lives that were so much more important than anything else.

It wasn't even a question.

The admission I was initially going to make fell silent on my tongue as my heart and mind processed who Ian was. Somehow, Ian found comfort in it, and I could feel the rigid lines of his body slowly relax.

His breaths evened out, even though he didn't lessen his hold, and when I carefully extracted myself from the cradle of his arm, he groaned and rolled fully onto his stomach.

I sat up at the edge of his bed, looking down at him, eyes memorizing every line of his muscular back, all of it again covered in ink.

My stomach pitched.

Tossing me into a freefall.

No parachute.

Nothing under my feet.

Praying he might be there to catch me when the man was completely unprepared for what I was going to ask of him.

All of it felt so wrong and so right.

But I guessed he'd been spot on when he'd sat in my chair at the salon and teased that it was fate.

I hadn't believed him. Hadn't even given the idea a smidgeon of credit.

After all, I'd taken a chance on a stupid party and then had Kenneth Millstrom laugh in my face.

I'd run because of him, my things scattered on the ground. And this mysterious, dangerous man had been the one to help me back onto my feet.

My heart expanded, overflowing with hope.

A chance.

One my gut told me had always been worth taking. I just hadn't fully been prepared for what kind of chance that it would actually be.

I slipped off his bed and quietly sneaked out of his room, nothing but longing in my gaze as I paused at the doorway to peer back at him sleeping.

Yes. Yes. That's what it had to be.

Fate.

Because I didn't think I'd ever felt so safe in a man's arms before his. Had never felt so sure of the goodness that radiated from inside.

Trusting someone was nothing but a chance thrown into the wind, and I didn't think I'd ever wanted to put my trust in someone so fiercely.

I just had to figure out how to convince him to take a chance on me.

IAN

"*This* is bullshit. I told you I was finished with all of this," I hissed below my breath where I sat in my office at my desk, mashing my teeth together so hard I didn't know how they hadn't ground to dust.

Anger had become a raging vortex in that hole carved out in the middle of my chest.

I hadn't thought it could get deeper.

I was wrong.

Wasn't surprised, either. I mean, fuck, what did I think?

Invite a girl into my bed and think she was gonna stay? I knew better than that.

Thing that bothered me the most was that I'd even wanted her to.

Still, I was the pathetic fucker who'd panicked when I'd woken and found the spot next to me empty. Jumping out of bed and running around my house like she was playing a twisted game of hide and seek.

I'd been just as prepared for the scenario that I was going to have to throw down some blows to protect her.

Fight for her.

The fact I was itching to showed just how fucking stupid I was.

Taking a chance.

What bullshit.

But the problem was, I hadn't lied to her. Being with her that way? Closer to a woman than I'd ever been?

I'd lost a piece of myself.

A goner.

Last night had been unlike anything I'd ever experienced. The way she'd made me lose control when the only thing I had going for me was self-discipline and restraint. Determination and grit and tenacity.

Nothing could touch me.

I consumed what I wanted without it even causing a spike in my pulse. With greedy hands and a black, barren heart.

No care.

No responsibility.

No attachments.

And there I fucking was, getting *attached.*

Attached to that feeling and that body and those eyes. Her spirit shimmering all around me, glowing into the darkest recesses of my spirit.

Had the sinking feeling she might be the *angel* that wielded the power to bust through the calloused shell and seat herself on a throne in the middle of it.

It was for the best. God, I should have been kissing the ground on which her pretty little feet had walked out on—without so much as a fucking note, mind you—saving me the grief.

But it was there.

A ball of unspent hurt. Exactly what I couldn't afford. Exactly why I couldn't do this.

I clung to it. The knowledge that I couldn't let some girl get in my way.

Distract me.

Stray me from course.

Didn't mean I wasn't still feeling pissed and surly and bitter, either.

What better asshole to take it out on than Lawrence Bennet.

Bennet chuckled one of his dark laughs. "You're my attorney. You represent me. It's your job."

"I also have an obligation to the state bar. To my firm."

"Your obligation is to me." He said it so hard and fast that I felt the impact of it through the phone.

I was firing right back. "You don't own me. No one does. No one will."

His short shot of laughter was deep. Ominous. Far too knowing.

That was what happened when you laid yourself at someone's feet.

They walked all over you.

"Just because you say it, doesn't make it true. I'm certain Kenneth would be crestfallen to hear I'd grown unhappy with my representation. He'd be downright brokenhearted if he learned his most promising protégé was nothing but a common criminal."

Lawrence didn't hesitate to throw out the loaded threat.

He knew my intentions.

Who I was going to be.

"Don't fuck with me, Lawrence. Blackmail isn't going to win you any favors. And anything you have over me was instigated by you in the first place."

Asshole had been influencing every move I made from the get go.

All the way back to when I was just a kid. A fucking kid who didn't know any better. A kid who was trying to survive.

He laughed a mocking sound. "Don't forget who you're talking to, Ian Jacobs. I picked you up off the ground and dried your tears when you were nothing but a sniveling, starving brat. Put shoes on your feet and a roof over your head. You'd be nothing without me."

"Out of the goodness of your heart, right?" Bitterness bled free.

"Maybe I should have left you in the gutter where you belonged. Just like your whore mother. But I didn't . . . because I saw something great in you. You'd do well not to forget it."

My eyes slammed closed as visions assaulted me. A violent rage boiled in my blood. A seething anger that coiled my guts into a thousand knots.

Hate and grief and regret.

Everything whirled, walls spinning faster.

I struggled to breathe as I shot blisters of hatred from my tongue. "Something great in me? The only thing you saw in me was a scapegoat. The days of my doing your bidding are numbered."

He laughed like everything I'd just said didn't matter. Like I didn't have a say.

We both knew I didn't.

If he went down, I was going down with him.

"Have those documents on my desk by five."

The line went dead, and I tossed my phone to my desk and propped my elbows on the wood. Digging my fingertips into my eyes, I tried to stop the visions.

The memories.

The smell.

"Wake up. Please, wake up." Hands shaking. A cold sweat. Nausea rolling. Vomit on the floor.

I bit down against them, letting the anger surge in to take their place. Focused on Bennet. God, I detested the piece of shit in a way I wasn't sure I'd ever felt before.

Dirty.

Just having an association with him made me dirty.

I knew that I was.

A demon.

The devil.

A light tapping sounded at my office door.

I dug my fingers a little deeper into my eyes to try to quell the sting, voice scraping as I tried to keep it level. "I'm busy, Marcus. I don't want to be disturbed."

My executive assistant knew well enough when to step away and not interrupt.

So, I rocked back in surprise when my door snapped open anyway.

That surprise shifted to a straight shot of disbelief.

Shock and anger and relief.

A tidal wave of that crazy energy flooded across the floor. My mind was rejecting the fact that she was standing there.

Part of me wanted to shout at her to get the fuck out. To scream that I didn't have time to play games, that I didn't want to listen to a goddamned thing she had to say, but my body was definitely on board.

I could still feel her on my skin. Taste her on my tongue.

My dick twitched, and I swore beneath my breath.

Not good.

Fuck me if I was going to let this girl have the upper hand.

She stood in my doorway, wearing a floral wrap-around dress that hugged all those curves and a pair of heels that made the girl look like she stood a mile-high, tall and proud and somehow vulnerable.

All those lush waves were twined in a neat knot on the back of her head, and she was gripping a big black bag she had slung over her shoulder.

Still, everything was completely off from yesterday.

Like she'd gone to a different place.

That energy alive, but brimming with hesitation.

Disturbed.

Confused.

Purposed at the same time.

Anxiety fisted my guts.

She pushed her way in, lifting her delicate chin like she was trying to make a statement that she had every right to be there.

Shit.

She was pretty.

So damned pretty that I could physically feel some of those hard spots going soft, and my heart was doing some stupid, wayward thing, beating faster than it should. Getting caught up in her presence.

With my hands planted on my desk, I pushed to my feet. "What are you doing here?"

Why did you leave?

Did I fuck it up already? Were you terrified of me last night? Did I prove just what an asshole I am?

She snapped the door shut behind her and eased deeper into my office, chewing on that bottom lip that I had half a mind to kiss. To just grab her and kiss her senseless the way she was driving me.

And that right there was the very reason I should turn my back. Tell her to walk.

Nerves blazed across that soft flesh, and she anxiously twisted her fingers. Then she was taking a desperate step forward and watching me with those eyes.

They were like looking into a bottomless aquarium.

Diving into the deepest sea.

"I need your help," she rasped, the words so tight and emphatic that they sank in and took hold.

Possessiveness swelled. So fast, I felt consumed by it. Suffocated by the need to hunt down any fucker who might have hurt this girl.

Anyone who'd even had a single thought about doing something that would harm her.

I'd known it from the start.

This girl had been running.

If that was the reason she'd left last night? Someone was going to pay.

"Anything."

Shit.

What was I saying?

But the promise was out before I could reel it back in.

My fucking resolve shot. Emotions tossed from one extreme to the next.

Hate. Hope. Lust. Anger.

Her gaze flashed in adoration.

The girl was looking at me like I could be her hero.

Her savior.

When the only thing I'd ever done in my life was destroy the things around me.

She took another pleading step forward until I was inhaling her, pink sugared petals pressed to my nose.

"You're an attorney," she said.

A statement.

I raised my arms out to the sides, irritation latching onto the word. "Obviously."

Unease stirred. A feeling climbed my legs, telling me that I wasn't going to like what she'd come to ask of me.

"I want to hire you," she said, voice just as resolute as the firmness of her nod.

Uh . . . no. I was most definitely not going to like what she was going to ask. In fact, I was feeling a little pissed off.

What did she think, I was some kind of fuck for hire?

Another one of those steps, and she brought us so close she'd nearly erased all the space. So close that I could touch her. Get lost in her the same way I'd done last night.

The second she did it, I was slammed with urges, ones of bending her over my desk and pushing that dress up over her hips. Taking her from behind. Hard and fast and rough.

Could almost picture me having to cover that sweet mouth while I made her scream.

Incredulous laughter rambled around in my chest. "You want to hire me?"

It came out sounding more like an accusation than a question.

She nodded, the decisiveness from the second before wavering, her tone slipping, verging on something frantic. "I don't just *want* to, Ian. I need to. I need someone who's willing to stand up for me. Fight for me."

Those eyes were pleading, begging for help.

How was I supposed to ignore that?

An itch started in my throat, and I reached up and yanked at the collar of my shirt where my tie had become too tight.

Someone was playing a cruel joke. Choking me out.

"I can't represent you, Grace. I think you know that." There was no softness to the words. No sugar-coating. Frankly, she was out of her mind if she thought I was all of a sudden going to be standing in a position of influence over her.

Not unless the influence I was exerting was in my bed.

My head angled down, my mouth at her ear, voice tripping into sex. "I fucked you last night, remember? And now you're coming here asking for me to represent you? I'm sorry, but it doesn't work that way."

I could scent her, the way desire seeped from her pores and her breaths turned short from my proximity.

One of those hands came up to the pounding at my chest.

Not helping matters.

"Please . . . I don't have anyone else."

A swell of protectiveness washed through my insides, this nudging to do what was right for once. My mind raced. Seeking a solution.

Okay, fine.

I might not be able to represent her, but at least I could make some calls, right? No big deal. Set her up with someone who could help her through whatever issue she needed help with.

"What do you need help with? I'll see what I can—"

"A custody battle." She cut me off before I could get the rest of the sentence out.

I froze, shock a boom in the middle of my brain.

A custody battle.

I let it sink in for a second.

Then I went fumbling back, trying to put space between us when white-hot panic went streaking through my veins.

Fight or flight.

I didn't know which one I was more inclined to give in to.

To run right the hell out the door or get in her face for fucking setting off this bombshell in the middle of my office.

"Excuse me?" I demanded, voice going hard.

Harsh.

Fueled by hate and fear.

A cold sweat broke out on my forehead.

She started shaking. First her hands and then it spread to the entirety of her body. A storm. Everything she'd been holding inside working its way out.

Secrets.

Motherfucker.

"I need . . . I need someone to represent me. My babies . . . he's trying to take them away."

She kept coming closer with every word that she said while I continued to back away. "I . . . I made a mistake. I fought him in a way I shouldn't have, and he turned it around on me. I should have known he'd fight dirty. That he'd lie and cheat as a way to threaten me, to control me, to get me to do what he wanted. He's trying to have me declared as an unfit mother. Saying I'm crazy. That I'm a thief. That I'm no good for them. Of course, he'll gladly drop the whole thing if I go running back to him."

Panic ridged with anger had taken possession of her, a desperation so thick I was inhaling it with every word that fell as a frenzy from her tongue.

"I think the only reason he wants me there is to control what I say. To make sure I don't leak the things that I've seen. But I've seen them, Ian. I've seen them and I know them, and there is no way I'm letting my children get placed permanently in that house. It nearly kills me every single time they go for their visitations."

It only had those volatile, conflicting emotions crashing harder. Careening. Making it feel like my insides were being battered.

"He . . . he's a monster. I didn't know . . . I didn't know until it was too late . . . but I don't know how to prove it." A hand fisted in my suit jacket. "Help me prove it."

It suddenly made sense. The fact that she was there. At the gala. Sitting so pretty and looking for easy prey.

What a goddamned slap to the face.

Maybe I had it coming.

Karma.

I'd always been warned that it would come around. That it would bite me in the ass. That I couldn't take and take and take and not end up without someone taking from me.

What a fucking fool that I was.

And here I'd thought it was me who was doing the stalking.

Hostility lit.

Spread.

This crawling sense of being used.

Fists. Feet. Fury. Lashes and blows. The pain. The pain. "Mama needs you, Ian. Just this one time. I need you to do it for me."

I tried to squeeze my eyes against the sensation. My spirit tossed into the throes of a motherfucking flashback. I swallowed down the bile and pried Grace's fingers from my jacket.

"Is that what this was all about? Your plan? Get under my skin? Sleep with me? Make me start falling for you so you could get your way? Weasel your way in until I didn't have a choice but to feel sorry for you?"

Horror seized her expression, that goddamned mouth parting in a surprised, offended O. "God . . . Ian . . . no. I didn't even know until last night that you were an attorney. I . . . I'd just assumed you were one of the business owners who was attending."

Rejection drummed at my lungs, leaving me on a scoff of distaste. "It seems awfully convenient to me . . . you just so happen to need an attorney? Go after the first one who looked your way."

"No." It was a whimper, and guilt flamed somewhere in my spirit when I saw the tears gather in her eyes. "No. Never. I would never do that to you. I swear. I'm . . . I'm falling—"

I flew toward her, getting in her face when I realized what was rumbling there. Getting ready to erupt. It wasn't going to happen.

"Don't you dare fucking say it."

She wasn't falling in love with me. Wasn't close to it. Like she'd told me last night, we didn't know each other.

She'd fucking used me. Hunted me. Went in for the kill when I was weak. Playing coy when really, she was suckering me in.

She started grappling, hands going back for my shirt. Like she could get inside.

Under.

In.

Sink in those claws.

Looking for a hostage.

"Please, Ian . . . I need you. For them."

She started talking so quickly I shouldn't have been able to keep up. But every word pierced me like a barb.

"Thomas and Mallory and Sophie. They are nine and five and barely two. My babies. I can't stand that they are in the middle of this. Being used. Dangled over my head like some kind of bait. Every time they go there, they cry, begging to stay with me, and they're a little more broken every time they return. They're scared . . . terrified that one day they're going to go over there, and they're never going to see me again. Help us. Please."

I wanted to slam my hands over my ears. Punch the words from my brain. Pretend she wasn't feeding me this line of bullshit.

I spun away from her, trying to keep my cool, rage turning my hands into fists.

No.

I didn't care.

This wasn't on me.

"Reed . . . he—"

I whirled back around, entire face pinching, words nothing but a shocked wheeze that gusted from my lungs. "What did you say?"

She stumbled back a step. "Reed."

Low laughter rocked free and bounced from the walls. "Tell me you aren't talking about Reed Dearborne."

Reed Dearborne.

All it took was that name to send the blood draining from her face. My recognition of the mess this girl had gotten herself into.

"Fuck."

Mother-fuck-fuck-fuck.

Spinning on my heel, I turned away, yanking at my hair like a fiend, pacing, before I was back in her face. "Tell me I didn't fuck *Reed Dearborne's* estranged wife. You know, the guy who's running for senate and is one of the most powerful men in South Carolina. Tell me we aren't talking about him."

The last I spit an inch from her face.

This girl wasn't just fucking with my heart and head. She was trying to destroy my career.

She blanched, her hands running up and down her arms. "Please don't talk to me like that."

I laughed again. Bitterness and bile. I wanted to fucking hurl. "And what do you want me to talk to you like, Grace?"

"Like the girl you made love to last night."

I pushed her against the bookcase that lined the wall, and she was gasping, torn between lust and fear.

Like she was feeding off the exact same thing that was oozing from me. "Let's be clear—love didn't have a thing to do with what went down last night."

Hurt blanketed her face, her throat bobbing frantically with short, jagged pants. "Good, then we can pretend like it never happened."

Was she serious?

Ignore this?

Forget it?

More likely, it hadn't mattered to her at all.

For a beat her eyes closed, softly, like maybe the girl was issuing a silent prayer.

I wanted to reach out and shake her.

Then she was slowly opening them, turning that mesmerizing gaze in my direction. A tidal wave to knock me off my feet. I was going to need a fucking anchor to survive this girl. "You asked me to take a chance on you, Ian Jacobs. Now, I'm begging you to take one on me. You are the only chance I have. I can pay you. A lot."

Fierce determination burned from her spirit. Somehow, it was muddled with shame as she rushed to unzip the big bag at her side.

My chest nearly caved.

Stuffed inside was nothing but stacks and stacks of bound cash.

My eyes about bugged out of my damned head. Holy shit.

Clearly, the girl was a whole lot more like me than I wanted to admit.

Willing to do anything.

Anything to get her to her goals.

But hers were that desolating kind.

Dreams that would crush you. Leave you nothing but rubble

and ash. It was the kind of risk definitely not worth taking. But for her? There was no question that it was.

A gutting worry almost clouded my mind, toyed with my senses.

What did you do, Angel Girl, what did you do?

Then a rush of anger boiled back to the surface. I couldn't let this girl get under my skin.

Obviously, she'd go to any length to get what she wanted. Use anyone. Just like she'd done me.

I roughed a palm over my mouth to break up the insanity. Then my voice was dropping, my head angled as I gritted the words so close to her face that our noses were touching as I roughly zipped back up her bag.

"It doesn't *matter* how much money you can pay me. I can't do this. You know it. I know it. We *slept* together. I could be suspended, or worse, disbarred, and the last thing I'm going to do is jeopardize my chances at becoming partner."

Not for her.

Not for anyone.

I swallowed hard. "And Reed Dearborne on top of it? Not for all that money you have in your bag would I take him on. I'd be a fool if I tried, and I'd still turn you down even if this was the first time I'd seen you. Taking that case would be career suicide."

Her chin trembled, and that same hopelessness I'd witnessed the first night I'd seen her doused her expression in defeat. She looked up at me, words so quiet, so low.

A sharp, hot dagger.

"I never took you for a coward, Ian Jacobs."

"And I never took you for a whore." It was a knee-jerk response. Defense against her criticism that went bone deep. Against the truth of what she'd said.

The second I released it, I regretted it. The way her entire being was rocked. The quiver ignited all the way into her soul.

Like I'd physically injured her.

I thought I must have.

Hurt her in a way I could never take back.

It was for the best.

It was for the best.

I needed to get her out of here. For good.

"Wow, you really are an asshole, aren't you? I shouldn't have let myself forget it after the first time I talked to you." Tears gathered in her eyes. She tried to fight them, but one streaked free, gliding down her cheek and dripping from her chin.

Fuck me, I wanted to reach out and wipe it away. Tell her I'd give her hope if there were any to be had.

But it was impossible.

Only a fool would get involved in that kind of high-profile custody case.

Against an asshole like Reed Dearborne.

Especially a man like me with a girl like her.

This girl who'd touched me in a way she couldn't.

The girl who was standing there with that big heart bleeding out all over my floor.

An angel with a broken halo.

This woman with *three kids.*

Three kids.

That right there had me wanting to crawl into the back of my closet and get cozy with all my skeletons. Snuggle up close. They'd be much cozier than dealing with the consequences of this.

There's so much we don't know about each other.

"I never claimed not to be an asshole," I forced out through clenched teeth.

Grace twisted out from between the bookcase and me, head dropped low as she headed for the door.

I forced myself to stay rooted.

Right then was not the goddamned time to grow a conscience.

I was chanting, *she did this, she did this. She knew all along. It was an ambush. A set up.*

But I knew that was nothing but a lie when she opened the door and looked back at me.

Grief.

Sorrow.

It was signed on her just as boldly as my name was signed on Bennet's falsified documents.

She swallowed hard, and her face twisted in remorse. "And there you went and had me believing in fate. I guess I really am a dreamer, after all."

She sent me the saddest smile before she stepped out and quietly latched the door shut behind her.

Both my hands went to my forehead, jerking through my hair. "Fuck!" I roared. I flew around and kicked the wall like it could take the brunt of what I was feeling.

I threw myself into my chair, body rocking forward as I bent at the waist and buried my face against my palms.

That motherfucking feeling was present again. Though this time it was stinging in my eyes and burning in my chest.

A groan pulled from somewhere deep inside. Deeper than my guts. Deeper than my lungs.

What the hell was I supposed to do?

GRACE

Trying to remain upright, I quickly glanced both ways before I rushed across the street toward where my car was parked at the curb about a half block down. My heels dragged along the pavement, held down by the piece of my heart and soul I'd left back there.

I'd cut myself open wide. Exposed myself. Put everything on the line.

Trusted him.

That dirty money was burning a hole into my side where I had it tucked against my body, the rash decision I'd made the day I'd left Reed the final time. But if I was going to fight him, I needed money. What better money than his own.

A car horn blared, the screech of tires coming from out of nowhere on the nearly desolate side street, and I lurched forward, fumbling to get out of the way.

Tears burned in my eyes, the heartache and sorrow that I'd tried to keep shored up by the flimsy blockade I'd made around my spirit trying to leak through the cracks.

I'd been doing my best to keep that well full of hope and belief and faith.

Ian Jacobs might as well have punched a fist into my chest and ripped the barrier down.

A dam that had burst.

Toppled.

Devastation underneath.

I never should have let him in.

The second I'd seen him, I'd known the man could wreck me with the barest brush of his hand.

And oh, had he done a whole lot more than let those fingertips caress my cheek.

A flashflood of memories from last night invaded my senses, my blood still pulsing with desire, with the remnants of that ecstasy he'd evoked in me.

Skin tingling, my heart and belly took turns doing wild things. Thumping and thudding and turning upside down.

Then he'd turned around and accused me of the most horrible thing. Acting as if I'd sought him out, used my body as a weapon against him.

Anger and hurt twisted around my heart, ribs constricting, everything too tight.

Had he actually been serious?

As if I could possibly wield the power to tie that man around my pinkie finger. Just a big red, sexy bow.

Yeah right.

I doubted that was even possible.

He was untouchable.

That heart so brittle and cold there was no chance of getting through.

I'd given him myself. Offered him a part of myself that I never should have after I'd already known exactly how that was going to make me feel. How I'd already known I was falling when he'd shown up at my salon yesterday evening.

Hell, I'd been falling all along.

That should have been warning enough.

Then I'd gone and pinned all my hope on him. A fool who'd deluded herself into believing that the connection we'd shared had been intended for something more. That it might have a greater purpose.

Gasping for a breath, I fumbled to get my keys free from the small front pocket of the bag as I approached my car.

The bag bounced around on my hip as if it were trying to break away from me.

What the hell was I thinking carrying around the proof of my extortion as if it were a tube of lipstick that'd been forgotten at the bottom of a purse?

My running lights flashed as I pressed manically at the fob, needing to get out of there before I lost my mind in the middle of the street.

Jerking open the door, I tossed the bag across the console to the passenger front seat.

I had to get away.

Put space between me and the man who was making me do irrational things.

A shriek ripped from my tongue when a hand landed on my forearm. Curling forcefully. Fingers painfully digging into my skin. Yanking me back.

Fear burst.

Volatile and violent.

I whirled around, half led by my anger and half compelled by the force being exerted on my arm.

I was sucking for the missing air when I saw who was standing there, the one who was pushing me back against my car and acting as if we were involved in nothing but a simple embrace.

Oh, but I could feel it . . .

His wrath spilling out over me.

It was there in the short, jagged breaths that heaved from his lungs, from the clench of his jaw, and the hatred in his blue eyes.

Hair flawlessly styled.

Suit perfectly tailored.

But where Ian oozed sex and intrigue, he did nothing but make my stomach curl with disgust.

"Reed." I tried to keep the whimper from my voice. The last thing I wanted was the bastard to think he could intimidate me.

Sway me.

But that didn't mean every cell in my body wasn't trembling, the man digging into my arm while he sent me a smile that any passerby would think was filled with affection.

The seething hatred and the shock of fear that was rippling through invisible to the naked eye.

But I knew that Reed was scared. And right there only made him a more dangerous man.

"What are you doing here?" I tried to make it come off hard.

He laughed a brittle sound. "You want to know what *I'm* doing here, when you just came out of one of the most prestigious law firms in Charleston."

I tried to yank out of his hold. He only tightened it.

"It seems I'm in need of an attorney, doesn't it?" I spat, his face so close to mine I was sure he could taste the venom that came with it.

He tugged me closer to him. "You have no idea what you're getting yourself into, Grace. Just showing your face here."

"Are you threatening me?"

He laughed a noxious sound, the man blond and tall and wide. Classically handsome, like any other hometown boy who was trying to make his small-town world his bitch.

I refused to be any part of it.

"I'm trying to knock some sense into you before it's too late," he gritted.

Bitterness bled free, and my teeth were grinding, the tears of hurt that had flowed upstairs turning into something else entirely. This steely abhorrence that made me want to spit in his pretentious face. "I think you already know it's exactly that. Too late."

"You're wrong."

"Where are my children?" I challenged.

The asshole.

Showing up here when he'd given that sob story to the judge about how I'd tried to steal his children from him, how when I had, the only thing he'd felt was a gaping hole in his life.

I'd like to show the prick a gaping hole.

"They're safe. That's all that should matter to you. I hope you want to keep them that way."

Rage churned at the deepest depths of me, and when I jerked my arm this time, I ripped it free from his disgusting hold. "You're right. That's the only thing that matters to me. And I won't stop until you are out of their lives."

"Don't tell me you're that delusional. You don't actually think that's going to happen, do you? That I'd let my children go? That I'd let you go?"

Before I could make sense of it, he had me backed against the car, his hand on my chin forcing me to look up at him.

My heart tumbled in fear, and I hated it, hated that he had the control to exert it. That I'd ever put myself and my kids in this position in the first place. "You're going to regret complicating things. Come home. Where you belong. I love you."

If the way he treated me was love, I wanted no part of it.

Nausea swirled in my stomach and sent bile climbing my throat. "And you're a fool if you think I'm going to back down."

He brushed his fingers down my cheek. As if he adored me and his soul wasn't deadened with greed. "I wish you wouldn't say that. I'd hate to hear that something horrible happened to my children's mother."

Terror rambled around in my chest and pushed against my ribs. I refused to let him see it.

His voice dropped lower, sharp as a knife. "Where's my money, Grace, and the folder you took from my safe?"

"Who knows," I told him, sending him my own threat.

It was the only power I had. Those few pictures I'd found in his safe that day—the evidence I'd found that gave me the courage to run. I'd taken the money at the same time.

It was the day I realized I had to be brave. That I could no longer cower and submit. I had to fight my way out of the castle or my children would be prisoner to it forever.

"Wrong answer." He tightened his hold.

Fear surged and any firmness that had been in my tone turned to a trembling plea. "Just let us go, Reed. Forget that we ever existed, and I'll do the same. You won't hear from me, and neither will the press."

His body ticked in aggression when I mentioned the press, the man stepping back, releasing me, but his mouth was right there, at my ear. "You think you have the upper hand? You think your flimsy accusation is going to stand? You even step in the direction of a reporter, and things aren't going to end well for you. The same as if I find out you've come back here. I'm finished playing games with you."

"Our lives aren't a game."

"No, you're right. Your lives are mine." He took another step back and meticulously straightened the cuffs on his jacket. "You have two weeks to come to your senses, Grace. Two weeks to end this stupidity."

He started to walk away before he turned around, pointing at me. "Two weeks." Then he jumped into the dark gray Jaguar sitting at the curb on the opposite side of the street.

Frozen, I watched as he started his car and jumped out onto the small side road. Not a single car had passed in all that time, not a single soul to witness our altercation.

Even if they had, it wouldn't have looked like anything more than a lover's spat, anyway.

No one would know my world was crumbling under me.

Time was running out.

I slumped into the driver's seat of my car, clinging to the steering wheel for dear life, as if it were a buoy, a life raft.

I refused to buckle. To surrender.

I was going to race time.

And I was going to beat it.

Hands shaking, I finally got the key into the ignition and started my car. I drove back through Charleston and to the quiet neighborhood where I had been raised. I pulled into the narrow drive and stared at the little house that always seemed to radiate emptiness when my children were away.

I forced myself to kill the engine and stepped out, the adrenaline that had been lining my bones draining, making me weak.

I unlocked the front door and stepped inside. I went right for the comfortable living room, which was decorated exactly the same as it had been when I was a child. The only difference were the pictures of my children that had been added to the walls.

Their toys scattered about.

It only made the lack of their presence seem all that more profound.

The second she caught the expression on my face, Gramma frowned and set aside the quilting project she was working on. She patted her lap as if I were four and just her holding me could chase all the demons away.

I moved across the room and curled up on the couch, hugging that stupid bag to my chest and resting my head on the top of her thigh.

She gentled her fingers through my hair. "I take it your meeting didn't go well."

There was no stopping it. The dam that burst.

Mostly, it was a result of the showdown with Reed. Hopelessness trying to find its way inside. To seed and plant and take root until nothing was left but weeds that had snuffed out beauty and life.

But I'd gone and let a piece of my heart get broken, too.

I'd opened myself up and made myself vulnerable.

I might as well have stretched my arms out to the sides and welcomed the pain.

A sob erupted from my chest, and I curled deeper into my grandmother's hold. "No, Gramma. It didn't go well. I was told again that only a fool would take my case."

Ian being the one who'd said it only made it all the worse.

"Well, good thing there are a whole lot of fools out there," she almost chuckled, my grandmother gifting comfort in a way that only she could.

I smiled through my tears. "They run rampant, don't they?"

"Sure do. Whole world is nothing but a bunch of blundering idiots who don't know their heads from their asses. I'm sure we can find one attorney with their head shoved up there somewhere."

Silence filled the room. Our spirits' quick acknowledgement that this wasn't a joking matter. Sometimes, the only thing a person could do was laugh their way through it.

My voice tripped into sorrow. "I think it was me who was the fool."

She softly brushed her fingers through the hair at the top of my head. "Shh . . . don't say that. You think with your heart, not with only two brain cells. Big difference."

"But I thought Reed was a good man."

Even though I was facing out, I could feel her give a sharp shake of her head. "You married Reed because that's what his parents pressured you into doing. You went along with it because you thought it was the right thing to do."

"And what did you think?" I breathed.

"I thought you were settling."

"I tried to love Reed with all of me. I did. I thought . . . in time . . . together we'd create a home. I thought it'd be a good choice," I admitted. "You and Grandpa took care of me my whole life. The last thing I wanted to do was burden you with the issues I'd created for myself."

Reed and I had been married in a flash, and I'd been pregnant a month later. It wasn't until I had a ring on my finger that I'd seen the true side of the man he was. Of course, I hadn't given myself any amount of time to really get to know him before I'd gotten myself into that situation.

I should have slowed down.

Listened to the worried wisdom that my gramma had tried to give.

She nudged me, forcing me to sit up and look at her.

Through bleary eyes, I gazed at the woman who'd always been my everything.

My rock.

My anchor.

She brushed her knuckles down the side of my face with her weathered hand, which bore spots of age but possessed more love than should be possible.

"You listen to me, girl, and you listen good. Not for a second were you ever a burden to us. When we lost your mama, we were crushed in a way that I wasn't sure either me or your grandpa were gonna survive. But she left behind the most precious sort of gift. This tiny baby girl who filled our lives with more love and blessings than either of us could have imagined."

In emphasis, her head tipped to the side, gaze penetrating to make sure that I understood. "I'm your family, and you're mine. There's no shame in leaning on each other in times of need. You weren't a burden then, and you aren't a burden now. Not you or your children."

She turned up my chin. "And my time is coming, sweet girl. I'm going to need you to take care of me. That's what we do. We take care of each other. So, don't you dare sit there thinking you were trouble then or that you're trouble now. You've always done the best that you could, and you did it with love the whole way. You work harder than anyone I know. You love harder than anyone I know. Put those two things together, and you're unstoppable."

A tear slipped free, and my chest expanded as she continued to speak. "You might have settled then? But you're not gonna settle now. You fight for it with all that love shining inside of you, and I promise you, it's all gonna turn out right."

"How do you know?" I whispered, searching for that hope when the vacancy cut so deep while my children were away. The terror of what my life would be like without them in it. When everything felt like a losing battle.

"Because there are some things in the world that are just too right for them to go wrong."

I wanted to believe her. But I'd experienced enough horrible things to know life wasn't that simple.

She smiled, her blue-gray eyes so full of belief and love. "I got my gift when I needed it most. When I was sure there was no chance of survival. You've got one coming, too. I can feel it."

"I hope so, Gramma. I hope so."

But even I wasn't fool enough to believe that every gift didn't come with a cost.

sixteen

IAN

A just before five p.m., I strode into Lawrence's office, which was two miles from mine. He was behind his desk, puffing at a cigar and talking on the phone.

"I need to call you back," he said, dropping the receiver into the cradle where it sat on his desk.

"Why don't you come in?" he offered sarcastically.

I didn't pause, didn't wait, I just moved for his desk. I set my briefcase on top of it, clicked it open, and pulled out the documents. I slammed them down onto the wood. "Three sets. These will be the last."

Laughing, he rocked back in his executive leather chair, looking at me like he thought I was cute.

I had the intense urge to smack the smugness from his face.

"Oh, Ian, you were always such a defiant boy. I do hope you realize it's my favorite thing about you. When I found you, you were nothing but an angry, bitter kid with nothing to lose."

But that was the problem. He knew that now I stood to lose everything.

"And you should know that I'm no longer anything like that boy."

A dark chuckle, and he rocked forward, stubbing his cigar into an ashtray and slowly shaking his head. "There are some things that can't be unbred. They just evolve. Become something bigger and badder and darker. You've become exactly the type of man I knew you'd be all along. It's time you stop denying who you are. The man you are."

"And what kind of man is that?"

"Wicked. Corrupt. All the way to the core. Men like us will do whatever is required of us. That's why you belong with me. The way you always have. I'm not entirely sure why you've decided to fight this now."

He wasn't wrong. I was corrupt, all the way to my soul. Still, there was something that stirred in that ugly pit, something rejecting all of this. I pointed at the documents. "Because one day that is going to ruin both of us."

A smile pulled at the corner of his mouth. "No, Ian, that is where you're wrong. It isn't. Because I won't let it. My connections are greater than you know, and it's time you stopped questioning my power. It's time for you to step up. Stand at my side in this business where you belong."

He kept spouting that ridiculous shit. Like I was actually going to join him. Set aside my goals for him. He was delusional.

My jaw clenched, and I jabbed at the stack of papers I'd set on his desk. "I want to know where this money is coming from and where it's going."

What the fuck he was actually involved in. At first, he had me on a bunch of bank accounts. Making transfers for him. I assumed he was moving money around, evading taxes and shit like that, details I didn't want to know about.

But, lately, I had felt myself getting dragged into something that went too deep. Dark, dark waters climbing higher and higher until I was swallowed. Sucked to the bottom.

Lawrence scoffed. "Since when do you think you get to ask the questions?"

"Since you put me in this position."

"You'd do well not to worry about it."

I huffed out a biting sound. "Don't worry about it? That's your solution?"

"You don't actually think your concerns have any bearing on my business, do you?" Arrogance seeped from him. Ancient and thick and callous.

Rage pulled across my chest, old, old pain mixed up with that emotion Grace had managed to evoke in me. It was something brutal and wild and confusing.

Maddening.

I pressed my palms flat on his desk and leaned in his direction. "I think you might be underestimating me. You might think I'm that same kid you pulled out of the gutter and dusted off. But I wasn't going to become him, whether you came along or not. No one controls me. Not ever. I've helped you because you helped me. But be clear, I won't stand aside and let you destroy what I've built."

I pushed off the desk, grabbed my briefcase, and headed for the door.

When the low threat hit me from behind, I stopped, not looking his way but tucking his words away deep in my chest. Where they could grow and fester, and the hatred I'd started to feel could expand.

"I could ruin you with the snap of my fingers, boy. Make you disappear with a simple call. Don't make me go that far. Not when I actually like having you around. I'd hate to lose the asset."

Asset.

Bitter laughter bounced against his walls.

I'd once looked up to him like he was the father I never had.

From over my shoulder, I looked back at him. No fear raced my veins. No hesitation. The fucker had no idea the threats I'd endured. The blows and the punches and the pain. "Don't think I would hesitate to do the same. Come after me, old man, and I promise, you'll regret it."

I walked out without looking back, his door slamming shut behind me and my heart clawing at my chest. I flew past his secretary without a word and stumbled out onto the sidewalk in front of his building.

Guilt unlike I'd felt in years crawled beneath the surface of my skin.

Worst part was knowing it was the girl who'd gotten there. Sinking and seeping and making me contemplate things I couldn't keep.

Agitation sped, muscles twitching. Anger and hostility seethed through my veins.

I was so sick of this bullshit.

Being someone's puppet.

I'd promised myself I'd live for myself. Then I'd gone and earned myself another debt.

Worse than that?

I couldn't get Grace off my mind. Couldn't scrape her from my skin. Couldn't evict her from the crack she'd found in my mangled heart.

I was . . . worried. Was that what this bullshit was? I guessed I'd been since that first night I'd seen her. The girl whipped something up inside me that shouldn't be possible.

I hated it.

Hated that she held that power, too.

I still couldn't believe she was Reed Dearborne's ex-wife.

The news hadn't reported the separation.

Shocker.

A local story like that paid off and swept under the rug because the bastard didn't want to tarnish his name.

But there was enough talk around town for us to hear rumblings of it in the office.

I'd met him twice.

Let's just say shady recognized shady.

And the guy skeeved me out.

But now? It felt personal. Like I wanted to hunt the fucker down for ever touching her. For hurting her. For claiming her.

Couldn't stand the thought of his hands on her. On that sweet skin. Fingers sinking into that soft heart.

Three kids.

Three kids.

Irritation stretched thin, everything feeling so goddamned off-kilter and foreign that it had my mind spinning with all sorts of bullshit I couldn't entertain.

Getting soft.

So goddamned stupid.

I knew better.

Still, that feeling was chasing me, thoughts pushing me one direction and then shoving me the other. Wanted to claw my goddamned eyes out, imagining it all, Reed and her family and the girl who I'd first seen sitting at the bar.

The opposition of the girl who'd been in my bed, blowing my goddamned mind, and the girl who'd been standing in my office with all that cash.

I couldn't reconcile the two.

I lost my jacket and brief case in my car and was driving back through town, unable to go back to my hollow condo.

Knowing her scent would still be there. Knowing my ears would still be howling with her pleas.

I needed an outlet.

A reprieve.

I hopped out of my car and paid the cover at the seedy club.

Like I said, shady called to shady.

And it wasn't like I was in the mood to hit Monty's. Mack would show, and there was no way I could explain away the mood I was in.

Didn't fucking get it myself.

I entered the dark club.

Nothing but sleazy air and flashing lights.

I moved through the pricks that filled the place, sordid fantasies playing through their minds. I found a secluded spot in the back, in the darkness, and welcomed it, the partner to my heart.

I sank down into the plush, deep chair. Maroon, crushed velvet.

Dancers were on the stage, glued to their poles. Lights strobed and music blared.

My attention was on the stage, eyes roving over the mostly naked bodies, sucking down the feeling that held fast to the atmosphere.

Greed and lust and desperation.

It didn't make me hard. Didn't turn me on. It just made me remember that I wasn't the only one who would do what they had to in order to survive. That there was no shame in doing whatever it took to make sure there was food in your stomach and a roof over your head.

When a cocktail waitress appeared at my side, I ordered a scotch, guzzled it down and asked for another. Told her to keep them coming.

If I was going to drown in my own self-inflicted depravity, I was going to do it right.

I drained glass after glass. Until I couldn't feel my fucking fingers or my toes or that blackened, mangled ball that was supposed to be my heart.

I didn't even reject the dancer who came over and asked if I wanted a private dance, let her take my hand and lead me to a back room, let her grind her body all over mine.

I watched her.

Detached.

Numb.

Verging on something else.

Like I was hanging on a sharp edge and getting ready to be cut in two.

Hating every second.

Wanting more.

Punishment.

She leaned in, hands on my shoulders as she ground on my dick, her lips on my ear. "I have somewhere we could go."

Revulsion spun, loathing rising to the surface. My hands instantly shot out, and I gripped her by the waist. "No."

The word was harsh.

Hard.

It only made her try *harder*. Her pussy barely covered as she rubbed herself all over my two-thousand-dollar suit. "Oh, come on, don't pretend like you aren't here for one thing. I see it written all over you. I promise to make it worth it."

"No," I said again.

"Come on, baby. Let me help you out." Through my pants, she stroked my limp dick.

Disgust.

Rage.

They spiraled. Twisted and bound.

My body was barely even reacting while my mind tossed me into the pit of my past.

Darkness.

Fear.

Sickness.

She grabbed both my hands and pressed them to her breasts.

Nausea tumbled in my guts and rolled up my throat.

I pushed her off my lap. Harder than I should have, and she stumbled back onto her five-inch heels while I stood, dug into my wallet, and pulled out a wad of cash.

I grabbed her hand and stuffed the bills into it, curling her fingers around the wad. "That should be more than enough to cover the dance."

She looked at me as if I were crazy.

Sounded about right.

I headed for the draped exit, needing to get the hell out of there before I lost my mind. Unable to understand what was happening to me. Why I felt like I was five seconds from coming unhinged.

I threw aside the heavy fabric, and I flew out, coming to a quick stop when a shadow stepped out in front of me, blocking my path down the narrow hall. "Are you showing disrespect to my girl?"

The asshole was wiry and thin, trying to play it big, jutting out his chin.

Begging me to put my fist in it.

My head cocked, aggression a blister rushing across my skin.

"Disrespect your girl?"

"That's right. You touched her. That means you're goin' to pay. One way or another."

"Just drop it, Cody. He didn't mean no harm." I could feel her behind me, cowering, attempting to get her voice to come out strong, but there was no missing the fact it wavered.

He sneered at her from over my shoulder. "Shut your fuckin' mouth, Cocoa. Unless you're opening up for dick, it stays closed. No one gives a shit what you have to say."

He turned back to me. "Here's how it's gonna be. You're either gonna take back out that fat wallet of yours and give me the rest of what's in there, or you take her with you, do what you will, and still give me everything left between the leather. Your choice. Makes no difference to me."

Hostile laughter rolled up my throat, coating him in my venom. "I'd think twice before you start throwing ultimatums my way."

He tried to get in my face, like his pathetic being held an ounce of intimidation, pushing up onto his toes.

I was still looking down my nose at him.

"What, like the fact you're about to get your ass handed to you out in the alley?" he tossed out.

Saw another figure step up behind him. Another piece of shit asshole lurking in the shadows.

Motherfucker.

My mind spun and my heart thundered, and I could taste the bile on my tongue.

Hate. Hate. Hate.

I turned on my heel to get a look at the girl who was fidgeting on this side of the curtain. I was barely able to speak through the clench of my teeth. "You want to come with me? You're welcome to. But the only reason for it will be to get you away from this prick, and you won't be coming back. Do you understand what I'm getting at?"

Caught off guard, I floundered forward a step when I was shoved from behind. Filthy hands on the back of my suit, even filthier breath that hit the stagnant, stale air.

"The fuck you say? Because I think you were actually implying that you were going to take one of *my* girls."

This prick was right there, at my back, thinking I was nothing but a chump in a suit who wouldn't retaliate. Thinking I'd whip out my wallet and beg for mercy.

The last thing he expected when I whirled around was the fist I threw.

It cracked against his chin.

His head whipped back and tossed him from his feet. He tumbled to the dirty ground, and I didn't think twice.

No thought of consequence.

No thought of remorse.

The only thing I saw was red when I jumped on him and started pounding on his fuck-ugly face.

Nothing but delirium invoked in the first punch.

Memories assaulted me as I assaulted the prick.

Image after image.

Horror and hate and hunger.

Hits. Blows. Kicks. Scrapes. Screams.

And I couldn't stop.

Couldn't stop beating him bloody.

Knew he deserved every blow.

"You piece of shit . . . you think you own her? Is that what you think? Did you force her into this? Is that what this is?"

Motherfucking pimp prick.

Pain splintered across the side of my head and spread across my face.

Out of nowhere.

Knocking me back an inch.

I blinked in shock, trying to process what was happening around me. To see through the haze of fury that clouded my eyes.

Took me a second to realize the punch wasn't delivered by the pussy who I had pinned on the floor, but by the bastard who'd appeared at the fringes of the hall.

Two on one.

Bring it on.

I didn't care.

In half a beat, I was on my feet and had him rammed against

the wall. His face slammed into the black-wallpapered plaster.

A scream pierced the space. The girl who'd started this whole thing stumbled around the pile of bodies I was making in the hall, wearing nothing but a thong and heels.

People scrambled from the main room, some to get out the front door before the cops showed and others vying for a front-row seat.

Before I could make sense of it, another asshole was on my back. Hauling me away from the bastard and tossing me against the wall. I hit it with an *oomph*, all that aggression spiking high. My muscles pulsed, my eyes darting between all three of the guys who'd ganged up on me.

Calculating my next move.

The first pussy pulled his beaten ass off the floor, wiping at his bloodied face. With my body pinned to the wall, he stepped up and delivered a sucker-punch to my gut.

I fucking growled, welcoming the pain, and the adrenaline only grew.

Ready to tear through them all.

Didn't take a whole lot to throw off the piece of shit who held me against the wall. Nothing but a kick to his knee to send him fumbling back, howling in agony, and I went for the little bastard who was about to bear the brunt of the hostility roiling inside me.

Alcohol soaking my brain and repulsion saturating my spirit.

A hand landed on my arm, whipping me around. It was the same guy who'd served me up as a present for the little fucker I wanted to break in two.

"Get out of my club and don't come back. You got it. We don't do trouble around here."

Don't do trouble.

Fucking priceless.

I would have laughed if I wasn't irate.

They just pimped out girls in the back room like a bad rumor.

It didn't happen in the VIP room, my ass.

"That's too bad because I'm in the mood to cause a little trouble."

Just as fast as the crowd had gathered, they were being pushed back.

Shit.

There was Mack, tossing people aside as he stalked through the mass like a battering ram.

Talk about burly assholes.

He flashed his badge at the prick who had his meaty palm on my arm.

Everyone scattered.

Motherfucking rats with a light shined in their sewer.

The guy released me and backed away, his hands held up in surrender. But he clearly wasn't what Mack was interested in. My best friend grabbed me by the collar and started to drag me down the opposite side of the hall toward the emergency exit at the end.

He shoved it open and tossed me out into the cool night.

I stumbled across the pavement.

The aggression burning all the way to my bones surged, emotions thick, too much, so dark I couldn't see.

"What the hell are you doing here?" I managed to press out, my knuckle coming up to my mouth and finding I had a busted lip.

He laughed a hard sound. "I'm a detective in Charleston, Ian. It's my job to know whatever shit is going down. Have a connection who works here. She recognized you, gave me a text when you got in that prick's face and said things were about to get heavy. Was having a drink with Jace two blocks over since he's in town for business, and I booked it over."

"You have a contact? Inside? Here?" Incredulous, I spat the words at him, angry that he might have someone following me.

Paranoid and delusional, I knew. But when it came to Mack and me, we kept our jobs to ourselves. Our secrets tucked away because the two didn't mesh.

No doubt, he knew I'd done some questionable shit in my life. Last thing I wanted to do was put him in a bad position, to have to make a judgment call when it came to right and wrong when the guy was always in the right.

"Don't ask questions you don't really want the answers to." There was something in his expression, something that set me off kilter, a warzone in his eyes.

Like he was holding something back. Instantly, I was taken back to our conversation from two nights before that somehow felt like a century ago, when he'd warned me to cut ties with Lawrence.

God.

Maybe I really had gotten myself in too deep.

A loud truck engine rumbled at the head of the alley. It came to a stop, and Jace ducked out.

Great.

Just what I fucking needed.

My brother and best friend thinking they needed to wipe my ass.

Hold my goddamned hand.

I turned on Mack. "I was completely fine. Don't need you showing up here like the calvary. I am perfectly capable of taking care of myself."

He quirked a brow. "Says the guy who just about started a brawl. Those fuckers aren't to be toyed with."

"Seemed like good enough fun to me."

He scrubbed a frustrated hand over his face. "Fine, man, laugh it off. But there's shit going down in there that you don't need to get involved in. I'm serious." His voice went low.

"I was only there to have a drink or two to unwind after a long day's work. Prick tried to swindle cash out of me. You should know me well enough to know that wasn't going to end well."

Jace edged closer to me like he was corralling a caged animal. Like I just might attack.

Wasn't so far from the truth.

Adrenaline still pumped and burned, and I was itching to throw back open that door and hunt those pricks down. Easy prey.

Expendable.

Just like Lawrence Bennet was trying to make me.

"Are you okay, man?" Jace asked, caution in his tone, eyes searching me, forever the protector. He zeroed in on the cut on my lip, like I was a two-year-old who'd fallen and scraped his knee.

"I'm fine. You didn't need to come over here."

"You sure about that?"

"One hundred percent."

Jace turned his attention to the back of the seedy club and shook his head.

Not like it was some big-ass deal that a lowlife like me would show up at a place like this to see some tit at the end of the night.

But Jace knew . . . he fucking knew, and it grated on me.

He knew my predilection.

The compulsion.

Right then, it felt like he was reaching in and searching through all the shit I didn't want him to see, the scars and the agony and the bottled pain.

Too much like that girl who was driving me crazy.

Grace.

Sweet, sweet Grace.

Grace who had immediately filled my mind when the girl inside had been climbing all over me.

The one I couldn't have, and I was aching to take.

"You don't have to hang on to it any more, Ian. I know you blame yourself. By now, you have to have realized, it wasn't your fault. She chose that life, not you, and there was nothing either of us could do to stop her."

The second the words left Jace's mouth, a fiery bolt of fury shot through my body.

Flames at my insides.

I'd felt it coming. What he'd been wanting to bring up. Revisit what was buried.

Not a fucking chance in hell was it getting uncovered.

I pointed at him. "Don't fucking go there. You don't know. You weren't there."

He laughed a bitter sound. "Are you kidding me? You think I didn't go through it for all those years, too? You think I didn't do everything to take care of you?"

Of course, I knew. Of course, I did.

My chest ached, and he pushed on, not stopping as he angled his face toward mine. "You think it didn't kill me that I had to leave you, Ian? With her? You think that when I found out what happened, I wouldn't have given anything to be there with you?"

My throat locked up.

It was my fault.

It was my fault.

But I couldn't say it. Couldn't admit it. Couldn't stand losing my brother when he finally found out what I'd done.

He'd gone to prison to protect me. *Me.* And while he'd been gone, it was me who had committed the greatest crime.

I backed away. "Just . . . don't. Anything you've got to say? Save it. Because it's done and over and there isn't anything that will change it. I buried any pain I had with her, so don't stand over there thinking that you need to come and save me. I have everything I want. Everything I need."

Sorrow passed through Jace's eyes. Grief and injury, not to mention the protection he'd always felt for me.

My knees rocked.

I forced myself to stand. Not to show the weakness that threatened to knock me off my feet.

"Is that what you want to tell yourself?" Jace asked, no challenge in his voice, just pity.

I wanted none of it.

I pointed at him as I took a step back. "You got your family, Jace. Reclaimed what you needed. What you wanted. Set your life up the way you'd always deserved. Why don't you do me the favor of letting me live mine?"

Hurt blanketed Jace's features, and I blinked, trying to block it. Unable to stand the thought of causing my brother any more pain. Of him being disappointed in me when the only thing I'd wanted to do was make him proud.

Be as good as him.

What a fucking joke.

"Just . . . I'm going to go home. Let's leave it at that, okay?"

I swiveled toward Mack, throwing out a taunt. "Unless you have something to say about what went down in there and need to take me down to the station in cuffs?"

So yeah.

I was being a dick.

Dividing.

Distancing.

But I knew better than to allow myself to get too close.

"Come on, man, don't fuckin' be like that. We came because we care about you. Same as you'd do for either one of us." Mack took a big step forward like he was going to wrap me up in some kind of pussy embrace.

Before he could get to me, I spun on my heel and started to walk away. "I'll see you tomorrow."

This conversation needed to end.

"You're hurting, Ian. I see it. Mack sees it. Faith sees it. You don't need to suffer alone anymore. We all love you and want the best for you. Only thing standing in the way of that is you."

Leave it to Jace to get in the final word.

I slowed for a moment, eyes pinned on my shoes, before I shook it off and headed up the alley without looking back.

He knew better than to think I was going there.

I left my Mercedes in the parking lot, not even giving a fuck that it probably wouldn't have wheels come morning, and thumbed into my Uber app. A couple minutes later, I hopped in the back of it before it could even come to a full stop, and I slumped into the dingy seat. I didn't say anything the whole ride, just tried to breathe through the memories that nudged at my brain.

Trying to take hold.

At my building, I jumped out at the curb, rode the elevator, and moved into the emptiness of my condo.

Darkness and shadows.

The memories followed me there. No matter how hard I tried to stop them, they pushed to the forefront.

Squeezing my eyes against the onslaught, I went straight for the bar and poured myself another drink.

Hoping I'd be afforded some kind of mercy. Hoping I could bury it deeper.

Cover and conceal.

Forget.

It was no use.

They came harder and faster.

Closer and closer.

Panic started to set in.

God, night after night, I couldn't stop it. When would this bullshit end?

My lungs fisted, and I grasped my head in my hands, trying to refuse the images. The sounds that haunted me like phantoms stalking in the night.

I wanted to run. To scratch the fucking unbearable sensation from my skin. I stumbled into my bedroom. Such a fucking pathetic pussy because I went right for the desk and tugged open the drawer.

I pulled out the silver music box I kept hidden inside.

I lifted the lid, and the dancing angel popped up, one of the arms broken off and the entire body angled to the side, the music it twirled to warbled and distorted.

Just like the image I kept of my mother.

I turned the box over and ran my fingertips over the design engraved in the bottom. A full circle with a Roman Numeral one in the middle of it. It was the same design as she'd had tattooed on her shoulder.

It was the reason I'd gotten the date of her death marked on me the same way as she had this marked on her.

Because I'd never really known when she'd started living and when she'd started to die. If my father had been the reason for her spiral or if she'd been a junkie whore all along.

A rasp of agony left my lungs, and the room spun like a bitch. And I hated.

Hated her for being so weak. For making promises she never kept. For allowing the sorrow and pain.

I hated that I'd been the monster who had ultimately destroyed her.

I hated myself most that I didn't know how to stop loving her. *Forever and ever.*

seventeen

IAN
FOUR YEARS OLD

*Ia*n grinned and snuggled down under the covers. He loved the

way his mama's fingertips felt as she ruffled them through his hair. His mama was so pretty, the prettiest mama in the whole wide world.

Her voice was soft and made him feel warm inside. So soft as she read to him in the darkened room, on her knees on the floor next to the mattress where he slept. She almost sang the words of his favorite book, the one he begged her to read to him over and over again.

Love You Forever.

He'd accidentally ripped one page out, but his mama

remembered the words, and she sang about how he would always be her baby.

Page after page.

Even when he was a big, big boy.

And when she finished, she sat up on the edge of the bed, and playfully she pulled him onto her lap before she breathed out a long sigh and cradled him close.

She pressed her lips to the top of his head. "Love you forever."

"Wuv you more forever."

She hugged him and then settled him back in his bed, and he smiled when she leaned down and kissed him on the forehead, the cheek, the corner of his mouth.

"Kisses are forever, too," she whispered. "And they're only for the ones you love most."

Ian smacked a bunch of kisses all over his mama's pretty face. "I wuv you most forever and forever."

His mama sighed. "I have to go. Ms. Roseann will be here with you."

As soon as she said it, his chest felt weird, like it was too big and too small all at the same time. "You got to go?"

She touched his cheek. "Yes, baby, I've got to go. Work is important. Mama has to make money to feed you so you can grow as tall as a tree."

Ian tried not to cry, to be brave and big like she told him to be, like his big brother Jace was. But Ian didn't like it when she went to work. When it was dark outside and he wasn't sure she would be there when he woke up.

It made him scared.

She sent him a tender smile.

"Goodnight, Love Bug."

"Night, night."

She pushed to standing and slowly crossed to the opposite side of the room where she leaned down and tucked in Jace who was already sleeping, before she quietly inched back across the floor toward the door.

His Mama's shoes were high and shiny, as shiny as the white dress she wore that he was sure was covered in diamonds, just as sure as he was that she must be a princess from one of his favorite stories.

With one last glance back at them, she stepped out and left the door open a crack. Ian strained to listen to the muddle of voices out in the living room, their apartment small enough that he could hear most anything.

The front door shut and Ms. Roseann turned on the television. She laughed from the other room, and Ian pressed his eyes together. Quick to fall into sleep.

Glass shattered, and Ian jolted awake.

Fear drummed in his heart. He tried to swallow, to press his eyes together tight and pretend he wasn't there.

"You fucking whore. You do what I say, when I say."

"Screw you. I don't belong to you."

Something crashed, and the walls shook, and he could hear his mama crying behind the man's mean voice. "That's where you're wrong. I own you. Don't fucking forget it."

Tears leaked from Ian's eyes, and he tried to burrow under his covers. To cover his ears. He wanted to disappear when his mama came home from work with a man.

Their voices different but always the same.

Terror rippled through Ian's spirit, and he wanted to save his mama. But he was too scared.

Quiet footsteps moved over the carpeted floor.

His big brother was there.

Ian breathed out in relief.

Jace pulled back Ian's covers, crawled into bed beside him, and wrapped him in his arms.

"I've got you, Ian. Don't be scared."

Don't be scared.

Don't be scared.

Scared was the last thing Ian wanted to be.

GRACE

I was already out the front door and running for the curb when the car came to a stop. So, what if it made me look desperate and needy. That was exactly what I was.

It really didn't matter all that much if I was showing an iota of vulnerability, anyway. I should have known it wouldn't be Reed who'd take the time to deliver his children back to me at the end of their visit.

I refused the spike of anger that wanted to climb into my feelings. Not right then. The only thing that mattered was they were home.

Safe.

Where they belonged.

We were going to make it. We would. Whatever it took.

Reed's driver, Riggs, put the big sedan in park and climbed out. He really didn't need to bother. My children were already pouring out, Mallory darting across the lawn with her arms thrown in the air.

My pulse spiked, joy hitting me hard.

I didn't even stop walking as I scooped her up, hugged her close. Breathed her in.

"There's my Mal Pal. I missed you so much."

I knew there was no way she could understand just how much that was.

Her little arms wound around my neck. "I missed you all the way to the moon!"

"All the way to the moon?" I teased. "Well, I missed you all the way to the sun and the stars and right back again."

"No way. You didn't have time to get that far."

"But what if I had a spaceship?"

"A spaceship?" Her little voice lifted in excited awe, as if we were already writing another chapter in our story.

We just might need one for a getaway.

I was holding her as I moved across the lawn and toward the car, my eyes on my Thomas, who looked like he was holding the weight of the world on his little shoulders.

I knew he was.

Our fragile world.

The child trying to be the caretaker, the protector of his sisters while they were away, continuing our stories as if they were here, as if it was me who was whispering in their ears.

He helped Sophie down.

Only she immediately tripped and fell onto her hands and knees.

I was hit with the urge to run for her. To shield her from any pain.

But my wild thing popped back up as if nothing had happened, sending me a smile with a row of her tiny teeth, gaps in between them, happiness radiating from her little body. "I do it, Momma!"

With a brush of my fingers through her hair, I set Mallory onto her feet, and she ran over to Riggs who was unloading her little pink suitcase from the trunk.

Sophie lifted her hands in the air, those chubby legs toddling my direction. "Momma now."

Momma now.

Momma forever.

I picked her up, filling my nose with her sweet scent, baby powder and the promise of spring. I spun us around, and she squealed, "I fly!"

Soft laughter rolled from me, at one with the peace of the late afternoon air, and I carried Sophie the rest of the way over so I could set my hand on Thomas's back.

I leaned in to whisper at his ear, "There's my brave boy."

He grimaced, and I knew he was contemplating playing indifferent, the big man who shouldn't show his feelings, which I was sure Reed had fed into his brain over the last two days.

"Sweet boy," I murmured, trying to reach him.

For a second, he hesitated before he threw himself at me and burrowed his face against my belly. "Mom. I missed you."

"It's okay, Thomas. I'm right here. I'm so sorry." I let him cry, these big, angry sobs that erupted from him, one of my arms around his shoulders while I kept Sophie situated on my hip as I tried to silently give him all the encouragement I could find.

The promise that we would be fine. That this would soon be over.

The faith that it would work out.

No matter what.

Like Gramma had said, some things were just too right to go wrong.

Riggs tried to hide the sympathy in his face, the old man always so kind in all the years I'd lived at Reed's house.

"Here you go, ma'am," he told me as he pulled the rest of their things out of the trunk. They had stuff at Reed's—ridiculous, expensive things—and I made sure to send them with familiar toys and clothes that would make them feel comfortable every time they went.

"Thank you," I told him, my voice hoarse, part of me wanting to beg him to tell me anything he could. To give me any ammo. I was sure he had plenty.

But his loyalty had always been to the Dearborne family. Born into it, his mother had been Reed's nanny until he no longer required one, and Riggs had quickly acquired a spot.

"It's an honor to drive your children."

"I wish it wasn't necessary." The admission hung between us. A bridge I was asking him to cross.

He slammed the trunk closed. "I do hope you and Mr. Dearborne find a resolution soon."

He glanced at all the children, giving them a soft wave and a big smile.

Mallory giggled when he did. "Bye-bye, Mr. Riggity Rigg! I see you soon."

At least Mallory could always find the bright side. The child so full of love she didn't know anything else.

Thomas grabbed his and Sophie's suitcases and turned toward the house.

My grandmother was there at the end of the walk, arms wide open. "There are the greatest great-grandchildren in all the land."

Mallory danced across the lawn, doing a twirl and a jump, and landing at my grandmother's feet like a prize. "Did you see that, Grams? One day, I'm going to be in the Russian Ballet."

Thomas snickered as he headed toward them. "Don't you have to be Russian?"

Mallory scowled at him, and I chuckled under my breath, heading back up through the lawn.

The engine hummed as Riggs pulled from the curb.

Halfway to Gramma, I froze.

Awareness nipped at my senses and sent the fine hairs at my neck spiking with electricity, stomach turning itself into a thousand knots.

Oh.

My heart started to race, and I slowly shifted to look over my shoulder.

Wary and terrified and filling right up with the hope that seemed so impossible to find until I saw him standing there.

The most gorgeous man I'd ever seen. The most gorgeous man I'd ever touched.

He was across the road with his hands stuffed in his pockets.

Dressed in a suit, polished, his face masculine and rough.

A perfect package.

A perfectly, imperfect gift.

nineteen

IAN

I stood on the opposite side of the road with a lump the size of a meteor in my throat. It might as well have been. Knowing the feeling that had put it there was going to completely wipe me out.

Desolate and destroy.

Those eyes were on me.

A blue, mesmerizing sea. Soft and sweet and filled with so much relief that my first inclination was to turn and run.

Especially when I was looking at the evidence of her kids.

The little girl in her arms. Two children standing at the feet of an old woman who was watching me, too.

A chilly breeze weaved through the colossal trees of the quaint neighborhood, while I was pretty sure I was being burned alive.

At the stake.

Grace slowly set the tiny, white-haired girl onto her feet, saying something to the woman who stretched out her hand for the little girl.

The older woman wrangled all three kids, shooing them and trying to get their bags into the house, sparing me a glance before she disappeared inside.

A warning.

That same kind of protection I so often found Jace watching me with.

Fierceness.

Loyalty.

The kind you didn't mess with.

Message received.

Grace watched until the door shut before she slowly turned back to face me. Fitted jeans and a pink chunky sweater and that sweet, sweet heart.

Fuck.

I was in trouble.

Had no idea what I was doing there. What I was thinking. The only thing I knew was I'd been doing all this shady shit for Lawrence, fostering God knew what, how could I not help her?

Maybe I could do something good in the middle of all my bad. Right a wrong.

Didn't mean it wasn't going to be brutal.

Gathering myself, I started across the road while the girl just stood there with the wind rustling through her soft, soft hair, so damned pretty she was again making it hard to breathe.

God, that pissed me off, too.

She was too much.

More than I could handle.

Some kind of motherfucking test.

I felt it.

I was either going to pass or fail, but I had to do this.

That energy tumbled along the ground as I approached, a shiver across her skin that she passed right off to me.

Teeth clenched, I stopped two feet away, and shoved my

damned hands back into my pockets so I didn't reach out and touch her.

"Ian," she whispered.

"You need an attorney?"

Her eyes moved over me. "Yes."

"You want me to represent you?"

She blinked. "I'm not sure I could trust anyone else."

Trust.

She really didn't know me, did she?

She glanced over her shoulder. "They're my life, and no one wants to take a chance on that."

She looked back at me.

"Except you?" Her tone shifted into a question.

A plea.

Adoration.

My stomach fisted.

Yup.

Brutal.

I took a step closer, breathing her in, delicious plum and sugared petals. "You know I can't touch you. Never again. And no one can know that I did."

Something decadent flashed through her eyes. Like she was watching it in rewind.

Against the wall.

In my shower.

Me holding her in my bed.

Her delicate throat bobbed as she tipped her face up so she could meet the steely determination in my gaze. "I know that. They are worth the sacrifice."

Slowly I nodded, voice coming out harder than it should. "They'd better be."

Wasn't exactly the type of sacrifice I was eager to make.

Not when I wanted to revisit all those scenes on repeat.

I rocked back on my heels, trying to get some space between us before I shoved my nose against her throat. "Not exactly a fan of kids."

Surprise had her stepping back. "How's that?"

I waved at the small house. "Because then they get wrapped up in shit like this."

Hurt dimmed her features. "You think I ever meant for them to get hurt?"

Old anger simmered in that pit inside me. "Not sure anyone does. It's all the bad choices people make along the way that get them there."

She slowly nodded, rubbing her lips together, glancing into the distance as a mini-van drove by.

Without question, I was wounding her.

But she needed to know where I stood.

And that was with distance between us.

I had to do this without emotion. Without caring about her or them. Nothing but the job.

That was what this would be.

Finally, she shifted her attention back to me, something fierce slashing across her face. "I might have begged you yesterday, Ian. I don't regret it. Not for a second. I've always been willing to do whatever it took for my children. To erase the bad *choices* I've made. And I won't stand here and pretend as if I haven't made terrible ones. I was responsible from the beginning. Settling when I shouldn't have. But *everything* I did was because I wanted the best for them. Because I've always loved my children more than anything else."

She crossed her arms over her chest, seeking distance, too. "And if you're not willing to fight for that? Believe in that? I will find someone who will."

"This is just another case, Grace. You can rest assured that I will give it everything I have. Just like I do with every client I represent. I work my ass off for my clients. Not because I am a champion of their cause, but because it's what they pay me to do."

With a streak of fiery disappointment, she turned her chin up at me. "So that's how it's gonna be?"

"That's how it has to be. This is going to be hard enough."

I was already crossing so many lines, I'd left sanity behind. Representing her was like volunteering to stand in the front row of a firing squad.

Wasn't sure I was going to make it out of this one standing.

Going against Reed Dearborne.

Risking Kenneth flaying me alive for putting the reputation of the firm on the line.

Not to mention the only thing I wanted to do was peel her out of those jeans and sink my dick right back into all that sweet heat.

But I was going to do this. For once in my life, I was going to do something that didn't benefit me. For once, I was going to do one thing right.

Another nod, and she inhaled a deep breath, the girl plastering neutrality onto her face. "Well, then, Mr. Jacobs. It's so kind of you to come all the way to my grandmother's home to take on this case. How do we proceed?"

The breath I took in was steeling. On the name of all things holy, what had I done? "I'm going to need to interview you and your children. Get a history, and then we can formulate a plan."

My voice dropped, and I angled my head. "You tell me only what you want me to know, do you understand?"

Shame flickered through her eyes.

No question.

She'd taken that money.

Those fat stacks of cash in that bag nothing but a confession.

God, I really was insane.

"I understand," she whispered.

"Do you?" I murmured.

"Yes." It was a wisp.

I lifted my chin. "Good. We'd better get started."

She led me into the modest house that hailed straight out of the eighties and smelled like freshly-baked biscuits.

My mouth watered, and my stomach growled.

Voices rambled from somewhere down a hall, a babbling baby and a boy and the older woman, a little girl butchering the lyrics of an overplayed pop song as she sang over the top of them.

Warmth and peace and complete chaos.

Irritation bubbled in my blood.

"This will probably be the most comfortable." Grace made an immediate right through an archway that led into a dated kitchen.

There was a worn round table under a window that looked out front.

"Have a seat. Can I get you anything to drink?"

I cleared my throat that was still sporting that meteor. "A water would be nice."

She gave a tight nod. Tension wound between us, the fact we were trying to be something I was pretty sure we weren't intended, client and attorney when really, we were kindling and fire.

She went to the sink and filled a glass with tap water. Her fingers brushed mine when she set it down on the table in front of me.

My dick jumped while the rest of my body flinched.

She breathed out a heavy sound, her chest lurching forward, no doubt feeling it, too. Her voice was soft when she murmured close to my ear, "Before we start, I want you to know how much this means to me. That you're doing this for us. I've felt so alone for all these months, waiting for a miracle. I had no idea that miracle was going to be you."

I tried to block her words from seeping into that crack in my chest. The girl getting her fingers right in there and tugging it apart. Trying to bust it wide open.

"I'm no miracle, Grace. I could be your worst nightmare. This could all blow up in your face. You need to know, this will not be an easy win. They are going to try to smear you. They will drag out every secret you have, parade around your skeletons."

Her trembling chin lifted defiantly. "I'm not the only one with secrets."

Hatred churned. I'd done a little research on Reed Dearborne this morning, stared a little too long at the pompous ass, his record as clean as the floor his maid surely scrubbed every day.

But it was all *too* perfect.

Wrapped up in a pretty red bow.

An illusion.

I knew it.

Was betting Grace knew it in a way that made my guts curl.

"You're going to need to let me in on that."

She breathed out a shaky sound and slumped into the wooden

chair beside me. "I'd like to avoid using that if at all possible."

"He won't hesitate to destroy you, Grace."

And that made me want to destroy him.

Her head shook. "I just . . . need to figure out how to do this with him thinking he's getting the best thing for himself. For his campaign. For his life. I think he'd much rather keep this on the downlow than have the whole thing explode on the media."

"I think you're fooling yourself. I think you're a threat to his pride, and that's something he won't settle for."

"It's more than that. He's afraid if I'm outside of his control, I'll expose the things I know."

Anger boiled. "Has he ever hurt you before? Physically?"

Wounds streaked through her eyes, and I was half a second from flying to my feet and out the door.

Fuck the case.

The asshole could die by my bare hands.

"Once," she said, her voice a tremor. "I'd left him back before Sophie was born. He didn't take so kindly to it."

She coughed out a horrified sound, like she was taken back to the memory. "He . . . forced me back into the house. Forced himself on me. Made it clear if I ever left again, I was going to regret it."

That lump throbbed in my throat, my chest squeezing too tight. I really didn't know if I could stomach any of this. Not when there was this ugly, nasty part of me that wanted to claim her as mine.

Take her and keep her.

My hands fisted. "He forced himself on you as in—"

The hostility on my tongue was cut off when a shouting voice broke into what I was going to say. "Mommy, Mommy!"

Grace's face split into a forced smile when a little girl came bounding around the corner and into the kitchen.

The child skidded to a stop when she saw me sitting at the table.

My heart got scrambled in my chest.

Big, blue eyes stared back at me. The same color as her mother's. Kid exuding nothing but love and hope and excitement.

Bile worked its way around that lump.

This . . . this was what I couldn't reconcile. The fact this woman I wanted to own, to take, had three children.

Three children she was responsible for.

For their safety and their happiness and their wellbeing.

Foolish.

That's what this was.

Part of me couldn't help but hold it against Grace. This recklessness on her part. Bringing these kids into this world and then turning around and dumping them into this mess.

"Hey, mister! Who are you?"

She was holding a big brown drawing pad, two times wider than the width of her entire body, little arms stretched around it. Blonde hair straight as a pin and perfectly trimmed at her shoulders, short bangs framing her curious face.

There was no hesitation when she rushed forward and climbed onto the chair on the other side of me. She set the thick pad in front of her on the table.

Instantly, I had the weight of the two of them bracketing me on either side.

My collar felt too damned tight.

Grace stood and moved around me to the little girl and ran her palm over her head. The child tipped her head back, grinning up at her mother like she was the sun.

Grace glanced at me, so much tenderness in her expression that it nearly knocked me from my seat. "This is my Mal Pal. Mallory Paloma."

Mallory gave an extravagant wave of her hand in her mother's direction, like she was some kind of gameshow hostess. "And this is the best mommy in the whole wide world. She loves me to the sun and the stars and back again because she has a super-fast spaceship."

She threw open the heavy cover of the pad and flipped through a ton of scribbled on pages.

It looked like . . . like some kind of storybook.

Picture after picture of the same characters with words written across them, some in children's hand and other's in a scripty font

216

that my gut instantly told me belonged to Grace.

Mallory pointed at the last page with a drawing. "I just colored this one right now. Mommy's spaceship goes a million miles an hour and uses fairy dust for gas and can find all of us in the night if she is looking for us because it has super-secret seeking powers."

She ran her index finger over the lines of the picture she'd drawn, completely excited when she looked up at her mother. "I need you to put in all the words, Mommy. Just like I said. Exactly like that. Don't mess 'em up. See that fairy dust right there?"

On her knees, she leaned toward me, her voice lowering like she was letting me in on a secret. "I don't know how to spell it because it has way too many letters and my teacher hasn't taught me yet. But I'm still a writer even if I don't write the words."

The last was absolute.

No room for interpretation.

The child was like a bottled soda that had been shaken and opened under the pressure. Everything flooding from her at the speed of light.

I gave her a tight nod. "I'll remember that."

"You better."

I choked back a laugh.

Okay then.

Grace stifled one too, her smile going soft when she angled her head toward me. "Mallory, this is Mr. Jacobs. He's going to help us talk to your father so that you'll be able to sleep here most of the time. He needs to ask you a couple of questions."

I could hear the air rushing down the kid's throat as her eyes grew round. "You mean we got our hero?!"

She rammed her hands together, threading her fingers and pushing them up under her chin like she was thanking God for an answered prayer.

Then she got serious. "Guess I got a lot of work to do in the story, Mommy."

Good God. How was I supposed to handle this child? The fact that they were relying on me for something so important? Her presence alone was about to bowl me over, and there she was, tossing ball after ball.

Those big blue eyes were on me. "Mr. Jacobs, what is your hero name? We got to get it right."

I cleared the roughness from my voice. "Ian, I suppose."

Her brow twisted up in some kind of abject horror. "Ian? That's a terrible hero name."

Of course, it was. Maybe the kid was reading me clearer than I thought.

She tapped her chin and looked at her drawing before she gasped out a thrill. "I got it! How about Ian-Zian the Great?"

"I'm not sure Mr. Jacobs wants to be a part of our story, Mal Pal," Grace hedged, that knowing gaze bouncing between the two of us, almost apologetic every time it landed on me.

I kind of wanted to shout at her. To tell her to quit calling me that. To tell her this was all going to be too much.

I'd made a mistake, coming here.

Hell, I'd made one that first night. Chasing after a girl when I didn't play chase.

Mallory looked at her mother like she had lost her mind.

"Why would he not want to be a part of our story? Our story is the funnest, most best adventure in the whole universe."

Her attention darted to me, voice so matter-of-fact that this time there was no stopping the laugh. "It's going to be a bestseller."

"I have no doubt," I told her.

She shrugged a little shoulder. "Doubts are for worriers."

This child was something else.

Grace suddenly shrieked. "Gah, Sophie, no!"

She flew around, and I shifted just in time to see a child who wasn't more than a baby running into the kitchen, three crayons fisted in her chubby hand.

All three tips were being dragged across the wall.

She squealed with laughter as her mother chased her.

"Sophie! No. Coloring is only for paper."

She swiped the kid off her feet, but not before she'd left squiggly lines of blue, red, and orange on a quarter of the wall about a foot from the ground.

"I *cowar*." She was all grins and small teeth.

"Yes, you can color, but only on paper."

Mallory shook her head. "My little sister is nothin' but a handful. Ask Grams."

Grace pried the crayons from the baby's hand. The child screamed and stretched her arm back out from them. "Give, Sophie! Mine!"

Sighing, Grace tossed the crayons on to the table, where they promptly rolled off and landed on the floor. She bounced the baby on her hip and looked at me. "This is Sophie Marie, who is, in fact, a handful."

With the last she smacked a kiss to the child's temple, the kid going from screaming to giggling in a second flat, Grace nuzzling her nose to the child's fat, rosy cheek.

I just sat there.

Realizing this all had to be a bad dream.

That was it.

I'd drank too much last night, and none of this was real.

Grace was a figment and her kids were a fabricated illusion sent to test my mind.

My will.

Then my eyes were going round, and a shocked shot of air jumped out of my lungs as cold liquid pooled on the front of my pants and soaked through to my dick, which was already having a really terrible day.

My attention jerked to the little girl who had crawled on top of the table to get an apple from the fruit bowl and had knocked over my glass of water in the process.

"Oopsie," *Mal Pal* said with another one of those little shrugs and a grin.

Motherfuck.

It wasn't an illusion.

It was just hell.

I glared at the kid. She and I were definitely not *pals*.

"Oh, goodness, Mal, look what you did," Grace said, blowing out a frustrated sigh that somehow sounded like love.

She set Sophie on her feet—the kid who immediately went for the crayons rolling around on the floor—and grabbed a dish towel to clean up the mess.

Didn't take but a second for the *handful* to start scribbling on the old linoleum floor.

Towel in hand, Grace rushed for me, not giving it a thought when she started rubbing the wet spot on my crotch.

Not helping things.

Because it was instant. The way my wayward dick reacted, desperate for the girl to give it a little love and kiss all this bullshit better.

A needy groan rumbled in my chest, and Grace inhaled sharply, like she felt the lust start seeping from my skin and climb to the air.

My jaw hardened, and I grabbed the towel. "I think I can manage, thank you."

She bit down on her bottom lip. I couldn't tell if she wanted to laugh or cry.

Crying sounded like a great idea.

Two seconds more, and I'd be rocking in a corner, sucking my thumb.

"Oh, God, I'm sorry," Grace whispered as she tried to hold back the amusement that was clearly playing around her pretty face.

"Ian-Zian the Great and his pee-pee pants."

Mal Pal.

I sent her a glare.

"What?" the child asked, way too sweet. "You got pee-pee pants."

Grace barked out a laugh, no longer able to keep it contained.

My teeth gritted, and I buried my face in the towel. Like maybe I could up and disappear into it.

Refuse this craziness I was feeling.

Suffocated and warm and cold.

Made me feel like I was being stretched thin.

Torn apart.

I choked down the emotions and forced myself to grab on to the professionalism I'd perfected. That was the only thing I could do. What I was there for in the first place. "Mallory, since you're an author and all, would you happen to have a notebook I could borrow?"

"Yes! Oh, yes, oh, yes, I got the best one ever as a present for my birthday and it's really pretty and since you're the hero, I'll give it to you." She scrambled down with a fist pump into the air and a leap.

Ballerina or unicorn, I couldn't tell.

Either way, the kid apparently thought she was saving her crazy imaginary world.

She disappeared through the archway, her feet pounding down the hall, and I went back to dabbing the towel on my still hard cock I was half inclined to beat into submission.

Or maybe I could just ask Grace for the favor.

Yeah.

Not going to happen.

Not ever.

And that shit was just sad.

I was still looking down when I felt those eyes on me. That energy zapped between us.

A live wire.

Thrumming through the space.

I was pretty sure it was going to be the biggest problem of all.

Bigger than these damned kids or her damned situation or her damned mouth that I wanted to devour.

Because I couldn't help but look up. Couldn't help but get lost in that overpowering gaze and that tender smile. "Thank you, Ian. Thank you so much."

"I haven't done anything yet."

"Except show up at my door. That's the most important thing of all."

I turned away, scrubbing some more at my pants, unable or unwilling to respond.

Wasn't sure which.

The only thing I knew was I couldn't take her gratitude. Didn't deserve it.

A minute later, Mallory was back with a pink pad and an array of pink pens for me to choose from.

Awesome.

"Here you go, Ian-Zian."

Grace reached over, tore a piece of paper from it, and gave it to the little girl on the ground who rolled onto her belly and started scribbling on the blank sheet.

"I get paper!" the tiny girl hollered up at me from the floor. She stuck out one of the crayons she gripped in her chubby fist, grinning at me like I wasn't some kind of stranger and she knew me and she was eager for my approval.

I was pretty sure Grace's children had declared anarchy.

Didn't think it could get worse.

Oh, but it could.

Because my lungs locked up tight when a young boy came around the corner.

All scowls and bad attitude and messy, sandy-blond hair.

He reminded me so much of myself at that age that it took about everything I had not to go bolting out the door.

When she saw him, Grace softened and moved to where the kid had come to a stop in the archway. He stood there, taking me in with nothing but hostility.

She touched his cheek, his chin, so soft.

I didn't want to watch it.

That real kind of love every kid deserved to feel.

To know their mom would be there for them when they woke up, no matter what.

And this kid might have that taken away.

I couldn't stand—

"Thomas, this is Mr. Jacobs. He's an attorney who is going to represent our case." Grace started talking before I had the chance to finish the thought.

There was no missing the way her words had changed for him, no doubt the boy far too aware of the direness of their situation.

The hopelessness.

From out of nowhere, an overwhelming emotion charged through my being.

Determination girding every cell.

Emphatic.

Different from dedication and tenacity.

This felt like . . . purpose.

And that right there scared the living shit out of me.

The kid looked at me as if he were adding me up. Calculating the threat.

Wary, he looked back at his mom. "What if he works for him?"

I frowned. "What does that mean?"

Thomas laughed. "Everyone does. Dad gets what Dad wants. Right?"

Scorn. It oozed from his every pore.

"And what is it you want?" I asked, grabbing the notebook, knowing the kid was going to be a challenge, but he was also probably my best source.

My best witness.

Hell, the little girl could probably be swayed by a lollipop and a trip to the local bookstore.

Not this kid.

He lifted his chin. "I want to protect my mom."

Huh.

Guessed the kid and I were on the same page, after all.

GRACE

I hovered.

Chewing at my nails and fighting the ball of emotion that had my insides twisted in a knot, every part of me wound up and held in Ian's hands.

Thomas sat in the chair beside him, antsy, knee bouncing a hundred miles a minute under the table while Ian remained calm and casual, as if our worlds weren't hanging in the balance.

But that didn't mean I didn't feel the intensity radiating from him.

The care.

Even when he didn't want to admit it.

This beautiful, rough man who I wanted to reach out to and

just . . . hug. Let him hold me and pray I could maybe hold a bit of him. But I knew that was impossible.

Our lines had been drawn.

Boundaries made.

"And how do you feel when you have to visit your father's house?"

Thomas scowled and crossed his arms over his thin chest, which I was sure one day would be massive. My little boy who I knew would become a good, good man. "I hate it. I mean . . . I don't get why he even wants us over there. He's always busy and working and we don't even see him. Eva takes care of us the whole time."

Ian jotted something on the pink pad. "Who's Eva?"

"Our nanny."

Ian glanced at me. I paced a little more, hugging myself, trying not to get too excited, too hopeful, because I knew what Ian had said was true.

This wasn't going to be an easy win.

But we were going to fight it. Win it. I knew it.

Could feel relief spinning through the air, getting caught up in the power of that energy.

"How does that make you feel . . . that the nanny takes care of you?"

Thomas shrugged. "Like it's a waste of time. And when we do see our dad, he's always asking questions. Wanting to know what our mom is doing. Telling us to tell her that we want to go home. And then other times, he says mean things about her. It makes me . . ."

Thomas glanced over at me, his lips collapsing in a grim line. I got the distinct impression he didn't want to admit it in front of me.

As if he were trying to protect me.

My big, brave, little man.

He turned back to Ian and lowered his voice. "It makes me angry and mad and worried. I don't like it."

Ian shifted the pad, his question carefully constructed. "What is it about what he says that makes you worry, Thomas? Can you remember anything specific that he has said?"

Thomas worked his jaw, hesitating, the words cracking when he finally forced them out. "He said she was going to regret it. That she was never going to get away with blackmailing him."

That word pierced me like an arrow.

It wasn't what it was supposed to come to. Wasn't what I wanted. But I had been left without a choice.

I also knew Reed would make good on that threat.

He wanted to make me regret it.

He thought I'd made him look bad.

Put him in this position.

Left him.

He should have known there was no chance I'd stay.

Ian looked down and fidgeted with the pen before he looked back at my son. "Have you ever heard him say anything . . . specific. About how he might make your mom regret the choice she made? Any sort of threat? Anything about hurting her physically?"

Every cell in Thomas's body froze, and I swore I could see it.

A cold dread that visibly shook down his spine.

In pain, he looked back at me, and I saw the hint of tears brim in his eyes, as if maybe my child thought he was the one who was hurting me.

It's okay, I mouthed.

I could almost hear his back creaking as he turned to lean toward Ian. He whispered so low I wasn't certain I'd heard him right. "Not my dad . . . but . . . but his friend."

Horror raced through my being, my mouth going dry when I realized this was no longer intimidation thrown around by Reed.

I could feel the blast of fury that shivered through the air. This protective anger unlike anything I'd experienced before.

It came from Ian in violent waves.

He edged forward, clearly trying to keep his cool when it was completely fading. "What friend?"

Thomas shook his head with unfound guilt. "I . . . I don't know. I didn't see him. They were in Dad's office. The man . . . he said . . . he said bitches who don't obey need to bleed."

Shock jetted from my mouth, and I tried not to show my fear. The way chills skated my flesh and nausea roiled in my stomach.

Ian's eyes squeezed closed, and he clutched the pen, seeming to have to brace himself.

Remorsefully, Thomas looked back at me, his voice half apology, half defense. "I'm sorry for saying a bad word, Mom, but he asked."

"You aren't in trouble, Thomas. Not at all."

Ian shocked me when he reached out and touched Thomas's arm. Thomas jerked his attention that way. "You're not in trouble. I promise. You can tell me anything, and you won't get in trouble. You can trust me. Do you understand?"

Thomas gave a shaky nod.

"Can you remember anything else?" Ian prodded.

Shame drooped Thomas's shoulders. "No . . . I . . . I should have gone right in there and punched that guy in the face. But I was too much of a coward, like my dad told me I am. God . . . I . . . sometimes I hate myself."

Anger and sorrow.

They surged.

Washing me through.

Tears sprang to my eyes.

That bastard Reed.

I hated him.

Hated that he was manipulating our children every bit as much as he had manipulated me.

"You aren't a coward, Thomas." Ian's voice resembled a growl, his words muttered as he inched closer to Thomas, as if he wanted them to sink inside. "Not even close. Don't let anyone tell you that. Don't let anyone make you think you're less than you are. You're showing how brave you are, right now, telling us all of this."

Hesitation rolled from Ian, the man clearly trying to find his words, his tongue swiping across his bottom lip before he started to speak again. "The only thing confronting your father or his friend would accomplish would have been you getting hurt. Our main concern is your safety. The safety of your sisters. Okay? So, if you hear anything, you pretend like you didn't, and then you come to me. Do you understand?"

Thomas nodded again. "Okay."

"Okay," Ian agreed, and I could sense the urgency that rattled him to the bones.

The man so powerful.

So fierce.

The intensity of it ricocheted from the walls.

It made me both afraid and comforted.

"I think that's it for now. But if you think of anything else, need anything else, or are ever in trouble, I want you to call me. Can you memorize this number?"

Ian shifted forward, took out his wallet, and pulled out a business card. He handed it to my son.

Thomas stared at it, his mouth silently repeating the numbers over and over as he committed them to memory. "Got it."

"Good boy."

Thomas grinned in pride.

My heart almost shattered.

Thomas pushed to his feet and glanced over at me. "Can I have my tablet now?"

"Yes, just be ready for dinner in an hour."

"Yeah, yeah." He lumbered out the archway.

There was my grumbling boy.

I watched him until he disappeared, my eyes pinned on that spot, unable to look back at Ian who I knew was watching me.

I could feel it.

The heat searing across my flesh.

The way my heart tumbled and thrashed and sped.

Finally, the lure of it was too strong, and I looked his way.

Ian held me in the grips of his gaze. There was something so hard and angry there. Something so volatile and explosive. All of it for me. For my children.

Ian blinked as if he had to break himself from the trance we were under, and he pushed to his feet and flipped the cover of the notebook closed. He lifted it in the air. "Let's hope Mack doesn't see me with this."

A giggle burst free, coming from the depths of the strain and butting against the absurdity of it all.

How had we ended up here?

"Don't laugh," he said, but there was something playing at the corner of his mouth.

"How can I not?"

He waved it around. "I better get out of here before she draws me into your story with a tiara and a pink cape."

"No capes. Don't you know anything?"

A twitch of a smile danced around his gorgeous mouth before he staunched it and tucked the notepad under his arm.

There he was.

So good under all that brash.

I followed him out of the kitchen and into the small foyer. Voices drifted in from the living room, my grandmother keeping the girls busy while Ian had asked Thomas questions.

Ian opened the door and stepped out into the cool, late afternoon, fall approaching quickly, the leaves on the trees spinning from green into gold.

Stepping out behind him, I hugged myself as another rush of gratitude prepared to gush from my lips.

I didn't get a chance before I was gasping, shocked when Ian suddenly spun around, the powerful man backing me into the far corner of the stoop.

We were hidden behind a large shrub that crawled up the trellis and reached all the way to the eaves.

He kept coming toward me until my back thudded against the wall, and there was nothing I could do but breathe in the man.

Cinnamon and orange and delicious, mind-numbing sex.

I could almost taste him on my tongue.

My mouth watered, and my tummy tilted.

"You and I . . . we need to talk. Lay this all out. I need to know everything."

I could barely nod. "I know."

"I . . ." Ian curled his fist against the wall at the side of my head.

It was palpable.

The way violence skated across his skin.

"I hate him, Grace. I hate him for putting you through this. For putting that fear in your son's eyes." His voice dropped in menace. "I hate him that he ever touched you."

He dipped in closer, his breath gliding across my face and sinking into my soul. "How fucked up is that? That I want to destroy this guy, take him out, because you once belonged to him?"

Emotion tangled around my heart. Tightening and tightening. "I thought you said this was just another case?"

Ian laughed a bitter sound. "I think you and I know better than that. You . . ."

His head angled to the side, the man searching for restraint. "You drive me insane. How's it possible I let you get under my skin like this?"

"Do you think I don't feel the same? I don't even recognize myself around you."

He dropped his forehead to mine. "I can't have you."

"I wish you could. Maybe in another life."

Somberness bled out, his lips parting on a soft chuckle that rang with pain. "That's too bad, considering we're only given one."

A tremble rippled between the two of us.

He inhaled against my temple. "You're going to ruin me, Angel Girl."

"And you're going to save me."

"That's the intention." He pulled back, gazing down at me with those penetrating eyes. "Do you trust me? Do you trust me to do this? If I fail you—"

I reached out and pressed two fingers to his lips before he could get it out. "The only thing I ever asked is that you take a chance on me. On us."

He was still right there, in my space, the distance between us bare and alive. Blistering and boiling with that energy. He ran his nose up the curve of my jaw and to my ear.

Oh God.

This was so not good.

His lips moved against the sensitive flesh. "Just one thing . . .

230

did you love him?"

He pulled back to take in the truth he knew he would find in my eyes.

"I did . . . once I did . . . before he ruined all the faith I had."

He stepped back and nodded. "Tomorrow. Be in my office at nine. You tell me everything."

"Okay."

He reached out and grabbed just the tip of my two fingers. He swung our arms between us for a moment, so much there, electricity in his touch.

Fire and need.

The hardest part was feeling the undercurrent of sweetness that passed through it all.

"Tomorrow," he told me.

Then he spun on his heel and bounded down the single step, leaving me standing there against the wall heaving for a breath.

I shook myself off and forced myself to go back inside.

I could hear *Wheel of Fortune* blaring from the family room, my grandmother's favorite show. Of course, she wasn't even in the room, instead moving around the kitchen as she started to prepare dinner.

Mallory's voice was elevated over the television, the child singing about an affinity for big butts.

Apparently, our lives really had spun out of control.

I went into the kitchen where my grandmother had put Sophie into her high chair, my baby girl shoveling orange slices and dry Cheerios into her mouth. I kissed her head and then looked up at my grandmother, who stood facing away at the stove.

"Good meeting?" she asked.

"Yeah, I think so."

She looked at me, one hundred percent appraising and just as accusing. "He's awfully handsome."

"Yes, he is, but that doesn't have anything to do with what he's doing for us."

She arched a brow as she dumped fresh green beans in to boiling water. "Doesn't it?"

"No."

She chuckled under her breath. "I might be old, but I'm not senile."

I moved across the kitchen and leaned against the counter.

"Where were you the other night?" she asked so casually. As if her question didn't punch me in the gut.

God.

The woman was a bloodhound.

"Out." I went for casual, too.

"With who?"

I shrugged and murmured, "No one special."

She shook her head. "You think I didn't notice you sneakin' in here at four in the mornin', hair all matted and wild, looking like you'd gone a round or two with the devil. What's that they call it these days? Freshly fucked?"

Horrified, my eyes darted around the kitchen, praying my daughter hadn't heard. "Gramma," I hissed under my breath.

She shrugged, all nonchalant. "Oh, come on, Grace, you have three children, so I don't think it's necessary for me to sit you down and give you another talk about the birds and the bees, and there you are with your cheeks as red as a clown's."

My lips pursed. Maybe she was right. That was what it'd felt like with Ian. New and overwhelming and perfect.

Being touched that way.

Powerfully controlled and knowing I couldn't be in safer arms.

Letting myself go.

Getting lost.

It was something I'd never experienced before.

My grandmother grabbed me by the chin and searched my face. "That's what I thought. You did take a tumble with the devil."

I'm the devil.

Ian's warning spun through my mind. I wondered if my grandmother had heard it, too.

"Is that what you think he is? Because it sure seems to me as if he's here to help us."

"Or get back into your pants."

"The exact opposite. Us never mentioning what happened the

other night is one of his stipulations for helping."

Still smiling, she shook her head. "All I'm saying is he *is* a man. Most men know exactly what it is that they want. And that one looks at you like he's bound to eat you."

I wished.

"Two of you were about to light up this room. That's why I didn't start dinner . . . couldn't risk turning on the gas stove. Whole place might have blown."

"Gramma." It was all a scolding. "Besides, what were you doing up at four in the mornin' when the kids weren't here?"

"Might have been out taking me a tumble with one of those old devils myself." She winked, stirring the pot.

I faked plugging my ears with my fingers. "Na-na-na-na."

"Na-na-na-na," Sophie mimicked, laughing manically when I looked her way.

I turned back to my grandmother. "You're a horrible influence."

"Nothing wrong with a little fun." Something went soft about her, and she was watching me in a different way. "You know that, right? Especially with a man that looks like that."

She was right back to waggling her brows.

I rolled my eyes. "That's not going to happen. He's my attorney. That's it. It can't go any farther than that. He's doing this for me, and the last thing I want to do is get him into trouble. He laid out the rules, and we're going to follow them."

"Didn't anyone tell you rules are made to be broken?"

"Says the woman who had me grounded for half my life."

"You were a troublemaker." Her voice was all a tease.

I huffed out a sound, words going dry. "I'm pretty sure I've broken enough rules."

Gramma shook her head as she placed breaded chicken legs into sizzling oil in a frying pan. "You broke Reed's overbearing rules because that's what a mother does—anything it takes to protect her children."

She was right.

And I'd gladly do it all over again.

IAN

I jumped when my office door swung open without warning. Was it wrong I was disappointed that it wasn't that gorgeous girl blazing through like she did a couple of mornings ago?

Especially with the irate expression Kenneth Millstrom was sporting.

Was I surprised?

Nope.

Irritated and worried and fucking itching like a motherfucker?

Hell yes.

I sat back in my chair and acted like it was any other day. "Good morning, sir."

He stalked in to stand across from me at my desk. "Don't good morning me."

With a frown, I looked up at him, trying to play it off that I didn't have a clue what he was talking about.

"I'm sorry?"

"You're going to be. Care to tell me about the contract I saw you signed with one Grace Dearborne?"

I tugged at the tie around my neck and cleared my throat. "I'd be happy to. I was contacted a couple of days ago by the potential client. We spoke, and I felt hers was a case I could represent. One that deserved to be represented. One that will be an asset to our firm."

He planted his palms on my desk. "An asset?"

I kept my chin lifted, refusing to cower. "Yes, an asset."

"How the hell is going up against Reed Dearborne an asset?"

"You know the kind of recognition and attention a case like this will bring to our firm."

"Yes, and I also know the kind of trouble it will bring. We're talking about Reed Dearborne here. He has the entire state eating out of the palm of his hand. We go up against him, and we become the enemy."

"He's scum." I tried to staunch the emotion that wanted to become a part of the word. It trembled with violence anyway.

"Maybe. But you and I both know that doesn't matter. It's all about perception. And his ex-wife is about to get dragged through the mud. We take her on, and we're going to get dragged right along with her."

"She deserves to be represented, just like anyone else in this country. If we refuse her based simply on who her case is against, we become the bad guys. And you know I'm not afraid to get *dirty*."

His eyes narrowed, searching my face.

The guy was a bulldog. There was a reason he was in the position he was. I could only pray he couldn't sniff me out.

The fact I'd been lost in all that skin and that body and that sweet, broken heart.

"Do you know she came to me the night of the gala and asked me to represent her?" he demanded.

A hard swallow and a short shake of my head. "No, I didn't."

"Reed Dearborne showed up that night as well. Introduced himself. You know in this world, a shake of a hand is an alliance. You understand the position this puts me in?"

"When I win this case, you won't care about that position. The win will speak for itself. You taught me from the beginning that we don't climb to success by taking the easy route. The easy cases and easy wins. We get there by achieving the impossible. By beating every odd. This one might not be easy, but I assure you, in the end, it will be worth it."

A win against Reed Dearborne would give the firm an allusion of power and strength.

Tenacity.

Exactly what men like Kenneth and I were made of.

He pushed off my desk. "You better hope you win. Because if you don't? You're done. This loss won't be pinned on me."

Throat growing dry, I gave a tight nod.

I was putting myself on the line.

My career.

My partnership.

My future.

Everything I'd worked for.

But I refused to consider it a risk.

I was going to win this case. Whatever it took. This win would be the last rung on the ladder to the top.

"I won't let you down."

I wouldn't let myself down.

And for the love of everything that was right, I wouldn't let Grace down.

He moved for the door and pulled it open, pausing to look back at me. "I hope not."

He started out, only to fumble a step, and my heart went racing when I saw her. She was dressed in some kind of goddamned skirt suit, pink and cream and gold, the jacket fitted and the skirt not quite landing at her knees.

A motherfucking vision.

"Ms. Dearborne," he said, agitation lining his posture when he looked back at me as he held the door open for her, the guy sending me a clear and distinct warning.

Don't fuck this up.

"Mr. Millstrom, it's so nice to see you again," she said as she moved into my office, standing on a pair of cream-colored heels.

I tried to remain unaffected.

To pretend like her standing there didn't have me wanting to do crazy, crazy things.

"I only wish I could say the same," Kenneth muttered, not saying anything else as he stepped out and closed the door.

Only thing that managed to do was shut me in with her presence. The feel of her a ripple through the room. She took a step forward, and then another, each one sending another shockwave through the air.

Hammering into my chest.

Blow after blow.

She sat in one of the two chairs that were angled toward my desk, tucking her skirt under her legs as she crossed them at the knee. "Good morning, Mr. Jacobs."

I cleared the roughness from my throat.

Everything raw and hard.

Predominantly my dick.

"Good morning, *Ms. Dearborne*." Couldn't keep the scorn out of my voice when I uttered that name.

She let her teeth scrape over her plump bottom lip, the flesh slicked with something shiny and tinted the color of a plum.

I was going to lose my head.

"I trust you slept well."

Translation: I pictured you all night in your bed, touching yourself while you were thinking of me. Exactly like I did.

"It was a little rough, honestly."

"I can only imagine." There was an innuendo there. Something I couldn't keep out of the words.

"I'm . . . nervous," she admitted.

The anger returned. A vat of hostility poured into my already boiling blood. A chemical reaction.

Possession and this protectiveness I couldn't afford to feel. I reached into my briefcase and pulled out a white notepad.

Grace smirked. "No pink today?'

A soft chuckle rippled free when I thought of the whirlwind that was her child. The tornado that was her life.

"Not today. I tend to go for a more . . . streamlined and organized look."

Maybe there was a warning there. That I couldn't handle the chaos that was their lives. The noise and the love and the responsibility.

My mind was already screaming that I'd taken on too much. But there was something about this girl that made me want to hold it all. Her world and her needs.

God.

I had to stop looking at her like she meant something to me.

Not when she couldn't mean anything.

Not when there was so much at stake.

I needed to put on armor. Put distance between us. Convince myself to treat this as just another case. If I didn't, we were both going to lose, and that wasn't a fate I would entertain.

I cleared my throat. "Shall we get started, Ms. Dearborne?"

"I think that would be a good idea."

"Why don't you start by telling me how you first met Mr. Dearborne."

She hesitated for a moment, looking away, seeming to gather herself. "I was a freshman at The University of South Carolina. Reed was working on his masters. We met in the library of all places. He was older than me by six years. Good looking. Sweet. When he asked me for coffee that same night, I agreed. He was nice to me, and it was easy to fall into a relationship with him."

Every cell in my body tensed. On edge and unprepared.

This was bad.

So goddamned bad.

I focused on taking notes rather than the urge to come unhinged.

But the thought of her touching another man had something cutting me open wide.

I've only been with two men.

Her low laughter sounded of doubt. "I guessed I should have been wary when things started moving so quickly that I couldn't keep up. One day, I was attending school, and the next, he was putting a ring on my finger and telling me he wanted to spend his life with me. It was only a couple of months after we'd met. I'd tried to convince myself that it was because he was older and more mature. That he was ready for things to progress faster than me."

Regret dimmed the light on her striking face. "I should have known I was nothing more than an easy target. A naïve girl who was blinded by his promises."

Her tongue darted out, glancing across the sticky sweetness on her lips. I couldn't help but become fixated on the action. "It became clear pretty quickly that he had his life mapped out. He needed a wife. Someone to stand at his side and make him look like the perfect guy. The perfect husband and the perfect father. I think I was nothing but a diversion to cover who he really was. It kept people from digging deeper into his personal life."

Those eyes found mine over my desk. "I just wanted a regular family, and Reed wanted to rule the world. He was committed to doing absolutely anything he needed to do to achieve it."

I cringed, hating the idea that I could have one thing in common with that asshole.

Her head minutely shook. "You asked me yesterday if I loved him, and I did. But it was never as deeply . . . as passionately . . . as it should have been. But that didn't matter anyway because Reed had his own penchants."

My eyes tracked the way her delicate throat bobbed when she swallowed. "He'd be gone at all hours of the night . . ."

A small hiccup climbed her throat, and tears blurred her eyes. "I'd been certain he was having an affair. I followed him once . . . and I . . . he was actually hooking up with a prostitute. I was shocked, but as time went on, I realized it went deeper than that. My gut screamed that he was crooked. Involved in things that he shouldn't be. Our house full of whispers. All of his meetings carried out behind closed doors. Everything was a secret. He'd begun to threaten me. Trying to control my every move. Mold me into who he wanted me to be, and that was someone who kept her mouth shut and turned a blind eye."

She sucked in a shaky breath, twisting her fingers so tightly that they were turning white. "But that's not me, Mr. Jacobs. It's not me, and there was no way I was going to raise my two small children in that kind of environment. The problem was that I had no proof. I'd never seen anything solid. Reed made sure of that. But still, I knew. I knew."

"Do you think I don't know that?" I told her, unable to keep my mouth shut when I knew I should. "That I don't feel that in you?"

"I need you to. I need you to believe I'd never willingly put my children in this situation." She touched her chest like she wanted to offer me part of it. "The first time I left him, Thomas was four and Mallory was only a few months old. I left in the middle of the night while he was gone on a business trip."

My hand was moving across the sheet, taking down every detail, teeth grinding the whole time.

Trying to convince myself it was just another case.

Just another case.

Her voice was shaking as she continued, words barely scraping free of her throat. "I'd gone to California, thinking if I got far enough away, he wouldn't be able to find me, or maybe I was just hoping that he'd forget. Take it as an easy out. It only took him two days to track us down. It was the first time he . . ."

Her words trailed off, and I felt the last piece of sanity slip.

"Grace," I whispered.

She squeezed her eyes closed, gave a sharp shake of her head, and opened those gorgeous blue eyes to me. So deep and good, and I knew right then and there that I was drowning.

"Let's just say he forced me to go back with him. He told me I'd never see my children again if I didn't. I relented, not because I was weak, but because I had no idea what else to do. No way to fight a family as powerful as his. I was a twenty-three-year-old girl who had a cosmetology license, which was a miracle he'd even *permitted* me to get, with two children, and his family owned half of South Carolina. And he wasn't exactly painting me in a pretty light. But I knew one day, one day I would find a way."

"God, Grace."

Her lips pinched, and she exhaled. "After that, I fought him every inch of the way. Refused to let him touch me, and he'd force me, anyway. I just kept praying he'd get tired enough of it that he'd let us go. Or, that I'd find proof. Something to hold over his head."

Disbelief shook her head. "And I still don't know that I did, I went on a hunch, but what I found has been enough to scare him. Enough that he's kept his distance. But I know that his pride is taking hits, and he's about to crack."

My hand stilled over the notepad, voice too eager. "What did you find?"

"He was always neurotically secretive about his office." She bit out a scornful laugh. "We weren't *allowed* inside. I had a gut feeling that if I could just get in there, I would find something . . . something to use against him. He'd left to Washington, and I was able to sneak in. I went through everything, thinking I had nothing, until I found a safe hidden behind a big picture."

Disbelief flashed through her expression. "I'd thought there was no chance I'd get into it, but he'd actually used the kids' birthdates. I found . . . I found a picture. A picture that I knew meant something, even though I wasn't sure of what. So, I took it, Mr. Jacobs. I took it."

She fumbled in her bag and pulled out an enlarged picture.

She slid it across the desk to me.

I picked it up, guts twisted up in a thousand knots when I saw what she'd found.

It was shadowy and grainy as fuck, but I was ninety-nine percent sure it was Reed Dearborne down on the docks in the middle of the night, standing with his back to the camera, surrounded by a few men who I couldn't make out.

Large metal containers were being unloaded from a cargo ship. But it was the men facing the camera holding machine guns across their chests that had the breath punching from my lungs.

My body shot forward as I tried to make sense of what Grace had found. "You . . . ." I was barely able to look up at her. "You found this in his safe?"

It wasn't like I wasn't well aware of the shady shit that went down at the docks. The mess my brother and his wife had gotten themselves into was proof of that. The cases I'd represented. The things I knew. Almost touching, but always on the fringes.

But this?

This could be a bombshell.

My spirit shook. What was this bastard involved in?

Terror ripped through her body when she nodded. "Yes . . . it was in a secret compartment at the bottom."

She started to rush, leaning forward, "This was why I said that I didn't want to use it unless absolutely necessary. I don't want my children involved in this. Honestly, I don't even know what it means. All I know is that my having it is the only reason my children and I are still at my grandmother's. I went there because I didn't want him to think I was cowering or hiding. That I would face him out in the open. I . . . I told him I made a bunch of copies and, if anything happened to me, they were going to be sent to every news media outlet that I knew of."

"And he backed down?"

She exhaled heavily. "I think it was the only reason he didn't find a way to stop the divorce. He was scared. But over time, I think he's come to believe I'm bluffing."

"Are you?" I challenged, not sure how far she would be willing to go. The danger something like this might pose.

Nausea swirled through my guts, my mind riddled with what Thomas had told me he overheard.

Bitches who don't obey need to bleed.

Her chin lifted, and she shifted, switching the legs she had crossed. My eyes got locked there, snagged on the motion.

On all that smooth, silky skin.

I could still feel it burning under my needy hands.

I was slammed with it—a convulsion of lust.

"I think you know by now that I will do whatever it takes to keep my children safe."

She dug back into the same bag that she'd pulled the folder from, the same one she'd come in with the other day. She started pulling out a wad of that cash.

I flew out of my seat and was around my desk in a flash, sitting down on the edge of the chair next to her and shoving her hand back into the bag, my voice lowered to a hiss. "For the love of God, woman, put that money away. You think I don't know where it came from?"

And if it did come from where I was betting, there was no chance that piece of shit was going to let it go.

Taken aback, she blinked at me. "We already discussed that this is just another case for you, Mr. Jacobs, and I know your services don't come cheap."

"I'm not taking your money."

There I went again with the crazy talk. Seemed that, when it came to her, I couldn't stop it from flying from my mouth.

Still, that mangled, black spec in the middle of my chest was making the decision for me.

Grace blew out a surprised breath. "Yes, you are, Mr. Jacobs. You're taking this money, and you're going to pretend you don't know where it came from. I can't sit here in good conscience and let you do this."

"I don't want your money."

"Everything changed when you took me on as a client."

"Everything changed when I saw you sitting at that bar."

More craziness.

Unstoppable.

But no one had ever made me feel the way Grace did.

I tucked the money back into the bag, reaching over her so I could zip the satchel closed. It brought us too near, her spirit dancing out from her flesh, the girl's presence so profound I could feel it shaking through me.

Our eyes locked, and I got lost there. In that deep, teal-blue ocean. The depths of her gaze unfathomable.

Entrancing.

"I'm taking this case on, pro bono." My words lowered with the command, my lips moving two inches from hers while she watched me with some kind of awe and shock and horror.

Our bodies were so close, I could physically feel every erratic beat of her heart. Could almost hear the swoosh of the blood thumping through her veins. Could taste the desire that came off her skin.

"Mr. Jacobs."

I grabbed her by the back of the neck, hauling her to the edge of the chair, our noses touching. "Call me that again, and I'll have you bent over my desk," I warned.

I'd lived all of my adult life in control.

Self-control, that was.

And this woman had single-handedly made me lose it.

Gone.

Obliterated.

Threatening the most reckless of things. But the only thing I could see right then was the image of doing exactly that, bending her over that wood and pushing her skirt up over her ass. Maybe making it mine.

What it might cost really didn't seem to matter that much.

A tremble rolled through her. Her lips parted, and her eyes darted to mine, and I knew she was contemplating her own wicked things.

Pushing past all my boundaries.

Climbing over my walls.

Getting under my skin.

My teeth nipped at her chin. Never before had I wanted to eat a girl up more than I wanted to devour Grace right then.

She gasped, and her hands found my shoulders where they curled into the fabric of my suit jacket. "Mr. Jacobs."

Need rumbled in my chest. "You are begging for trouble, aren't you, Grace?"

I set my hand on her knee and ran it up the inside of her thigh. Parting her legs as I went.

My other hand twisted up in that mass of blonde hair.

What the fuck did I think I was doing?

"What are you doing to me, Grace? I have no control when it comes to you. You make me want things I can't have. Make me want to risk things I can't risk."

Her fingers dug deeper into my shoulders, words nothing but wisps of need against my face. "What do you want?"

"I want you. I want to explore every inch of your body. Taste and lick and fuck."

I want to keep you.

"I thought you said that couldn't happen?" The question was nothing but jutting rasps from her mouth as my hand continued to slip higher beneath the fabric of her skirt. I played my fingertips across the damp material of her satin underwear.

"It can't."

The girl was on the edge of her chair, the same as I was. Her legs were parted only enough to allow me to run my fingers over her panties, lightly, where I caressed the line of her slit with each pass.

Her legs were shaking so bad I was sure she couldn't decide if she wanted to clamp them shut or spread them wider.

We were nose to nose.

Breath to breath.

This woman the only thing I could see.

Long legs and high heels and lusty pants.

"Ian."

It was a plea.

A question.

She was asking for the answer to everything I didn't understand myself. My tongue darted out to wet my dried lips, and I was sucking down her every exhale as I nudged the silky fabric aside and pushed two fingers into her pussy.

Slowly.

Deeply.

A low moan rolled up her throat.

I pressed my mouth there, up under her chin, kissing along the flesh of her trembling neck. "Shh," I murmured. "Spread for me, baby. Let me make you feel good."

Her grip cinched down tighter as she opened for me, and I began to drive my fingers in and out of her sweet body, my fingers fucking her slow and hard and greedily.

Coaxing all these little mewling sounds from her.

I just wanted to make her lose her mind one more time. Exactly the way she was making me lose mine. I wanted to feel her come on my fingers. To know I could draw out her pleasure.

See to it that she was wanting me just as desperately as I wanted her.

She was so soft.

So wet.

So right.

So perfect, I couldn't help but tell her.

"You have the sweetest cunt, Grace. Did you know that? Did you know I haven't stopped dreaming about it since I had you? Do you know how many times I've fantasized about it? All the ways I'd take you if you were mine?"

She moaned a needy sound.

My dick pressed painfully at my pants.

It took everything I had not to rip off my belt and do exactly what I'd warned. Bend her over my desk and take her from behind. Take her lush cheeks in my hands as I drove into her.

Hard and possessive.

That was what I felt.

Possessive.

This girl mine.

I wanted to own her.

Take her.

Keep her.

Deeper.

More.

"More," she whimpered like she was a partner to every single thing I was feeling, to every thought, and I was watching her face, tugging her back by the hair as I drove the girl wild.

Her eyes were doing that mystical thing.

Drugging me.

Or maybe it was me who was drugging her.

Because she was grinding on my hand, ass barely hanging from the edge of the chair, desperate to get closer. Her head started to shake back and forth as she tried to make sense of what I was doing.

Energy flashed, and her entire body tightened. The woman rode the razor-sharp edge of pleasure. One I got the sense that she wanted to cling to forever.

"You want me everywhere, don't you, Angel Girl? Would you let me take you? Take every single thing that I want?"

"Yes."

I flicked my thumb over her clit.

It was instant. The way I felt her shatter.

Spasms rocked through her body.

Her pleasure in my hand.

Pooling and throbbing and speeding.

She curled her fingers into my hair, yanking hard, a scream locked in her throat. I ran my lips over it, across the vibration that blazed under the soft, delicate flesh, silently commanding her to keep it bottled and contained.

She rode on that ecstasy, tiny whimpers slipping from her mouth while all the wicked things I wanted to do to her welled up to feel like something precious that I held in my hands.

Like it would be okay to sink into her.

Claim her as mine.

And I knew I was losing it.

The way I had the intense urge to kiss her. Hold her. Promise her it would all be okay.

Instead, I slipped out of her body while I promised myself this could never happen again.

I lifted my hand and sucked my fingers into my mouth.

All fucking woman on the tip of my tongue.

"One last taste." It was a warning and a growl, and Grace was watching me as the shock of what I'd just done to her came crashing down.

She tried to gather herself, drawing in a bunch of breaths as she quickly fumbled to readjust her clothes. "I . . . I . . ." She stuttered, looking everywhere, maybe for an escape. "I need—"

I grabbed her by the chin, running the thumb I'd just had on her body across her lip.

She emitted a tiny groan when I dipped it inside and pressed it to her tongue.

"Shh," I told her. "I won't do that again. I just . . . needed to touch you one last time."

She could barely nod, but those eyes went soft in a sad sort of surrender, the words choked when they floated out in the inch of space that separated us. "You could wreck me, Ian Jacobs."

I brushed my fingers through her hair. "Too late, Angel Girl. I think it's you who's already wrecked me."

GRACE

"*Jammies!*" Sophie grinned her sweet, sweet smile as I pulled her nightgown over her head, her snow-white hair sticking up with static electricity as I situated it over her tiny body. She pressed her hands to her chubby belly and jumped, giggling as if it were the funniest thing in the world.

I poked her belly where she was holding it.

"Are these Sophie's favorite pajamas?" I asked her, voice twisted in close to a song.

"Pink horsie!" She giggled again, the sweetness that rolled from her expanding my heart.

So big it sometimes made it hard to breathe.

Mallory shook her head from where she was on the floor

dragging our storybook out from under her bed. "It's not a pink horse, Silly Sophie. It's a unicorn. Unicorns are magic and horses have no magic and you've got to know the difference because it's a big one."

Sophie giggled again and galloped around the small room. "Horsie!"

Mallory sighed and held her head in both of her hands, looking at me as if she were an adult and I would totally understand. "Hopeless."

I tried not to laugh, but there was no stopping it. Not after I'd carried around so many uncertainties throughout the day.

My meeting with Ian had gone a direction I hadn't anticipated.

A direction we both knew it couldn't.

And still, it seemed as if there were no chance of stopping it. The overpowering connection that wrapped us in chains every time we were in the other's space.

The man felt so vitally important. As if my heart remembered how to fully beat when he was there, his touch safety and sanctuary and fire, the feelings he evoked in me too conflicted and at odds for my mind to make sense of it all.

The only thing I knew was that we needed him.

All of us.

My children most.

I knew he'd been put in my world for a reason. For a purpose. And that wasn't for me to fall in love with him, even though I could feel pieces of myself continuing to slip, slivers carved away and given to him with every moment that passed.

Thomas came into the room, dressed in sweat pants and his hair wet from his shower.

"Did you brush your teeth?" I asked.

He rolled his eyes.

At least there was that.

"I'm not a baby, Mom."

"I know you aren't a baby. But you're my child, so that means I'm going to ask you if you brushed your teeth."

He huffed an irritated sound as he went to sit at the edge of his twin bed. "You'll probably still be asking me when I'm thirteen."

"Thirteen," I gasped, as if what he said was an atrocity. From where I'd been on the floor, I scrambled for him on my hands and knees. I started tickling his sides. "Thirteen? I'll be asking you if you brushed your teeth when you're thirty!"

He tried not to laugh, but then he rolled onto his back on his bed, trying to fight me and cracking up at the same time. "Stop it, Mom. You're crazy. I'm . . . I'm going to move away and change my name and my number, and you can never ask me if I brushed my teeth again."

I tickled him harder. "And I will find you. You can't get away from me!"

Sophie and Mallory jumped up and down.

"Get him, Mommy!" Mallory shouted.

"Get him, get him!" Sophie parroted, clapping her little hands and laughing more.

"You'll never catch me," Thomas shouted, wiggling and laughing.

"You're the crazy one, Thomas! We got the magic and we will find you." Mallory climbed onto his bed, shouting it at his face where she was on her knees looking down at him from over his head.

It was almost too much.

The way love and adoration and devotion poured free.

Taking everything over.

My voice softened to wistfulness, and I stopped tickling my son so I could run a hand over his damp hair. "I will always find you. No matter where you go. All of you."

It was a promise.

A promise that we would all be together. No matter what that took.

Thomas sobered, and Mallory climbed off his bed and opened our picture book, wanting to continue our story the way we did each night.

"What's this?" Mallory asked, waving a piece of paper in the air that she'd found pressed between the pages.

The smile I was wearing slid off my face, horror taking its place.

Heart crumbling.

Spirit failing.

Oh God.

My trembling fingers ran over it.

It was a crude image of the maze near the castle.

But that was where the similarities of our story ended.

Because the prince and princesses and the handmaiden had been slain, the king standing over them holding a knife that dripped with blood.

A lump locked in my throat. I looked at my son who was now hunched over on the side of his bed, hanging his head in shame.

"Thomas," I whispered, touching his knee and urging him to look at me. "What is this?"

Tears filled his eyes. "What if there isn't really magic? What if this is the way our story ends?"

"I won't ever let anyone hurt you. Do you think—"

He shook his head, and frustration bled out in his voice. "What if we don't get to leave? What if we have to stay there forever?"

And I realized this drawing was his own metaphor. The idea that Reed held the ultimate power.

"Nuh-uh, no way, we got a hero now and we don't have nothing to worry about because he's going to save us and we're going to get free and fly away on our unicorns. Ian-Zian the Great to the rescue!"

Mallory was pointing at the picture she'd had me help her draw last night after Ian had left. When he'd walked out of our house and left it brimming with hope.

I should have known it would be my worrying little man who would have all the questions. The one who'd toss in his sleep and contemplate the way everything could go bad.

I took his hand and pulled him off his bed. I didn't care that he was nine, and he thought he needed to be a man. I tucked him close to my chest, held him even harder. Sophie hopped over and climbed into my other arm, and Mallory threw herself onto my back, wrapping her thin arms around all of us.

I drew them all as close as I could get them, the words emphatic as I let the promises permeate the room. "I won't let you go. I won't let any of you go. You are my babies. You are my life.

You are the reason I live. The reason I breathe. And I will live every breath that I have for you."

It didn't matter what the circumstances were or how powerful Reed might be.

I had to have faith that everything would turn out right.

We belonged together, and there was no power in this world that could change that.

Especially when we had our hero fighting for us.

twenty-three

IAN

"What the fuck is this?" Lawrence tossed the newspaper onto his desk.

I wanted to tell him that no one still unwrapped a newspaper and read that shit, but the fact this was splashed all over the online news media and was getting special broadcast time on about every news channel in the state made the point moot.

Flippantly, I flicked it back toward him. "Don't tell me you had me come all the way over here because you wanted to ask me about my new client."

He pitched forward. "Drop it."

Incredulous laughter rocked out of me. "Excuse me?"

"You heard me. Drop the case. Give it to someone else. I don't care. I don't want you anywhere near it."

My head shook. "I'm not sure how you think you have any say in the clients I take."

"I do when they're this high profile. You can't be drawing attention to yourself. People look too deeply into you, and they will see more than I want them to. Do you really think I want you associated in any way with a man as powerful as Reed Dearborne? It's suicide."

I didn't know if he meant that in the literal or figurative sense. With the way he was looking at me, it was literal. But clearly, the only thing the asshole gave a shit about was how it might affect him.

More laughter.

This time scornful.

All of it directed at myself. It was my fault I'd let this asshole exert so much control over me for all these years. Thinking I'd owed him something when he'd clearly only been using me.

Venom screamed through my veins. So harsh and hard that I'd put down bets he could feel it spurting from my pores.

I set my palms on his desk and leaned toward him, voice dipping in menace. "Let's make one thing clear, old man. You don't own me. I will take on whatever case I choose, and you don't have a say in it. Do you understand me?"

Especially when it came to Grace.

Grace.

Bastard laughed and shook his head. "You really are clueless, aren't you, Ian?"

One of those old-school intercoms squeaked on his desk, and he pushed the button to answer it. "Yes, Mimi?"

"Sir, you have a delivery you need to sign for."

"I'll be right out."

He pushed to standing, his glare clearly ordering me to stay put as he moved out his door.

The second he did, I was around his desk and punching the code into his computer.

Needing . . . something. I didn't fucking know what. I just wanted more. More than what I was involved in because without a doubt that shady shit went deep.

Something big and ugly.

If the asshole thought he was going to push me? Guess-fucking-what? I was going to push right back.

Hard.

My fingers quickly clicked over the keyboard.

The guy had a system and was meticulous.

Luckily, I'd spent my life being privy to it. The eight-digit password wasn't that hard to decode.

I hacked into his computer in a flash. I started clicking and moving. Eyes darting and gathering anything I possibly could. There was nothing that really stood out that I didn't already know about.

Then my heart rate spiked when I popped open a minimized file.

It was code. Not quite making sense. Which told me I'd stumbled upon exactly what I'd been looking for. It wasn't like the dirtbag was going to have "Illegal activities" stamped on the top of the file.

The document was a list of addresses, and there was another file with names.

All female.

I blinked at it, mind whirring as I struggled to add up when it meant.

I could hear Lawrence's low voice echoing from out front, and I fumbled to pull my phone out of my pocket and snapped a couple pics.

Footsteps came closer and closer, his voice drawing nearer as he shouted something at his secretary like the asshole he was.

Shit.

I was running out of time.

Breaths turning hard, I clicked through the documents, minimizing them both and putting his computer back into sleep mode, all but jumping over his desk and onto the other side by the time Lawrence pushed back through his door, carrying a flat overnight envelope.

My pulse raced like a bitch, the close call a little too close for my taste.

He moved back around to his executive chair, sighing out a contented sound as he rocked back in it. He tossed the envelope carelessly onto his desk.

"You want to make things clear, Ian? Fine. Know this. I could take you down with a snap of my fingers. I own you. I've owned you since the second you started working for me. I have *always* owned you. You just didn't know it."

My head cocked. "Is that so?"

"It is."

I planted my hands back on his desk, leaning over far enough that I could get in his face. "Then you can take this as my resignation."

The address stared back at me.

It was in the middle of the others. Nothing special about it except for the fact that it was so goddamned important to me.

One I'd never forget.

One that I couldn't help but move toward, drawn back to a memory that I wanted to slay.

A stone sank to the pit of my stomach as I got deeper into the city, buildings becoming shoddier and the characters walking the sidewalks and loitering at the end of the alleys growing shadier.

Could almost taste the despair and despondency in the air.

Memories slammed me.

Heavy and vile.

I'd sworn to myself I'd never come down here again. That I'd outrun the poverty and depravity. That never again would I be looked at like I was trash.

Worthless.

Scum.

Hungry and begging.

Emotion raced my throat as I made a left and then a right.

My last memories as a boy sped up to meet me.

Rushing.

Hitting me head on.

I slowed as I approached the old building, and part of me wanted to ram on the accelerator and get the fuck out of there before I was taken back to that time.

A hostage.

A prisoner.

Instead, I forced myself to slow, and I cracked the window of my car, which was so out of place that people kept turning their heads, distrust in their postures as they stopped in their tracks to watch me drive by.

The sounds of the inner city came at me in waves. A baby crying and a woman shouting. Music thumping and a fight down the street.

Maybe it was shock I felt when I came to a stop at the address in front of the rundown building where everything had changed.

Where my life as I had known it had come to an end.

This was where I'd become someone else.

This was where I'd become a man.

A man who had chosen to take what he wanted for his life rather than a boy who had scrounged for any scraps he could find.

A fire burned in my eyes and raced my throat.

I fought the sensation because it made me fucking weak.

My hands clamped down on the steering wheel and sweat poured from my brow when I saw the three women stumble out of the building. It was early, but I guess some jobs were never done.

Men always breathed. Ready to degrade and take and overpower.

Didn't matter the time of the day.

I squeezed my eyes closed. Like it could stop it. Staunch it. But it would never matter how far I went or how calloused I became or how many years had passed.

She was always right there.

My greatest sin.

Treason and betrayal.

twenty-four

GRACE

"You have a walk-in haircut."

Melissa was smirking at me as she walked into the salon area from the front waiting room.

My heart skipped and sped in a million wayward beats when I saw who followed behind her.

Foolish, foolish heart.

But there was no stopping the reaction to the man, so tall and powerful and commanding that he made the ground tremble beneath my feet.

"It seems someone's hair grows really fast." The words falling from Melissa's mouth were perfectly wry, delivered with a silent, *Plan on dishing the details later.*

No doubt, she would pin me down and pry it out of me.

"Okay," I managed to mumble, looking back to the older woman sitting in my chair. "Let me finish up with Mrs. Galvez, and I'll be right with you."

Ian nodded, those hands in his pockets, the energy speeding between us like it was fuel for an out-of-control train.

I finished styling Mrs. Galvez, quickly dusted off the hair from her robe, and unsnapped it. She pushed from the chair. "Thank you, dear. I'll see you in six weeks."

She reached out and stuffed a five-dollar tip into my hand before she scurried around Ian, who looked as if he was half inclined to chase everyone out of the salon.

As if he needed me alone.

As if he just . . . needed me.

There was something unhinged about him, so raw and abraded and sensitive beneath all that hardness.

Those eyes flashed, and I gulped as I quickly swept up the mess under the chair and tossed the bill onto my station. I angled my head. "Let's get you washed up, Mr. Jacobs."

His nostrils flared the second I said it, and he strode across the salon, his legs taking long, purposed strides as he moved toward me.

I could feel it.

The shift in the air.

A hot intensity that spun and shivered and shook with every step that he took. He passed by, brushing my arm, sending shivers skating across my flesh.

This was so bad. So, so bad, because I couldn't stop my reaction to him. The way my body ignited with the simple touch.

I wanted this man in a way I shouldn't.

In a way that was wholly profound and wholly impossible.

He sat at the same basin as the one he'd occupied just a week before. I did the same thing I did then, turned on the water and tested its temperature before taking the nozzle and slowly wetting his hair.

It turned dark beneath my hands, as dark as his eyes that watched me carefully.

"What are you doing here?" I finally whispered.

Anger stormed across his face, the emotion just as distinctly marked in his voice. "I want to submit for an emergency injunction. I don't want your children anywhere near Reed."

A gust of surprised air left my lungs. "That . . . seems impossible. That would mean having him declared as unfit, and the only thing Reed cares about is his reputation. He's not going to take lightly to us trying to make him look bad."

We were both whispering, held in our little bubble as I gently washed his hair, and he issued words that filled me with too much hope and too much fear.

The two collided.

Turmoil that clashed in the center of my chest.

I wanted it . . . so badly . . . to permanently remove my children from Reed's control. And I realized I was conceding to that fate, believing that would be the only way for me to maintain custody of my children.

To share them.

But that meant Reed having influence on them, too.

That meant telling them goodbye each week and seeing the fear and questions and sadness in their expressions.

Ian sat completely still, all except for those eyes that were flickering across my face, as if he were watching all of those exact fears play through my mind.

My own questions, and my own sadness.

And I realized my children and I were just passing that back and forth to each other. Each time they left and returned, it only grew.

"He's dangerous." Ian's jaw clenched, and I froze, watching the way the chiseled stone of his face hardened more.

"How do you know that?" Of course, I knew that. He was a man capable of doing wicked, horrible things. It was the reason I'd left. It was the sudden urgency coming from Ian that had me shaken. "Did . . . did you find something out? Do you have proof?"

"I don't have solid proof yet. But I will find something. The only thing I'm going on right now is my gut, plus what Thomas confided in me. That's big."

Something flashed through Ian's eyes.

A vulnerability unlike anything I'd ever witnessed in him before. I searched the depths, silently begging him to let me in, when the best thing for both of us would be for him to keep me out.

But I wanted to know him. To hold him a little in the way he was holding me.

"I . . ." His voice cracked as he struggled to find the words, and he pinched his eyes as if he couldn't look at me when he admitted them. "I lived in fear my entire childhood, Grace. I never knew when I'd be hugged or when I'd be hit. I never knew who would protect me and who would hurt me. I don't want that. Not for them."

Horror locked in my throat. I slowly rinsed his hair, my fingers threading through the soft, soft locks, my own words wobbling as I released them from my throat. "I'm so sorry, Ian. I'm so sorry you went through that."

His teeth ground, and I could feel his breaths turn ragged.

All I could picture were the scars littering his skin, covered with shadows and ink.

Gaze opening to me, he reached up and grabbed me by the wrist. "I told you not to pity me."

My voice turned so shallow I could barely speak. "I don't pity you, Ian. I'm in awe of you. Of who you are and who you became."

His eyes squeezed closed again. "I'm not a good man. I've done horrible things."

I turned off the faucet and grabbed a towel, tenderly rubbing it over his head, my face so close to his that our noses were touching when I quietly said, "You were only trying to survive, doing the best you could. I don't know your whole story, Ian, but I know you are good underneath it all. I see it."

My mouth fell to the shell of his ear. "I've felt it."

A shudder rolled through him, and I could feel the pain emanating from his spirit. Something old and hidden ripping free. But it was anger that came tearing from his mouth like a curse. "My mother . . . she was a junkie and prostitute. I have no idea who my father even was."

Grief.

It streaked through me.

A thunderbolt.

Rending me in two.

Instantly, my mind was back on the confession I'd made to him in his office. He was the first person I'd ever told that I suspected Reed was involved with illicit things. Taking women because he could afford to buy them.

It left something sour on my tongue.

I could almost sense Ian as a child, a sweet, sweet boy who'd been shaped and molded and formed into a hardened man.

A deep-seated realization crashed over me.

This was why he thought of children has a burden. As too great a risk.

"I would never neglect my children." I was almost begging him to believe me when I said it.

Emotion twisted through his expression, anger and hurt and fear. Gruff words breezed across my face. "Sometimes, it's already happening before someone realizes it's too late."

"It's okay to love her and be angry with her for the way you were raised." I knew I was going a direction I shouldn't go.

Tumbling.

Tumbling.

But I couldn't stop, wanting to hold the grief that thundered through his veins and thrashed in his spirit.

He barely shook his head, fighting opening up. "I did love her. So much, Grace. So much. And I failed her."

Confusion pulsed, and my hand went to his face. With the contact, those eyes flashed open for a beat, giving me a view to what was buried deep inside.

Torture.

Torment.

"No, Ian. There's no chance," I murmured, the two of us still caught up, taken away, elevated to another plane where it was just him and me.

His pain was so palpable, I was finding it difficult to breathe.

"You're wrong, Grace. You're wrong. And I'm fucking terrified I'm going to fail you. I fuck everything up. Ruin it when it matters most."

"You won't fail us. I know it," I was close to begging.

Those strange-colored eyes flashed, cinnamon and orange and the setting sun. "I won't. I promise you, I won't. We have to take that bastard out so your kids don't ever have to experience the agony of losing their mother."

It flooded me.

Love. Love. Love.

My spirit screamed it.

My tongue wanted to confess it.

But I knew it would be refused. Ian was in no position to accept it. Instead, I took his hand and guided him to standing, the man towering over me from behind. I started to lead him into the private waxing room.

I was overcome with the need to touch him. To hold a little of his pain. To show him he was worthy of so much more than the self-loathing that he held onto so tightly.

The soles of our shoes echoed over the floors, and there was no doubt in my mind that every head in the salon turned to watch us go.

I didn't care.

The only thing I cared about was him. The frenzy that worked up inside me. A need greater than any other.

I nudged him into the dimly-lit room, and he was still stumbling back as I clicked the lock on the door.

Typically, the atmosphere in the small space of this room was quiet and subdued so the clients could relax.

Ian looked anything but relaxed.

Every molecule between us charged.

Getting ready to blow.

That jaw twitched, and I watched as he grew hard, the outline of his massive cock pressing at the thin fabric of his pants.

I flew for him, undoing his belt buckle and unzipping his pants before I could control the impulse.

A surprised *whoosh* gushed from Ian's mouth. "Angel Girl, what do you think you're doing?" His voice was grit and need, and it only spurred me on.

I dropped to my knees, needing this man to feel half of what he made me feel. The way he'd commanded my pleasure back in his office. The way he kept me up at night, tossing and turning as I dreamed of what it might be like to be loved by a man like him.

I wanted to return some of it.

Show him what it would be like to truly be adored.

Loved.

Give it and offer it.

Lust sped, mixed with the frenzy of emotion that gripped my heart, the realization of what he'd become to me. I jerked his pants down around his thighs, taking his underwear at the same time. His cock sprang free, thick and full and long, bouncing in my face as it pointed for the sky, the tip already glistening with his need.

"Fuck, Grace, you don't have to—"

I wrapped my hand around him, stroking once, looking up into his eyes. "I know I don't have to, Ian. I know you don't expect anything from me. And I know we can't do this. But I need you to feel this. To feel me. Let me. Please."

I licked across his engorged head, tasting the saltiness of the man.

On a groan of surrender, his fingers threaded into my hair.

And the timid, vulnerable boy he'd shown me out at the sink was gone.

In his place was that dominant man.

He surged his cock forward in a possessive stroke.

I welcomed him, swallowing him down into the back of my throat as far as I could take him.

For a moment he just stared down at me.

His gaze doing something different.

Something soft and adoring and my heart was whispering stupid, foolish things.

I'm falling in love with you, Ian Jacobs.

Then he fully let go, grabbing me by the sides of my head as he began to fuck my mouth.

Every thrust deep, dominating, and measured.

Desire spiraled inside me, a hot vortex that sucked me in, making my mind spin and my spirit sore.

Desperate to get closer to him.

"Grace, God . . . you feel . . . fuck . . . your mouth is perfect. So sweet. God, you're sweet."

I sucked him and stroked him and palmed his balls.

Ian growled.

Low and menacing.

Tingles sped, fire across my skin. With the stark expression that took hold of his gorgeous features, I knew I was in trouble.

This man was going to devour me.

There was no missing it, the way he was watching me with all that lust he'd been watching me with that first night.

With something akin to anger.

Possession in the muscles that bowed and flexed and pulled taut.

Tension stretched the air thin, severity bounding through the enclosed space.

He suddenly pulled out of my mouth and jerked me off my knees. His hands went under my skirt, and he ripped down my panties, winding them off my heeled boots in the same second as he was spinning me around and bending me over the waxing table.

"You don't have the first clue what you're doing to me, do you, Angel Girl? Ruining me. Little by little. I want to mark you, Grace. Get so deep inside of you that you'll never forget my name."

Oh, there was no worry of that.

Surprise left me on a gasp, unprepared for the pleasure that sheared through me when he bunched up my skirt and thrust himself deep.

Hard and fast.

I jolted forward, hands darting out to the opposite side of the table, hanging on as he began to pound into me.

Relentlessly.

So deep and desperate, I could feel him capturing all of me.

Taking it all.

He rocked and jutted and fucked.

Driving me to the brink, pulling back, slowing and teasing,

before he was driving me out of my mind again.

I was whimpering, hands clinging, heart a thunder where it beat through the confines of the tiny room.

"Do you feel that, Grace? What it's like to feel like you're losing your mind? This is what you do to me. Every second. Every day. You make me crazy. Make me forget myself. Make me think I might want things that I can't have. You make me believe in the impossible."

"You have me. You have all of me." They were pleas falling from my lips, panted into the thick, dense air, and Ian was inhaling a rasping sound.

"Don't say things you don't mean," he warned, driving his dick deep, spreading my bottom wider, angling in a direction that had me losing all control.

Bliss so bright I was seeing spots.

The man holding me.

Controlling me.

Liquid. Fluid. A river that washed through the middle of me.

"I'm yours."

Surprise heaved from his lungs, and his hands tightened their hold, and he drove deeper, harder, as deep and hard as his voice. "Say it again."

"I'm yours," I rasped.

"All of you?" he demanded.

"All of me."

He spread me wider, the feel of him almost more than I could bear.

So perfect and wrong.

The man my heaven.

The man my hell.

Everything I wanted, a tease of what I could never keep.

"You make me forget everything that's important to me," he grated. Confusion and anger spiraled out like a complaint, and he was running his fingers through the crease of my bottom, fingers touching me in places I'd never been touched.

I groaned out a surprised sound, half mortified, the other half pushing back. Begging for more. For everything this man could give me.

"Ian," I whispered through my own confusion.

Delirium.

The man the fever that raced through my veins.

"Do you like that, Grace? I've had that mouth and that sweet pussy. Would you give me this, too? If you belonged to me, would you let me take it?"

Rawness bled from him. Sheer, masculine dominance. Power and strength. Anger and ire.

But I wasn't afraid. Not even close. The only thing I was afraid of was him letting go.

"I already do. I belong to you in a way I've never belonged to anyone else."

He instantly slowed, yanking a mournful cry from my mouth as his strokes became long and measured. As measured as when he swirled a fingertip around my ass before he was slowly pressing in two.

"Like that?" he murmured. A caress. A promise. A threat.

I wanted to moan. To beg. To weep. All I could say was, "Please."

He pushed his fingers deeper and deeper.

More and more.

Taking and filling and ruining every inch of me.

Because just like I knew when I'd first met him, I was never going to be the same. Ian Jacobs was going to scar me in the best of ways. In the most profound of ways.

"Yes," he hissed. "Fuck, you are perfect."

It felt so full and so wrong and so perfect, and I swore, I could feel every cell in my body come alive.

As if every single nerve ending was riding the sharp, bitter edge of ecstasy.

Everything alight.

Fire and flames and need that glowed white hot.

Pleasure as he began to rock and fuck, fingers moving in sync.

His breaths shallow and his pleasure palpable, the man barely hanging on by a thread.

"Nothing . . . nothing has ever felt better than you, Grace.

Nothing. Not once. Not ever. Everything is better than the last. Every look. Every touch. Every time I take you. You. Are. Everything."

That's what I wanted to be.

His everything.

But I knew it was impossible, and still I wanted it all.

So, we rode on our blissful torment, my hands planted on the bed as I began to meet his thrusts. As he touched me in a way that made my sight blur at the edges and my heart speed out of control.

Energy ricocheted through the tiny room.

Bounding.

Gaining momentum with each rock of his hips and every tremble of my body.

His other hand slipped around to find that sweet spot that instantly lit.

Fireworks.

Rockets.

I was burning alive.

Unsure I could take it. Needing more. My head swished back and forth, and I gripped tighter as the man possessed me.

Owned me.

I guessed he'd owned me all along.

Shivers raced my flesh, and I was shaking.

Shaking and shaking and shaking.

So close. So close. I couldn't take any more.

"Come for me, sweet girl. Let go. Let me see how perfect you are. Show me that you love feeling me this way. So lost in me that you don't know where you end and I begin. Tell me it's only me. It's only me. Tell me you'll never forget what this felt like. You and me."

"It's you. It's you, I'll never forget." I was whimpering frantically, the last word floating away as everything gathered at my center.

A ball of pleasure.

A pinpoint of ecstasy.

A burst of light.

And I was shooting.

Falling.

Somewhere in the sun.

In the clouds.

Weightless.

Ian jutted and his thighs shook, his rough grunts taking to the dense atmosphere. "You're mine, Grace. I don't care if you can't be. In my mind, you'll always be mine."

Both of us were lost in this wilderness.

No hope of safe passage.

Crashing in the middle.

He came, the feel of him pulsing inside me so overwhelming that tears sprang to my eyes. Reckless, reckless, reckless.

With him, I had no other idea how to be.

I couldn't keep him.

I couldn't keep him.

We'd both be ruined if someone found out.

This beautiful mess we were in was breaking every societal rule. The oath he'd made as an attorney.

He was in a position of influence over me. And God . . . I felt influenced. The man holding me in the palms of his hands.

I wanted to turn around and kiss him and hang on and never let go.

My name was nothing but a deep, guttural moan from his plush lips.

He slowly pulled out, and I slumped over the table, keeping my face hidden.

Because the last thing I wanted him to see was the evidence of what was written there.

He leaned over me, panting, gasping for air, the words so rough when he murmured them at my ear. "I'm losing myself, Grace, and that's the one thing I can't do with you."

twenty-five

IAN

Heart hammering, I tried to catch my breath. To reel in this goddamned feeling that was speeding out of control. I could feel it thundering through the space, bounding against the closed in walls.

I wanted to hold her. Wrap her up and tell her this would all be okay.

That I was going to protect her and her kids. That's what I needed to do.

What I needed to focus on.

Protecting her and her kids.

Instead, I'd completely slipped.

Lost all fucking control.

Needing to possess her. Some place in my mind had snapped when I'd driven away from that apartment building. Too much shit twisted up in my mind, memories coming at me fast, ghosts bringing up the rear.

Felt like I'd been being hunted on every side.

My first instinct had been to come here. Seeking out her comfort. Desperate for a touch of that soothing *grace*.

Knowing with just a look, she would take away some of what was haunting me.

We weren't supposed to end up in this room.

Not like this.

Treading dangerous, dangerous waters.

Every touch, and I was putting her at risk.

Putting myself at risk.

Everything I'd ever wanted.

Everything I'd worked my ass off for.

Lived for.

This woman was forbidden. Off-limits. On top of that, she represented everything I didn't want.

She had three kids, for God's sake.

Three fucking kids.

I gulped around that meteor that was still crashing to Earth.

On a heavy exhale, I turned and took two steps across the confined space to the sink. I washed my hands, grabbed a white hand towel from the folded stack in the cupboard, and ran it under warm water.

I fisted it over my dick, cleaning myself, hissing as I did, sensation still racing out of control.

Then I stuffed myself back into my pants, zipped up, and fastened my button and buckle, trying to figure out when I had completely spiraled.

Seeking pleasure. Willing to do anything for another taste of it.

I grabbed a fresh towel and ran it under the water, pulling in a deep breath because God knew I needed some clarity before I could turn back around and look at her.

No use.

Because my pulse spiked, and my stomach twisted when I

turned. The girl had pushed up to sitting, wearing this cream-colored, tufted dress that she was attempting to get back down around her waist, that blonde hair mussed, her gaze unsure and timid and still full of all that courage that she possessed.

Sexy as all fuck.

Beautiful, inside and out.

A battered Cinderella.

My broken angel.

And there I went, breaking her more. Tainting all that goodness and trust that oozed from her skin.

Slowly, I edged back across the space.

Our eyes gauging the other.

Carefully.

Warily.

Setting my hand on her bare thigh, I nudged her legs back apart as I pulled her to the edge of the bed. The softest moan left her when I pressed the warm towel between her thighs, the act like some kind of twisted apology.

"I can't believe I did that to you." It sounded of a confession.

I'd become rash and negligent. Goddamned careless.

Shyness bled through the small sound that slipped from her mouth. "I'm the one who dragged you in here, Ian."

"And I'm the one who came to you when things got too heavy in my life. I'm the one who keeps pushing it farther and farther. Taking more when the last thing I should be doing is asking you to offer it."

Her voice was soggy and rough. "And what if I want you to have it? This part of me? I don't want to give it to anyone else. You make me feel things I've never felt before. Things I'm not sure I fully understand."

Those eyes washed over me. So soft and tender and full of trust.

This time, it was me dropping to my knees, and I was staring up at the girl as I continued to clean her.

Softly.

Gently.

I kissed the inside of her knee because I just needed to kiss something, my nose at her flesh, breathing her in.

She threaded those sweet fingers through my still damp hair, the girl watching me with all the things she couldn't feel.

Everything I couldn't receive.

In sheer honesty, I gazed up at her. "I want to help you, Grace. I want to be there for you in a way I'm not sure I've ever wanted to be there for anyone in my life."

Something streaked through her expression. Something so intense and real, I was certain I'd never seen it directed at myself before.

It speared me.

Gutted me.

The most foolish part of me wanted to reach out and make it mine.

I climbed to my feet and grabbed her underwear from the floor. I handed them to her and helped her resituate her dress. Like a fool, I moved to stand between her legs like I might belong there, brushing my fingers through that soft, lush hair like I'd do anything for the connection.

"We can't let this happen, anymore. There's too much at stake." The words were low and hard and loaded with regret.

Sorrow moved across that pretty face. "I'm so sorry. I never wanted to put you in this position."

I dipped down to capture her attention. "Don't ever apologize for this. Ever."

I pressed my lips to her forehead and whispered, "In another life."

She nodded against my lips, and I peeled myself back so I could resituate my coat and tie. "I'm filing for an emergency injunction this afternoon. I'm going to have to use Thomas's statement that he is worried about your safety. They're probably going to want to talk with him, but if we're going to win this, we're going to have to use any weapon at our disposal. Including everything you know. If it comes down to it, you're going to have to be prepared to use that photo."

Worry shivered through her body, but she warily nodded. "Okay."

"I have no idea how he's going to react, but I don't trust Reed not to come after you on this. I need you to promise me you'll be careful. Call me if you hear or see anything. This is all coming to a head, Grace. To the end. And I'm going to do whatever I have to for that result to end in your favor."

Fear streaked through her expression, every heinous scenario playing through her mesmerizing eyes.

I touched her face. One last time. "It's going to be okay. I promise you."

She nodded again. "I trust you."

I trust you.

I looked at the door, wanting to fucking punch it. I looked back at Grace. "Come out right after me, and restate how much my services were as we go to the register. Make sure everyone hears it. Do you understand?"

Her throat wobbled, as much as her legs did when she slid off the bed. Fumbling, she yanked off the sheet and tossed it into the dirty clothes hamper. She quickly laid out a new one and fluffed the pillow. "Yes, Mr. Jacobs."

Jesus.

This was out of control.

What I felt.

I didn't even think I recognized myself when it came to her.

I roughed a hand through my hair. "Okay."

I unlocked the door and strode out. Just like I'd expected, every goddamned eye was on us, some blatantly gaping and others trying not to stare, their whispers instantly silenced when I strode out.

Grace was right behind me, her heels clicking on the floor. "The haircut is twenty-five and wax is fifty."

I rounded the corner, and she slipped in behind the register. "So, seventy-five total."

She was a shaking mess.

I pulled out my wallet and passed her a hundred, the tip of my index finger running over the back of her hand, praying it might calm her.

Just fucking needing to touch her.

The last thing I wanted was for her to feel ashamed in any way.

The two of us had been forced into a closet.

One where we could no longer meet.

For a moment, her eyes squeezed closed before she nodded frantically, accepting our fate, and she took the money and shoved it into the drawer.

I forced myself to turn and leave.

I had a job to do.

And it was time I remembered it.

GRACE

I hadn't been able to stop shaking for two hours. Not since Ian

had come through the salon door. Not since I'd asked Melissa to reschedule my clients for the day and left five minutes behind him because there was no chance I could stay there cutting hair and acting as if it were a normal day.

Not when I knew everything was about to change. We were going to go charging over a boundary I'd set for myself, no longer just praying that Reed was going to go away, but fighting back.

Taking a stand.

Doing whatever we had to do.

Though now—now it felt as it were a true statement. Maybe a dangerous one, but one that was worth it.

I pulled into the driveway in front of my grandmother's house. Today was the day she played bridge with her friends, so she'd be gone most of the day. I couldn't help but be relieved.

I needed to . . . be alone. Process and come to terms with the hand life had dealt me. The fact I was falling in love for the first time in my life.

The true kind.

Not an easy kind or a slow kind or a loyal kind. It wasn't the kind a person settled for, and I knew, with every part of me, that it wouldn't be fleeting.

It was the all-encompassing kind. The kind that hit you fast and came on hard and scored itself so deeply in your heart that it'd forever beat with it.

Blowing out a strained breath, I killed the engine and clicked open the door, pushing out to standing in the quiet, cool air.

I gasped out in shock and pain when a blur of movement spun from behind me, my body flying back when I was pushed against my car.

Hard.

I blinked, trying to orient myself, not even being able to clear my thoughts before Reed got in my face.

His was red and raging mad.

"What the fuck do you think you're doing?" he spat.

Fear raced.

Oh, God.

"I . . . I don't know what you are talking about."

He pushed me closer against the cool metal that felt like shards of ice against my back.

Expression murderous. The cool he typically wore had vanished. "Don't bullshit me, Grace. I just got a call from the judge. Did you really think I was going to stand aside and let you get away with this?"

"I'm just doing what is right for my children."

"They are *my* children." Arrogant indignation flashed through his expression.

I scoffed out a bitter sound, tried to stand tall, to stand my ground.

He needed to know I wasn't backing down.

"Are you kidding me, Reed? You barely even see them when they're at your house. You don't spend any time with them. They don't want to be there, and I sure as hell don't want them in your space. Just . . ."

I searched his face for any understanding. For him to make rational sense of this. "Just . . . let them go. Let me go."

"You're out of your mind if you think that is going to happen. You're coming home with me. Now."

My own anger flared, butting up against the terror slingshotting through my veins. "I think it's you who is out of your mind. I'm never going back to you, Reed. Not ever. You think I don't know the things you're involved in?"

I was reaching. Hoping he'd stumble and admit something I could use. Give me something I could take to Ian to serve up as proof.

Rage blistered across his flesh. "You don't know anything. And even if you did, no judge will believe you. Don't you get that yet? I own this town. Every bit as much as I own you."

Dread made my spirit want to falter. The cruel actuality of what he said.

He possessed all the power.

I lifted my chin, praying he'd bite. "I have proof. Pictures . . ."

His voice dropped into his own threat. "I warned you that you were putting your nose in places it doesn't belong. As my wife, you are there to stand at my side, not get involved in my business. Do you understand? You need to come home . . . where I can protect you."

Disbelief had my mouth dropping open. He was serious. He actually thought that I would find comfort and safety in his home. That I'd what . . . keep my mouth shut like a good little wife? "Thanks, but I think I'll pass on your brand of chivalry. And in case you need the reminder, I'm not your wife."

"Don't make me do something I'll regret."

Harsh laughter rocked out of me, all mixed up with the fear that curled and beat and thrummed in my blood.

He was insane.

One second, he was acting like he loved me and wanted to keep me safe, and the next he was threatening to be the one doing the damage.

I kept my chin lifted, refusing to cower. "Like what, Reed? Are you going to hit me? Have me taken out? Tell me exactly what it is you want to protect me from."

He shuffled on his feet, dropping down to get in my face. "From things you don't understand. And don't act like I'm the bad guy here. I'm the one who has five-hundred grand missing from his safe. I will have that money, and I will have you."

I cocked my head at him. Feigning strength. Defiance. Hating the way my knees were knocking. "You're delusional. I'll never let you touch me again, and I don't have that money."

A shriek flew out of my mouth when he twisted a hand in my hair and jerked it hard, venom grating from his mouth. "You think you're smarter than me? You think I don't know you took that money? It's mine. Just like you. It's time you remembered it."

His mouth slammed down on mine, violent as he tried to force his tongue into my mouth, his body pressing into me.

Depraved and perverted.

Just like I knew he was.

Nausea lapped in my stomach, and I groaned a defiant sound. My hands slapped out as I flailed and tried to break free of his hold. He grabbed me by both wrists and pinned them over my head.

"No," I screamed, no ears to hear it.

He kicked my legs apart and wedged himself between them. He held my wrists with one hand while one went to my breast. Squeezing hard.

I whimpered, tears springing to my eyes.

No.

This couldn't happen. It couldn't.

I struggled harder, trying to break free, kicking and trying to bite him when he pushed his hand up under my skirt. "Stupid girl."

It rang with so much ugliness. And I could almost hear the voice whisper through the choppy air, *Angel Girl.*

Angel girl.

"You're going to regret ever fucking with me," Reed wheezed, hand fumbling under my skirt. "No one leaves a Dearborne."

I kicked and screamed and wailed.

But he was stronger.

Crueler.

I was at his mercy.

That was a bad place to be when I knew he was merciless.

IAN

I rammed on the brakes when I saw the Jaguar parked two houses down from Grace's.

Awareness scattered across my flesh, a dark, black plague that pulsed with hostility.

That motherfucker was here.

The second I'd gotten word that the petition had been denied, I'd jumped in my car and headed over here.

Exactly like I'd promised myself I wouldn't do.

I cut the engine and jumped out.

Adrenaline spiked, every muscle in my body curling with aggression as I moved up the sidewalk toward Grace's house.

Trees and hedges surrounded the property, concealing the

front.

But still, it was in the air—the taste of her fear.

I followed it, moving faster and faster with each step.

A scream broke in the air.

Grace.

That spike of adrenaline I'd felt when I first got here dumped like a vat into my system.

Brimming and overflowing.

I started to run, vision clouding with red when I rounded the hedge and found Grace caged against her car.

Bastard was plastered to that sweet body, grinding himself all over my girl. Hand under her dress while he tried to kiss her.

He was trying to kiss her.

Sweat slicked my skin, images flashing, my heart whipping and my spirit thrashing.

I sprinted for them.

There was no thinking it through. No calculating the risks or the consequences. I grabbed him by the back of the collar and yanked him away from her.

The asshole stumbled, so wrapped up in defiling the girl that he hadn't even realized I was there.

Took him about two seconds to add it up.

"You fucking prick." He came right for me.

I welcomed it.

The way his body slammed mine, the fucker wider than me, but he wasn't close to being a match.

Pussy-bitch clean and polished.

He'd probably never even been the brunt of a schoolyard scuffle.

I let him take me to the ground, dick thinking he had the upper hand. He scrambled to get on top of me, and I lifted a foot and planted the sole of my shoe against his chest, sending him sailing where he thudded to the concrete.

Instantly, I spun, crouched before I attacked, on him in a second flat. My fists flew with all the fury I felt.

With all the hatred and the anger bottled inside me.

For Grace.

For those kids.

Memories spun as I pounded the fucker into the ground. Sight blurring at the edges.

My mother.

I pummeled his face. Strike after strike. Blow after blow.

My mother.

He was just like those pricks who'd used her. Kept her drugged and needy and bloody. The men who'd used me and my brother as punching bags.

Total disregard.

I was wholly game to *disregard* him.

Flesh split and blood gushed, and I could feel the splintering of bones.

Every part of me coming unglued.

Unhinged.

Screams were all around me. Hitting my ears.

That sweet, sweet voice begging me to hear.

The impact of it barely landed in the fringes of my manic mind. "Ian . . . please . . . stop. You have to stop."

"Asshole," I seethed. "I'll end you. You think you can touch her?"

From behind, Grace curled her arms around my neck, her mouth at my ear, her presence penetrating through the haze of violence that blinded my heart and mind.

"Ian, you've got to stop. Please, stop."

Another blow landed on his cheek.

"Please," she begged again. "You can't do this. Not like this."

I sagged, slowing, my last punch landing limp. My vision flickered, and my heart pounded harder than it had before.

With something different.

Something bigger than I'd ever felt.

I sucked for a breath, the cold air drawn into my collapsing lungs.

I staggered to my feet. Prying myself away before I went for him again.

"Oh, God." Grace pressed her hand to her mouth when she saw the mess I'd made of the piece of shit who was trying to destroy her life.

The piece of shit who was using her.

The piece of shit who was trying to take her from me.

He was coughing, gasping for air, groaning in pain. Finally, he peeled himself off the ground, staggering to one side and then the other, hand swiping across the river of blood dripping from one eyebrow and his chin.

He only managed to smear it all over his smug face that was now a little disfigured, nose bent and lip busted.

Blue eyes glared at me, blinking in disbelief, like he was having a hard time accepting that he'd just gotten his ass handed to him. Wondered if the fucker knew I'd only stopped because it was what Grace had begged me to do.

For her.

For her.

Every-fucking-thing had become about *her*.

I looked in her direction, my damned heart bleeding as badly as that bastard's chin. Wanting to crawl all over her. Wrap her up. Hold and never let anyone hurt her again.

I'd almost been too late.

My stomach roiled with what would have happened if I'd waited for five more minutes.

My gaze ripped from the girl when he bellowed out a deranged laugh. "Oh. I see how it is. You're fucking your attorney." He wasn't looking at me when he said it. "You think I don't know who this punk is?"

Frantic, Grace shook her head. "No."

He was back in her face in a flash. "You fucking slut . . . don't lie to me. You're fucking your attorney, aren't you?"

I had half a mind to finish him. Take him out. Erase the threat from her life.

Didn't give a shit what it cost.

I sucked it down, trying to latch onto the thread of sanity that was dangling somewhere in my brain, getting blown in the breeze, just out of reach.

I'd worked too hard to let this cocksucker ruin my life. And I wasn't going to do something that would ruin hers.

"No, asshole, I came over here to have her sign the paperwork in response to the petition I filed at the courts today. And low and behold, what do I find, the same scumbag she just made a claim against, the man she stated she was afraid of, trying to rape her. Wonder how that's going to look?"

It was my own threat.

Go on, asshole. Cry to the media that you got your ass kicked. I'll have your reputation fried in the blink of an eye.

Incredulous laughter rocked from him, and he was shaking his head, looking away before he turned his attention back on me. I thought maybe the man staring back at me was every bit as hard as I was.

Stone.

Willing to do whatever it took for him to get what he wanted. "You actually think you're going to go up against me? A pathetic, scrounging at the bottom of the barrel, wannabe attorney who thinks he's a hot shot, thinks he's actually going to go up against me? Funny how you're the only attorney in town who was willing to take her case."

I lifted my chin. "I took it because it was one I knew I could win. One that I will win. When I rip your fucking name to shreds in court, I'll be the one all you piss-ass politicians who think they know what's best for everyone want on their side. It was a calculated risk. After today?" I squeezed my fist that was screaming like a bitch. "I'm pretty damned glad I took it. It's looking like a sure thing."

He looked between Grace and me. The girl was getting rocked by quivers of unrest that speared through her body, her spirit in turmoil, that energy so fierce I wasn't sure how I was still standing right there pretending like I was still doing this for myself.

He backed away, nodding. Knew from the expression on his face that it wasn't in surrender. He pointed at Grace. "Warned you."

Then he turned and stormed away.

Grace and I stood there in the breezy silence of the quiet neighborhood, watching him go.

The fact the judge had called Reed told me the law was not

going to be our best asset.

This was going to be a harder fight than I'd first anticipated, and I'd already been sure it was going to be a shitshow.

Hell, I'd known it was close to hopeless from the get go.

Reason I didn't want to take it in the first place.

Not when I felt like every part of me was wrapped up in the middle of it.

My fists clenched in agitation when his engine roared and his tires squealed as he flipped around and tore down the street.

Every muscle in my body was rigid, antsy and angry and hungering to go after him. But it was the worry I felt for Grace that had everything breaking down around me.

She stood in some kind of terrorized, numbed state.

Her jaw slack and her gaze vacant.

"I'm so sorry I didn't get here sooner." It rumbled out of me, so low it became one with the whip of the wind.

Grace turned my way, emotion so thick in her expression that I was having a hard time standing in her presence.

Especially after this afternoon at the salon. After what I'd just walked in on right then.

"You're sorry, Ian? You saved me."

My face pinched as I let the admission free. "I want to kill him, Grace. I want to get in my car and chase him down and end it all. Destroy him so he has no chance of hurting you or your children again."

She edged my way, locks of long, wavy hair whipping around her face, the girl a tornado of energy.

She reached out a trembling hand and touched the spot over my eye where the prick had gotten in a shot. "You're here. That's the only thing that matters."

"Grace," I whispered, unable to stop, overcome with this swell of emotion that filled me up. Bubbling from the deepest part of me, in that vacant place that had been left for ugliness that now glowed with something warm.

She reached her hand out for me. "Come on, let's get you cleaned up. You're a mess."

I followed her into the house. The walls echoed with a

profound stillness. Or maybe the intensity that beat between us was so alive that it was the only movement I could feel.

Pulse after pulse.

She moved down the hallway, and I followed. She turned into the first door on the left that was a small bathroom.

She shut the door behind us.

It closed us in.

Swore, I could taste her on my tongue.

That I was inhaling her spirit and imbibing her goodness.

That this woman was ruining me.

Those hands found the buttons of my shirt, and she was peeking up at me as she worked through them.

Slowly.

One by one.

Her heart battered so hard I could feel it drumming against the walls.

Ricocheting.

Slamming from her and into me.

Beat after beat.

She pushed the shirt off my shoulders.

Shivers rushed, and my breaths turned shallow. "Grace," I whispered again.

Her head slowly shook. "I don't know what would have happened if you hadn't have shown up here."

Rage burst in my blood. Flames of fury and hatred.

Incinerating.

I reached up and ran the pad of my thumb across her bottom lip.

Wiping hard.

Like I could erase the bastard.

"He tried to kiss you."

I knew he'd intended more. Way more. His hands all over her. Slipping under and trying to get inside. All of it . . . it made me crazy. Self-control chipped away as I pictured what could have happened.

That he'd hurt her. Touch her. Force her.

Could feel that thread fraying, spinning, getting ready to snap.

I brushed my thumb across her lips again, entranced by the motion.

Kisses are for who you love most.

Emotion bottled in my chest.

So tight.

So big.

So real.

And the girl, she ran her fingertips over my mouth, tenderly, in a way I wasn't sure I'd ever been touched.

I breathed out, lips parting.

Those blue eyes watched me with something vast. Something endless.

A toiling sea of all the things she couldn't feel.

The things that I couldn't feel.

But it was there.

Brimming in the space between us. Lapping like the lull of her waves. Rising higher and higher. So comforting and quiet that I was under before I knew I was drowning.

Our bodies had begun to move, circling, hovering, magnets that attracted and repelled.

Not quite touching.

So close. So close.

Unable to resist the connection, I dropped my forehead to hers, a choked sound leaving me, pain and wounds and the overpowering desire to protect her.

To keep her and hold her.

I squeezed my eyes closed, rocking forward and rocking back, pained pants leaving my lungs as I warred with this feeling.

With the compulsion.

Compelled to find this girl in a way I'd never found another.

There was nothing I could do.

My mouth slanted over hers, and I felt myself slip into oblivion.

Our lips pressed softly.

Once.

Twice.

God, she tasted so good. So right. So perfect.

The sweetest, juiciest plum.

It was instant. The way delirium raced.

A need unlike I'd never had before.

Wanting to consume all of her.

Like taking of her could fill up the hollowed-out space in my chest. Provide and sustain.

My hand twisted in her soft hair, and I slanted my mouth over hers, swallowing her needy gasp as I kissed her.

I kissed her.

"Ian." On a raspy moan, her fingernails sank into my shoulders, raking my skin, trying to get closer.

Her tongue sought mine.

A soft, sugared petal.

Swirling so deliciously.

Ecstasy.

I'd never known it quite like this.

I kissed her harder, possessively, lips and tongue and nips of teeth. I wanted to devour her, gulp her down and gorge on her beauty.

She kissed me back just as recklessly. Hands everywhere. The two of us spiraling. Spinning as we banged into the wall, the door, the sink.

Hot, hot kisses.

A fever in my veins.

Need, want . . . love.

Oh, God.

Was pretty sure that was when the thread of sanity finally snapped.

When I lost all control. Mind gone. Insanity taking over. Everything I'd fought and overcome and put behind me finally caught up to me.

There were some things in life you couldn't outrun.

Fear.

My oldest friend. My constant partner. Cold and hungry and afraid.

It gripped me everywhere, in a way I hadn't felt since I was seventeen.

My chest tightened and everything came crashing down.

Raining.

Pouring.

Annihilating.

Panic gripped me by the chest. A steely vice. Crushing.

I couldn't do this.

I couldn't.

I pressed my hands to her shoulders and pried myself away, lungs jerking as I sucked for the air that had gone missing, horrified as I stared down at the girl who was watching me with what I couldn't receive.

Panic took control of my shaking movements, and I snatched my shirt up from the floor, shrugged it on, and flew out the door.

IAN
TWELVE YEARS OLD

Ian shot upright in his bed. Darkness surrounded him. He blinked, disoriented, his sight almost completely taken by the deep, desolate night.

But he knew he'd heard it.

The front door bursting open and banging against the wall.

His heart took off the way it always did, fear creeping up behind him like a monster that would jump on his back and sink its fangs into the side of his throat.

Drain him dry.

Ian struggled to breathe.

He wanted to burrow under the blanket. Hide. But that's what cowards did, and Ian was no coward.

His brother told him he had to be brave.

That he had to take care of himself.

He shoved off the itchy fabric and stood, his knees shaking so badly he almost dropped to them when he heard a crash of shattering glass and the whimper of his mother, all of it muddled together with another voice.

Gulping down the terror, Ian inched to the door, squeezing his eyes closed as he turned the knob and sneaked out into the hall. A hazy light glowed from the main room of the apartment.

This one was nicer than they'd had for as long as he could remember, the refrigerator full and the water always warm when he wanted a shower.

His mama said she was going to take good care of them from now on. She'd promised that she hated it when they were cold and hungry, and that she was going to make sure it never happened ever again.

She said she was clean. That she was going to stay that way. That she wasn't going to touch that crap ever again.

Best part? His mama . . . she'd seemed . . . happy. Smiling so much that it made Ian think it might be safe to smile, too.

But the sounds coming from the kitchen didn't sound like she was smiling.

"Fuck you," she whimpered. "Get out of my house, you piece of shit."

Ian pushed his back up against the hall wall and slid that direction, wishing his big brother Jace wasn't still off with his friends.

He'd know what to do.

There was another crash, and his mother screeched. Her footsteps pounded on the floor. Heavier ones were right behind her.

Fear raced across Ian's flesh like the prick of a million needles when he heard the man's low, menacing voice. "Your house? I bought you, you stupid bitch. You think any of this comes for free?"

Ian peeked around the corner, and the man was trying to put

his mouth on his mother, his body way bigger than his mom's, so muscly and hard, Ian was worried he could break her in half.

She kept moving her face away from him, head jerking one way and then the other, trying to stop him from putting his gross mouth on her lips. "Stop."

Sickness crawled through Ian's belly.

Kisses are for who you love the most.

That man didn't love his mother.

His mama flailed and kicked while the man tried to put his hand under her shirt, and his mother cried out, "Get off me, you sick prick. You disgust me. I told you we were over. Over!"

Ian flinched when he heard the crack.

He'd heard the same thing before, and he knew it was a strike across his mother's face. That her cheek would be blue tomorrow, and she'd spend the day in bed crying.

It only took that flash of realization, and he was no longer afraid. He went barreling out into the other room, roaring at the top of his lungs, "Leave my mama alone!"

He might be skinny, but Jace told him he was a fighter.

A scrapper who was gonna take everyone by surprise.

He jumped on the back of the guy who had his mother pinned against the kitchen counter, climbing him like he was a jungle gym. He locked his arms around the man's neck. He cinched down as tight as he could. "Run, Mama, run. Get out of here. I'll save you."

Horror streaked across her face, just as dark as the mascara that ran in messy lines down her cheeks. "Oh my God, Ian. Let him go. Get down. Let him go."

Ian fought harder, tightening his arms until they were trembling with the force he was trying to exert.

But he guessed it didn't matter all that much because the man growled and grabbed Ian by the wrist. He gripped him and swung at the same time, tossing Ian across the kitchen like he didn't weigh anything at all.

Ian slammed into the refrigerator, hitting it like a rag doll, arms and legs flopping around like they weren't attached. Pain splintered across his shoulder and the side of his head.

He slid down and slumped to the floor.

He tried not to cry from the pain.

But Ian realized he didn't really know what pain was.

Not until the man ripped his belt from his pants and came for him.

An hour or a minute or a day. Ian didn't know. All he knew was agony.

His mama was screaming. Begging for the man to stop. It only made the man hurt him more. That was the last thing Ian knew before everything went black.

Ian couldn't move, everything hurt so bad. He tried to pry his eyes open, but they were too puffy and swollen, every part of his skin feeling like it might burst.

"Shh, baby, shh. I'm so sorry. I'm so sorry." His mama's voice was right there at his ear, and he realized he was in her arms, and she was rocking him. "I won't let nothin' bad happen to you, not ever again."

He drifted in and out, lulled by the sound of her singing softly in his ear. "Forever and ever."

Her lips fell on his temple as she gave him a soft, soft kiss.

It stung.

But to Ian, it was the best thing he'd ever felt.

twenty-nine

IAN

I jolted awake where I'd fallen asleep in the driver's seat of my car where I'd pulled it up to sit right in front of Grace's house. Gasping for air and disoriented, my eyes darted around the shadows leaping through the darkened neighborhood. The trees were a bluster where the wind pummeled and pounded, clouds building in the starry-sky, a storm to bring on the winter.

Creeper mode.

Protector mode.

Wasn't sure I even knew the difference any longer.

The only thing I knew was I hadn't been able to force myself to drive away from the spot since I'd ran out her door hours upon hours earlier. I'd just . . . sat in my car.

Guarding.

Refusing to leave in case that weasel-dick showed his mangled face.

Grace's grandmother had gotten home with the kids about an hour after I'd left, and I'd sat there, watching the lights come on at twilight before they'd finally dimmed at around ten-thirty.

The house going silent.

Didn't mean I hadn't been able to feel Grace. Her gaze searching for me from out the window. Her spirit nothing but worry, like I could feel it radiating out to gather me up.

Wasn't sure when I'd drifted. But there I was at after one in the morning, gripping the steering wheel, sweating like a motherfucker. I might as well have been that twelve-year-old kid getting his ass beat to within an inch of his life rather than the man I'd become who refused to allow anyone or anything to touch him.

That man had just been another in the long line of men who had come in and out of our lives. Depraved and deranged.

I scrubbed a hand over my face to break up the exhaustion and grabbed my phone where I'd tossed it to the passenger seat.

Part of me hoped Grace had texted me.

Another was wondering if I'd hear from Mack, my mug plastered all over their alerts, wanted for assault.

Reed's pride was too bloated to let me get away with it.

I blew out a sigh when I saw that my phone was void of any messages, eyes moving, everything silent except for the howl of the night.

Still, agitation lined my bones. Deep and cold. Filled with dread.

Everything felt . . . off.

I didn't know if it was the recurrence of that dream, the scars lining my body screaming in agony, or if it was the girl who rested inside that house.

The only thing I knew was I couldn't sit idle.

I had to do . . . something.

Make the first move.

Not wait around for the bastard to have the upper hand.

I pushed the button to start my car. A spray of headlights lit the road, and I eased by Grace's house, carefully searching, making sure they were safe before I made a U-turn.

The powerful engine of the Mercedes roared as I accelerated. Streetlamps glared from above, casting the pavement in a hazy white glow, not a soul around as I sped beneath the flash of streetlamps that shined from above.

Had no clue what the fuck I was doing except for crossing all kinds of lines. So many of them, I was sure there was no other outcome than one that was going to be bad.

I was getting myself in so deep there would be no resurfacing.

No reclaiming what I'd worked for. Strived for. Lived for.

Stupid.

Goddamned stupid, but I didn't know how to stop this out of control train as I flew around a corner, making a sharp right, not even slowing when I did. Tires squealed as I skidded, the rear fishtailing for a second before I caught traction and barreled down the street.

Anxiety climbed with every second. With every mile.

I took a couple more turns the same way, flying through the night like I was invisible.

Invincible.

That's what it was going to take to win this case.

No fucking fear of what would be waiting for me at the end of the street.

As I approached the ritzy neighborhood, I slowed. I made a left and then a right, thanking God my car didn't stick out in a place like this.

Here, the houses were set back, surrounded by spiked wrought-iron fences, some surrounded by stone, all fucking pretentious and oozing old money.

The house had been in the Dearborne family for more than a century, Reed's great grandfather one of the first bankers in the area. Politics had quickly become synonymous with their name. Reed's father had once been mayor, and Reed seemed all too eager to take it one step farther.

Knowing the prick, he probably just wanted to show him up.

My hands fisted tighter around the steering wheel, my knuckles torn to shreds and starting to scab, a reminder of the sleaze the asshole really was.

Thomas's voice had become a constant whisper in the back of my head.

Bitches who don't obey need to bleed.

What the fuck did that even mean?

Didn't know if it was some chauvinistic bullshit tossed around like banter or some kind of true directive or command.

Probably wasn't going to find the answer to it by creeping around his house in the middle of the night, but I couldn't help but drive to his address.

Maybe I'd sit guard.

Cut him off first if the asshole was stupid enough to even think about going back over to Grace's place.

I eased alongside the estate. It was at least four acres surrounded by a stone wall that was broken by sections of blackened wrought-iron. A passerby would only get blinks of the rambling lawn and expanse of massive, ancient trees that stretched over the property. That and the hint of the grandeur of the white house tucked inside was all a person could see.

Like they got off on the tease. Giving a tiny glimpse to those who weren't quite good enough to take a look at the whole thing.

My chest fisted.

I hated this pompous shit.

Hated that Grace had been lured into it. Hated that her children were subjected to it.

I pulled to the curb at one of the breaks in the fence, peering into the muted lights that shown through the hedges. I could make out one side of an enormous fountain in the middle of the round drive and the very edge of a step of the front porch.

But it was a shadow off to the side that caught my attention.

I straightened, straining to see through the wisps of darkness that swayed and moved over the property.

What the fuck?

I had to be hallucinating.

Squinting, I angled to get a better look.

My heart took off at a sprint.

I was sure it would be impossible for me to mistake that posture. That overbearing demeanor of the man who stood facing who was clearly Reed Dearborne.

Lawrence Bennet.

Fear climbed my throat.

Locking it up in an excruciating kind of terror.

Not for me.

For her.

It felt like I was going to suffocate in the cabin of my car. Inhaling, I tried to break up the frozen shock, and I forced myself to shift into gear, releasing the brake so my car could roll away from the curb, barely accelerating and praying the rumbling engine wouldn't draw attention.

When I got to the corner, I gunned it.

One sight in mind.

One reason.

One answer.

I'd promised her I would protect her.

And that was exactly what I was going to do.

GRACE

Frantic pounding echoed from the front door, cutting into my sleep and sending me bolting upright. With my palms pressed to the mattress behind me, my eyes darted around my room, confusion clouding everything. That was when I noticed my phone continually lighting up from where it sat on the nightstand.

Blip after blip.

Quickly, I fumbled for it. My heart that had spent the evening being subjected to the worst sort of turmoil jumped into an erratic rhythm when I saw who the string of texts were from.

Ian: Open the front door.

Ian: You have to be pissed at me. I know. I'm a dick.

Ian: But you need to open it right now. This isn't about us.

I didn't even question it. I threw off my covers and raced for the door, not taking the time to put on pants. I was barefoot, wearing just a tee and my underwear, fumbling down the darkened hallway to the door that a heavy fist was banging on again.

On the other side of the house, a light flickered on, and I knew Gramma had to have been awakened, too.

I rushed through the two locks and tossed open the door.

Ian was there, pacing on the stoop, gripping at mounds of that soft hair.

The man so menacing. So big and powerful where he raged at the door.

"Ian," I whispered the shock, my mind struggling to catch up with what was happening. Why he would be standing there in the middle of the night after he'd spent the rest of the day and evening out in his car.

I knew keeping watch. Needing distance and not having the ability to fully walk away.

But after whatever had happened in the bathroom, my soul had ached with the reality that it had to. That after all of this was said and done, after the trial, *after he saved my family,* he had to walk.

He had to protect himself.

His career and his heart.

I knew, without a doubt, he didn't have the full capacity of loving us.

Not the way I'd come to realize that I loved him.

His thick throat bobbed. The man stood in the wispy shadows of night wearing the same bloodied shirt, though the buttons were askew, the sleeves shoved up his arms. The man was a disaster.

His beauty so intense it was almost a tragedy.

"Grace."

"What's going on?"

His jaw clenched, anger blistering and crude, brutal

possessiveness flashing in those strange-colored eyes. "We have to get you out of here."

A bolt of terror stumbled me back. "What?"

Without being invited inside, he pushed through the door, angling as if he couldn't stand it if our bodies were to touch. Like that might be the one thing that would finally push us over the edge.

As if we hadn't already arrived at that point the first time we'd met.

"We have to get you out of here. You and the kids. Right now."

I swiveled to watch him stalk into the house, and my sight caught on my grandmother who was standing off to the side, wringing her frail fingers together with her white hair sticking up all over the place.

I wanted to tell her everything was fine. To go back to bed and not to worry. I didn't think I could pull off a lie that great.

Because I felt it—the disorder howling in the space.

Reaching out, I snatched Ian by the wrist before he had the chance to go busting down the hall. "Tell me what's happening."

He whirled around. I was taken aback by the fierce agony cut into every line on his face. "You're in danger."

"How . . . how do you know? What happened?"

"I don't know, Grace. I don't fucking know . . . but I *know*." He stabbed his fingertips against his heart. "*I know*."

He rushed for me and gripped me by the face with those big hands. Stealing my breath. Shattering my world. He'd been shattering it all along. "Please . . . you have to trust me on this."

I couldn't tell him that I trusted him more than I'd ever trusted any other man in my life. I couldn't tell him that he was the one who felt like safety. Couldn't tell him that he felt like the goal we were running for.

The only thing I could do was nod frantically.

Then his eyes raked down my body.

So hot, they licked across my flesh like the searing of flames, everything turning dark when he realized I was standing there in almost nothing.

He dropped his arms as if he were being burned and stepped

away. "Get dressed."

I nodded again and darted down the hall. He was right on my heels, moving into my childhood room. He filled it with that presence, bounding and pulsing, pouring into my lungs and strumming my heart into a frenzy.

I pulled on a pair of jeans, and the man was at my closet, throwing the doors open and grabbing a bag. He moved to my dresser and started to frantically stuff clothes into it.

I shoved my feet into my shoes, my nerves frazzled where they tumbled from my mouth. "Where are we going?"

"Somewhere safe," he told me, giving me no details.

It didn't matter. I trusted him anyway. Trusted him with my life. With my children's lives.

And I realized that was the most significant thing of all.

That I'd place them in his hands and trusted that he would do them no harm. That he would be the one to stand for them. Protect them.

Even when he had absolutely nothing to gain.

I wondered if he had any idea what type of man that made him. If he had the first inclination that when I looked at him, I saw someone giving and selfless and good, when he believed himself rotten and vulgar.

The devil when I saw a shattered saint.

He zipped up the bag and tossed it to me. "Take that."

Then he was moving back out of the door and into the hall, going straight for the door that had been left open a crack.

As if he already knew exactly where they rested. As if he could sense the lulled thrums and magnified dreams of their sweet, sweet hearts.

He softly pushed open the door. Light from the hall spilled into the room.

Thomas instantly stirred, sitting up in bed and rubbing his fists in his eyes. "Mom?" He blinked, trying to focus. "What's wrong?"

Ian went directly to him and knelt. He set a reassuring hand on his knee.

That might have been the very moment when my heart completely burst.

A million pieces fragmenting.

Scattering.

Spilling.

Seeking a new home.

Finding him.

The moment the man owned every part of me.

Heart and body and soul committed to his hands when I knew full well that he couldn't hold me. That he couldn't keep me. That what we were was hopeless except for what we were both fighting for.

But *they* were worth it.

Every sacrifice and every loss.

Ian's voice was quieted. "Thomas, I need you to listen to me very carefully. We're going to pack a few things, and then we're going to leave. I'm taking all of you to a safer place where I can protect you. I want you to know it's okay to be afraid, that all of us are sometimes, but I also need you to be brave for your sisters because this is something they can't understand. Can you help me do that?"

"Are you taking us away from our dad?" Thomas asked, words a muted croak.

Ian didn't waver. "Yes."

Thomas slid off his bed and pushed back his shoulders. "All right."

My chest pressed full, and my throat tightened, and I struggled not to cry.

My spirit was being pummeled by so many things.

By so much love and hope and belief.

All mixed up with a torrent of terrorized fear. The undoubted risk we were taking. The truth that Ian would never show up here in the middle of the night, frantic, if we weren't in danger.

Compounding it was that I could feel myself already being crushed by the gutting loss that I knew was to come. The gaping hole this man was going to leave at the center of my soul.

Ian pushed to standing and patted Thomas on the shoulder. "Get the things you want to take with you."

Instantly, Thomas jumped into action. It was no surprise that he grabbed his tablet and charger first and then stuffed a few books and some clothes into the same small suitcase he used when he went to Reed's.

I quickly packed the necessities for Sophie, diapers and her shampoo and her pajamas, her favorite doll, and then I hurried to get Mallory's things that she would want most.

Ian was right there at my side, as if he belonged, shuffling through her drawers and stuffing everything he could into her bag.

We did it all quietly. Barely making a sound as we packed side-by-side. Still, a severity rang between us. The low, pulsing toll of an alarm.

"Ready?" Ian asked as he zipped Sophie's diaper bag.

I could barely nod. "I think so."

Ian walked over to Mallory.

For a moment, he froze, looking down at my sweet child where she slept face down on her bed, sideways, one leg kicked up and all her blonde hair spilled out in rivulets of golden locks over her bed. He seemed to hesitate, fighting some kind of war, before he released a shaky exhale and scooped her into his arms and hugged her against his strong chest.

Break. Break. Break.

I just kept feeling all those pieces creaking inside me. Coming loose. Getting lost forever. Scattering to the wind.

Mallory sighed in contentment, releasing a tiny yawn as she lifted her head in bewilderment before a massive smile lit on her face. She was whispering in a dreamy voice when she claimed, "Ian-Zian the Great."

Ian blanched, almost frozen solid as he rigidly held my daughter.

"What are we doing? Are we going on an adventure?" she asked, far too excited.

He cleared the roughness from his throat, but his voice was still raw and low. "Yes, we're going on an adventure to a special, special place. Is that okay?"

"Yes! I love adventures!"

"Okay," he said, the word thick as he wrapped his arms tighter around her.

He glanced at me, and I picked a sleeping Sophie up from her crib. She didn't even stir as I nestled her into my arms.

We all started for the door.

"Wait!" Mallory cried, a frantic whisper as she wiggled down out of Ian's hold and raced for her bed. She dropped to her knees and pulled the sketchbook out from under it. Holding it against her chest, she went right back for Ian, eager for him to pick her up.

Carefully, he did, and she tucked the bulky book under one arm and snuggled into his arms, her face pressed to his neck.

His eyes dropped closed as his arms cinched tight around her small body, the man so clearly in his own private battle.

Lost in an old war that he had become a prisoner to.

Finally, he turned and walked toward me, mouthing, *We need to go*.

We ushered Thomas out ahead of us, my big, brave man wheeling both his suitcase and Mallory's. I was right behind him, Ian towering over us from behind like a wraith that thrashed and whipped.

His darkness a hedge of protection.

We stopped at the end of the hall where my grandmother was still waiting.

"I'm so sorry, Gramma, for all of this," I rushed.

She moved for me and softly pressed her lips to my cheek before she ran a weathered knuckle down my sleeping baby's cheek, looking between me and my child. "Don't you dare apologize, my girl. You are my gift. Now, yours has come."

Her gaze traveled to Ian.

Overt and unabashed.

"Take care of them," she told him.

I could feel him shifting uneasily on his feet. "That's exactly what I intend to do. I think you should come with us."

She gave a tight shake of her head. "No one is running me out of my house. I'll be here to let you know if someone shows up sniffing around. Don't worry about me. I'm a tough old girl. That coward knows it, too. I'm the last person he's going to mess with."

"Are you sure, Gramma?" I asked, not knowing if she was

better off with us or without us.

"I'm sure," she promised.

She moved to Thomas and lifted his chin with her finger. "You be a good boy and watch over your sisters, Thomas."

"I will, Grams."

"Has anyone told you lately you're a good, good boy?"

Thomas blushed and kind of huffed. "Only you, Grams, and my mom about a million times."

"You just keep proving to the world that you are."

He nodded tightly, and I saw my son's fear and ferocity.

She turned her attention on me. "Go on then. Call me in the morning and let me know that you're safe." She looked back at Ian. "I expect you to keep them that way."

A flood of energy gushed from Ian. A promise that was felt rather than heard.

We all shuffled out the door and into the chilly night, the wheels of the suitcases zipping on the sidewalk as Thomas hauled them toward the street. Without saying anything, we moved to Ian's car that was parked at the curb, the headlights still on and cutting through the dense, deep night where it idled.

Clearly ready for a getaway.

Leaving the suitcases at the trunk, Thomas opened the backdoor and climbed in, and Ian sat Mallory next to him.

He barely cast me a glance as he went to my car and removed the car seat that he quickly installed.

He buckled in my children.

Sophie stirred when he took her from me. "It's okay," he murmured softly.

Something hard and rigid lining his muscles as he did.

The gentle actions so at odds with the clear violence I could see pushing at his flesh, muscles bound and nerves on edge.

Those demons on his arms screaming.

The cross crying out.

Once the kids were secured, he placed the baggage into the trunk and then we both climbed into the front seats. I looked back through the window as we pulled away. My grandmother stood in the doorway.

Your gift has come.

Everything tightened.

My heart and my chest and the knots that continually fisted my stomach.

I looked over at Ian.

So gorgeous where he sat at the wheel. So fierce and dominant. The sinister man who oozed sin and seduction who'd come to mean everything.

A hero I'd never expected.

He made a few turns, quickly but safely driving through the city, eyes darting around to take in our surroundings. He continually glanced in the rear-view mirror to check on my children, the girls fast asleep and Thomas sitting there stoic, the way that he did.

Knowing more than I wished he had to.

So brave when the only thing I wanted was for him to get to live his childhood without these overbearing cares and worries.

Ian reached over the console and took my hand.

He squeezed it.

Warmth.

Care.

A quiet hum of need.

Ten minutes later, we broke out of the city. The buildings had grown sparse and the marshlands grew thick as we hit a two-lane road. Random houses surrounded by trees were lit up by porch lights where they were tucked off the country road, the yellow, dotted stripe down the middle of the secluded road our guide as we raced through the night.

I didn't ask him where we were going.

I trusted him. Trusted him more than I'd ever trusted anyone.

Ian began to slow as we came into a small town, a big painted sign boasting a population of twenty-three hundred that welcomed us to Broadshire Rim.

I'd heard of it, but it was an area I had never visited.

Ian kept our speed slow as we drove through the quaint town. It felt as if we'd been taken back a century. Storefronts lined the main road, different colored awnings stretched out over the sidewalks with parking spaces angled in front.

He squeezed my hand as if he felt all of my questions. "Almost there."

We took a right and then another onto a dirt road.

The car bounced along the uneven road, the headlights cutting into the night, illuminating another big painted sign on the left.

Broadshire Blooms Bed and Breakfast.

Ian slowed and made a left onto the narrow, tree-lined lane. On either side, mammoth oaks reached for the sky, their old branches stretching out to create a canopy of welcome overhead.

The car rounded a slight curve and a three-story plantation came into view.

Clearly restored and just as striking as it had to have been back in its original day.

It had two stories of wrap-around porches and massive pillars holding them high, the third-story roof arched in three different areas, like three mountain peaks jutting for the speckled, shimmering sky.

It had to be the most gorgeous thing I'd ever seen.

Coming to a stop in the rounded drive, Ian stared over at me, emphatic as he said, "You'll be safe here. These are the best people you'll ever meet."

I looked back at the house as one side of the double doors opened. A man who looked so much like Ian stepped out onto the porch. A beautiful, dark-haired woman with a newborn cradled in her arms followed him.

Love and support shone fast in their eyes. Care and concern that flooded through the night.

And I wondered if Ian knew he was a part of that equation.

Because some people came into our lives because they were meant to be.

I squeezed his fingers.

And I knew Ian was always supposed to be a part of mine.

IAN

I cranked open the door and slipped from my car.

My brother barely lifted his chin at me in a gesture so slight that only I would notice it. His promise that he would always be there for me, no matter what I needed.

Even if it meant dragging his ass out of bed in the middle of the night.

Suffice it to say, he'd thought I was drunk and playing some sort of sick prank when I'd called him on the way to Grace's and told him to get ready for us.

Three kids in tow.

Not exactly my style.

"Jace," I said, voice grit, filled with nothing but stark gratitude and the quiet fury I felt at finding Lawrence with Reed. Hating not knowing what was going down, but not fool enough not to realize whatever it was, it was bad.

Lawrence would strike someone down in a blink.

In a flash.

In the second it took to cock a gun.

Two of them together equaled the type of depravity I didn't want to contemplate.

Jace tried to keep his footsteps light as he bounded down the porch steps. "Ian."

I rounded the front of my car, and he came right for me, pulling me into a tight hug. He clapped me on the back and muttered at my ear, "You've got some explaining to do, brother."

Obviously.

"Let's get them settled. Then we can talk."

Nodding, he stepped back.

Faith, Jace's wife, slowly came down the stairs, protecting her youngest child against her chest, my sweet niece Bailey Button undoubtedly sleeping and not having the first clue about the inn's newest guests.

Faith pressed up on her toes to plant a kiss on my cheek. "We're so glad you came to us."

I almost laughed. "Don't thank me yet."

Who knew what kind of shitstorm I might be dragging into their home.

Turning this old plantation into a bed and breakfast had forever been my brother and his wife's dream, since they'd first met when we'd moved to this small town when I was sixteen.

Our *mama* had gotten another wild hair, moving us out of the city and thinking we would actually find a better life. Like she wouldn't be the same useless mess wherever we went.

We'd only been here for a short time before things had gone south for Jace, but during that time, he'd found his destiny.

His fate that had been stolen from him.

The guy had fought for it until he'd claimed what was always meant to be, even with years of heartache and loss separating the two of them.

I'd call bullshit on the whole *happily ever after* bit except for the proof of it that was standing right there. Shining from their faces, so real it was impossible to miss.

I moved to Grace's door and opened it.

I extended my hand to help her out.

A flashfire raced my arm.

Every fucking time.

Every touch.

Every brush.

Nervously, she stood, a little more flustered than I'd ever seen her. "Grace, this is my brother Jace, and his wife, Faith." My tone was a gentle encouragement.

"Welcome to our home," Faith said, stepping forward. The girl was all warmth. Oozing comfort.

Grace stepped forward and accepted her embrace, the baby snug between them. "Thank you so much for having us here. I'm so sorry to wake you in the middle of the night."

Faith giggled a soft sound and bounced Benton. "Oh, not a whole lot of sleep happening around here these days, anyway. This little guy thinks the only time he can sleep is when I'm rocking and pacing with him. Second I put him down, he starts to scream."

Jace wrapped an arm around his wife and nuzzled his face along her cheek. "My little man has good taste."

Grace glanced at me for reassurance. No doubt, she'd thought I'd steal them away to somewhere secret and far, where no one could find her. But if anyone would stand up and fight with me for them it was Jace, Mack a phone call away.

Without a doubt, we were going to need those connections.

"Why don't we get everyone inside so y'all can get some sleep?" Faith offered. "We only have one other guest right now, and he's checking out in the mornin', so it'll just be you and your family staying. My daughter Bailey is going to be beside herself when she finds out she has a friend to play with."

Faith's gaze turned to the backseat of the car where Grace's little girls were conked out, Sophie's head dropped all the way forward in her car seat and Mallory with her mouth gaping open wide where she was buckled in her booster.

And Thomas.

Thomas was watching us with all that worry and speculation.

My chest tightened.

The kid had had to grow up too fast. Had seen too much. Hated it in a way that few could understand.

My hands fisted with the thought that he'd ever have to endure any of the pain and agony that had been inflicted on me.

Just the thought of someone striking him was more than I could tolerate.

It was instant.

Fury clenching down on my ribs and twisting in my stomach.

It wasn't going to happen.

I jumped when I felt the hand on my arm. Grace looked up at me, worry swimming in the depths of those teal eyes. "Are you okay?"

Not even close.

I cleared my throat and roughed a hand through my hair. "Yeah. Let's get them inside."

"I have all the rooms ready," Faith said, turning for the porch steps.

Jace went to the trunk and pulled out the bags.

I opened the back door, and Grace leaned in and unbuckled Sophie, shushing her and whispering at her temple when the tiny girl whined in her sleep. "It's okay, Sophie Marie. Mommy's got you. Shh."

That meteor in my throat raced faster.

I moved around the car, opening the other door where Thomas waited like the poor kid didn't know if he belonged.

I fucking hated that, too.

That he ever had to question who he was. Question his worth.

"Come on, buddy, let's get inside so you can get some sleep."

His eyes darted around the property, into the billow and rustle of the leaves of the trees. "Are you sure this is a good place?"

"I'm sure. My brother is the nicest man you'll ever meet."

He looked up at me, blinking, his question all too genuine. "Nicer than you?"

The laugh I choked out tasted of bitterness, and I knelt so I could help him gather his charger and tablet that he seemed to cling to like a lifeline. "Yeah, buddy, nicer than me."

A million miles and a lifetime away. Our paths, which had once seemed linear, diverted. Parting in the middle. Him going one way and me the other.

It pushed at that dirty space that echoed with that hollowed-out vacancy.

Threatening to spill.

Breaking through the cracks where it was supposed to be bound and subdued.

Fucking Grace. Fucking Grace with her tempting body and her sweet heart and adorable kids.

Whittling their way in where I couldn't let them.

I swallowed it down and stood.

"Come on. Let's get you inside."

Thomas slid out, and when he did, I set my knee on the backseat so I could reach in and unbuckle Mallory, who was pretty much wedged between the two.

God, when I'd purchased my AMG, the last fucking thing I'd pictured was a herd of kids buckled in the backseat.

Never expected for my heart to fucking quiver when I pulled the little girl into my arms.

For everything to rush and expand when she wrapped her tiny ones around my neck and whispered, "Ian-Zian the Great. The most bestest hero in all the land."

Faith showed us to our rooms, where she'd given us the four bedrooms that ran the left wing on the second floor of the massive plantation.

I'd told Jace implicitly that Grace and I weren't together. That she was a client. That we sure as hell wouldn't be sharing a bed, no matter how goddamned badly I might want to.

He'd instantly caught onto what had felt like a lie grinding through my teeth, the fact that the girl felt like mine. Didn't change the fact that she couldn't be.

The kids were tucked into their rooms, and the rest of us stood outside of Grace's door where she was again profusely thanking Jace and Faith.

Faith touched her arm. "It's our honor. Now, get some rest. I know it has to have been a long night for you."

"Thank you," she said, and Jace sent her a smile. "Good night."

Faith and Jace stepped out of the hall, leaving me and Grace there alone.

She looked up at me with those trusting eyes.

So bright and beautiful and good.

That feeling stretched tight between us. So intense that I was having a hard time not giving in to the pull.

"Good night, Grace."

A somber smile pulled at one side of her mouth. "Good night, Ian."

Stepping back into the room, she snapped the door shut. It took every ounce of willpower I possessed not to bust it open.

Tear through it like some kind of wildman set on staking a claim.

Take her.

I stood there, glaring daggers at the wood. Cursing its existence, hands clenched in grueling restraint.

I jumped about fifteen fucking feet in the air when the voice hit me from the side. "How about a drink, brother?"

My head whipped Jace's direction where he'd moved to the head of the hall, arms stretched out to rest on the walls as he watched me with a mix of speculation and amusement.

I ran both my hands over the top of my head. "Need about ten of them after the day I've had."

Jace's gaze traveled over my disheveled appearance. Shirt fucking shredded, soiled with blood, and my pants wrinkled and covered in dirt. "Found yourself a bit of trouble, yeah?"

A chuckle almost slid free. "You could say that."

He turned and started for the curved staircase. "Won't act like I wasn't shocked when I got your call."

Following behind him, I huffed out a sigh as we hit the first-floor landing of the enormous home. Everything restored, oozing character and charm and an old-world Southern elegance.

Still, there was something haunting about it, like the walls held a thousand secrets, and if you put your ear against one, you could hear the voices screaming out.

Jace led me into the parlor where an old-fashioned bar was set up. Wasn't too hard to imagine the shit that must have gone down in there over the years.

Today, it still had all the original dark, carved wood, and it was furnished with antique sofas and a vintage settee.

I sank into one of the ornate stools while he went behind the bar and poured a tumbler of my favorite scotch. He slid it to me. I took a big gulp as he poured one for himself.

He took a sip and then pressed both his palms to the bar.

"Well?"

Another sigh, and I dropped my head, shaking it. "Got in deep, man."

"No shit."

I ran the back of my hand over my lips and tried to figure out what to tell him when I felt like I didn't know a goddamned thing. "She's going through a nasty custody battle."

"That's rough." But he was eyeing me, clearly knowing there was more.

I exhaled all the air from my lungs before I was sucking for more. Like it might offer some clarity. "Reed Dearborne."

He choked on his scotch, liquid spewing out and splattering on the glossy wood. He grabbed a napkin and ran it over his mouth. "You're serious?"

"Do I look like I'm joking?" I took a deep pull of the amber fluid, welcoming the burn as it raced down my throat.

"He's trying to declare her an unfit mother and using it as a lure to force her back to him." Could barely cut free the explanation.

Jace pursed his lips. "From what I've seen, the guy's a prick."

That feeling knotted up in my throat, and the words were raw when I forced them out. "He's a sick bastard. I . . . I found him trying to force himself on her yesterday afternoon. I'd filed for an emergency injunction granting her full temporary custody until we could go to trial. An hour later, he was tipped off by the judge. He showed at her house."

He pointed at the blood splattered on my shirt. "And I take it that was the result."

"Yup," I said, taking a swill.

"God, you weren't lying when you said you got yourself in deep."

"Gets worse." I looked at my older brother, shaking my head, anger and fear strangling my heart. "I went over to his place tonight, just to stake it out. Make sure the prick wasn't contemplating a repeat."

Alarm tightened everything, guts screaming. "Bennet was there."

The bottom of his glass thumped on the wood when he dropped it away from his mouth. "Ian."

Fear climbed into his voice. The same kind of fear I was feeling. An affirmation that I wasn't being crazy and linking things together that didn't fit. That I wasn't off on some crazy tangent and making assumptions.

Scum found scum.

Just like I'd always said.

Just the way Bennet had found me, no doubt he'd found Reed.

"Reed could just as easily be involved in Bennet's legitimate business as he could the shady. Doesn't prove anything." Jace was trying to sound resolute. Clearly trying to come up with a solution that didn't put my neck on the chopping block.

"You and I both know *legitimate* doesn't go down at two o'clock in the morning."

"How the hell would those two be tied?"

"Not sure, but I will find out. No question in my mind that whatever it is, it will be the key to setting Grace and her kids free from that bastard. Don't care what it takes to figure it out. I'm going to do it."

Jace just stared at me. Shock written all over him.

"You love her."

"No." It shot from my mouth with the velocity of a bullet.

He laughed out a disbelieving sound. "You think I'm an idiot, Ian? You think I don't know there's something more going on between you two? It's so thick, the rest of us are choking on it."

I blinked out what I hoped looked like denial.

"You going to sit there and tell me you haven't slept with her?"

My tongue locked up, so fat and thick it got stuck to the roof of my mouth.

A rough chuckle escaped him. "You're sleeping with your client . . . that's the one thing you'd never do . . . put your career on the line for a piece of ass."

"She's not a piece of ass." The rebuttal whipped out harder than I intended, teeth gritting as I leaned his direction.

He nodded. "Exactly my point."

He huffed out a frustrated sigh, and he lowered his voice. "There's no shame in loving someone, Ian, and there's nothing wrong with letting someone love you in return. You deserve it. You are the most loyal man I know. You've lived alone for too long. You think I don't see it? The way you've been filling your life with meaningless things? You think I don't know that you're covering up for everything that we went through as kids?"

His head shook. "But pretending that it didn't happen doesn't take it away. Those scars are always going to be there until you face them. You deserve to live again."

In another life.

In another life.

Pain lashed through my insides, and my face pinched in disgust.

All of it was aimed directly at myself. "You don't know me, Jace. You don't know the things I've done. I don't deserve anything but to rot."

He scoffed. "I know you better than anyone, and I know you care about that girl upstairs. And I know you care about her kids."

"I can't," I choked, fear constricting. Tightening and suffocating. I wheezed in a breath. "I won't be the one to ruin them."

Jace downed the rest of his drink. Setting his empty on the bar, he pointed at me. "Think the only thing you've ruined is yourself."

If he only fucking knew.

He planted his hands back onto the wood, angling his head. "Maybe it's time you stop and figure out what it is you really want. Because believe me . . . once you love, there's no going back. And when you realize you let that go because you were too stupid and stubborn to hold on to it? When you missed out on the only thing that really mattered? Believe me, brother, that's when you'll discover what it's like to really hate yourself."

"I have one goal, and that's to become partner. To get one step closer to taking over the firm. That's what it's always been. I win this case, and I gain everything I've ever wanted." Every word was goddamned sand. Lies I couldn't tell myself fast enough to make myself believe what I was saying.

"That so?" he challenged.

"That's so."

He pushed away from the bar and walked toward the carved archway, pausing to look back at me. "Then I guess you're a bigger fool than I thought."

Disappointed, Jace walked out, thinking he knew me. That I deserved more.

Thinking I was being selfish.

What he didn't get was I could never keep them.

Not when I didn't deserve anything at all.

IAN

I stumbled down the sweeping staircase, roughing a hand through my bedhead and subduing a yawn as I followed the clatter of noise banging around from the bottom floor.

All the bedrooms had been empty.

At six o'clock in the damned morning.

I tried not to shake my head, tried to fight all the anxiety surrounding all of this. Tried to shove it down into that deep pit where I knew it would only fester.

I'd woken up—feeling different. Like maybe I was a heartbeat from changing a philosophy or two. Clinging to that ridiculous notion that everything would turn out the way it was supposed to.

Yeah fucking right.

It was the only thought in my head as I walked into the enormous kitchen and was slammed with the chaos going down inside.

I froze in the middle of it, mouth gaping open and eyes going wide.

Beyoncé was blasting through the room from the overhead speakers, giving all the single ladies instructions on how to wrap their men around their finger. Mallory was dancing around, waving her hand in the air, and Bailey was following her around like she'd found her long lost BFF, trying to keep up with the lyrics that she clearly didn't know.

Oh, but Mallory did. She was singing them at the top of her lungs.

Sophie Marie was standing in place, bouncing low, her diapered butt nearly hitting the floor every time she dropped it like it was hot.

My eyes just got wider when my attention landed on my *badass* brother. He held Benton facing out, the baby kicking his arms and legs and letting loose the tiniest sounds of laughter, while my brother danced and bounced his son as he sang along.

Dude was waving his free hand in the air—his very ringed finger, mind you—right in the middle of the little girls.

Wasn't even sure who was the instigator of this madness.

Thomas stood at the island singing just below his breath while he cracked some eggs into a bowl, listening intently while Faith gave him instructions.

As easy as could be.

Obviously, the entire world had lost its mind overnight.

Oh, wait, no, that was me.

Because my damned breath hitched, and my pulse went haywire when my gaze continued to glide across the country kitchen that was the heart of this historic home, and I found Grace standing at the stove, pouring round dollops of pancake batter onto a griddle.

Her tight ass rocking all over the place.

Rocking me.

Tossing me from solid ground.

I took a step forward into the alternate universe. Not a damned familiar stone beneath my feet.

Mallory was the first to notice that I'd entered.

She danced right over, throwing her hands in the air. "Ian-Zian, I thought you were going to sleep the whole day and you were going to miss our adventure and it's the best adventure in the whole world. I got a new best friend. Her name is Bailey. She loves adventures, too."

She waved an exuberant hand at my niece like she was introducing me to a stranger. The second Bailey saw me, she started jumping around, too.

"Uncle Ian, Uncle Ian, you spent the night! I've been missin' you. Did you go huntin'?" She looked around the room, her voice turning serious. "My uncle is a dog. Just ask my dad."

That was the exact time Faith lowered the volume. You know, just in time for Bailey to emphasize the fact.

All eyes locked on me.

I was pretty sure I needed to find some slippers and tap my heels three times or some shit because I'd been swept into a tornado.

Problem was that those would be the wrong damned kind of shoes. Because my battered Cinderella turned around.

The second those eyes landed on me, they set me on fire. But it was the softness playing around her lush mouth that had the dark spot in my chest doing crazy things.

She looked so damned happy, like she belonged right there in the middle of my family.

Like this was the place where she felt safest.

Like she was getting lost in the warmth. Adding to it. Shining all that light and understanding.

"A dog?" Mallory asked, twisting the word around and drawing it out like she was completely confused.

"Yup. Daddy said his *brover* is *nofin'* but a dog. Isn't that right, Daddy?"

A smirk climbed to Jace's smug mouth, and he was looking directly at me when he said, "Yup, nothing but a dog who looks like he could use a good scratch."

Asshole delivered it with a load of innuendo. None of his disappointment from last night came through. He was back to being my big brother who thought it was his job to give me shit.

Grace cupped her hand over her mouth like she was trying to hold back a laugh, and Thomas was looking on with overt fascination. Didn't even want to consider whether he might be able to pick up on any of this. The kid was so smart and intuitive and protective.

If I wasn't careful, he'd probably kick my ass and with good reason.

Hell, I kind of wanted to kick my own ass.

"Jace," Faith chastised softly, barely heard over the music as she angled her head.

Jace shrugged. "What?"

Faith glanced at Grace and then back at him. "We have guests."

Grace waved her off with the spatula that was in her hand. "It's fine. I only wished I had a brother or sister to give me a hard time."

"And sometimes I wish I didn't have one," I grumbled under my breath.

Jace laughed, not offended for a second. "Ha. You'd be flipping burgers if it wasn't for me."

If only that were the case.

Jace believed he'd gotten out of prison and worked his ass off to give me my dream.

For years, I'd lied to my brother.

Told him I was just a smart fucker who kept getting scholarships and grants.

In reality, it'd been Bennet who'd funded most of my college.

At the time, I'd believed I was taking a load off my brother but, really, I'd only been digging myself a deep grave. Looking back, I wondered if it wouldn't be better if my ass wasn't still working some pathetic, bottom-of-the-barrel job.

At least it'd be honest.

My gaze moved to Grace, who watched me with soft affection, like she wasn't standing right in the middle of a raging storm.

Trying to brave the surge.

Keep her head above water.

My chest tightened.

No.

I wouldn't take any of it back. Not for a second. Helping her family might be the only truly honest thing I'd ever done. Didn't matter what it cost me. It'd be worth it.

Everything about Grace softened, and she looked at me standing there in all my discomfort like I might be the best thing she'd ever seen.

Like I was better.

Different.

Her genuine gaze traveled to my brother, words nothing but adoration. "Thank God you helped Ian become who he is today. I'm not sure what we would do without him."

"We kind of like him," Faith said, affection in her voice.

I wasn't sure I'd ever felt like such a fucking imposter.

Didn't these people know me at all?

I wasn't a good guy.

And there I was, in their house, acting like I could be. Like I was someone else.

Never was there more proof of that than when Sophie was suddenly at my feet, her little hands tugging at my sleep pants, the child all toothy grins and white pigtails when she looked at me. "Ian. Up. Up!"

Unease sloshed through my veins. God damn it. But there I was, reaching down and picking her up.

Excited, she smacked at my cheeks with both her hands, trying to get my attention when the only thing I could focus on was the feel of the child in my arms.

"Hi!" she squealed, smacking my face more, her eyes searching mine, like she was trying to climb right inside.

Didn't think any of this had fully hit me until right then. What was truly riding on me not fucking this up.

These were Grace's *babies*.

The beat of her heart and the reason of her being.

Fear clamored through my senses, and I was suddenly having a bitch of a time breathing.

She shifted in my hold and pointed at Grace. "Mommy make

pancakes!"

I choked down the overwhelming emotion that thrashed and spun and proceeded to force out the words. "Is your mommy making pancakes?"

Could feel everything constricting. Pressure rising.

I couldn't fail them. Couldn't. I had no idea where that would leave me if I did.

Sophie nodded emphatically, still pointing at her mother. "Ian want?"

Yeah, Ian wanted. So goddamned bad.

But Ian couldn't have.

I kept having to remind myself of that shit.

Grace let loose a soft giggle. "I hope so because I'm pretty sure there is enough food here to feed an army."

I moved that way, not even able to stop myself from edging up behind her. I was still holding her kid as I looked over her shoulder.

A selfish asshole could get used to this shit.

My voice lowered, and I breathed that energy in, letting it sustain me, knowing we were undoubtedly going to need that army she was about to feed. "Did you sleep okay last night?"

She peeked up at me. Blue eyes fathomless. Rays of sunlight streaking through to touch the bottom of the deepest sea.

Chaos had struck up in the kitchen again when Mallory called to Faith, "Turn it up, Auntie Faith! This one is my favorite, favorite!"

Surprise, surprise, The Spice Girls.

But what really tilted the floor to the side was the fact the kid was calling my sister-in-law *Auntie*.

She and Bailey were back to dancing with my brother, and Faith laughed her encouragement as she helped Thomas make another batch of pancake batter.

Still, Grace's voice left her on a whisper, like it was meant only for the two of us.

Well, the two of us and Sophie who'd fully wrapped her little arms around my neck.

"I don't think I've slept so well for as long as I can remember.

Thanks to you. Thanks to your family. You're right, they're the best people I could ever meet."

I'd started to sway.

That's the way whirlwinds were. You were caught up and spinning and getting tossed into a realm you'd never expected before you had the chance to prepare yourself. To stop it.

Just like right then.

Because I let my nose drop to the delicious slope of Grace's neck.

I inhaled.

Sweet, juicy plum that I'd come to realize was just an overflow of her heart.

I wanted to suck it down and keep it forever.

She took in a sharp breath before she leaned back into me.

Flesh searing into mine.

I wanted to wrap my arm around her waist and hold her there. But that was just foolishness.

I forced myself to take a step back. That was when I noticed Jace watching us from across the room. I thought he might smirk. Rub it in that he was right again. Instead, he sent me a sympathetic smile.

Like he got that, no matter how this turned out, it couldn't turn out in my favor.

One way or another, I was going to lose, and I was pretty sure that was going to hurt worse than anything else had in all my life.

GRACE

"You love him?"

Faith's soft voice broke into my thoughts where I was sitting on the porch. I was watching my children play on the back lawn with Ian and his brother and his sweet little girl, Bailey, this family so wonderful I was having a hard time processing all the emotions threading through the middle of me.

Stitching and binding.

I glanced over at her. The gorgeous woman was holding a bouquet of fresh-cut roses that she'd harvested from the rose garden off to the side of her magnificent house.

Everything about her screamed beauty.

Her face and her home and her spirit.

While mine swam with turmoil. I tried to swallow around the surge of it that was threatening to wash me away, and I cast her a weary smile. "I'm trying not to."

She grimaced and came to sit on a chair next to me. "Not so easy to tell love what to do, is it?"

A weak sigh blew from my lungs. "No, not so much."

Rambunctious laughter rolled through the cool air, and Ian chased after Thomas, who was running with all his might, Ian just barely *missing* him as he reached out to tag my son.

It seemed crazy that just last night Ian had swept into my home. A dark savior. Today, it felt so much that way.

As if we'd been rescued.

Lifted directly out of the storm.

"Ah, man, Thomas, you're way too fast for me!" Ian hollered, his smile freer in that moment than I'd ever seen him wear.

My chest stretched tight.

Squeezing and binding.

Silence spun between Faith and me as we watched them play.

Sophie Marie tottered around, trying to keep up, while the rest of the kids ran circles around her. Jace was holding their son again, so protectively, as if the man refused to let him go.

Faith finally broke our quiet bubble. "Ian is . . . complicated."

I almost laughed, my gaze flitting to her before it was back on Ian, who'd swept Sophie back up into the strength of those arms. He ran with her, chasing after Bailey, soaring Sophie through the air as if she were flying since she now was "it."

As if the man was her champion.

Her hero.

She kicked and flapped her arms and laughed.

"That much is plenty obvious," I said, looking over at her, my lips pressing into a grim line. "But he also might be the most transparent man I've ever met. He's so fundamentally good, but all the fear and regret he carries around makes him believe he's someone bad."

Faith nodded slightly, contemplating, not sure what she wanted to confide in me. Her voice dropped, so low I had to struggle to listen. "The first time I saw Ian, he was stuffing a sandwich into his mouth, crying because it hurt to eat since it'd been so long since the last time he had."

Agony cut me right in two.

Physical.

This pain that took me over at the thought of this powerful man a boy.

Scared and hungry and afraid.

All those scars that covered his body.

I didn't have the first idea of what he'd gone through. The only thing I knew was I wanted to go back and wrap him up and stop it from ever happening.

I wondered if he knew that was exactly what he was doing for my children.

Protecting them from torment.

Different than his, but the kind that would leave scars all the same.

"Jace had stolen it for him," she mused quietly, rocking on the porch rocker, as if she'd been taken back to that time. She glanced over at me, tears shimmering in her dark eyes. "They took care of each other that way. Their childhood . . . it was a battle. A warzone. One they were forced to fight even though they'd never enlisted. The aftermath left them completely different and so intrinsically the same."

Her throat bobbed when she swallowed. "Fearful. Scared. Thinking they have something to prove. And really the only *proof* they need is for someone to show them that they deserve to be loved. Not because they earned it, but because of who they are."

Hesitation buzzed around her, and she glanced away, her words careful. "But I think Ian's wounds go deeper than either Jace or I can see. The man's terrified of loving or being loved in return, so that heart of his doesn't know what to do. How to give or how to receive. It's grown dark and bitter. That might be the greatest tragedy of all."

Mallory's squeal broke through the air, capturing our attention when she was tagged. "No fair! No fair! You're a superhero, and I'm only a princess!"

"What are you talking about, Mal Pal? I thought you were a

magic princess?" Ian bounced Sophie. "And your little sister is a magic princess, too. That's how she caught you, isn't it, Soph?"

Sophie clapped. "Sophie win!"

My heart went crazy. Shaking and shivering and stretching out. Because the risk I had wasn't in not being able to love someone.

It was in how desperately I did.

I knew it from the start. Even being in his space was dangerous. That I was going to fall.

Hard and fast and completely.

But none of that seemed to matter because I stood anyway when Ian gestured for me to come and join him.

Rays of wintery light streaked through the sky. But it was the light radiating from Ian that speared me. The man's presence a force I didn't know how to stand under.

It only shivered brighter the closer I came, and he tugged at my hand. "You're it."

God, just the rough cadence of his voice sent me into a swoon.

Somehow, I let myself laugh as we ran and played, darted and diverted and tagged.

I lost my breath when Ian tackled me. His big body pressed against mine where he had me pinned on the ground. The pants from his mouth rough and his heart racing. With my eyes, I silently begged him to kiss me. To show me why he'd run from me when we'd been in the bathroom.

Faith's concerns remained fresh in my mind. Though they didn't scare me. They felt like a buoy.

As if I'd gotten one step closer to this man when I already felt lost in the middle of him.

He froze for a moment, those eyes so tender yet confused as they flicked between my unwavering gaze and my mouth.

The air shivered and shook.

Kiss me.

Squeezing his eyes closed, he dipped his head before he peeled himself away, stretching out a hand, refusing to meet the silent questions rushing from me as he helped me to stand, though I could feel the torment in the squeeze of his hand.

"You're it, Momma! Ian Zian caught you, you're it!" Mallory

shouted.

Oh, God, did he catch me.

I darted for my daughter. She squealed and ran.

We spent the day that way.

Together.

Faith and Bailey and Jace took us to their favorite stream at the back of the property where the kids splashed and played, and Thomas looked as if some of the weight had been lifted from his shoulders.

Only because Ian was holding some of it.

In the late afternoon, we returned to the house, and Mallory pulled out our big book so we could add a new chapter. The great escape that had turned into an adventure where we'd all been whisked away to a secret castle hidden in the sky, her little mind running wild as we continued our story and new characters were introduced.

Faith and I made dinner while the guys played a board game with the kids, and I was sure that my life had never felt so full.

So right.

As if I were coming up on eternity.

We ate and we laughed and we talked, and I quickly fell in love with the people at the table.

Ian's family so fundamentally a part of him. The devotion between them all so distinct.

The kids had baths, and we tucked them in, and then Ian and I went back into the kitchen to do the dishes together, telling Faith and Jace to take the night for themselves.

It was the least we could do for their hospitality.

I got the stupid inclination that this was the way it was supposed to be. Ian and me, side-by-side.

Then my phone buzzed in my pocket at the same time Ian's buzzed in his.

Still wearing a satisfied grin, I pulled it out and thumbed into the messages without giving it any thought.

That was right when my heart that had grown too big cracked right down the middle.

Speared.

Spliced and split into a million pieces.

Ian went pale when he looked at his screen. No question, his exhibited the same images.

Ones of Ian with a woman in a dark, depraved room. Those big hands were on her bare breasts as the woman straddled him on a chair.

A prostitute.

The same one I'd seen Reed with.

The tattoo on the back of her shoulder was exactly the same. A broken ring with the number 7 in the middle of it.

I could only see it from behind, but it was clear what they were doing.

But it was the time stamp on the bottom that sent me reeling. Hot knives driven into my flesh. Splaying me open wide.

I might as well have bled out right there on the floor.

Sickness twisted through my stomach. Speeding out to saturate every cell.

A cold, lonely disease.

It was the day I'd first gone to Ian to beg him for help. The very next day after I'd gone to his apartment and spent the night.

Where he'd fucked me, just like he was clearly doing here.

Reed: This is who you have my children with? I'd think you'd be smarter than that. I told you, you'd regret this. I expect you and my children on my doorstep within the hour. I'd advise you to have every dollar of that money, too. Don't say you weren't warned.

Grief climbed into my throat, and I couldn't even look at Ian. Couldn't meet his face.

Couldn't fathom the pain that gripped and tore and shredded my insides.

So, I fled, not even saying a word when I pounded up the stairs and into the room where I was staying.

Because Faith was right.

It wasn't so easy to tell love what to do.

And mine had just been slaughtered. Left for dead where it'd just spilled out all over the floor.

thirty-four

IAN

I stood gaping at the bullshit that lit up my screen from the unknown number. Blood draining from my face. Rage flooding out of my soul.

Unknown: You fucked with the wrong person. Did you actually think I'd let you get away with it? Do you actually think you have the power to go up against me? I'd think again.

Coming in right behind it was a grainy picture of me with that stripper at the club. It was captured right in the moment she put my hands on her breasts, right before I'd pushed her off my lap after she'd propositioned me.

Most likely nabbed by a security camera.

From the angle, it looked like I was balls deep and having the time of my life rather than being completely disgusted.

Rage clamored through my being. Like a ship tossed from side-to-side. Rocked in an unstable ocean.

I didn't even have time to process what was going down in front of me until Grace tried to smother a shocked sob behind her hand.

Oh, fuck.

She darted for the swinging doors of the kitchen, her feet pounding down the hardwood floors of the hall, leaving a trail of that energy hammering the walls behind her.

Consuming in its disorder.

Fire and lashes.

Hate and heat.

I tried to force myself to stay rooted to the spot. I'd done enough damage. But there was no resisting the riot that spun, barbs and wires that hooked into my chest.

I flew out into the hall to the weight of her footsteps and the slam of her door.

The girl a turbulence only I could feel.

Let her go.

The rational part of my brain shouted it, but my heart wasn't fucking having it.

There was no slowing, nothing I could do but go after her.

I bounded upstairs, my heart beating a million times a second, right out of my chest. I didn't even hesitate when I burst into the first room on the left where Grace was staying, coming up short when I found her standing at the big window that overlooked the rose gardens below.

Moonlight streaked in and cast her in a milky halo. From behind, I watched as her shoulders heaved, her face in her hands, heartbreak radiating from her body.

My broken angel.

I clicked the door shut behind me and flicked the lock like it could keep out the rest of the world.

I eased into the unrest that spun through the room.

Slowly.

Like if I gave her enough warning, she wouldn't startle. Or maybe it would offer me a little more time in her presence before this all came to an end.

All that intensity rippled back, and her spine tensed in awareness. Our bodies recognizing the other.

"I told you I'm not a good guy," I finally forced out, voice nothing but grit.

The sob she was trying to contain finally made a break for it. She hugged herself tighter, looking out over the beauty of the yard like if she wished hard enough, she might get swept away.

Disappear.

She'd wake up and all of this would be a bad dream.

Problem was, I knew that was exactly what I was.

I took another step deeper into the room. Wisps and shadows stroked and whipped across the floor, a moon dance colored on the wall.

"I did go to that strip club that night. It's where men like me belong, Grace. Where our sick hearts and our depraved spirits feel most at home."

Another step closer.

Swore I could feel her spirit tremble.

"But I didn't fuck her. I wouldn't." The last cracked. Like just the word split me open.

This girl was the only one who'd ever managed to get inside me.

Her head shook. "You don't owe me anything."

It was a brush off.

Chains and armor to shut me out.

I was behind her in a flash, our bodies separated by a mere inch, that tiny sliver charged.

A live wire ready to burst.

"Bullshit," I hissed. "I owe you everything."

Goose bumps prickled across her flesh, and she slowly spun around to face me, stirring the air up more.

Sadness streaked across that face. There was nothing I could do but reach out and hold it, pray I could somehow erase the hurt.

My thumb stroked across her cheek. "I've never lied to you, Grace, and I'm not going to start now. I went to that club thinking I might be able to outrun what you'd made me feel the night before. What you'd made me feel when you'd come into my office. As a reminder of who I was, and where I belonged. But I promise you, that picture? However the fuck Reed got ahold of it? It's a lie. I was pushing her off my lap. Nothing more. I've never paid for a woman, not once, and I never will."

A tear slipped from the corner of her eye and landed in the web of my hand.

Grace's mouth trembled. "I hate all of this, Ian. I hate that Reed has this control. That I'm living in fear constantly, waiting for the other shoe to drop. But maybe what scares me most is how badly it hurts to see you with someone else. After you'd touched me. I . . . why does the thought of you touching someone else destroy me?"

My thumb traced the angle of her cheek.

God, why did she have to be so pretty?

"I'm so sorry," I whispered. "I don't want to hurt you. It's the last thing I want to do."

Soft sorrow moved across her face. "I'm the one who dumped my mess at your door. I'm the one who didn't listen when you told me not to fall. I'm the one who wants all the things you promised you could never give me."

The rawest vulnerability took hold of her expression. "It's me who wants more."

More.

The idea of it shivered beneath the surface of my skin.

So intense.

Overwhelming.

"I want to. I want to so goddamned bad that it physically hurts, Grace. It's killing me, wishing I could be the kind of man who could hold you. Protect you."

I gulped down my reservations. Or maybe it was just the girl who'd scaled right over the top of the hundred-foot wall surrounding my heart. Toppling it. Nothing but rubble at her feet.

I grabbed her hand and splayed it across the erratic drumming of my chest.

"Do you feel that, Grace? It doesn't fucking beat right, but still, it beats for you."

Those eyes blinked up at me in the softest kind of affection. She splayed her hand out wider, eyes tracing over my face when she whispered, "I feel it, Ian. The way it beats. Can you feel the way it beats perfectly with mine?"

And I knew I was lost.

Gone.

Completely gone to this girl.

I dropped my forehead to hers, breathing in her sweet heat, her aura.

Memories flashed.

So bright.

All the reasons I'd sworn to myself that I'd never allow my heart to love.

That it was never worth the risk.

And still, with her there, so close to me, her sweet spirit whispering to mine, my mouth was moving a breath from hers.

"Kisses are forever, and only for the ones you love most."

I swore, she fell into the words.

Became one with them.

The surprised breath coming from her both hard and soft and covering me whole.

Did she get what she'd done to me?

She'd become the air in my lungs.

The blood in my veins.

The beat of my heart.

Every part of me would be shattered when she was ripped away.

But none of that mattered right then.

The only thing that mattered was I was overcome with it. With what I'd been fighting since I first met her. Since she'd seeped in and taken over.

The only thing that *mattered* was her.

I swept my mouth over hers.

Softly at first.

Relishing in this slow kiss.

This kiss that meant everything.

Kisses are only for the ones you love most.

It was a shout from the heavens.

A claim of my soul.

Delicate brushes of lips. The gentlest tangle of tongues. Giving and taking.

Emotion swelled from the depths, boiling up.

"Kisses are only for the ones you love most," I murmured in the middle of our kiss.

Lost to it—her passion and her surrender.

Her mouth was a whisper against mine. "I want to kiss you for the rest of my life."

It was her own confession.

I gripped her by the sides of the face so I could stare down at her, my eyes moving over her gorgeous face, my words so raw as they scraped from the bottom of my soul. "I love you, Grace. I fucking love you, and I love your kids, and it's going to destroy me. I know it. I know it. It will, and I don't care. The only thing that *matters* right now is loving you. If I get to feel this for even one day, it will be enough."

"Oh, Ian." It was a wisp from her mouth, her hands spreading over my chest, riding up to grasp my face. "There will never be a day when I don't feel this. When you won't matter. You've become everything."

We were spinning.

Crashing.

Kissing.

Kissing, kissing, kissing.

Nothing had ever felt so good. So right.

Hands everywhere.

Frantic and needy and unhinged.

I gulped her presence down, kissing her hard and possessively as I backed her toward the bed.

That crazy energy thrummed between us. But tonight—tonight I swore that it glowed. Brighter than ever before.

Those hands found my shoulders, and she pressed her tight body against mine, whimpering as she tried to get closer. "Ian . . . my sweet broken man. How am I supposed to live without you now? How . . . when you've changed everything? What I want and who I am?"

"I love you." It was the only answer I had.

"I love you," she rasped, the words winding through me like the most passionate caress. Delirium on my ears. Perfection on my soul.

All I wanted was more.

And she was giving it to me. Like she knew how desperately I needed it.

"I love you so much it hurts, Ian. So much that I can feel you etched on my skin. Written on my heart. Marked on me forever. You are my *gift*. The hero I never expected."

I knew that was the moment Grace finally shattered me.

Pieces spilled out and poured into her hands.

Part of me wanted to deny it, to tell her again that we couldn't do this.

But I was swamped by the truth that oozed from her body. Overcome by the devotion that poured from mine.

The crazy realization that I would do anything, give up anything, if it meant she found the joy she deserved.

Freedom with her children.

Her sweet, sweet kids.

Barely even knew them. Didn't matter. It was all-consuming. The instinct to wrap them up and protect them the way I wanted to protect her.

To love them.

To love them.

Derangement clouded my mind, distorted my judgment.

I kissed her harder, and she gasped out a throaty sound, and I didn't stop, didn't slow as I devoured her delicious mouth.

I wanted all of her. Every inch. To possess and claim and mark.

I growled and hoisted her into my arms.

Mine.

She wrapped those lust-inducing legs around my waist.

Blood pounded south, and my dick grew so hard, it was close to painful.

Pained, perfect bliss.

That was this girl.

Flawless desolation.

"I won't let him hurt you," I promised as I carried her to the massive bed set against the far wall, the bedding plush and thick and soft.

As soft as this girl.

While every inch of me was hard and rippling with possession.

"I won't let him take them from you. I promise you. He has nothing. Nothing. I'll die before he gets the chance. Do you understand?"

Teal eyes found mine. So real. This girl life. "I trust you, Ian. I trust you."

"I need you. Now." It was all a mumble between my impatient kisses. My lips tugging and nipping and moving in a frenzied dance with hers.

I shoved down the misery when my thoughts traveled to the truth that I couldn't keep her. That I was still her attorney. If the courts even caught a whiff of what we were doing, anything I could do for her would be null.

Void.

"I'm yours," she whimpered. "I think I have been since the moment you chased me down on that dancefloor."

"Mine," I mumbled back. "You've been mine since the second I looked up and saw you. God, Grace . . . it's you . . . you who changed everything inside me."

Kisses are for the ones you love most.

Standing at the foot of the bed, I laid her down in the middle of it. Her blonde hair spread out across the pillow, her lush body rocking with her own need.

Her hand fluttered toward me, that charm bracelet on her wrist tinkling as it slipped up her arm, the connection binding us pulling taut, her voice comfort and seduction. "That man's been there all along. You just needed someone to believe in him. I believe in him. I believe in *you*."

I stood staring down at the girl of my dreams.

A fantasy.

Everything I'd never believed I deserved or even wanted.

And there she was, spread out like my idea of eternity.

A partner to this place that screamed of purity and safety and love.

Faith told us last night that magic happened in this room.

Miracles.

I'd become a believer.

Because standing there, I knew I'd never be the same.

Grace. Grace. Grace.

I needed it in my life.

I needed *her* in my life.

How had I been so blind to what I was missing?

I climbed over her, and those long legs parted, making me room.

Hands planted on either side of her head, I stared down at her in the moonlight.

My chest expanded, so wide I was sure it was going to burst.

Those fingers trailed down my face.

She angled up to brush her mouth across my bottom lip. "I love you, Ian Jacobs."

Hands diving into her hair, I captured her mouth.

Kissed her wild.

With the type of passion I'd never allowed myself to experience.

Unbridled.

Raw.

Real.

Emotion pitched and rocked and drove us higher.

Her heart was drumming an erratic thud, thud, thud, and I spread my hand out over it, feeling it pound for me.

"I love you," I said again.

Because I couldn't stop.

She moaned through a small laugh and whispered, "I love you so much."

I drank down her words like they were the water of life.

God.

She was exquisite.

Her tongue temptation.

A sweet, juicy plum.

Every flick of it sent shockwaves of lust racing through my body.

"You are delicious, Grace." I couldn't help but tell her.

Another giggle slipped up her throat and landed on my tongue.

Like she was offering me her joy.

Joy.

That might have been the first time I felt the fullness of it. The wholeness of what it meant.

I edged back so I could peel her shirt over her head, leaving her in her bra and jeans. Her hair mussed and her lips swollen from my kisses.

Her spirit danced and lapped, at one with the shadows, glowing in the darkness.

Wrapping me up in ribbons and bows.

Sitting back on my knees, my eyes rode up and down her perfect body.

"Grace," I murmured, reaching out to stroke her cheek with my thumb, running it under the hollow of her eye, down to that mouth.

Back and forth.

Back and forth.

"Look what you've done to me."

I pressed my hand behind her back to rid her of her bra before I edged up a fraction so I could reach down to flick the button of her jeans.

I left her only long enough to rip them and her underwear down those legs.

Those legs that were nothing but miles of silk and curves and seduction.

I'd gladly get lost and roam them forever.

My own sacred promised land.

I continued to kiss her while everything between us intensified.

Growing more desperate by the second.

Wasn't like I hadn't been inside this girl before. Taking her. Owning her.

But this . . . this was different.

We both knew it.

It was the pinnacle we'd been climbing toward.

Where everything melted and then melded.

Where me and this girl became one.

This was where I offered everything.

Where it was only Grace and me.

This . . . this was where love lived.

Her fingers trembled as she worked through the buttons of my shirt, the girl shaking as she pushed the fabric off my shoulders. I twisted out of it, tossing it onto the floor with the rest of her clothes, the girl making short work of my pants, shoving them down my thighs so I could kick them free.

I hovered over her body, my eyes devouring every inch, cherishing every second.

"You're so beautiful," I murmured, dipping down to nip at her ear. "So sexy. I can't see straight when I'm looking at you, because the only thing I see is my perfection. Everything I've ever wanted. But it's this heart . . . this sweet, sweet heart that changed mine."

Her chest heaved.

I dipped down to kiss along the slender column of her neck, and her head rocked back. Fingers sank into the flesh of my shoulders.

Lips traipsing, I moved lower, roving over the wild thrum of her beating heart. I licked a path across one breast until I was taking it into my mouth, sucking and laving and making her moan.

"Ian." Hands found my hair, tugging. "Ian."

"What do you need, Angel Girl, what do you need?"

"You. The only thing I need is you. I don't think I know how to keep living without you. Not when the meaning of life now includes you. You're a part of me. Forever."

Her fingertips traced over the designs marring my flesh like she could read everything that was etched into my skin. Like she could grasp the story, dip her fingers in deep and feel every scar. What they meant. Where they came from.

Her fingers traced over the demon on my arm.

A shiver rolled through the darkest depths, and the confession was pouring out, "With you, I don't want to be him. Not anymore. If I could be someone else for you, I would."

"You're the man I fell in love with, Ian. You. Not who you could be or who you were in the past. But the man who's shown me time and again who he really is. The man who's stood up for me. For my children. The man who's taken a risk when I know what I'm asking for is more than anyone should have to give. That's who you are, Ian."

She was back to pressing her palm against the thunder that roared in my heart.

And I was taken.

Delirious.

I positioned myself at the welcome of her sweet body before I drove home.

Her body arched, and she softly cried out my name.

Home.

I gasped out at the stark pleasure that sizzled through every nerve.

I could stay in that spot forever and be content.

But I was dropping down and hooking my arm over the top of her head, holding her by the back of the knee with the other, opening her up for me as I began to move.

Hard and slow and deep.

Different.

So different from how I'd ever been with another girl. Who fucking knew how many girls I'd fucked. Hundreds? A thousand? I didn't know. The only thing I knew was none had compared to this.

"You are the best thing I've ever felt. This . . . this is the gift, Grace. That I get to experience this with someone, even if it's only one time."

I rocked into her, and the girl met every thrust.

I dipped down. Kissed her long and slow and with everything I had.

Forever and ever.

With the truth that she'd come to mean everything, and still I wanted more.

Our breaths turned shallow, and she was releasing these throaty pants into the air that I swallowed down. They only wound me up more, my stomach in knots and muscles flexing and bowing and rippling beneath her touch.

Because the girl . . . she was touching me everywhere.

My scars and my skin and my heart.

"Ian." She started to jut up into my body, needy for more. That was the one thing I could give her. I edged back, angling to hit her just right, holding myself up on one hand while I stroked her clit with the other.

The girl clawed and whimpered and moaned, her body stretching tight below me. Everything cinching down.

Bliss taking hold of the air.

Taking us with it.

"Ian," she gasped one more time, and I captured her mouth to silence her scream.

The girl came undone.

Billows of her pleasure streaked through her body and directly into me.

Sinking in and setting me free.

Pleasure knotted at the base of my spine, my balls lifting as they slapped against her body.

Harder.

Faster.

More.

With Grace, I would always want more.

But this was what we had.

This moment.

I gripped her tight when I came. Exploding into her body. My cock surging and pulsing and pouring into the wet, warm welcome of this woman.

My mouth dropped open on a silent roar.

Nothing . . . nothing had ever felt as good as that.

Giving myself to her. Letting her hold it. My body went rigid, both of us hit with tremors and aftershocks.

Floating somewhere high where I wished we could stay forever.

She clung to me, holding me as close as she could as we both floated back down.

Still, it felt like reality couldn't touch us. Because it was just me and Grace and the ghosts in that room.

I kissed her again.

Nothing but the soft press of lips.

Adoration.

Then I rolled to my side and took her with me, tucking her into my side, refusing to let her go. I ran my fingers through those silky locks as she stared at me in the shadows.

Hope blazed from the depths of those eyes. "Where do we go from here?"

Guessed we both knew there was no going back from what we'd just shared.

My words were gruff. "I don't know, Grace. The only thing I know is I have to protect you and your kids from that bastard. That is the only thing that matters right now. Beyond that?" I gripped her tighter. "We will figure it out."

"I don't want to lose you," she admitted through a whisper, burrowing deeper into my side. "Not when I've finally found who I've been looking for."

I kissed her forehead. "And you're exactly what I've been running from all along."

A frown pulled to her brow, understanding winding into her expression.

The girl taking me under. "Will you tell me about her?"

A tremor rolled through my body, and I opened my mouth, because somehow, I'd allowed this woman to cut me open wide.

IAN
Seventeen Years Old

The apartment door creaked open slowly, and the dread and worry that Ian had been tossing in all night shifted into anger. His hands balled into fists, and he pushed to standing from the couch as his mother walked through the door.

A whole twenty-four hours since the last time he'd seen her.

She was wearing a skin-tight dress and no shoes, and her hair was ratted and her makeup smeared under her eyes. She hobbled inside, limping on her left leg like she'd been injured.

Beaten down.

Worn and used up.

That anger gripping Ian's chest shivered in a flash of repulsion.

How could she do this?

She'd promised when they'd moved back to the city after Jace went to prison that things were going to be different. That she'd never touch drugs again. That she was going to take care of him, just like he'd promised he was going to take care of her.

Things were going to be better. They had to be because Ian couldn't fathom anything worse than the emptiness he'd felt when his brother had been taken away.

Jace had been the one person he could rely on, his protector and his best friend, and now Ian was trying with all his might to step up and take his place.

How was that ever gonna happen when his mama kept doing this?

Ian's jaw clenched, staring at his mother who was just repeating the same bullshit he'd spent his years growing up in.

She lifted her face to him. There was a scratch down her cheek, and part of him wanted to run to her, demand to know who had hurt her so he could hunt the asshole down.

Fight for her and protect her.

But he was so over it. So over her promises that were nothing but lies.

His lip curled and the hurt and hatred came spilling out. "I can't believe you. You're into that same bullshit again?"

Rage thrummed with the heartbreak, fractures cracking through the middle of him.

It was supposed to be different.

She'd promised. She'd promised.

A soft whimper left her mouth, and she edged forward, dropping her purse directly onto the floor as she inched toward him. "I had to, Ian, you don't understand."

Disgust shot out of him on a hot breath. "I don't understand? What's not to understand, Mama?" He spat the last like it was a filthy word. "That you're nothin' but a junkie? That you'd rather leave me here to worry about you, worry you're dead in a dumpster somewhere, while you go get your fix of dope and dick? Is that what I don't understand?"

She gasped out a tortured sound, and her body bent in half as if Ian had physically injured her.

But he'd never do that. It was his mother who'd allowed it to happen to him again and again. His own body covered in scars that would never heal. The ones that couldn't be seen only went that much deeper.

He could almost feel it, the deep grooves carved out in his back, the years of black eyes and busted lips and broken ribs.

The marks that had been written on his soul.

She took a pleading step forward, and the smell of her cheap perfume and men's cologne slapped him in the face. He wanted to puke.

"Please, don't say things like that to me, Ian. Not when everything I do, I do for you."

Scornful laughter rocked from him, and he took a step her direction. "For me? That's rich, Mama, when the only thing you've ever cared about was yourself. Everything you've ever done was for your benefit. You let me and Jace starve so you had the money to fill your worthless body with drugs, or you let men use us as punching bags just as long as they kept you supplied with that shit."

"No," she wheezed. "No, Ian. I never, ever wanted you to get hurt. There are some things you can't understand."

He gripped two handfuls of hair, tugging hard, at his end. He got in her face, spewing the words, "God, I'm so sick of your excuses. You might have kept me hooked on your every word when I was a little boy, desperate for a little love and attention, but guess what? I'm not a kid anymore, and I can see right through you."

A sob wrenched from her. "No, Ian. Please, don't say things like that. You're the only thing I have left. The only reason I breathe. The only reason I have to keep going."

He shook his head and snatched his wallet off the end table, unwilling to listen to her justification when none of this bullshit could ever be justified. He shoved it into his pocket. "Whatever. I have to go to work."

A frown pulled across her brow. "Work?"

His smile was full of his resentment. "I got a job. So I can take care of myself. So I don't have to sit around here praying my mom will actually give a fuck and think to feed me."

"Where?"

"Clover's Italian Restaurant . . . Lawrence Bennet offered me a job in the kitchen."

She paled. "I won't allow it."

Sickened, disgusted laughter bounced from the walls, the anger that had been simmering in him for years rising to a boil. "You won't allow it?" he challenged, a sneer on his face. "You won't allow me to make a little money for myself? What are you worried about, that I won't be around here to pick you up off the floor and clean up your puke? Or that I won't be here for one of your Johns to beat on, and he's going to turn that beatin' on you?"

Her entire face went white. "No, Ian, you got to listen to me. That man is no good. He's tryin' to sink his claws into you."

A scoff ripped from his tongue. "What, now you're the authority on *good character*?"

He started for the door, rounding her to get to it. His mama flew around and grabbed him by the arm. "You've got to listen to me, Ian. *Trust me.*"

He ripped his arm away. "Trust you? I fucking despise you. In case you didn't know it, trust is earned, and you've never done a single thing to get it from me."

He flung open the door.

She locked herself on his arm. "Ian, please, listen to me. That man . . . he is bad."

He shrugged her off, unable to believe that she would do this to him.

Again and again. Over and over.

Hurting him at every turn. Rage burned at the base of his throat. She'd been responsible for Jace getting sent away.

"Go to hell."

The only thing she wanted to do was hold him back. Keep him poor and hungry and pathetic like her.

Desperation clogged her words. "Ian, oh, God, please, you've got to hear me. Listen to what I'm sayin'. Everything I've ever done was for you. Everything."

He whirled around, voice full of spite. "And look what that got me."

She whimpered, and his eyes fell over her.

His heart hurt.

Hurt so damned bad looking at her. Skinny as fuck, all bone, fucking spreading her legs for the bag he was sure she had tucked in her purse.

She'd promised. She promised it was going to be different this time. That they were coming back to the city so she could actually take care of him. But it never was. It was always the same. It was never going to change.

Old agony thundered in his blood. She'd let them hurt him. *She'd let them. She'd let them.*

His face twisted in hatred. "Why don't you do us a favor and end it. Because I'm finished with this."

He turned around and started out the door of the crummy apartment.

Home-fucking-sweet-home.

Repulsion shivered across his skin when she reached out again and grabbed his hand, yanking him back. "Please, Ian, don't go, don't go."

"Let me go."

"No," she whispered. "I won't let you go. I love you."

He tugged his arm, hard enough that she stumbled forward. "Yeah, well I wish you were dead."

Stricken, her shoulders sagged and tears ran down her face.

Guilt streaked through Ian.

Just like it always did.

Every time she cried, he'd feel guilty, like it was his responsibility for the choices she'd made.

He was finished being responsible for her.

It was time he took responsibility for himself.

He turned his back on her, storming away to her whimpers and cries that started to jut from her mouth. "I'm sorry, Ian. I'm so sorry. I tried to be a good mama. I tried, but I failed, but I will always love you. Forever and ever."

Her words impaled him the whole way, and he hurried to

outrun them, banging through the stairwell door, like he could stop himself from hearing what she's said.

Because Ian . . . Ian couldn't take one more lie.

Ian finished running the last of the dishes through the industrial dishwasher. He was drying his hands when his new boss walked by, pausing to squeeze him on the shoulder. "Good job tonight, kid. Keep working hard like this, and you're going to do big, big things."

"Thank you, sir," Ian told Mr. Bennet, dipping his head, trying not to grovel like a pathetic fuck when the man handed him a folded hundred.

His mouth watered, thinking about the food he could buy with it. That he was finally gonna be able to stand up and be the man Jace had always told him he'd be.

Maybe his mama wouldn't change, but maybe he could be the one to make a change for them.

So when he left, he swung by the fast food restaurant, and instead of ordering one meal, he ordered two.

He'd feed her.

Care for her.

Make her see they *could* have a better life.

He was going to make sure of it.

He bounded up the stairwell of the noisy apartment complex, ignoring the fights and the wails and the loud music that beat through the space. The only thing he was thinking about was how he was going to apologize for what he said. Explain how he felt.

That he was mad. Disappointed. That it hurt so much when she let him down.

That he was gonna help her.

Help her get clean.

Whatever it took.

He rushed the rest of the way to the fifth floor and hit the hall, smiling with the smell of the french fries rising up from the bag.

His mama was gonna be happy. Proud. She'd see this was a good thing.

He went for his keys in his pocket, frowning when he realized the door was already unlocked. He pushed it open.

His heart seized, and he could feel the blood drain from his head as a roll of dizziness nearly knocked him from his feet. He dropped the bags of food, rushed across the room, and fell to his knees where his mama was passed out in the middle of the floor.

His hands reached out, shaking her. "Mama, Mama, wake up."

There was no movement. No response.

He shook her harder. Her head lolled back. "Mama, please, wake up!"

Tears blurred his eyes, and he started to scream. "Mama, please. Please! Wake up!"

Hands shaking, he pleaded with her, prayed, shook her harder. "Oh, God, Mama. Wake up. Please, wake up!"

Nausea swirled, and he gathered her up in his arms, hugged her limp body against his chest.

He wailed.

"Mama, don't leave me."

Please, please don't leave me.

But his Mama . . . she was gone.

Gone.

A needle still in her arm.

Ian's body wrenched, and he scrambled back, unable to see through the violent stream of tears that ran hot down his face. His body recoiled, and he vomited on the floor, the memory of the last thing he'd told her forever emblazoned in his head.

I wish you were dead.

GRACE

A thousand pounds of panic weighed down my chest as I shot up in bed.

Dread spiraling all around me.

I could feel it.

The riot of turbulence that roiled in the stagnant morning air.

Without giving myself time to clear my head, I fumbled out of bed and struggled to get my legs into my pants and my shirt over my head.

All the while, the disorder that had shaken through my sleep continued to echo from downstairs.

Shouting and clamoring that broke through the hint of morning that peeked through the window.

An upheaval that I could feel bone deep.

Anxiety blazed through my body, and my pulse was a jackhammer of nerves galloping at breakneck speed.

I scrambled out the door, tripping around the corner as I tried to hurry.

Manic, I started to fly downstairs.

It only took two seconds for my heart that had felt as if it had finally been made whole last night to go crumbling to the ground.

The scene in front of me one of my worst nightmares.

"No," I begged, my hand on the railing to try to keep myself standing as I raced faster for the bottom floor. "No."

Mallory was wailing, my sweet, happy girl nothing but a ball of fear and screams. "Please, Mommy, I don't want to go. I want to stay here. Tell them I don't have to go anywhere because I want to stay with you and Ian!"

She tried to jerk her arm away from a man. He was wearing a suit, not even giving her any comfort when he struggled with her flailing arms and legs to pick her up.

To restrain her.

To take her.

Oh my God.

My spirit roared.

A mother's cry.

Outrage and hate and fear.

The cruelty that was being imposed.

The vile selfishness that would drive a man to do something like this. To his own children.

Appearance so much more *meaningful and important* than their happiness.

Used as bargaining chips.

No. I wouldn't let this happen.

But that dread was spiraling through the middle of me when I met the malice in Reed's eyes.

He stood firm in the middle of the porch with his arms crossed over his chest.

Smug.

A bastard with the upper hand.

Callous and inhumane and merciless.

As if he'd just executed a hostile takeover.

That was exactly what this was.

Hostile.

A hot frenzy burned through my blood.

Desperation took over. Mind racing frantically, searching for anything to say or do.

For my own weapon against the atrocity.

But my own fear only grew greater when I realized what Jace was trying to do. Getting in the man's face who was tussling with Mallory in a bid to intercede. "You can't just show up here like this. This is private property."

An officer stepped between them and pushed Jace back by the chest. "Sir, we have a warrant and orders to remove these children from this premises. If you interfere, I'll be forced to put you in cuffs. I hope you don't make me do that."

He gestured to the infant Faith was rocking where she stood appearing frazzled and shocked to the side of him.

Wanting to do something but utterly helpless.

I refused to be.

I hit the ground floor, my bare feet pounding on the worn wooden planks as I threw myself toward the double doors.

"Mommy!" Mallory screamed, one arm reaching out for me as her small body thrashed.

Sophie was already outside with another officer, her blue eyes wary as she sucked her thumb.

Confused and scared.

My pulse careened, hatred howling through my senses, the need to get to her—to them—more than I could bear.

"No, let them go. You can't take them. I won't let you."

A gasp of pain shocked through me when I saw Thomas on the porch, too. Standing beside them with his face turned toward the ground as if he somehow thought this could be his fault.

"No," I cried again. The same officer who'd pushed back Jace stepped in my way when I went for Mallory, my arms flying and hot tears streaking down my face as he pushed me back.

A barricade between me and the reason for my life.

"Ma'am, you need to stay right there."

"No . . . these are my children. You can't just come here and take them."

Sympathy flashed through his expression, but still, he lifted his chin. "An emergency injunction was signed this morning by Judge Hirrod. These children are to be placed in the care of their father."

Judge Hirrod.

Jonathan Hirrod.

One of Reed's oldest friends.

Oh God.

Reed's expression filled with cruel satisfaction. "Don't stand there and act like I didn't warn you, Grace."

"You." I started for him, hands balled into fists, only for Jace to reach out and snag me from around the waist. "Don't do it, Grace. I know you want to fight, but you need to fight this in a different way."

Pounding rattled the stairs behind us. I didn't have to look to know that it was Ian.

That powerful presence surged from behind.

Anger and ire and barely contained rage.

He immediately was in attorney mode. "Under what order?"

"Parental abduction," the officer replied.

"Bullshit," Ian spat, reaching his hand out for the piece of paper. He snatched it out of his hand, his eyes roving over the document.

Hostility came off him in agitated waves, growing stronger as his attention darted over the words.

Mallory was still screaming, begging for me. My heart shattering and shaking.

How could I just stand there?

I had to do something.

Something.

Oh God, please, please help us.

In all his arrogance, Reed moved forward. "I went to pick my children up for their visit yesterday, and they were gone. Nowhere to be found. What else could I do?"

Ian was right.

Bullshit.

It oozed off Reed in nauseating pulses.

I wanted to puke.

Or fight.

Fighting seemed like a much better option. When he let my babies cry and wail and beg, and didn't give what they were going through a thought.

Twisting out of Jace's arm, I pushed around the officer and got in Reed's face. "How could you do this? To your own children? This is ridiculous. We can . . . we can work out something."

I was frantically scrambling to come up with a plan to waylay him. To assuage the situation.

I just . . . I just had to make him think he was getting his way.

"It's too late for that, don't you think, Grace? Considering the whole world knows my ex-wife is fucking her attorney?" He tsked. "Such an abuse of power, wouldn't you think? Or is it you who was buying him off with the money you stole from me?"

Dizziness spun my heart, that nausea pushing at my throat.

This couldn't be happening.

He had no proof. No proof.

I battled with my faltering spirit to regroup, to fight this man.

"You're being absurd. I'm only here with him for safety. For the safety of my children. To protect them from you."

His cold smirk only grew. "Huh, that's not what the news is reporting right now."

No.

No, no, no.

Dread dripped like ice into my veins.

Sickness clawed at my flesh.

The room spun, and my hand darted out to the doorframe to keep myself standing. "What did you do?"

"What I had to. You should do the same, Grace. Stop being a fool and get in my car with our children."

Ian stepped in front of me. He pushed a hand behind him to keep me back, a physical shield. "She's not going anywhere with you."

Reed cracked a vicious smile, twisted derangement when he

looked at me. "It's her funeral." Menace streaked through his expression when he turned his attention back on Ian. "Actually, it's yours."

Rage flashed through Ian.

I could feel it.

So intense and powerful.

The man barely hanging from a thread.

His teeth gritted when he hissed the words. "You won't get away with this."

"Watch me."

Reed snapped his fingers in the air like the sick cliché that he was. "Let's go."

"Daddy . . . no . . . please, I want my mommy!" Mallory squirmed in the man's hold.

"That's your mother's fault," he grunted at her, not even glancing at his daughter as he stalked down the steps ahead of everyone else. Her feelings and needs didn't matter in the least.

The exact way as it'd always been.

"Reed, please," I begged again.

Sophie started crying, her confused, worried sounds piercing my heart. "Mommy! Mommy, need you!"

Daggers and stakes.

How could I explain to a baby what was happening? That it was going to be okay? How could I convince her when I had no idea how to make it true?

I could feel the walls of this old house crashing down around me.

Ian raged at my side. Every muscle in his body rigid and hard, body shaking, held in restraint.

"Please!" I pleaded. But no one was listening.

That was right when I got trapped in the swamp of misery that swam in Thomas's eyes. At the sorrow and the fear that wracked his little being.

I darted for him. "Thomas."

The officer stepped in front of me and pinned my arms to my sides. I flailed against him, fighting and begging, unable to see through the mask of tears that blinded my eyes.

I couldn't let this happen.

I couldn't.

The officer's voice was at my ear. "Please don't make me arrest you in front of your children. That's only going to be harder on them."

Oh God.

Oh God.

Thomas's little voice hit my ears, so contrite and filled with guilt. "I'm sorry, Mom. I didn't mean to. He just asked where we were on my messenger. He said he wanted to make sure we were safe. I didn't know I was going to ruin everything. I always ruin everything."

A sob crashed out of my throat, the words stretched thin, praying they could touch him from across the space. "No, Thomas, no, it's not your fault. Mommy is the one who's sorry. I'm so sorry."

My whispered pleas turned to fractured screams as they hauled my children to Reed's car.

"I'm so sorry! I'm so sorry. Mommy loves you. I'll fix this. I'll fix this." The cries just kept coming as the sound of the car doors slamming ricocheted like bullets through the hazy morning, the officer still holding me back, while Ian, Jace, and Faith had to watch.

No one with a word that could change a thing.

The barest gray glowed above the trees, birds chirping and flitting from the branches, a hint of the sun chasing the stars from the sky.

It felt like every single one of them were crashing to the ground.

I screamed and wailed as Reed's car began to pull away, fighting the officer as the crunch of tires sounded over the gravel drive.

He kept me there until the cars disappeared.

"I really am sorry, ma'am," the officer said as he released me, holding his hands up in apology as he backed away.

The second he let me go, I dropped to my knees.

Torment ripped from me as my skin dug into the hard wood.

Sobs reverberated through the dull morning light, and agony sliced me in two.

Gutting.

I couldn't breathe.

Arms circled me from behind and pulled me from the unforgiving ground, words abraded and raw. "I won't let him get away with this. I will destroy him, Grace. Destroy his world before you lose those kids. I promise you."

My back was to the thunder of his chest, my feet not even touching the ground as he held me pinned against his body as my cries climbed for the sky.

Slowly, he set me back onto my feet, not releasing me as he placed a massive hand on my throat, drawing me back, voice vicious at my ear. "Whatever it takes."

It was cold and hard and terrifying, and I clung to it.

Believed it.

He released me, and I slowly turned around, shoving back the hair that was matted to my forehead, sniffling and trying to clear the tears from my eyes.

Trying to gather myself when I kept getting rushed.

Wave after wave of agony.

I blinked back at the faces staring at me.

Faith wearing nothing but heartbreak on her expression, the woman hugging her baby boy to her chest as if she were terrified that he might be stolen away, too.

Bailey was nowhere to be seen, probably still upstairs asleep and having no idea of the atrocity that had just been committed.

Jace stared at me. Fury shivered from his skin. But it wasn't close to what was coming off of Ian.

The man a storm.

An inferno.

Jace's face was hard, gauging his brother, before he turned and strode down the hall with purpose.

Ian guided me to follow.

He moved into a sitting room down the hall where he flipped on the television to the local news.

A reporter's voice came through the speakers. "Dearborne's

children were reported missing late last night. Dearborne shared joint custody with the children's mother, Grace Dearborne. Grace was spotted leaving her attorney's home, Ian Jacobs, in the early morning hours on November eleventh just before dawn. It's speculated Jacobs and Grace Dearborne initiated the affair in a bid to damage Dearborne's senatorial campaign. More news on this breaking story at the top of the hour."

The whole time she spoke, a reel played. A picture of me leaving Ian's building in the middle of the night, my hair a sexed up, matted mass, another of us on my grandmother's porch, hidden away in the shrubs and somehow still in plain sight of a camera, another of Ian at the strip club.

Ian froze at my side.

Ice cold.

Rigid.

Detached.

"Ian," I whispered.

Without saying a word, he turned on his heel and strode out the door.

And I was sure I'd never felt so alone in my whole life.

GRACE

Silence hung in the cab of Ian's car, the only sound the hum of his engine and the tiny tremors of sorrow that kept scraping up my raw throat.

Everything hurt.

Excruciatingly severe.

Torment wracked through every cell in my body, steadily pumped by the slivered remains of my heart.

Ian stared straight ahead as he sped down the road, one hand gripping the steering wheel, his bloodied knuckles white and blanched as he squeezed the other fisted on his thigh.

The man was emitting so much energy he could light up the entire town.

But that energy had morphed.

Had become something dark and bitter and ugly.

His soft words from last night vanished with the reality of what we'd done.

He hadn't said anything during the time we'd been forced to watch the evidence of our affair play out on the screen as if it were sordid and dirty. As if it were made of greed and corruption when I was sure I'd never experienced anything so pure and right.

Jace, Faith and I had just stood there.

Shocked.

Broken in the truest sense.

Ian had left me there to listen to him where he'd roared and moaned, his fists pummeling the wall as he'd raged outside.

Five minutes later, he'd returned.

Hatred and vacancy in his eyes.

It was the first time I'd thought he'd resembled what he believed himself to be.

A demon.

Capable of anything.

He'd simply said, "We have to go. Now."

Faith had scrambled to gather my children's things, and we'd loaded them into Ian's car.

The whole time, Ian hadn't uttered a single word.

Now, the car screeched as he took a corner hard. I swore, my mind had to be racing just as fast, searching for a solution.

Fighting the hopelessness that threatened to seep in and take over.

I refused to succumb to Reed's demands.

Refused to succumb to the despair that crashed and covered, the weight of it making it impossible to breathe.

The tires squealed again as Ian took the last turn into my neighborhood, and he slowed as he navigated the suburban streets to my home.

A sanctuary.

A place of peace and love.

And somehow it was Ian who'd come to feel like home.

He pulled to the curb, and my shattered heart heaved in a shock of pain when I looked over and saw the utter devastation on his face.

Different from mine.

A shroud of guilt covered him whole. The man vibrated with self-condemnation. A dark cloud crawling his flesh.

Shaking, I fumbled out of the car, still barely able to stand.

My bleeding heart was somewhere in my throat.

Thick and knotted.

Suffocating.

A crisp breeze twisted through the intense blue sky that murmured of the coming winter.

Like a cold, quiet whisper.

A premonition.

Chills flashed across my skin, and my stomach twisted in awareness and dread.

I couldn't control the shaking in my hands as I opened the back door of his car.

Grief streaked through my insides, and I nearly fell to my knees when I looked at my children's things.

Their little suitcases and their seats.

The unbearable reality slammed me.

He took them.

He took them.

Grief took over everything.

Every cell.

Every molecule.

He took them.

A sob ripped from my chest, and my eyes blurred with the tears that I couldn't keep at bay.

They fell. Fell as violently as the anger that infiltrated to the marrow.

Ian came around to my side, the man a dark, gray storm, those crazy-colored eyes the strangest I'd ever seen.

Swirling with rage and anger and a terrifying sort of desperation.

He gathered up everything in one fell swoop, shifting on his heel and stalking up the walkway, rigid anger as he waited at the door.

I felt as if I were crawling as I followed. Moving against the current. Cutting against the grain.

Everything wrong.

So wrong.

Legs heavy, I moved around him and unlocked the door, and he set everything just inside.

He refused to look at me, jaw clenched and muscles bunched and twitching, the designs etched into his skin alive, exposed by the tee shirt he wore.

My soul wept.

Cried and howled.

Couldn't he see that he was only making it worse? That he was only hurting us more by doing this to himself?

Blame would win us no points.

But it was there in the firm set of his chiseled jaw as he stepped back, there in the anger and the fury that roiled and tossed and turned my world into disorder.

A gust of wind screamed through. Burning my flesh. Freezing my bones.

He glared off into it, still refusing to look my way.

"Ian," I finally begged, unable to take it any longer.

He stayed frozen.

The man carved of stone.

Stone that was roughened by the world. Gaping holes underneath. "I'm sorry," he grated, the words just as hard as the rigid lines of his body.

"What are you sorry for?"

Bitter laughter punched the air.

Haunting.

Echoing through the space.

"What am I sorry for?" In a flash, he whipped toward me, and he was angling down, coming so close that I could taste his savage words. "I'm sorry for being me. For fucking this up. I knew I would. I fucking knew I would, and I went after you anyway."

He straightened as soon as he said it, putting space between us.

Agony twisted my brow into a tight bow, and I hugged myself.

"No. You are what I needed. What I was waiting for. We needed you."

Bitter laughter rumbled low, and that gorgeous face twisted in disgust. "Your kids are gone because of *me*. You're alone because of *me*. Everything I've worked for since I was seventeen, all the blood, sweat, and bullshit I've taken . . . gone. Because. Of. Me. Gone because I couldn't keep my goddamned dick in my pants."

He might as well have slapped me.

"You know it was more than that," I wheezed through the desperate plea.

"It wasn't anything but a mistake." He gritted it so close to my mouth I could taste the venom coming from his tongue.

A sob climbed my throat, so big I was suffocating on it.

I couldn't take any more.

"No . . . don't say that. Please, don't say that."

"This ends. Now."

I reached for him, and he stepped back.

"Please, Ian, don't leave me. Not now. I need you."

His expression turned cold, distant, and I swore the earth shook, the last pieces falling away.

Destroyed.

Desolated.

Pain splintered and spread. Veins of devastation that crawled and exterminated.

Uprooting all the hope I'd put on this man.

My fingers clawed at him. "No . . . no . . . you . . . you said you were going to fight for them. With me."

I was begging.

Pleading.

Praying,

How could he do this to me?

He laughed more, this low, disgusted sound. He tipped his head to the side, bleeding antagonism. "You really think a judge is going to listen to what I have to say? I *fucked* my client. Guess what, Grace, that means I've lost all credibility. I can no longer touch this case. I've *ruined* my career. It's over. All of it."

Desperation sped through my blood.

"No, you can't do this. You can't just walk away from me. From *us*. You love me. You love us." I was floundering, the despair too great as I tried to reach for him.

To get ahold of him.

To make him see.

"That's exactly what I'm going to do."

"No . . . please."

He lifted a defiant chin, all the tender goodness I'd come to recognize in this man obliterated.

Standing in his place was the predator.

The man who would do absolutely anything to survive.

It didn't matter who got in his way.

Including me.

"I don't want this mess, Grace. I never did. Now, I'm walking away. Believe me, you'll be better off."

"So . . . that's it? Things get rough, and you run like a coward?" I choked around the accusation.

He didn't even flinch. "I warned you who I was."

Selfish.

Greedy.

Incapable of love.

The devil.

Maybe I'd been the fool who hadn't believed him. The one who'd seen more in him. Something better than the powerful, callous man who stood in front of me right then.

I hugged my arms across my chest as if it could shield me from the brutality of his words. As if they could protect me from the truth I should have seen all along.

Still, I was stumbling, pleading with him. "No, you're wrong. You're so much more than that. I know you are. I've seen it."

"You only saw what you wanted to see."

"You told me you loved me. I trusted you. I trusted you with everything."

"And look what that got you."

A gust of wind whipped through the narrow street. The spindly branches of the ancient oaks hissed and howled, sending a tumble of dead, dried leaves across the ground.

It stirred the chaos that raged inside me.

I don't believe you.

I don't believe you.

My spirit screamed it while my mind struggled to accept the reality. The truth that he could hurt me this way.

That he would just . . . turn his back and walk.

It ripped and tore at my insides.

Loss.

A grief unlike anything I'd ever felt.

Hope scattering like the leaves.

"How can you do this?" I forced myself to look at his beautiful face.

Too beautiful. Too mesmerizing. Too dangerous.

"How can you, when you know what is at stake? When you know how badly I need you? *I trusted you.*" The last raked from my throat that was raw and aching.

As raw and aching as my heart.

My eyes squeezed closed when he reached out and brushed his fingertips down the side of my face.

Tenderly.

A stark contrast to the wickedness that blazed from his soul.

Then his voice twisted with that dark, bitter hatred—hatred I was sure was completely directed at himself.

"You shouldn't have."

thirty-eight

IAN

"What the fuck are you going to do?" Jace demanded below his breath.

Ripping at my hair, I paced the parlor at Jace's place. A goddamned panther who was going to claw his way out and take everyone down with me when I did it.

Mack was sitting at the bar, grim expression on his face.

My attention darted their way. "Whatever the fuck I have to do."

Mack shook his head. "This is messy, brother."

"You think I don't know that?" I spat.

It was a motherfucking mess.

A disaster.

That meteor I'd felt coming had finally broken through the atmosphere, nothing but a ball of obliteration that had made landfall.

An implosion no one had seen coming.

But I should have.

I fucking should have.

Fury boiled my blood, the hatred so intense the only thing I saw was red.

Worst part was Grace's face when I'd walked away.

When I'd left her standing there like the asshole I'd warned her I was.

Her giving heart bleeding all over the ground after I'd trampled it.

But I had to.

I had to so there would be no mistake.

She was better off without me.

What could one dance hurt?

Everything.

Everything.

Ruin it all. And I was the bastard who'd gone after it when she'd warned me she couldn't get involved. When she'd told me there was more going on than I could see. Then like some kind of arrogant fucker, I'd thought I'd be the one who'd right her world.

Steady it on its spinning axis.

And I would. If it was the last fucking thing I did, I would. Didn't have anything left to lose, anyway.

Mack sighed and ran his palm over the scruff on his face. "They are painting you as the bad guy here, Ian. Reed has garnered the sympathy of every damned voter in the county. They think the poor guy almost lost his kids over the election."

I paced some more. Rage blistering out with every violent step. "It's right there, man. It's right there. I just don't know how to put my finger on it. Everything I need to put that fucker away is right there."

Mack studied me while Jace nervously ran his hand over his head. He'd been in the middle of his own bullshit not long ago. The last thing he needed was a repeat.

"So, what . . . she has some photos that could be construed as incriminating?" Mack hedged, the insinuation that her evidence didn't prove anything hanging in the dense air. I had little to nothing to go on.

Especially when a man like Reed made things that didn't look so pretty go away.

Disappear.

My head shook as I tried to calculate. "But it's more than that. Thomas . . . her oldest. He overheard someone in Reed's office who was threatening Grace."

"Who?" Mack's entire demeanor went rigid. The guardian coming out to defend.

Frustration pursed my lips. "He didn't get a look at him."

His eyes moved over my face. "Not a whole lot to go on there, either, man. We have to have something solid to get a warrant."

I whirled around, chest nothing but a jackhammer that'd sped out of control. "Night before last . . . I went by Reed's place in the middle of the night. Lawrence Bennet was there . . . outside his house . . . having a little powwow with our *friend* Reed." It was a scrape of icy sarcasm.

In shock, Mack reared back. "Fuck. Are you sure?"

I gave him a tight nod.

Awareness spun. Like the guy was adding it up. Solving a riddle he'd been trying to piece for years. "Goddamn it, Ian. I told you to get away from that piece of shit. He's dirty as fuck."

No shit.

Same as me.

"You think he's involved with Reed in some way?" he pressed.

My voice was tight. "I don't know. The only thing I know is none of this sits well. Lawrence has been pushing me harder, and I've been pushing back. Then he showed up at Reed's place the night after I kicked Reed's ass? Gut tells me something is going down."

A heavy sound pulled from Jace's chest. "Reed knows the whole town. It wouldn't be that odd for a man who owns as much property as Lawrence does to be an associate."

Mack was watching me when he answered Jace, "Don't know

about you, but in my experience, not a whole lot of business goes down in the middle of the night other than the dirty kind."

Worry tripped through Mack's expression. "Need you to tell me straight. How deep are you?"

"Not deep enough," I told him.

But I knew I was about to get deeper.

Agitated, fucking broken in a way I never should have allowed myself to be, I scrubbed a palm over my face. "Listen . . . I'm going to get out of here. See if I can figure anything out."

Mack stood and slowly walked over to me and set a hand on my shoulder. He squeezed. "Think you should lie low, man. With this shitstorm of a media frenzy, the last thing you need is to be drawing more attention to you or Grace. Let me dig. See what I can find. It would be best if you could remove yourself from the whole situation. Let the cops do the footwork."

"I can't just sit idle, man. I have to do something. I know I'm missing something. I can feel it right there, just out of reach."

Understanding dawned in his eyes. "You love her."

Agony pulsed through my spirit.

Grief.

Sorrow.

I bit it back.

"Doesn't matter what I feel. Only thing that matters is her getting custody of her kids."

Warily, he nodded. "I get it. I get it. But you've got to be careful. Don't make this worse than it already is. Gut tells me Reed would love to see you go down."

"I'm already down. Not sure he could kick me any farther."

Mack sent me a look that called bullshit. He knew my connections went deep, tied to Bennet in a way that was dangerous.

I stared right back. Promising she was worth it.

He nodded again. "Call me if you think of anything, and I'll see what I can pull together."

Jace rounded the bar. "Both of us . . . we're here to back you up. Just . . . don't do anything stupid. Two of us will be here for you, however you need us to be."

My attention bounced between the two of them. "Thank you."

Jace shook his head. "You're my brother, Ian. From the beginning, we've had each other's backs. That's not ever gonna change."

He squeezed my shoulder. Tightly.

I nodded.

Mack pulled me in for a hug, his voice low at my ear. "Call me. I'm on standby. Let's take this fucker down."

Bastard already had me on my knees.

There wouldn't be any standing.

Only standing I could do was for Grace.

I walked out and headed for the door.

I froze when I heard the soft voice hit me from behind. "Ian."

Slowly, I turned, not really wanting to see the pity that would be written all over Faith. The woman was too kind for me to handle.

Not when the only thing I wanted right then was blood on my hands.

To get dirty.

Depraved and wicked.

The way I'd always known myself to be.

Her lips twisted into a sad smile. "Here. I found this in the kitchen. Thomas left it."

Didn't think it was possible, but the spec that was my blackened heart sank to the pit of my stomach.

Chest a fist of heartache.

Thomas's tablet.

I reached out and took it, trying to keep my damned hand from shaking. "Thank you."

She looked to the ground, tentative when she peeked back up at me. "I'm so sorry, Ian. I saw you with Grace. With her children. There's nothing more terrifying than the people we love most being in danger."

I wanted to refute it.

Tell her there was no love lost.

Didn't have it in me to tell a lie that big.

I just opened the door and stepped out onto the porch.

Cold air blew in low. A shiver raced my skin, but it didn't have a fucking thing to do with the wind.

I started for my car, only to stop halfway down the porch steps when Faith called out again from the doorway. "They're worth it, Ian. I know your life hasn't always been easy, and I won't pretend to have a clue what you've been through. But what I do know is you've had to fight to survive. That it never made sense to let your heart go when there was never anyone there who you could trust to hold it."

My spine stiffened, and I locked my muscles, refusing to look her way.

"This place is made of magic and dreams. I have never stopped believing that. Not once in my life. Yours are here, too. I felt it, between the two of you. How *real* you are. That you both are fighting for the chance to live again. You will, Ian. You'll live again. That life is right there, waiting to break free, to take its rightful place."

My head swiveled in her direction, and there was no anger in my voice, only pain. "I think we both know it's too late for that."

Faith sent me a tender smile. "Love never comes too late."

GRACE

I ran into the bathroom and dropped to my knees. I vomited so violently I was sure my guts had to be coming up with it.

Everything. Everything.

Tears burned and stung where they dripped down my cheeks, and my body heaved and clutched. A tight sob wheezed out of my throat while my insides squeezed in the most excruciating kind of pain.

I clung to the toilet, knowing I had nothing left.

No ammunition. No fight.

How could I fail my children this way?

I guessed I really had been a fool. Because I was absolutely staggered that Ian had just walked. Turned his back on me in the moment I needed him the most. Maybe I did have the worst intuition when it came to men.

But I'd believed in him so wholeheartedly that, when he brushed me off, it felt like the cruelest sort of blow.

Total devastation.

Ravaged by anguish.

How could I have hope when the man who was supposed to advocate for us believed there was no hope left?

Another roil of nausea slammed me, and I heaved again, bringing up nothing, my stomach expanding with the void.

Sobs ripped and tore, and I didn't have the strength to lift my head when footsteps shuffled in. And I didn't think things could get any worse until I felt my grandmother's heart shatter right there.

Her grief mine and mine hers.

"Oh, my girl."

A soft hand was laid on my back, stroking down my spine, voice coaxing in its soft timber. "It's okay. It's okay. Tell me what happened."

I clung tighter to the cold porcelain, the only relief for my skin that felt as if it were on fire. "I wasn't enough, Gramma. I wasn't enough. My babies . . . Oh, God, my babies."

I doubted she could understand a word I said, everything fragmented and broken.

An extension of me.

She hadn't been home when I'd stumbled through the door after Ian had driven off without so much as a backward glance. I'd originally intended to tell her about what had happened with the kids with Ian at my side. I'd envisioned we'd gather at her table and together we'd form a plan.

I could feel her trying to be strong, but her own torment shone through, her voice growing craggy and thin. "Reed got to them?"

My face pinched in agony, and I nodded, sniffling, raking my forearm across my face in an attempt to see through the bleariness. Moaning, I pushed myself back and flopped against the tub. "He said he came to pick up the kids yesterday and they weren't here. That going to the judge was the only thing he could do. Of course, that judge just so happened to be Jonathan."

Anger gusted from her being. "He did nothing of the sort."

I could only nod again. There was no surprise in hearing the bastard had lied about that, too.

It wasn't as if it wasn't obvious that he'd been having me followed this whole time. That my private life had not been private at all.

But it stung, just the same, that the man could spew lies and blasphemies and claim it as truth and the world would take it as fact.

"It doesn't matter. The only thing that does is that my kids are gone, and I have no idea how I'm going to get them back."

She reached out and tipped up my chin. "You dry your eyes, pick yourself up, and remember you have the power to go after what's right."

Helplessness bled free. "I'm not sure that I possess that power anymore."

"Nonsense. Of course, you do. Your last name might still legally be Dearborne, but you're a MacNally at heart. We might get beaten down, but we always get back up."

Unable to fully focus, I blinked at her through the haze of misery. "And sometimes we make mistakes, Gramma. Terrible mistakes that are selfish and stupid, and we ruin any chance that we had, and once we realize it, there is absolutely nothing we can do to take them back."

Her gaze deepened, and she inclined her head. "Are we talking about that looker of yours?"

Her words were nothing but a jagged blade driven into my side. "He's not mine."

"You sure about that? Because it definitely seemed that way to me when he came for you in the middle of the night a couple of days ago. Not many men step out like that, not unless they've already put their heart on the line."

"We put everything on the line. Both of us. And we both lost. We lost everything." My voice was a wisp.

She brushed her knuckles through the tears that blanketed my cheeks.

Unchecked and unending.

"Don't you know the bleakest times are making way for the brightest sunrises?"

"I'm not sure the sun can rise when there's only darkness left."

Her head shook. "The sun always comes. It might tarry, but it will shine. Now that's a *gift* we can always count on."

"I'm sorry, but I don't think my life is gonna end up wrapped in a pretty red bow." I swiped frantically at the tears that kept falling. "Maybe the best thing I could do is give in to what he wants. Go back to him."

The thought of Reed ever touching me again made my skin crawl. But my children were worth any sacrifice.

I'd trade joy for their safety.

Happiness if it meant I was there, watching over them.

She huffed out a loathing sigh. "You will do no such thing. You left because you knew that's what you had to do. Because your children deserve better than that life. Because you deserve better than that life."

"But what if it's the only option?" I whimpered, hugging my knees to my chest.

"It's not. It's not. So, here's the plan. You're going to get in that shower and clean yourself up, curl up in bed and have yourself a good cry, and when you wake up in the morning, you're going to be ready to fight again. Because I promise you, even though you can't feel it right now, the sun will be there to welcome you."

I gave her the weakest smile. "It shouldn't be possible to keep crying, but I can't seem to stop."

Sadness wedged into the lines of her aged face. She reached out and cupped my cheek. "Tears for our children don't go dry. Our cares don't dissipate. Until they're safe, those tears will go on forever. But you will smile again, sweet girl. I know it. My heart knows it. You just have to believe it, too."

IAN

There are moments in our lives when we gain evidence of everything our souls had forever screamed was our truth.

Call it a reaffirmation.

An underscore.

Motherfucking proof.

Or maybe it was just providence cinching down tight on the collar it had wrapped around your neck. A noose reminding you who you were. Who you were destined to be.

Changing—becoming someone better—wasn't in the cards.

I'd wanted to. God, I'd wanted to.

A week had gone by, and there I was, in my darkened condo in the middle of the night, responsible for the very thing I'd promised myself I'd never be.

The joy of children.

Innocent children who had no way to fight. Children who were sitting across town waiting for someone to be their hero when they didn't know our only fate was tragedy.

I knew it.

I'd known it all along, and then I'd gone and gotten stupid and thought there might be something better out there. Some bigger purpose.

What bullshit.

Alone, I sat on my couch, drinking straight from the bottle because the burn that slid down my throat was the only companion I could ever rely on.

Sure as shit couldn't rely on myself.

Grace had to learn that firsthand.

Most pathetic part was I somehow thought I had the right to ache and hurt and wish there was something I could do when they only thing I'd hit through the entire week was dead end after dead end.

I couldn't find shit on Reed.

Fucker was squeaky clean when he was the dirtiest bastard around.

I took another pull of the warm liquid. Wished it was Grace's hands. Grace's sweet hands that could chase away any storm. The girl peace and light and everything I'd never known I was missing.

Missing.

That's exactly what this was.

I was missing her like a bitch.

Really, what she'd done was summon a whole new storm. God knew that the girl had turned my life upside down.

The truth was, I'd never have been good enough for her. For them. I knew it to my core.

Misery beat through my body. Was pretty sure stumbling upon that girl was nothing but another penalty for what I'd done. A tease of what I could never have.

I knew it.

I knew it.

Chest aching, I looked over at the tablet that sat on the couch next to me, that fucking jewelry box sitting next to it, trying to stop the hurt lining my insides.

I needed to accept defeat.

This was over.

Just to punish myself a little more, I pulled the tablet onto my lap and swiped into it, a soft smile pulling to my mouth when I saw the background picture.

Grace and Thomas and Mallory making goofy faces where they sat on the floor in the bedroom where all the kids had been staying, Sophie with her little arms around Grace's neck as she clung to her back.

Grace was angled toward the camera.

Felt like I could reach out and touch her.

Like she was right there and nowhere at the same time.

So damned lonely, missing them so goddammed much, I clicked into Thomas's photo folder. Invading his privacy, the same way as I'd invaded their lives, an intruder who wouldn't do anything but cause them pain.

Had I not chased Grace down that first night, this never would have happened. She wouldn't have my name to tarnish hers. She wouldn't have the media going wild with scandalous stories about her sleeping with her attorney. Wouldn't have this bullshit that made her look like she was indecent and dirty, when the girl had the purest heart of anyone I'd ever met.

Her children her priority.

Her life.

Exactly what they were supposed to be.

Emotion surged my throat when the images popped onto the screen, the bright light glaring into my darkened apartment. Thomas had taken picture after picture of his sisters. Mallory being crazy and funny and the brightest thing on the Earth, and Sophie wrecking all that mayhem, the child nothing but a handful that I would do anything to hold.

There were some that Thomas had taken of himself. The boy stoic and proud and scared and too mature for his age.

My chest tightened.

Everything ached.

Then there was Grace. Always there. Always present. Always loving.

God, how could I have been so selfish to think I could fit into their world? That's what I'd fucking done, wasn't it? Started to imagine what it might be like to belong.

Really belong.

When the only thing I'd ever truly belonged to was selfishness and greed.

I clicked into a video.

Cringed a bit when I realized it was taken at the Dearborne estate. Still, I couldn't stop watching it, their little voices breaking into the unbearable silence of my condo.

"Thomas, Thomas, are you recording me? I'm going to sing you your favorite song!"

Thomas scoffed. "Pssh . . . all you're gonna do is ruin it."

"Nuh-uh! I'm the best singer in the world and I'm gonna go to New York and be an actress or maybe to Hollywood so I can be in movies and then you're gonna be sad you didn't believe my dreams when I'm famous and you want to be my best friend. And I'm going to write all my own songs because I'm a writer and I'll probably write all the movies, too. Maybe you can record them since you take such good pictures. Just don't make me mad," she warned with some of that sass.

A soft smile pulled at my mouth, while my shredded heart ached.

Mal Pal.

Pain sheared through the middle of me. And I just watched. Unable to stop.

"Sophie dance!" Sophie was bouncing around Mallory, always wanting to be in the middle of it.

Mallory started singing.

New Kids on the Block.

Good God, I was going to have to have a talk with Grace about that shit.

With the thought, a hot blade pierced my chest.

How the fuck had it gotten to the point that Grace no longer had the influence? That her right was taken away?

"Tom Tom,, dance, Tom Tom, dance!" Sophie chanted.

Thomas was angling his camera to get a close-up, her big blue eyes so excited and trusting.

The screen bounced around, and I could tell Thomas was setting up his tablet to record where he balanced it upright on a table. Then all three of them were in the middle of the room, dancing and singing and laughing.

My breath hitched.

It was the most perfect thing I'd ever seen.

Only thing wrong with it was the location and the fact Grace wasn't there.

A female voice called, "Lunch," and the three of them took off. Thomas had completely forgotten about his tablet, leaving it recording as they scrambled off to eat.

I started to click out of that video so I could move onto another one when a male's voice broke through the speaker, so distinct and recognizable my blood went cold.

"I told you she was going to be a problem."

Lawrence Bennet.

I shot forward on the couch, clutching the tablet in my hand, staring at the screen that only captured a stilled picture of a living room. But it was the voices caught from somewhere off to the side that had tension racing.

Gripping and clutching.

"And I told you she was my problem and not to worry about it," another voice hissed. One I wouldn't recognize if it weren't for the two foul interactions I'd had with him a little over a week ago.

Reed Dearborne.

"There's a point where you no longer get to make that call. You put everything at risk, and I'm going to step in. I think you should know me well enough by now."

Finally, finally, both of them stepped into the frame. Reed glanced around, his voice held low and hostility vibrating from his demeanor.

"You think you're going to come into my house and start

making demands? Do you know who I am?" Reed demanded.

Asshole was clearly offended Lawrence had the audacity to question him.

Lawrence lifted his chin like the cocky old bastard that he was. "I think the better question is, have you forgotten who I am? I built this company. This town. You. I own everything. So, when there's a problem? It's my job to fix it. Including when your pretty little wife goes rogue."

My blood that had run cold froze over.

Reed flew into his face, like the fucker cared. "Stay away from her. If she's an issue, then I will be the one to handle it."

"She's already an issue. The fact that she isn't here and you can't control her is proof enough."

"And what do you think the media is going to say if she goes missing? Shows up floating in the river? All eyes are going to be on me. No one gives a fuck if one of the junkie whores goes missing. But a mother of three who just so happens to be my ex-wife? You don't think that's going to look suspicious or raise some questions? You know we don't need that right now."

Panic pounded through my veins. Rage jumped in to take a ride, too.

Lawrence straightened his tie. "Car accidents happen every day."

"That's the mother of my children you're talking about."

"Who is a liability. She will do anything to get custody of her children, including hire *my fucking attorney*. She'll throw you under the bus faster than you can say go. Last chance, Reed. Get her back here by the end of the month or I will take matters into my own hands."

Vomit climbed my throat when I realized it was the last day of the month.

Thanksgiving gone without me even realizing it.

"Just like I had to do with Dear Industries," Lawrence continued.

Dear Industries.

My mind started to spin. I'd heard that company name before.

My chest tightened, and dread sank to the pit of my stomach

when I realized from where.

It was the last documents I'd signed off on.

Documents that made it look like Lawrence had legitimately taken over a business when it'd amounted to little more than a heist.

Documents that had come from a fake man's name with a fake social security number from a fake bank account with a huge transaction of cash that I'd filtered into some of his more legitimate companies.

One I'd forged as legit.

"My accountant went through those numbers a hundred times," Reed growled. "The numbers are good. Nothing is ever going to come out exact. A few dollars aren't going to kill anyone."

"I wouldn't call five hundred thousand dollars a *few dollars*. And I'm pretty sure that it would." The implication rode on the air, so palpable between the two of them I could feel it from where I sat.

"I won't be stolen from. I don't give a fuck who you are. Not to mention, you overdrew on Williamstown by two million. You had a deadline. Now I will take back what is mine."

Williamstown.

My head spun.

That was the name of the rundown apartment complex where my mother and I had lived when I'd met Bennet. When he'd taken me in and given me a job and treated me like a son, when really, he had been suckering me into his shady business that I'd been too naïve to see at the time.

Petty theft and sifting through people's garbage cans hardly amounted to my being shrewd enough to grasp the full extent of the debased wickedness and corruption and greed.

Evil.

Bennet had owned that building.

God.

What a fool I'd been.

I'd buried my head in the sand and stupidly believed that Lawrence had stumbled upon me outside that complex.

Noticing that I was half starved and wholly desperate.

I'd thought him a powerful businessman who would own half

of the city.

Realization slammed me.

What the fucker had been doing was running a prostitution ring.

One my mother had gotten involved in.

Sickness twisted my guts into a thousand knots.

Was that why we'd gone there in the first place? Was that why she'd packed us up and promised me we were starting a new life when, in reality, she was driving right to her demise?

Dead six months later.

Because of me.

Forever and ever. Her voice spun through my mind.

You left me, mine whispered back.

Did I really think I was any better?

I'd dived right into the middle of it, sucked under, never let up for air until it was the only thing I breathed.

I'd become the devil. Just like these two.

No fucking better.

My pen and my voice had been my weapon.

I was nothing but a flimsy piece of paper that amounted to a cover for the disgusting empire Lawrence had built.

"I needed that money for the campaign." Reed's voice was twisted in his own kind of hatred. "You know the deal. I get the guns here and you get me the money."

My mind immediately flashed to the picture Grace had been able to smuggle out of Reed's house.

Down on the dock.

The Dearborne money came from imports and exports. The reason his great grandfather had settled in Charleston to begin with.

It all crashed over me.

How deep this went. What was happening.

I shot to my feet while the video was still playing, a clatter of footsteps echoing across the floor as Mallory ran into the room. "Daddy, can we go to the movies?"

Both men jerked away from the other. Reed's expression showed nothing but annoyance. "I'm working, Mallory. Go back in the kitchen."

"But, Dad—"

"Go!"

Go.

Yeah, fucker, you could count on it. Because I was already running out the door.

IAN

My tires screeched as I flew out of the parking garage. Adrenaline surged, seeping into my muscles that flexed and bowed, at the ready for a fucking fight.

My sight clouded with rage, and my heart thundered with fury. I pushed the phone button on the steering wheel and instructed it to call Mack.

He answered on the third ring, voice groggy from sleep. "Ian, man, what's going on?"

"Heading to Bennet's office. Meet me there. Pretty sure that's where I'm going to find the proof that he and Reed have been working together. Wasn't some fluke that those pictures of me were snagged at that club. Lawrence and Reed are involved in some major shady shit."

"Pull over. I'll meet you."

"Not going to happen. I'm going. Bring backup. And get a cruiser to Grace's house. She isn't safe."

"Shit." I could almost see him scrubbing a big palm over his face to break up the sleep. "Are you sure?"

"Positive. I just need the papers to prove it."

"Give me five, man. Then I'm out the door and on my way to you. I don't want you to do anything that will get you into trouble."

Cold laughter rippled out. "Think it's too late for that, my friend. Just get down there. Be prepared to do your job, no matter what."

Worry bled through the line, Mack's hesitation thick. "What are you saying, Ian?"

"I'll see you in fifteen."

I ended the call and flew down the street. Ten minutes later, I screeched to a stop at the curb in front of Bennet's office. Didn't even try to hide my car.

This wasn't about going covert.

This was going all in.

The last thing I had to give.

Heart hammering wildly, I grabbed my phone and tapped out a text.

Me: An officer is on their way to your house. Stay put, don't let anyone inside until they're there. You're not safe.

Even though it was the middle of the night, her response was almost instant. Like she'd been lying awake like me, tossing in torment.

Grace: What's happening? Are you okay? Are the kids okay?

Me: It's all going to be okay. I promise you. But I need you to be extra careful right now.

I bit my lip, knowing I shouldn't do it, but I was unable to stop myself. Not with what was getting ready to go down. My fingers flew across the screen.

Me: If I could be a better man, I'd be him for you. If I could live a better life, I'd live it for you. I'm sorry for bringing this burden on your family. They are beautiful, Grace. The most amazing people I've ever had the honor of knowing in all of my pathetic life. Keep writing your story. Hold them close. Love them hard. That's the way I'm going to forever love you. Goodbye, Angel Girl.

I pushed send, threw open the door of my car, and slipped out.

Cold blasted across the fire that burned my skin and that adrenaline sloshed as I strode toward the building.

Didn't give two fucks when I grabbed one of the decorative rocks and smashed in the pane of glass to the side of the door. The sound of it crashing to the ground echoed through the night.

An alarm started to blare.

So loud.

So loud.

It only amplified the determination that lined my heart like a coat of steel. The willingness to do absolutely anything to save that family.

Guessed I hadn't really understood what that meant until tonight.

What it was really going to cost.

Everything. Everything.

I didn't care.

I stepped through the broken window in the brick wall, glass crunching under my feet, ducking down beneath the dangling shards that still hung from the upper frame.

I blew right by the front office desk and went for Bennet's office, which was locked up tight for the night. I picked up my foot and kicked it in. It flew open, wood banging against the interior wall.

I strode in like I owned the place, going right for his computer and punching in the same password as I had the last time I was there.

Only, this time, I knew exactly what I was looking for.

The alarm was deafening where it blared in the small room, stampeding my heart even faster.

Like every scream urged me to hurry.

I clicked open the file that was encrypted and moved through about fifteen options for passwords before I found the one that was right—a combination of Bennet's phone number he'd had when I'd met him and his mother's birthdate.

The file popped open.

Vomit pooled and sloshed.

Had to give the asshole credit. His blackmail skills were on point.

There was a copy of the same picture Grace had managed to smuggle out originally.

Reed down on the docks with the armed guards.

Only there was another one that had clearly been taken at the same time, Lawrence caught whispering with someone off to the side as they inspected the opened crates that had been brought up from the bowels of Reed's ship.

I continued to click through the photos kept in the hidden folder.

There were a ton of Reed with prostitutes climbing all over him, the man caught in the act of Bennet's depravity, clearly spanning years. I raced to click through them, the images getting older and older until it came to one where Reed couldn't have been much older than a teenager.

Clearly set up.

Hooks sunk into him just the same as Lawrence had done with me.

All of us corrupt.

Lawrence at the helm driving the debauchery.

Round and round.

I quickly flicked through the pictures of Reed.

My eyes squinted, studying the grainy photos.

Every single one of the women had a tattoo on her shoulder, a broken circle with a number.

The realization slammed me.

These women were numbered.

Possessions.

Marked.

Disgust churned, and I struggled to see through the haze of repulsion.

The proof of what Lawrence had been involved in mixed with the horrors of my childhood ripped me open wide, old wounds bleeding, that hatred and shame of what my mother had had to do right there at the forefront.

I tried to stop them. But images flashed.

Pulsing from where I'd tried to keep them trapped in the recesses of my mind.

The tattoo my mother had always had since I could remember.

On her shoulder. The full circle with a Roman numeral one in the middle of it.

It was the same as what had been engraved on the bottom of the silver box. The one thing she'd had left of my father.

Nausea rolled, so violently my body recoiled, lurching with a sickness, bowing me in two.

Oh God.

Oh God.

I could barely see.

Could barely stand.

I sucked it down. I could deal with the implications of this shit later.

Grace needed me.

Those kids needed me.

I pushed print on a few of the pictures, before I quickly clicked into the Dear Industries folder and started printing every document in there.

My own personal glowing accolades.

Document after document.

Companies I'd falsified, helped Lawrence create, laundered money through.

I found three that I realized could be directly tied to Reed.

Alarms continued to blare.

My blood pounded in sync.

Harsh and hard.

I froze when I heard the cocking of a gun at the back of my head. I'd been so caught up on this suicide mission, clicking through as many documents to print them before someone erased them, that I hadn't even noticed that I wasn't alone.

Sweat gathered at my nape. Cold and clammy. I swallowed hard.

"Having fun?" Bennet's voice was a growl at my ear.

Hatred flooded out with the low roll of my laughter. "Best day of my life."

"Make the wrong move, and it will be your last."

He grabbed me by the back of the collar, gun still rammed tight against the base of my skull, and forced me over to the alarm pad. He punched in the code and the alarm cut off. He reached over and grabbed the receiver from the phone on his desk and dialed a number.

"Yes, this is Lawrence Bennet. I came into the office in the middle of the night because I woke up realizing I forgot to do something *important.*"

He emphasized the word. Just for me.

"Apparently, I was a little too sleepy and tripped the alarm. I apologize for any inconvenience . . . All is good . . . No need to send anyone . . . Thank you for your help."

He tossed the phone back onto the receiver.

"Sounds good to me," I gritted out, facing the wall he had my face pinned against, going right back to the threat he had made. "Won't be able to look myself in the mirror after seeing all this shit anyway."

He scoffed. "Don't act like you didn't know full well what was going down. You did it of your own free will. Didn't take a whole lot of twisting your arm."

"I was a kid."

"You were growing into the man you were always supposed to be."

Anger boiled, and I tried to bite it back, biding my time, praying Mack at least got here before Bennet had the chance to take a shot and disappeared with the evidence.

With the gun still aimed at me, he stepped back, releasing his hold.

I slowly turned, hating the man I saw standing four feet away.

"No wonder I ended up with you," I gritted, bile on my tongue. He shook his head. Haughty and contemptuous. "Is it?"

I gulped around the fury that flamed at my insides. "Is it true?"

His eyes narrowed, and mine were frantically searching his face for clues, for the resemblance I'd been too much of a fool to look for all along.

"What? That you have always belonged to me?"

Revulsion shook my head. "I've never belonged to you."

"That's where you're wrong. You've been mine since the day you were born. Your bitch of a mother might have tried to get away with you. Steal you from your legacy."

He took a step forward. "From your destiny."

My spirit thrashed. "What are you saying?"

"Your mother belonged to me. She was mine. The first one. The only one I cared to love. Big mistake."

Sorrow pinched my eyes. I tried to fight it. Not to show any weakness in front of this disgusting man.

"I found her, homeless, living like gutter trash with a baby pressed to her tit. Wasn't all that hard to get her under my roof and into my bed. Only mistake I made was not treating her like the rest. Treating her like she was special. But that's what happens when you let someone get under your skin."

Everything drew tight, the air thin, the world spinning. "How?" Brilliant.

But I couldn't get anything else out.

Everything crashing. I was struck with the realization that I'd known nothing, and it'd been right there under my nose all along.

Bitterness twisted up his face. "She took off with you and your whiny brother when you were just two weeks old. I'd hunt her down, drag her home, and then she'd do it all over again. Refusing the life I offered, instead thinking she was giving you a better one.

What bullshit. She was a junkie, just like the rest. A whore. She never changed."

Rage coiled. "Why didn't you tell me?"

He shrugged a shoulder. "After your brother got arrested, she came crawling back. It'd been twelve fucking years since I'd seen her, and there she was, begging at my door, willing to do anything to put a roof over your head. I put her back to work, not because I gave a fuck about her any longer, but because my son was finally home."

Grief creaked through my bones.

Forever and ever.

"You were responsible from the get go? Got her hooked on drugs?" My face pinched. "Fucking pimped her out?"

My mind was adding up the fucked puzzle faster than my spirit could tolerate it.

Could feel it, splitting me in two.

Gutting.

Gutting.

I struggled to breathe.

"A woman's a lot easier to control when you're the one holding that control. Don't you get that? Which is why that bitch you've taken up with has got to go. I won't let her destroy what I've built. What I've built for you."

Disgust boiled in the pit of my stomach. "I want nothing to do with you."

A scoff bled from him. "Don't be dramatic, Ian. I've been shaping you into who you were supposed to be for years. You weren't ready to hear it. Not until now. Now it's time to take your place. Reed and his ex-wife have become an issue. Now you're going to fix it—end it—sweep it under a rug and make sure it disappears, and then you're going to take your place at my side."

"You're delusional."

Bile swam on my tongue, and I sucked the bitter taste down. "My mother—"

"Was in my way."

Wrong. Not delusional. He was just a monster.

"She came to me, begging for help like the pathetic piece of garbage she'd always been, and then turned around and actually thought she was in control. Making demands of me. Ordering me to stay away from you."

Ruthlessness oozed from his pores.

He lifted his chin and uttered the words like a slogan, "Bitches who don't obey need to bleed."

Agony sheared through my chest. Splitting me in two. Taking up the empty space was a horror and a rage unlike anything I'd ever known.

"What did you just say?"

His laughter was hatred. "Your mother would have done anything for you. Including fight me. That was her first mistake."

My head shook. "You're a liar."

"And you've always been a fool."

My mama's voice flooded my mind. *"Ian, you stay away from that man, do you hear me? He's not good."*

Anguish.

It constricted and mashed.

Tightening around my ribs.

No air found.

Suffocating.

"You killed her."

He shrugged like it didn't matter. "Well, I ordered it. Reed did the job. The first I gave him. I needed to make sure he understood he worked for me. That I would ruin him and his family. He had a thing for my women, you see, and I had a need for him. It was a win-win."

The pictures on the computer.

That's all it'd been.

Years of twisted blackmail.

My knees weakened, and I stumbled, the voice coming off my tongue a pained groan. "Mama."

Oh god.

My mother.

Forever and ever.

Savage words impaled my ears. "She was stupid enough to threaten me, saying she was going to go to the police with what was happening at the apartments if I didn't stay away from you. Problem was, you'd always belonged to me, Ian. I had no choice but to take matters into my own hands."

His head slowly shook. "It's time you stop pretending that you're different than me. That you're better. Stop pretending you have morals when we both know your hands are just as dirty as mine."

He took another step closer, his voice dropping. "You're just like me. My blood runs through your veins. My heart is yours. I gave it to you. I shaped you. Now it's time to accept who you are."

Rage.

They say it's blinding.

They were wrong.

Because I saw everything.

All of it coated in red. His blood on my hands. Restitution for my mother's that was on his.

It was my fault. It was my fault. It'd always been my fault.

I lurched for the gun.

Bennet smashed me across the face with it.

I didn't stop.

Didn't slow.

I dove for him.

My chest seized with the gunshot that rang through the air.

GRACE

Gaping through the shock, I stared at the messages that Ian had sent me.

It was the first I'd heard from him in a week. It'd been seven days that I'd spent lost to the worst sort of torment.

Floating through relentless waves of grief and worry and sorrow.

Unending.

Boundless.

Fathomless.

Fear had become the focus of it, Reed's constant texts shifting into callous warnings. Words about me running out of time. To make the right decision.

They didn't feel close to being a plea.

They felt sinister.

My gramma had promised me going back to him wasn't an option. But I didn't know how to keep hanging onto that when it felt as if everything I adored was slipping away.

How long could I remain at my grandmother's house alone, while Reed continued to dangle my children over my head like bait? While I didn't know if they were safe or cared for? While I couldn't kiss them and tuck them in at night?

But this? I squeezed my phone tighter. This felt like the first glimpse of hope I'd seen all week. The sun promising to break over the horizon.

A glimmer of light.

That gift my grandmother had been talking about.

All the while, his goodbye obliterated the remains of my heart.

What was he saying?

What did he mean?

Whatever it was, I wasn't going to question it. Even after everything, I still trusted him.

Wholly and completely.

The man he'd shown me was real, even if for his own survival he couldn't acknowledge it.

I pushed out of bed, pulled on a pair of jeans, and slipped my feet into tennis shoes. The night was all around me, pressing into the bedroom, and my heart began hammering out of control.

I swore I sensed something approaching in the howl of the wind and the whip of the branches raking on the eaves.

Something ominous.

Wicked and cruel.

Taking my phone with me, I slipped through my bedroom doorway and eased down the hall and into the foyer. I stopped there, my breaths turning shallow as I waited.

Listening.

Praying that the police officer would show up and tell me everything was okay. That my babies were safe. That I was safe. That Ian was safe.

I jumped about ten feet in the air when someone pounded on

my door.

Then I blew out a breath, relief bounding through my system when I realized that the officer had to be there.

It was short-lived.

Terror rippled through my bloodstream when I peered through the peephole and saw Reed standing there.

"Open the fucking door, Grace. I know you're there."

"Go away," I shouted. It was nothing but a plea from my soul. "Just . . . go away and give me my children."

"You know that's not going to happen."

A light flicked on from the other side of the house, and I could hear my grandmother shuffling through the night.

"That squirrely bastard," she hissed. "I have half a mind to go after that boy with a frying pan and teach him a lesson. Lord knows his mama must not have done it."

If only it were that simple.

But it wasn't.

I could feel the magnitude of this all the way to my soul. After tonight, nothing would be the same.

I could feel myself at the edge of a cliff.

Oblivion or paradise.

I had no idea which was waiting beneath.

I pressed my finger to my lips, begging my gramma not to say anything.

I turned back toward the door. "Go away, Reed. There isn't anything you can say that will make me go back to you. This is a losing battle."

A fist battered at the wood again, jolting me back. But it was his voice that shocked through me like a thunderbolt. "Fuck, Grace, listen to me. Please. You are in danger. And it's my fucking fault. I accept that. But if you don't leave with me right now, there isn't a way for me to protect you. I need you to come outside."

Dread whipped through my spirit. "Where are the kids? Oh my God, Reed."

"They're safe. But you have to hurry."

I reached for the lock.

"Don't you dare leave with that man." Gramma was right there behind me, trying to drag me back.

I turned to her, complete and utter desperation flooding from my pores, as heavy as the tears that immediately clouded my sight. "My safety isn't the concern anymore, Gramma. It's my children's. And I will do whatever I have to in order to make sure of that. I can't risk it."

"Oh, sweet girl." I thought it was her own surrender. The moment she realized I didn't have another choice.

Grief locking everything up, I wrapped her in the tightest hug. "I'm so sorry I dragged you into this."

"You couldn't have kept me out of it," she murmured.

Without another word, I threw open the door and rushed outside. Instantly, Reed grabbed me by the arm. His concern from a second ago completely wiped away. He leaned in toward my ear, hatred in his voice. "This will be the last time you disobey me."

I didn't even think it was shock that had the air bursting from my lungs or the fight lining my body like rods of steel.

Part of me had known he was playing me.

He'd been playing me all along.

But this wasn't me being naïve or a fool.

Like I'd told my gramma, I could risk it. Couldn't lay down bets on their safety.

I'd do anything for my babies.

And I knew right then going with him was doing them no favors.

I ripped my arm away, as hard as I could, summoning all the strength I could find. "Fuck you."

This was going to end.

Right then.

"You don't own me. You don't control me. I will never belong to you. I will fight you to the end."

"If that's what it has to come to," he sneered before he launched himself at me.

Fear raced, and I scrambled to get away, flailing my arms as I tried to make it back to the door.

I'd barely made it one step when he tackled me to the ground.

It knocked the air from my lungs. I wheezed in pain. Reed got to his feet, pinning my arms behind me and dragging me to standing. "You're going to pay for this, Grace. You really think you could leave me? A Dearborne? Make me look like a fool? I'd think again."

Reed jerked me toward the walkway, then we both became disoriented when we were blinded by the bright lights in our eyes.

"Freeze," an officer yelled as my entire body went weak with relief. "Let her go, and get on the ground with your hands behind your back."

"Do you know who I am?" Reed sneered, jerking me back harder.

"Let her go."

"Fuck you."

Another trample of feet surprised us from the side, and our bodies were being propelled forward by the officer who tackled Reed from behind.

His arms released me, and I was crawling away, sobbing in relief as I heard the tussle behind me, the words riding into the night air like a shout of mercy.

"Reed Dearborne . . . you're under arrest . . . "

Keep writing your story. Hold them close. Love them hard.

I thought I could actually hear Ian whispering it in my ear, his hand on my face. And I knew with every fiber of my being that the only reason we were going to be able to do it was because of him.

I didn't know what he'd done.

But I knew he'd given me this.

My shattered saint.

IAN

"*Drop* the gun. Get down on your knees." Mack's voice powered through the room, the shot he'd fired still ringing in my ear. Boots pounded into the room, and a group of officers surrounded us, lining up on either side of Mack where my best friend had his gun pointed at Lawrence Bennet.

My father.

The man who'd had my mother killed.

I was still on the ground, trying to fucking breathe through the bomb Lawrence had dropped onto my world.

Imploding.

Desolating.

Nothing left.

I'd always known her death was my fault. I'd just never understood the magnitude of the circumstances.

She had died for me. Been killed over me.

Because she'd loved me.

Forever and ever.

And I'd played right into Bennet's hand, signed my life away to the man who'd spent the last twenty years shaping me into a monster exactly like him.

I choked over the realization.

The gutting, ravaging devastation.

Bennet laughed, taunting, "Do you have any clue who I am?"

"Scum?" Mack tossed out with a shrug. Then he turned his attention on me. "You okay, man?"

No.

Not even close.

But I managed to push to my feet, hand going to my face that was dripping with blood from a cut on my lip.

Wished it was his.

Wished it was a pool of it.

Overflowing the room.

I'm so sorry. God, I'm so sorry.

Forever and Ever.

Kisses are for who you love most.

I was seized by grief. Every inch. Every cell.

One of the officers moved around Mack and knelt over Bennet, reading him his rights as he put him in cuffs.

I didn't even hesitate, didn't slow. I went to the printer and gathered the pictures and the documents.

Lawrence started roaring like a beast from where he was pinned facedown to the ground.

He needed to be six feet under it.

"Don't do it, Ian. I'm your father. Your family. You owe me. I made you. Don't you fucking dare."

My face twisted in disdain. "You aren't my family. Not ever. You are every single thing I'm ashamed to be. And be clear, I owe only one person anything. Actually, make that four."

Four perfect, perfect faces that deserved to live.

To be free.

Their lives joy.

Filled with *grace*.

"That should be everything you need." I handed the stack to Mack.

He stuffed his gun into the back of his pants, almost grinning when I handed him the evidence that would put Lawrence and Reed away forever.

But he wasn't smiling so big when he realized every single one of those documents also implicated me.

I was just as guilty.

My signature was on a ton of forged documents, my hands soiled, the proof clear in all the evidence I'd handed him.

"Shit, Ian," he wheezed. "Fuck, what is this?"

I could see the outright war play out on his face, his mind scrambling to come up with a different solution when there was none to be found.

I lifted my chin before he could do something stupid like put himself on the line.

"They're worth it," I said.

There wasn't even a tremor to my voice.

No wavering.

No question.

They were worth it.

"Are you sure?" Grief came out with his words.

I nodded tight. "I've never been so sure of anything in my life."

Mack gulped hard when he moved to where I was standing by the desk, and I turned around and put my arms behind my back.

His voice was choked, barely heard. "You have the right to remain silent . . . "

He continued through the words as he wrapped the steel around my wrists.

Cinched them tight.

Tugged me upright.

From behind, his voice was at my ear, "I'm so fucking sorry, man, I'm so fucking sorry."

"They're worth it," I whispered again.

My mother's face flashed through my mind.

She was worth it.

In all these years, I'd never known it, Jace had never known. Maybe she'd been fighting for us all along.

Mack squeezed my shoulder. "I'm so damned proud of you."

But I had none.

No pride.

Every goal, every aspiration had been wiped out.

Obliterated.

Loving Grace Dearborne had cost me everything.

And losing my freedom for hers was a small, small price to pay.

GRACE

Emotion ripped through the cold air.

Wild and frenzied and free.

I ran.

Straight out ran.

I didn't slow until I dropped to my knees. I didn't even care that they had to be bloodied from hitting the sidewalk.

Because Mallory was throwing herself in my arms. "Mommy."

Her little arms wrapped tightly around my neck.

Sobs wracked from my soul.

Flooding.

Pouring out.

This uncontainable love.

I pressed my face into her hair.

Warmth and light.

Awe and joy.

So much joy.

I was weeping with it, unable to see when I stood, taking Mallory with me, clutching her while I ducked down to get Sophie out of her seat.

Movements frantic as I undid the straps of the car seat, hands shaking and shaking.

She was chanting, "Mommy home, Mommy home!" Clapping like it was just another day.

Little did she know this was the first day of the beginning of our new lives.

I couldn't stop the tears as I gathered her close, my face in her hair, breathing her in, too.

My little handful that I wanted to forever have in the palms of my hands.

"It's okay, Mommy. You don't need to cry. Everything is okay. We're home, and we get to stay forever and forever," Mallory whispered, her voice hitching with her excitement, holding herself up high while I pulled Sophie out of the backseat of Mack's car.

"Mal Pal." It was the only thing I could get out around the clot of emotion locking up my throat.

Only thing I could get out around the outpouring of love.

The river of hope.

Everything. Everything.

A torrent of tears clouded my vision, but I was still moving, trying to get around the other side of the car.

Mack was already there, ushering Thomas in my direction.

I just stood there for a beat, watching my brave little man, his eyes a little haunted but brimming with his own hope.

For a few seconds, he just stood there, before he ran for me and threw his arms around my middle, burying his face in my stomach as he began to weep. "Mom. I'm so sorry. I'm so sorry."

I settled the girls onto the ground beside me so I could get back on my knees in front of my son. I took him by the outside of both of his arms, forcing him to look at me.

To see me.

To understand.

"None of this was your fault, Thomas. None of it. Not for a second. You are so brave. So very brave, and I couldn't be more proud of you. Do you understand?"

Through his tears, he nodded, and I gathered him back up again, squeezing him so tightly, my chest so full.

I fumbled to reach for the girls, pulling them into the same embrace.

Holding my babies close to me.

To the pound of my heart and the well of my devotion.

My voice was a haggard promise. "Mommy is the one who is sorry you all had to go through this. But I promise you, you're safe now. You don't have to worry about anything. Not anymore."

"That's because Ian-Zian the Great is our hero!" Mallory shouted, giggling, having no idea she was driving a knife into that wound that I wasn't sure would ever heal.

Right into that place Ian had taken. Carved out for himself.

I forced a smile, glancing up at Mack who anxiously waited at the back of his car.

Giving us a moment.

Easing back from my children, I touched their faces, just needing the connection, before I gathered myself and angled my head toward the house. "Why don't you go inside and give Gramma big hugs. She's been missing you like crazy. What do you want to bet she's making a big ol' feast for us to celebrate tonight?"

"A million dollars!" Mallory agreed.

Thomas scoffed. "You can't bet a million dollars if you don't have a million dollars to bet, Mal."

"You're just a party pooper, Tom Tom."

There they were. My bickering kids who I adored.

Somehow, I knew right then, that we were really going to be okay.

Pushing to my feet, I watched them as they raced for the house, Thomas taking Sophie's hand and making sure she got inside okay, Mallory singing and jumping and dancing the whole way.

"Be careful, Mal, you're going to bust your face on the porch if you don't watch where you're going," Thomas warned.

My little protector.

"If you fall, you get right back up again," Mallory just sang louder.

A smile pulled across my face.

Both brittle and beautiful.

Because in the middle of the most intense happiness I'd ever felt, there was sorrow, too.

I could feel it, so thick, as thick as the weight of Mack's presence. The wary heaviness that he wore like a shroud.

I finally forced myself to turn to look at him. He was the one who'd called to let me know he had the order to return my children to me.

The one who'd dropped me to my knees, my heart bleeding with relief.

But his voice had been grim when he'd told me that we needed to talk.

So, there I stood.

Waiting.

Winter whipping through the trees and me hugging my arms across my chest as I looked at the big man waver, a sadness I couldn't quite understand pouring from him in sheets.

He lifted his hand to gesture toward the house. "The best part of my job is when I get to see things like that happen. When wrongs are righted, and everything turns out the way it's supposed to be."

I could barely nod. "Thank you so much for bringing them back to me. They're my world."

"And that's why they belong here."

I waited because I knew there was more. Something that was going to break me.

A heavy sigh heaved his massive shoulders. "Reed Dearborne and Lawrence Bennet are both in custody. They're charged with multiple counts of racketeering, prostitution, fraud, and smuggling." He paused. "Also murder, Grace. Their crimes went deep and dark and farther than any of us really estimated, even though I've been on an undercover team investigating Lawrence Bennet for the last year. Don't think either of them are going to see the outside of a cell for the rest of their lives."

A gasp choked out in the middle of the stark relief that pounded through my blood stream. A buoy to my heart.

Revulsion at the depths of the wickedness. The realization that it had been much worse than I'd ever allowed myself to imagine.

"And?" I begged, edging forward, praying for news that wouldn't shatter me a little more.

Unsure of Ian's fate.

What he'd sacrificed last night.

The idea of him being hurt was more than I could comprehend. More than I could physically bear, my mind not allowing me to imagine an outcome so reprehensible.

Mack flinched. "Grace . . ."

I hugged myself tighter, and my mind spun. *They got to him. Oh, God, no, they got to him. He was gone. He was gone. No. God, please, no.*

My entire body tensed as I prepared to receive the news.

"Ian is also in custody."

"What?" The word rushed from me in a rasp of shock.

"He's charged with racketeering and money laundering."

"Oh. God." It was a whimper. A cry. Disbelief.

I clutched myself, trying to stand. Trying not to allow the man to knock me off my feet again.

"He . . . he was involved? The whole time, he was involved with them?" It didn't matter how I tried to hold myself steady.

Everything swayed.

My body and my heart and my mind.

Sympathy passed through Mack's expression. An age of it, as if he were dredging it up from the past. "Ian has had probably the hardest life of anyone I've known, Grace."

For a second, my eyes squeezed closed, riddled with the warnings Ian had given that I hadn't heeded.

I'm no good.

I'm the devil.

My mind hadn't even traipsed into the territory of this being what he'd meant.

"That's no excuse," I spat, trying to hold my anger back. To just put it all behind me since the only thing that mattered was my children were home.

That they were safe.

But I couldn't make myself budge from that spot.

Because my soul screamed with how much Ian had come to *matter*.

"He got involved with Bennet around the time he found his mother dead of an overdose. He was seventeen. Alone. Bennet swooped in. Became a father figure. Ian was seeded in that world before he even knew what being in that world meant."

My head shook, wanting to refute it, stomach tumbling with rolls of nausea that I could barely keep down.

Sorrow for Ian. Anger at Ian.

He didn't deserve my sympathy, did he? But I couldn't stop the way my spirit trembled in pain for the man I didn't think I'd ever stop loving.

Not after everything we'd shared.

In agitation, Mack speared his fingers through his hair. "Ian's done some shady shit, Grace. No question. He knows it. He's known it for a long time. I've been begging him to cut ties with Bennet, knowing things were gonna get messy and hoping he would get away before it was too late."

Mack paused before he rushed, "He turned over everything, Grace. All the proof we needed to put Reed and Lawrence away for a long, long time. He broke into Bennet's office. Produced all the evidence he could find on the two of them. By doing it, he implicated himself."

"What?" This time the word left me as a pained breath.

As it all started coming together.

What Ian had done. The goodbye of his text.

He'd given himself up.

For us.

He'd lost his career.

His freedom.

His *life*.

"Standing here, I'm making no excuses for what he's done,"

Mack continued, helplessness as he tipped his hands up. "He's done some bad shit. What I am telling you is it about killed me to have to put him in cuffs because at the core of him, he's one of the best men I've ever met. He proved that to me all over again last night. He gave himself up for you. For your family."

"What's going to happen to him?" A shiver shook my voice, horror and desperation and worry.

"Don't know, Grace. Only thing I know is that this is what he wanted. He's ready to pay for his sins. Because of you. For you. Because you were the one who showed him that he does have good inside. That he has something better to offer this world than taking from it. And I can only thank you for that."

He left me standing there with my tattered heart fluttering in the wind.

I knew all the scars that remained would be the one's scarred by Ian Jacobs.

And I wouldn't want it any other way.

"Ian Jacobs, you are hereby sentenced to a term of one year. A minimum-security facility is recommended."

A gavel cracked against the wood.

Faith whimpered at my side, and Jace's eyes squeezed closed, as if he couldn't look at his brother being sentenced for what he had done.

Ian didn't even flinch from where he was standing in front of the judge. No trial since he'd pled guilty.

Who knew how many years had been shaved off his sentence for his testimony against Reed Dearborne and Lawrence Bennet.

He just gave a short nod of acceptance and let the guard lead him away in cuffs with his head held high. Somehow both resolute and riddled with shame.

Not once in the last weeks had he talked to me, every attempt I'd made shut down.

You're better without me.

Go.

Live your life.

So, my breath hitched when he paused to look back at me.

That energy lashed between us. The same as it'd always been.

Alive.

Fierce.

Powerful.

Though this time bogged by the most severe sort of sorrow.

Cinnamon eyes flashed, and I swore I heard him utter the words all over again.

Goodbye, Angel Girl.

All I could silently whisper back was, *Thank you.*

I had no idea where I would be without him.

He'd taught us so many things. He'd shown my heart what it really meant to love a man.

Wholly and fully.

He'd shown us what true sacrifice meant.

He'd lost everything, and in return, given us a second chance.

Joy.

Peace.

Ian Jacobs.

Our unexpected hero.

forty-five

IAN

The gate buzzed, and I stepped out into the late afternoon air.

The air was hot from the summer heat, and I swore I could reach out and run my fingers through the heatwaves that sagged from the brilliant sky.

I blinked against it, the first time I'd seen outside a prison yard in six months.

Two steps away, and somehow the air felt different.

Half of my sentence had been shaved off for good behavior.

It almost made me want to laugh considering I hadn't played partner to a whole lot of *good behavior* in my life.

But I was finished with that. After all the shit I'd gotten myself wrapped up in, there was no chance I'd go that route again.

Wouldn't cause my brother worry.

Wouldn't unwittingly cause people harm.

Never again.

I walked away from the penitentiary, wearing the clothes I'd worn on the day I'd been arrested.

Jace and Faith were standing at the side of their SUV, all kinds of anxious love and anticipation radiating from them.

Couldn't help the one-sided smile that ticked up at the corner of my mouth when I saw them.

Jace stepped forward. What looked like amusement flitted across his face. "Well, well, well, if this isn't bringing back some bad memories I'd rather forget."

But there was no disappointment in his tone as he referred to the day so long ago when I'd picked his ass up after he'd been released from prison.

He'd gone for me.

Taken the fall for me.

All in his bid to protect me.

Because he was as selfless as they came.

We'd lost so much because of it. Because of our mother who'd made terrible choices. Had put us in unspeakable situations.

Part of me would never forgive her for what she'd done, but the other part would never forget her soft touch or the promise of her words.

Forever and ever.

"Guess I just wanted to be like my big brother," I tossed out.

"You just wish you could be as cool as me," he said, smirk riding onto his face.

"No wishing about it, asshole."

I was grinning by the time I made it to him, and he pulled me into a tight hug. He clapped me hard on the back.

All the amusement bled away. "I am so damned proud of what you did, Ian. I know it wasn't easy. That you lost everything because of it," his voice nothing but quiet encouragement.

"I'd do it all over again. A hundred times," I muttered back.

He hugged me tighter, and I just . . . let him. Let myself feel because I'd been refusing to allow myself to do it for too long.

Truth was, seemed the only thing I could do was *feel* anymore.

Grace had ensured that. Changed every-fucking-thing. Didn't regret it for a second. Not for a moment. The only thing I regretted was that I couldn't be better. Regretted that I couldn't be right for them.

My name nothing but tarnish and blame.

Grace had tried to make contact with me multiple times over the months. I'd refused each time, praying she'd move on. Live the kind of life that she deserved.

But a letter had made it through. The one that felt like a million pounds where I had it shoved in the pocket of my pants. I itched, thinking about the words that had been scratched on the page, the letters crooked and messy and all in pink.

Ian-Zian, you're invited to our party and it is the specialest party ever and the best one, too. Please come. We need you!

Love,
Mal Pal

Date was today. Gut told me it wasn't a coincidence. They'd planned it, knew when I was getting out.

Just wasn't sure I could stand in front of them now that all my sins were out there for the world to see. I mean, what kind of fucking influence would I be then?

I'd always known I wasn't good enough to be in their space. Now they had the proof of it.

I'd given up everything for Grace and her kids.

Maybe it was some sort of fucked-up atonement. A worthless soul trying to make amends for the weight of all its wrongs.

The reason didn't matter. The only thing that mattered was she and her family were safe. They got to live the kind of life they deserved.

It was the one good thing I'd ever done.

Thought it was best to leave it at that.

Faith stepped forward and wrapped me in the welcome of her

arms. Her sweetness all around. "Welcome home, Ian. We missed you."

"Where are my sweet niece and nephew?"

God, how much I'd missed them, too. Another effect Grace had left etched on me.

Faith stepped back and held me by my forearms, smiling so softly it almost made me itchy. "We dropped them off at my parents'. All Bailey kept saying was she couldn't wait for Uncle Ian to get home from his hunting trip. She can't wait to see you."

I choked out a laugh and shot an accusing glare at my brother. Asshole just shrugged. "What? Seemed like a plenty good explanation to me."

I laughed it off, glancing between the two of them, no pretenses left to find. "Thank you for being here."

Jace squeezed my shoulder. "We wouldn't be anywhere else, man. Told you, I couldn't be prouder of the man you are."

I could hardly speak, so I just gave a nod as I climbed into the backseat of the SUV.

He started it, and he pulled out onto the rural road.

As the prison faded into the distance, a tension filled the air, the awareness that things were never going to be the same.

Like he'd become a partner to my thoughts, Jace glanced at me through the rearview mirror. "Know your life looks different now, Ian."

I was no longer an attorney.

Disbarred.

With good reason.

Goals shot.

Thing was, it was all my doing. I'd been stepping on the wrong rungs when I'd been climbing that ladder.

Too much of a fool to realize I hadn't been climbing at all.

I'd been a puppet. Played by a man who'd wielded too much power and possessed nothing but wickedness.

I was still struggling with the fact that he'd fathered me. Was still trying to come to grips with the fact he had been responsible for the death of my mother, Reed in the middle of it, each of us pawns in his twisted game.

Agony lanced through my chest. Spikes and barbs.

I had no idea how I was going to forgive myself for what I'd done.

Jace sighed, roughed a hand through his hair. "I want you to consider coming to work with me."

My head mildly shook. "The last thing you need is my name associated with your business. You've worked too hard. Not going to fuck that up."

His eyes flicked my direction before his attention was back on the road. "And now I want to work with you. You feel shame over your past, Ian? Only thing I feel when it comes to you is pride. You are exactly the kind of man I want working at my side."

Faith glanced at me from over her shoulder, her smile soft. Her stance clear. She wanted me there, too.

"I . . . I think I'm going to have to figure shit out on my own. Who I am, and who I want to be. And I need to do it the right way. No skipping steps."

Jace smiled, a soft nod. "Well, if you want to figure out those steps next to me, that door is always going to be open. And this isn't your big brother doing you a favor. This is a businessman who knows when a partner will be an asset."

He had taken a few turns deeper into the city, the minimum-security prison where I'd been held only about twenty minutes out of town. Way too cushy, if I were being honest. But I'd had a ton of time to reflect.

But coming to terms with all this bullshit was going to take more than six months behind bars.

"I appreciate that more than you know."

"Just . . . tell me you'll at least consider it."

"Okay," I agreed, not sure how to even picture it. What my life was going to be like now that the one thing I'd chased forever was gone.

Funny thing was, I didn't even want it anymore.

It'd all come down to one case. One case that *mattered*.

One case that didn't even end up needing a trial.

Hers.

My pulse spiked as her face flashed in my mind. The girl written on me in a way that should be impossible.

Jace made another turn, and I frowned. "Where are we going? Thought you were dropping me off at my place?"

Faith shifted in her seat, and Jace didn't look at me when he took another turn into a parking lot. "You're going, Ian. You'll regret it if you don't."

God, they knew about whatever this party was. Were in on it. Unease tumbled through my guts. "I've been away a long time. Think it would be best if you took me home first. Think I need to wrap my mind around being free."

"You want to be here, Ian. Trust me," Jace said as he pulled into a vacant parking spot and killed the engine.

Trust me.

God.

I roughed a hand through my hair, shaking when I slipped out of the car, nerves instantly wracking through my body.

Like I could feel the shift.

Something big bounding my way.

Twilight hung on the horizon, the hot day giving way to the trill of bugs that were all too eager to welcome the cooler night.

We parked in a lot beside a local bookstore.

One that had been there for forever. One I'd walked passed a million times, doing little more than glancing at it.

The parking lot was jam-packed.

Cars lined the street when they couldn't find a spot.

It was the first time I'd noticed the way they were dressed. My brother in a suit, and Faith in a pretty dress and heels, her dark hair done up. But it was her expression that got to me, something that almost looked like sympathy all mixed up with a brilliant, shining hope.

Faith stretched her hand out for me. "You're supposed to be here, Ian. They need you. And I know you need them, too."

Jace lifted his chin at me.

No challenge in his stance but believing that I'd step up and be the man he'd always told me I'd be.

Agitation rushed through my veins, and my heart started pounding so damned hard I could feel my pulse in my ears.

Deafening.

Or maybe it was just my soul.

Crying out.

Feeling it.

That intensity I could feel rising up my legs.

Dragging me closer.

I swallowed hard, and my feet planted against the ground. Body frozen in a shroud of fear. "I'm not sure I can go in there."

I didn't have an answer as to why.

I just knew I couldn't.

That it was too much, the buzz of energy that radiated back.

"You need to see this, Ian. You'll regret it for the rest of your life if you don't," Jace told me.

Fear clamored through my senses. This shame that I could never be the good guy.

That I was bad.

The devil.

But I didn't want to be him anymore.

Beating back the demons howling from my soul, I gave them a tight nod and followed them around the old building.

Anticipation billowed, unease and excitement.

Could feel the greatness radiating from the brick walls.

Something good and right.

Jace swung open the door, guiding his wife inside, glancing back at me in some kind of silent invitation.

To step up.

To be the man he'd tried to teach me to be when I'd been just a kid.

I'd thought that meteor in my throat had already crashed to the ground and obliterated everything, nothing but dust and destruction in its wake. But there it was, bobbing so heavy I could barely see when I stepped into the old bookstore.

Tons of old books lined the shelves. Other displays boasted new titles and the latest bestsellers.

But I saw none of that. Only thing I could see was the crowd that had gathered for a signing at the back of the room, the long, excited line twisting all the way back through the aisles of shelves.

It was the woman sitting behind the table, her blonde hair tumbling down around one shoulder as she angled her head and signed a big book that stunned me.

Knocked the breath right out of me.

Kick-started my damned heart that until right that very moment had forgotten to beat.

My battered Cinderella.

My Angel Girl.

This girl who I'd had all wrong. She wasn't close to being broken.

She was real and perfect and whole.

The bright, bright light in the middle of my darkness.

She smiled and handed the book back to the little girl who was waiting for it.

It was big and square and illustrated.

A children's book.

My chest squeezed, and Jace and Faith started walking that direction. That was when I saw Faith's parents up close to the table, Mack dressed up and chatting with them.

The sweetest kind of torture speared me when I saw Thomas wearing a suit where he stood next to them, holding a cup of punch while he looked around in awe.

Little Sophie Marie was on the ground coloring something.

It was Mallory who saw me first.

Her face split into the biggest smile. Big enough to shatter the earth.

She gasped and threw her arms in the air. "Ian-Zian the Great!" She dropped the animated conversation she was having with Bailey.

She snatched one of the books from the table by her mother and came bounding my direction.

Energy and light.

She skidded to a stop a foot away, holding out the book, so proud. "Ian, look it, you got your very own book! *Ian-Zian the Great Saves the Ruby Prince and the Priceless Princesses.* That's because he's our hero and we love him so, so, so much! I got to help Mom write all the words and then she found someone so special to color all the pages and now we're going to sell them and it's going to be a bestseller! I told you I was a writer and I was going to sell all the books!"

My chest tremored. Ripples of waves. Quivers of emotion that kept rolling in. Getting greater with each second that passed.

No ebbing. It was just a constant flow.

My lips parted, awe taking hold of me when I reached out and took the book, eyes moving over the cover.

It depicted a toppled castle tower. A dragon circling overhead. A prince that wore a ruby crown, and two tiny princesses cheering, a big diamond pendant on the older one, a sapphire ring on the small, small child, the beautiful handmaiden who looked a whole lot like Cinderella at their side.

I was in the middle of it, holding the sword of a saint.

Staggered, I squeezed my eyes closed, not sure how to accept that this was the way they viewed me.

Like I was their hero when I'd been the one to blame. When I'd been so close to ruining everything for Grace and her family because I'd gone after a girl I knew I could never keep.

Then my staggered world froze when Grace looked up, that sea of bottomless blue capturing me.

Taking me over.

Flooding me with so much love I didn't know how to stand.

She stood slowly, like she was in her own shock, unsure that I would come.

Her sweet body trembled all over.

But it was her belly that was big and round that sent me reeling forward, feet barely functioning as I fumbled across the space.

Drawn.

Energy lashing.

Awareness and need and awe.

She rounded the table, those eyes so tender, her heart so sweet.

I dropped to my knees at her feet.

Because it was the girl who had knocked me off of mine.

My hands went to her round stomach, shivers streaking through me at the contact, and her fingers threaded softly through my hair.

"Ian," she whispered.

A prayer.

My solace.

Moisture gathered in my eyes, and I pressed my forehead to her belly.

Overcome.

"Grace," I murmured.

My answer.

Because there were some moments in your life when you knew things would never be the same.

I knew I was still messed up. That I had so much to conquer. To realize and forgive and learn.

And still, I knew, right then that this was where I had been meant to be heading all along.

For the first time ever, in all my life, I felt peace.

True, unmitigated peace.

Mallory was dancing around at my side. "And we get a baby! Did you know that, Ian? We get a baby and it's a boy and I think his name should be Zian Number Two, but Mom said we have to wait so you can decide with us. What do you think?"

I looked up at Grace who was gazing down at me.

Adoration covering me.

Rushing and pummeling.

I pushed to my feet, and her chest heaved, the hammer of her heart fierce, beating for mine. "I'm so glad you came."

She glanced around the room. "I needed you to be here for this. I needed it so badly, and I wasn't sure that you would. Still . . . I believed it. Believed in you, that you would come back to us."

My fingers fluttered down the side of her cheek. Unable to keep from touching her. "I'm not sure I deserve to be here."

Devotion oozed from Grace's expression, everything so intense as she spoke to me, "You deserve this more than anyone. You deserve everything. You saved us. Sacrificed in a way I never could have asked anyone to do. You've loved me in a way no one has ever loved me. You deserve to live, Ian. And I know I'm still asking so much of you. But I can't pretend like I don't want more. That I don't want it all. All of you."

Thomas had come to our sides, holding little Sophie's hand, and Mallory was dancing around, still holding her book.

Emotion surged.

Overpowering.

Everything I never imagined I could have.

A family.

I didn't think I'd ever been so scared in my life.

Or ever so sure of anything.

"I'm terrified, Grace. Terrified of what I feel for you. For them. For this." I touched her stomach that shouted of new life.

Of new chances.

Hands shaking like crazy, I burrowed my fingers into Grace's hair, cupping her on either side of the neck and running my thumbs along her jaw. No fucks given that we had an audience.

That people were watching.

Hell, I wanted the world to know.

"I love you, Grace. So much. I never wanted it. Not until I met you. You showed me what that meant. You showed me what *mattered.*"

Her mouth trembled with emotion, those blue eyes brimming with moisture. "I love you, Ian Jacobs. Stay with me. Forever. Let's live again."

"Forever and ever," I murmured, the quiet promise rising from my spirit. "You have all of me."

My eyes dropped to those sweet, lush lips. I dipped down and captured her mouth.

A profession.

A claim.

A promise.

Kisses are only for the ones you love most.

Pride billowed, and I was smiling against her mouth, unable to stop.

She was laughing under it, curling her fingers in my shirt.

Everyone cheered.

"I love you," I whispered again, looking down when I felt something tugging at my pants.

Sophie had her little hands fisted in the material, grinning up at me with her trusting smile. She lifted her arms, and I picked her up, my spirit trembling when I did.

Mallory wrapped her arms around one of my legs, hugging me tight. "I love you, Ian-Zian, the greatest hero in all the land. But you're a real kind of hero, did you know that? You saved us forever."

My heart tremored, and I ran my fingers through her pin-straight hair as she smiled up at me. "I think it's you who saved me."

I glanced around at all of them. "All of you."

Thomas didn't seem to quite know what to do, and I met his stoic gaze, praying he could see.

Like he got it, felt it, he rushed for us and threw his arms around Grace and me.

"I'm so glad you came back," he cried, his face buried in the lower part of my chest.

"Where else could I go?"

I pressed my face into Grace's neck, against the steady, unwavering beat of her pulse.

Where else could I go?

The five of us just stood there. Hugging tight. Refusing to let go.

Right where we belonged.

Forever and ever.

IAN

The barest breeze whispered through the branches, a slow, mournful cry that twisted through the heavens.

I stood at her grave that was marked by a cheap, flat stone, the etching only her name and the dates that marked her birth and her death.

There were no claims of beloved mother or daughter or wife. There were no scriptures or sayings about a soul lost too soon that would never be forgotten.

A shiver raced down my spine when the presence stepped up beside me. Grace threaded her fingers through mine.

My support.

My consolation.

My reason.

I squeezed her hand tightly, my chest stretched so tight I was struggling to pull a breath into my lungs, grief a blur in my eyes as I inched forward and knelt at the place where my mother had been laid to rest.

And I prayed that she was.

At rest.

At peace.

That she knew that I forgave her.

Grace eased up behind me and set her hand on my shoulder. I reached up and gripped it tightly, needing her comfort and her love and her support.

Eyes squeezed tight, I exhaled a tremor of remorse and my own peace.

Because kneeling there, I knew it was time to forgive myself.

I turned my head so I could press my mouth to the inside of Grace's wrist before I released it and pressed my fingers to my lips.

With that hand shaking, I reached out and touched my mother's headstone.

Kisses are for the ones you love most.

I knelt in front of Grace and slipped the cream-colored shoe onto her foot. "There," I whispered, gazing up at her. "To misplaced slippers."

She smiled down at me, all that blonde hair cascading around her.

My angel.

My Cinderella.

My wife.

She reached out and caressed my face, the bangle on her wrist tinkling as the charms knocked together as it slipped down her forearm.

A ruby, a diamond, a sapphire, and an amethyst.

I pushed to standing and held out my hand. Grace accepted it, allowing me to help her stand. She stumbled a little.

I smirked. "Knocking you off your feet."

"Good thing you're always there to catch me."

I leaned forward, pressed my mouth to hers, slipped my hand down her delicate neck. "Always."

"Always," she whispered back.

I stepped back, taking her hand. "We'd better go or we're going to be late."

"I still can't believe this is happening. Are you happy?"

I fiddled with an errant piece of her hair, staring at the woman who had changed everything.

The one who'd seeped in and got under my skin.

The one who'd breathed new life.

The one who'd taught me what it meant to love.

"I think I have to be the happiest man in the world."

Because Jace had been right.

Money didn't buy happiness.

I weaved my fingers through hers and led her out our bedroom door and down the hall. We slipped into the nursery, and I went right for the crib.

Collin gurgled and cooed, his little fist working with all its might to get to the giraffes that spun on his mobile. I scooped him up, lifted him out in front of me.

The sweetest smile pulled up one side of his crooked mouth, and I brought him to me, kissed him there, breathed him in.

Let my heart fill full.

I handed him over to Grace who nestled him in her arms, and the two of us headed down the stairs of the modest two-story house we'd purchased in Broadshire Rim, two minutes from Jace and his family.

We edged down the stairs, our house full of laughter as everyone was there in anticipation of our celebration.

My brother was there with Faith at his side. Bailey, Sophie, and Mallory were in the middle of the living room chanting an alternate version of ring-around-the-rosie, all of them bursting out into laughter when they fell to the ground.

Thomas was playing with Benton on the floor, helping him build large cubes of Legos.

Couldn't stop my grin when I saw Grace's grandmother flirting with Mack where they stood by the table.

Our attorney smiled when he turned around. The paperwork had been signed by the judge that morning.

My heart tremored and expanded, emotion soaring, pouring free and somehow filling me up.

My shattered world whole.

I dropped Grace's hand and moved for the table where the documents were spread out, ready for me to sign.

Mallory was suddenly at my side, jumping up and down, shouting, "Do it, do it, do it!"

My smile was soft when I turned to look at her.

Mal Pal.

I touched her chin, kissed her head, breathed her in.

Sophie ran over. I scooped her up into my arms and pressed my lips to her cheek.

Thomas appeared at my side, the little man that he was, eyes poring over the papers.

He looked up at me.

For reassurance.

For a sign.

For a promise.

I ran my hand through his hair, making his head tip back. I dropped a kiss to his forehead.

I lingered there for a beat.

This little boy who reminded me so much of myself.

Kisses are only for who you love most.

Mallory wrapped her arms around my leg and held on tight, Thomas at my side, Sophie hooked in my left arm.

For so many years, I'd scribbled my name across documents of shame. Had been the partner of disgrace and dishonor.

I glanced over at Grace.

She cast me the softest smile where she rocked our youngest son in her arms.

One in a billion.

That energy surged.
Rolled and expanded.
I finally got what it meant.
I leaned over and signed my name.
This family was mine.
Forever and ever.

THE END

Thank you for reading *All of Me*!! I hope you loved Ian and Grace's story as much as I did. These two are forever going to live in my heart! Aren't ready to let them go? I have an EXCLUSIVE BONUS scene available for FREE that picks up the night after the book signing!

READ HERE
https://geni.us/AOMBonusScene

Text "aljackson" to 33222
(US Only)
or
Sign up for my newsletter
https://geni.us/NewsFromALJackson

Ready for the next *Confessions of the Heart* novel? Fall for Mack in *Pieces of Us*!

More from A.L. Jackson

ABOUT THE AUTHOR

A.L. Jackson is the New York Times & USA Today Bestselling author of contemporary romance. She writes emotional, sexy, heart-filled stories about boys who usually like to be a little bit bad.

Her bestselling series include THE REGRET SERIES, CLOSER TO YOU, BLEEDING STARS, FIGHT FOR ME, CONFESSIONS OF THE HEART, and FALLING STARS.

If she's not writing, you can find her hanging out by the pool with her family, sipping cocktails with her friends, or of course with her nose buried in a book.

Be sure not to miss new releases and sales from A.L. Jackson - Sign up to receive her newsletter https://geni.us/NewsFromALJackson or text "aljackson" to 33222 to receive short but sweet updates on all the important news.

Connect with A.L. Jackson online:

FB Page **https://geni.us/ALJacksonFB**
Newsletter **https://geni.us/NewsFromALJackson**
Angels **https://geni.us/AmysAngels**
Amazon **https://geni.us/ALJacksonAmzn**
Book Bub **https://geni.us/ALJacksonBookbub**
Text "aljackson" to 33222 to receive short but sweet updates on all the important news.